DARK KISS

CASSANDRA BELLA

Jove Co. Press

This book is a work of fiction. Names, characters, places, and incidents are either the product of the author's imagination or are used fictitiously, and any resemblance to actual persons living or dead, business establishments, events, or locales, is entirely coincidental.

Dark Kiss

Jove Co. Press New York City, NY 10279

Book Cover by Novalarty

First JC Press edition 2024

ISBN: 979-8-2185-0452-6

ISBN: 979-8-2185-0453-3 (ebook)

"Please. Just go."

He should. Was prepared to. Something in the look of her stopped him. For all her strength, all her courage, she looked so vulnerable. The shadow of light and dark played over her delicate features. The breeze tossed long red curls around her gentle face.

He moved closer, watching her eyes widen. Her full lips pulled into a tight line. A mix of fear and defiance flashed in her dark gaze.

"I can't." The honesty of it burned. "I know I should. But I can't find the strength to."

He hovered close, his breath a mix with hers with only a slice of space between them. "I've spent so long trying to deny it, but I've missed you."

"Don't." Addie pressed her hand against his chest, wanting to push him away. Instead, she lingered, fingers molding over hard muscles through the thin cotton of his shirt.

She didn't want this. Didn't want any of it. Long ago she'd chased away her feelings for Reed. Buried them where they belonged. It was weakness now, the very thing she hated, allowing them a chance to return, reminding her of everything she'd once had.

BOOKS BY CASSANDRA BELLA

RELUCTANT ANGEL
PLAYING WITH FIRE
HUNTER'S CAPTIVE

GRADY BROTHERS TRILOGY

YESTERDAY'S PROMISE
TODAY'S DESIRE

For Tracie Salerno

For every best friend my characters find in their life, you are the inspiration. There is no friend who knows me better. Who can make me laugh till my cheeks hurt. Who, with just a look, can speak so much to me.

I am, always have been and always will be, so grateful to have your friendship as such a huge part of my life.

Here's to plastic pools and pool boys and many more years of friendship still to come! I love you!

A kiss that is never tasted
Is forever and ever wasted
-Billie Holiday

FORWARD

The storm raged, lashing heavy pelts of rain against the windows. Lightning flashed through the dark sky. Trees, hovering like beaten guards around the cabin, struck long branches over the weathered shingles, shaking their wrath through the tiny rooms inside.

The force of it fueled him. Gave him power.

He'd come home, something he never did, to this decrepit place lost in the backwoods. To the memories of hell.

Nothing but the memory of her remained. The hateful hag passed a month ago, her lifeless body buried under a mound steps from the back of the cabin.

He'd gone there when he'd first come. Not to pay respects, as she'd never deserved such from him. But to gloat. To show her he'd done something. Proven himself a man, the very thing she'd told him he'd never be.

Enjoying the treacherous weather, a match to his mood, he settled at the tiny table in the worn and beaten kitchen. Sipping from the lukewarm coffee in his mug, he read the words scrawled on paper.

Handwriting matches didn't worry him any more than fingerprints or DNA. For all that mattered, he didn't exist. Times were, he'd forget his own name as he picked up another alias to fit his place.

He pictured Special Agent McReily reading the letter. Imagined that cocky look of his draining away as his arrogance took the hit he deserved.

He'd thought he was smarter. Better at what he did.

It was time to knock him down a notch and remind him of who truly held the power. Who had held it all along.

Downing the last of the coffee, tasting none of it, he dropped the mug carelessly in the sink, letting it sit without a thought. Grabbing the letter, the addressed envelope beside it, he whistled softly as he put the two together and left it at the edge of the table for delivery come morning.

He felt good. Better than he had in months. He'd hit a down moment, unable to find the same joy he once did in his triumphs. He'd needed something to jolt him back, remind him of the thrill.

He hated coming back to the cabin of his childhood, a place he'd rather see burned to the ground than stand in its disrepair, but it gave him what he'd needed. A direction. A reason to celebrate again and look forward to what the next day held.

Perhaps that was the way it should be. Here was what spawned the man he'd become. So here would be what pushed that man to go further.

Poking at the fire, adding logs, he looked at the worn, tired couch. His bed for the night. He refused to sleep in the single bedroom. The memories were too strong, even now.

Just one night, he reminded himself, pulling off his jeans, throwing them to the side. In nothing but boxers and t-shirt, the old quilt his only cover, he settled across the thin cushions.

One miserable night inside the cabin would be worth it for the promises tomorrow held. His identity was good and tidied up. It would take nothing more than a quick trip to the post office in the morning, sending McReily's gift on its way. Then he'd work his way south, towards the gulf, until New Orleans became his home.

CHAPTER ONE

I t was proving to be one hell of a morning, following on the heels of one hell of a night.

Bachelor parties. Reed McReily cringed at the thought. An old tradition still so highly held. He'd considered not going, had all the excuses he'd need to bow out gracefully.

But Mitch Branson was one hell of a good partner. He'd spent the last eight years knowing him in the way only another agent could. It didn't sit well to miss out on celebrating such a huge event in his life.

So he'd gone. Done the partying. Now he paid for it.

At his desk, he drank from his coffee as if it were a lifeline, needing the jolt of caffeine more than he cared to admit.

He had work but didn't much find the desire to take care of it. What he wanted was to go home and back to bed. To sleep off the headache he'd earned from a few too many drinks.

"You look like hell." Branson, looking no better himself, hitched a hip against his desk.

"Try looking in a mirror." He snarled at his partner as he considered shoving him off, just for spite. "Who thinks it's a good idea to have a bachelor party in the middle of the week?"

"You try booking anything decent on a weekend around here without at least six months' notice and let me know how you do at it."

Reed didn't answer, having no experience in that area. He grabbed his nearly empty cup and pushed up from his seat. "You have anything more in those reports?"

"Nothing more than what's already there. Our guy's been quiet lately."

He bit back frustration as he refilled his coffee. The past year and a half, he'd tracked the one the media called the *Kissing Killer*. From Tennessee through Mississippi, Alabama and down into Georgia, he'd left a trail of dead bodies. Eight women total. Raped, tortured, strangled, and marked with a single red lipstick kiss on their right breast.

In all his years with the Bureau, never had one dug at him as this one did. The faces of those women stayed with him in dreams. Their families' tears a constant echo following him through the days.

"What's he up to? He's been quiet too long."

"Three months. Figured we'd be in Florida by now, staring over another body."

Tracking his path, Florida had been the next logical step. Even as he did all he could to find him before he had the chance to murder another, he waited for the call. Expected it.

"He's not done." Feeling it deep in his gut, he shoved away from the counter. "He'll be back. Unless, of course, we find him first."

The odds of finding him, at this point, were slim to none. But, for Reed, there was always hope.

A short walk and a bit of brisk spring air did him good.

Reed chose the deli down the street from FBI headquarters for that very reason. That, and they had the best pastrami on rye to be found.

No longer suffering from the drag of a night of too much liquor, he settled at his desk with another cup of coffee and the latest reports pulled up on his computer.

He hated this time of waiting. Hated feeling as if he was stuck spinning his wheels with nothing to show for the many long hours he'd put in.

His mind battled this one. Couldn't let go of it. Whoever this Kissing Killer was, he'd made it his personal goal to bring him down and pay for the senseless deaths he left behind.

All other cases had been shifted, handed to other agents so he could work only this, and the lull unnerved him, making him edgy. He needed to be doing something.

He was proving to be a ghost with nothing to link him to any database the FBI had access to. No clue of who he might be or where he came from.

Only a line of dead women, marked with a single bright red kiss on their breast.

"Marshall wants us in his office." Looking better himself, Branson nudged his partner on the shoulder, waiting for his attention to drift from the computer.

"Any idea why?" Closing the reports, he pushed from his desk.

"No clue."

Special Agent in Charge Alex Marshall didn't make requests without good reason. And since they were working on only one case at the moment...he ran through the possibilities as Branson rapped his knuckles against the door.

"Branson. McReily." Marshall nodded as he opened the door. "Take a seat."

He circled back behind his desk, settling in his own chair. "We have a problem."

He clamped fingers around the corner of a sheet of paper, holding it out for Reed. "This was delivered today. Plain white envelope. No return address. Sent directly to you, McReily."

He held the letter with one hand, his heart picking up a quicker beat as he read it.

I find myself at a crossroads. A bit bored with my current path and in need of some excitement.

For more than a year now, Special Agent McReily has spent dutiful time getting to know me. So, I believe it is my turn to give back and do the same.

You intrigue me, McReily. And as your past has shown, it has been for good reason. Your long, deep history with New Orleans has convinced me where I must travel.

The ladies there are amazing, I hear. And as your keen interest in me has been a great challenge, I will follow it and meet you there. Back where your life was formed, and my own history will be set.

Perhaps we will find ourselves in a marvelous game. One I have every belief I will win while you, again, come out on the losing end.

There was no signature. No name to go with the letter. They didn't need one. The Bureau knew, just as he did, who sent it. For his time in silence, it was clear the Kissing Killer was preparing for his return.

"He's made it personal." Reed handed the letter to Branson. "Not something we expected from him."

It irritated, knowing even the best in the Bureau playing with the mind of this one couldn't see such a turn. Never thought to expect it.

Who was he?

The question gnawed at the back of his mind as it had from the beginning. As often as he'd tried to get inside his head, he'd eluded him, creating a trail impossible to track.

Until now. Until he'd showed his hand.

"Some are pushing to take you both off this case. They don't like he's drawn you in. They'd prefer to leave this in the hands of our SAC, Burke, already in the New Orleans office."

"What do you prefer?"

"You head for New Orleans in the morning. And you—"

He looked at Branson, a slight smile easing the hard lines of his face. "No reason to upset your wife-to-be before the vows are shared. Keep your plans as you have them. Burke has agents in New Orleans to backup McReily until you're back."

Branson didn't like it. He'd known it was a risk, allowing his personal life to continue while on the heels of a serial killer.

"Don't go getting yourself into trouble while I'm gone. I don't like the sound of this. Part of me wishes you'd let the agents in New Orleans handle it rather than risking your own hide."

"My hide will still be intact when you're back. I promise."

With that, it was done.

Reed was going home. To New Orleans. To the past he'd left behind thirteen years ago. He thought of Addie, as he always did when memories of home came. Saw her as he always held her in his mind, so small and delicate. Soft red curls tumbling down her back. Deep brown eyes, the color of warmed chocolate, peering into his soul.

And as he always did, as had become a means of survival in the time he'd been gone, he pushed it away. Pushed her away to the place he'd let the memory of her rest for many years.

CHAPTER TWO

There was magic here.

Adelaide Monrose's entire life was New Orleans. Born and bred. And still there were days catching her in amazement, reminding her of the many reasons why she loved this place.

The Quarter shimmered as she hurried up St. Peter thanks to a light Spring drizzle through the night. The tumble of flowers inside Jackson Square lent their subtle scents to the air, following her down Chartres and into the shop.

Here, new smells greeted her. Soft and subtle, the incense and candles layered their fragrances through the hand-stitched tapestries. Glittering wands. Delicate charms.

"About time." Rosalie's emerald eyes sparkled playfully from behind the counter. "Send you out for lunch and soon I wonder if I'll see you again."

Working the plastic bag around the many displays, Addie made her way through the tiny shop, dropping their food on the counter in front of her aunt. "Spring's definitely back in force. The tourists are heavy out there."

"We're busy enough, ourselves. No time to break for lunch. We'll have to eat and work."

As if on cue, the gold bell above the door rang. Grabbing her Shrimp Po'boy, Addie tucked it on the small shelf beneath the counter and came around to greet the two young women making their way inside.

Magic Moon was a shop all to itself. Most didn't know what to expect when they came through the doors. Another gift store, like those littering Bourbon Street? Or a Voodoo Shop, so much a part of what was New Orleans?

This place, a dream of her mother and aunt, brought to life over two decades ago, wasn't the expected. It was the mystic. The mysterious. With the slightest touch of magic blended around the corners.

If one had a heart for the power of stones, they'd find it. If their mind leaned more to the gentleness of oils, they had a shelf to choose from. Angel oil to Bewitching Oil, it was there.

Whatever the desire, the belief, or the need, it was held inside the shop.

Giving the customers their personal space, she waited close without hovering. Greeting them with a smile as their questions came, she directed them toward the wall shelves where they'd find the Celtic Jewelry they'd come looking for.

It was second nature for Addie, all she'd ever grown up with. This shop, the intricate allure of it, the home that was part of it, was hers in every way. The only life she'd known.

Making their choices, she stepped back as they headed for Rosalie waiting at the counter. The sweet song in her voice, soft glimmer in her emerald eyes, welcomed them as it did every person walking through the door.

Before they finished, more came through the door, setting the pace for the day.

Thirteen years.

Reed guided his rental car down streets he'd never forget, no matter how long he'd been away. Tension collected between his shoulder blades. Barely back in New Orleans and the reminders came rushing back. Of who he once was. Of why he'd left.

It wasn't for here. Wasn't for now. Shoving the bitter feelings back, he pulled to a stop in front of the modest, brick building taking up half the block. He stepped into the muggy heat that was New Orleans, even in these early months of the year.

"You made good time." Edward Burke met him at the door. "I've got my two best agents waiting to meet with you.

He led the way down the hall. Dark in skin and heavy in step, he carried himself as a man comfortable in his power and strength.

"We haven't seen any sign he's here. I'm thinking that's the normal way of things when it comes to this UNSUB." He pushed open a door at the end.

"Unfortunately, it is."

Reed stepped in behind him, noticing the agents settled at the table centering the wide room. A conference room, he guessed, by the looks of it. One complete with a coffee pot, sending the enticing scent into the air.

"May I?" He steered away from them, grabbing a cup from the stack at the edge of the counter.

Slowly sipping from the black liquid, thick and bitter as tar, he found his way to the table where Burke took his place at the head with two agents at his left side.

The one closest to him stood and held out a hand. Blond wavy hair and bright blue eyes made him more fit for Hollywood stardom than an FBI agent. "Christopher Perry. And this is my partner, Linda Jackson."

Her smile reached into soft green eyes as she stood and shook his hand. She looked professional in her crisp, dark blue pant suit, but Reed sensed the Southern Belle hiding beneath the clothes.

"You have a hard one here." Burke waved him to a chair across from his agents. "Nothing I've read gives much information about your suspect."

"Our best behavioral are struggling on this one. He picks at random. No set choice on age, race, body type, or social standing. He kills the same but doesn't hunt the same. We've found evidence he stalked some of us his victims while others appeared to be an immediate grab."

"So, no pattern to follow." Perry spread out the pictures of the dead women.

"The only pattern we've been able to determine is the path he takes. From Tennessee down into Georgia. We were prepared for Florida next, until—"

"Until he made it personal," Jackson finished for him, taking in the pictures scattered around her.

"So, what's his next move?" Burke looked at the agents around the table.

"A hit at me. If he's going to strike, odds are, it will be on my turf with my past as his playbook."

The idea of it made him sick.

"You worried about your family?"

"It's only my parents when it comes to immediate relations. Their money already pays for the best security." He fought back the bitter taste in his mouth. "Better than what the Bureau has the resources to give.

"I have cousins spread out, here and there. You'd have to dig deep to know about them. I don't think our guy has that in him."

Perry drug the pictures back to a pile. "So, we have nothing to go on. An UNSUB who has broken the only pattern you had on him. And if we don't find him first, we'll have another victim to add to the list."

It was a truth none of them liked.

"I have a total of ten minutes to spare." In the flash and glamour so uniquely hers, AnnaBeth Turner burst through the door of Magic Moon. Her rich, seductive scent swirled in the air. Diamonds glittered in her ears, around her slender wrist.

"Working two conventions at the hotel." A shot of confidence in every step, she headed straight for the counter where Rosalie worked the purchases of a customer into the cash register. "Lots of power and clout going on. If I work it right, I'll guarantee a year's worth of reservations."

She flashed her famous smile at the older lady waiting for her candles to be bagged. "Those are some of my favorites. They smell simply wonderful."

"Really." Handed the bag, she opened it, taking a long sniff, the sweet scents of lavender and jasmine rising up. "Thank you for that. I was hoping so."

Closing the bag, she stuffed her wallet back into her purse and smiled. "Good day, ladies."

"I could have called, I know." AnnaBeth shoved thick, golden waves of hair from her face. "But I figured a walk would do me good. Make up for the early break I took from my workout this morning."

"Clay called. He's nervous about tonight." She shifted a hip against the edge of the counter, picked up a gently tossed stone, and twisted it through her long fingers. "He's got it in that dumb head of his that he won't draw a crowd. I told the fool his worries were useless. He's magic when he plays his guitar. Even more when he adds his voice to it."

"He is," Addie agreed. Friends with AnnaBeth since their first day of kindergarten, she'd grown up hearing him play. From a boy of only three to the man he was today, his music amazed her.

"He has no reason to worry. They'll love him."

"Told him that. He won't listen. So, I promised I would make sure you still planned on coming tonight. He claims one table full is better than none."

There wouldn't be empty tables. Teddy Kullen's bar, where Clay was to make his debut, sat well on a Bourbon Street corner. And on a Friday night crowds surged, no matter how good or bad the entertainment.

"You can reassure him I'll be there. I'd never break a promise to him."

"I know it. He knows, too. He's just blinded by insecurity at the moment."

"You're a good sister, worrying about him like you do."

"Yeah. Yeah. Don't go saying such things around him. I've worked hard to let him believe my single goal in life is to torture him into craziness."

"I used to do the same with Sophie," Rosalie added.

It was rare for her aunt to speak of her younger sister and Addie's mother. She and AnnaBeth fell silent, waiting for more.

Nothing else came, only a gentle smile, hinting at the memories she brought back.

Addie was used to it. An attempted robbery of the shop took her mom from her when she was only ten. Stole a sister from her aunt. While healing from her mother's death meant needing to speak of her often, her aunt's grief turned the opposite direction.

She rarely talked of her sister. She'd been the rock Addie needed, raising and loving her as her mother would have. If she'd needed to share her own love, Rosalie gave the time and freedom for her to do so, as often as she wanted. As many times as it took.

She came to realize as she grew older, for her aunt to speak of her memories was something too painful to do. She held her memories. Treasured them. But she didn't often share, choosing instead to keep it to herself in her own personal treasure of the sister she'd lost.

"I've threatened Teddy with physical pain if he doesn't reserve us one of his best tables." AnnaBeth slipped her arm through Addie's and started back for the door. "Clay's first set starts at eight. I'll meet you there."

She brushed a quick kiss against her cheek and waved goodbye to Rosalie before disappearing out the door and back to the crowded sidewalks beyond.

CHAPTER THREE

R eed hadn't gone back to his parents to stay. The thought of returning to the grand home he'd grown up in set his stress levels too high.

It was better to avoid that. He didn't need more added to what was already tugging at him. He booked a hotel off St. Anne's, trying hard not to wince at the amount that would come out of his own account after the meager expenses the Bureau was willing to provide.

Not that he couldn't dip into his generous trust fund, sitting untouched all these years. But the thought, as it always did, left a dirty taste in his mouth. He'd left it behind for a reason, hadn't yet faced a need good enough to change his mind.

Out of his suit, more casual in jeans and a cotton shirt, he pressed in with the crowds filling Bourbon Street. Though Uptown was where he was raised, here, in the Quarter, was where he'd spent so much of his youth. Usually with Teddy, finding an amazing excitement in life he never knew inside the stuffy, prestigious upbringing his parents placed over him.

A third cousin, removed from the responsibility—and a good portion of the wealth—of the McReily family, Teddy had the sort of life Reed craved. A freedom he never found in private schools, or the fundraising functions and fancy dinners carefully structured for the right appearances with the right people.

Teddy was the only one in the family he kept in contact with. The only one he cared to see now as he moved with the crowds spilling from the sidewalk to the street as another night of partying began.

Orleans House sat right where it always had through the years with different names and different owners. It was Teddy's baby now. An idea that still gave Reed a moment of pause.

He hadn't told him he was coming. Had come close to deciding against it as he sat in his hotel room, flipping through reports, fingers running tirelessly over the keyboard as he continued to search for more, always more.

What would be the point of reconnecting outside the phone calls they shared every few months? His time in New Orleans was limited. He'd be gone soon enough and back to the life he'd built away from the ties here.

He'd battled thoughts of whether it would be worth it.

In the end, it was his conscience making the decision. Being so close and not reaching out to the only family member he cared about didn't sit right.

He stood on the crowded sidewalk as a moody Rock classic poured through the row of open doors, drawing in those around him.

He joined those heading inside, taking a moment to look around and know the space.

A long stage butted up against the line of doors he'd come through. A small, well-worn dance floor centered it. Dark wood bars stretched along both sides, tables tucked between them, spreading out into more toward the back.

Low hanging lights were dim, creating dancing shadows over those who gathered around the tables or sat at the bars. Above the music, the hum of conversation and laughter mingled.

Pride swelled at what his cousin accomplished. Reed easily admitted he was impressed and a bit surprised. He hadn't expected—

He shook his head, not sure what he expected, only knowing it wasn't up to the reality of what he found.

"Ladies, what can I get you?" Over the loud, steady beat of the music, the familiar voice drew him to the bar on the right.

Teddy had aged, as they all had. Muscle taking where once there were only skinny limbs. A face hardened past boyhood charm. His hair, black as the night, fell in a tumbled mess over his shoulders. His green eyes glimmered, bright with the easy spirit he carried through life.

He turned, filling the order from the two at the end of the bar. Reed pushed in beside them, waiting for him to finish shaking the martinis. "Don't suppose you've got a nice Irish Stout?"

"Give me a moment and I'll—"

Teddy's words fell off as his eyes met Reed's. "Well, hell."

Quickly, smoothly, he slid two martinis on to the bar before flattening his palms along the polished top. With a quick shove, he was up and over, grabbing Reed in his arms as he landed on the other side.

"You're a sight I never thought I'd see again." Curving hard hands over his shoulders, Teddy held him out then drug him back for another hug.

Nearly suffocated under the force of his cousin's hold, he was happy he'd come. This was right. As it should be. "Didn't figure I'd be back. Caught a case that brought me here."

He wouldn't share the details of the case. It was not for Teddy, or anyone outside the Bureau, to know. "Figured, since I was here, and you've been carrying on about your bar, I'd come by and see what the fuss was about."

"Makes me damn happy you came by. It's been too long. Way too long. I'll get you that beer then round up one of my bartenders to take over. We've got catching up to do."

Addie couldn't say what drew her.

She and AnnaBeth sat at the table reserved for them near the stage. The bar was crowded, body to body. Clay's music pulled in more, needing to be part of the electric air pouring from the open doors.

He was good. She'd never had a doubt. She'd been lost in singing along with him when the first tug teased her.

Her first look around showed nothing to explain the strange sensation. Shrugging it off, she paired her voice with AnnaBeth's, belting out the chorus of a rich, lively melody brought to life by the talent of Clay's fingers strumming against his guitar, mingling with the rise and fall of his smooth voice.

He glided smoothly into the next song, picking up another beat, another tone, as if he was born to be the one to sing it.

While AnnaBeth continued, Addie dropped off as the pull returned. She looked again over the thick press of bodies. She caught sight of Teddy behind the bar, smiling from ear to ear. His hands fell and rose in easy conversation.

Addie's heart leapt into her throat. Her blood turned to ice, shivering her to the bone, as her gaze skimmed past him to the one he talked with.

It couldn't be.

Downing a long sip from her wine, she tried chasing it away. He'd been gone for years. She'd accepted, long ago, she'd never see him again. Had no desire to. He was nothing more than a bad memory from her past. One she'd successfully tucked away where her thoughts were not bothered by him.

But even with the changes the years brought, she recognized who stood at the end of the bar, wrapping long fingers around the bottle of beer Teddy set in front of him.

Reed McReily.

"Hey. Where'd you go?" At her side, AnnaBeth nudged her. "I thought we were working our duet skills here."

She looked at her best friend. Shock shimmered in her eyes. Her hand shook as she lifted her glass to her lips for a hefty drink. "What the—"

She followed the path of her gaze and understood immediately.

"Well. Well." She lifted her own glass for a sip. "He returns."

Addie's attention turned on her, a silent battle waging in her stormy gaze. "What's he doing here?"

Tossing another look over her shoulder, AnnaBeth shrugged. "Looks like talking with his cousin."

"You know what I mean. I didn't figure we'd ever seen him again."

Addie had counted on it. Had taken it for granted, getting her through in the rare, weak moments when memories of him snuck through.

"Looks like we'll find out." Over the rim of her glass, Annabeth watched Teddy swing a long arm around Reed's shoulders. "They're headed this way."

The urge to flee hit strong. Addie looked toward the doors, tempted to get up and walk out before they reached the table.

What a fool she'd make of herself if she did.

She knew the moment he realized she was there. His eyes, a deep, brilliant blue, darkened as a thousand memories swept through their depths. The smile, softening his expression, slid away, hardening the lines around his mouth and eyes.

He'd changed from the boy she held in her mind. A man now stood in his place. Age brought more definition to the lines around his face, chiseling features, leaving no hint of softness to him.

The lanky stance of a teenager had firmed and tightened, muscles rippling under the black shirt he wore, promising a strength that was close to frightening. AnnaBeth rose while Addie stayed frozen in her seat, unable to tear her gaze away from Reed's hard stare.

"Well, if it isn't Reed McReily come back to grace us with his presence." She grabbed him in a hug. He kept his eyes on Addie, staring at her over the delicate curve of AnnaBeth's shoulder.

"You're as stunning as ever." He curled long fingers over Anna-Beth's arms, held her out for a look. He dropped a soft kiss to her cheek. "I bet you break many hearts."

"That's my goal."

She scooted past him, moving out of the way as Teddy began snagging chairs to add around the table.

Reed noticed none of it, his attention held by Addie sitting and staring up at him, wonder and fear clashing in the depths of her brown eyes.

He wanted to reach out and touch her. Wanted to know, for just a moment, all that had haunted him for years.

She stood, slow and cautious. Her sweet scent, a mix of jasmine and roses, surrounded him as it had over a decade ago.

"I didn't think I'd see you again." Her smile forced, she shoved long red curls from her face.

He couldn't help but take her in. The long yellow skirt she wore flared at her ankles, shifting attention to her perfectly pink painted nails peeking out from leather-strap sandals.

Slender, creamy shoulders were his for the taking in the flower rich tank she wore, dipping enough to give him a hint of what was hidden beneath the thin cotton.

She still loved the jewelry. Emeralds sparkled in her delicate ears and around her slender neck. Rings covered her long, graceful fingers. Bracelets tangled around her wrists.

She was, had always been, soft and delicate. A magical fairy. That's how he'd once seen her in his ridiculous thoughts from youth. The first sight of her had him trapped, tempting him in ways he'd never known, desperate to be with her.

Of course, such naïve thoughts were long past him now.

"I didn't think I'd be back." As much as he tried, he couldn't look away. He needed the sight of her. Fed on it, satisfying a hunger he'd been unaware he still had.

He made a move as if to reach for her. Addie pulled back. Seeing him was enough. The touch of him would be too much.

"I'm thinking Addie and I need a refill." AnnaBeth pushed between her and Reed. She sent a quelling look Teddy's way as he tried waving down a waitress.

Away from the table, Addie sucked in a much needed breath. "Don't think I could have handled that any worse."

Stopping at the bar, using her charm to summon one of the bartenders, AnnaBeth threw a casual arm around her shoulders. "Darling, considering the past, you handled that like a pro."

It was far from the truth, but Addie didn't figure it was worth it to argue. She had greater concerns. Like the fact she still had to return to the table where Reed waited.

Reed watched her. He couldn't help it.

She'd come back to the table, making sure to take the seat furthest from him as AnnaBeth sat like a shield between them.

It was the way of it. The way, Reed figured, it should be, after the level he sunk to all those years ago. But hell, if it didn't poke at him, making him wish for the same kind of welcome from Addie he'd received from Teddy.

But his cousin…they were different. They were family. Blood. It was because of him Reed found this group of friends, so different than the relationships he'd had growing up as a McReily, having to remember the importance of his name. The expectations that came with it.

"He's pretty damn good isn't he?' Teddy thumped Reed against the shoulder, drawing his attention to the stage.

Hell. Reed hadn't realized who it was belting out the rise and fall of notes swirling around them as he played his guitar like it had a voice all its own.

He should have known. Where there was one of them, there was all of them. It was the friendship they shared. One he'd once found himself envious of.

On the stage, AnnaBeth's younger brother, Clay, ended the song. "We'll be taking a short break."

He swung the guitar from his shoulder, easing it against the edge of the drums behind him. "Don't go far. We'll be back."

With one quick hop, he was off the stage and headed their way. Of all of them, he looked most like what Reed remembered. Always the one with his own unique flair, Clay had a look it was impossible to duplicate.

His face still full of boyish charm, he wore a black Bowler hat on top of his light brown hair, tipped to the right, adding that bit of character Clay was constantly after.

"Well, look who came back to the lower class." Clay grabbed him in a hug then held him out, much as Teddy had.

"Couldn't stay away any longer." Reed looked him over as well, shaking his head in a mix of amusement and memories. His lemon-yellow blazer was pushed back just enough to give a glimpse of the paisley suspenders stretching over a dark red shirt.

He was so Clay, in every way he remembered.

"So, who's going to buy me a beer." Clay curled long fingers around the back of an empty chair and plopped down.

"Allow me." Since he was still standing, Reed turned for the bar. While he leaned against the edge, waiting for his order, he looked back at the four around the table.

Addie. It was always about her. The others too, they held their own mark and influence in his younger life. Their strange connection of friendship was so foreign to him. So lost in what he'd grown up knowing. And yet, they'd accepted him, taking him in as one of their own. Showing him a side of life, the pure fun in it, when he'd needed it most.

If it hadn't been for the tug of Addie against his heart, he might have come home sooner, rediscovering what he'd found in this strange group of friends.

Mistakes kept him away. Mistakes it was too late to fix.

He had pictures. Plenty of them.

It was his advantage. While the Bureau wouldn't know him from another on the street. He knew them. Especially one—Reed McReily.

He had plenty of news clippings to pick from, past and present, giving an intimate insight into the agent who'd followed him for more than a year.

It hadn't been hard to search him, learn about him.

He'd been lucky. It had only been a few bars and a couple nights wait before McReily had done as he'd hoped, walking through the doors, giving him the sight and incentive he'd needed.

Yes, this was good. Exactly what he needed to fight the boredom plaguing him.

Seeing McReily excited him, bringing back the need pulsing through his veins. The itch returned in a force it hadn't held for months. It fed the craving he'd satiated on from the very first killing, reminding him of what ran through his blood.

Tucked in the lingering shadows near the back of the bar while nursing his second beer, he kept his gaze steady on the table close to the stage.

The two women caught his eye. One was probably the most beautiful he'd seen. Thick, golden waves streaming over slender shoulders. A body screaming for touch and exploration. She stirred his more primitive instincts, screaming at him to act.

Even with that, she paled compared to the other. The one, he noticed, McReily gave most of his attention to.

She was a gentle beauty. Not the in your face as the other, but more subtle and crafty with her allure.

And she held McReily's interest. That, in itself, was all he needed.

Watching as she ducked her head, long red curls tumbling over as she spoke with the woman at her side, his decision was made.

Not only was it McReily's home he'd chosen. But his girl, as well.

CHAPTER FOUR

She wasn't brooding. It wasn't her.

Still, it came awfully close. Addie shifted in the wicker chair and sipped from her cup of hot tea.

This early in the morning the courtyard was quiet, peaceful. Ferns gracing the old, marble fountain swayed in the gentle breeze. Banana trees added shade, their roots thick and deep through the bricks at her feet.

Inhaling, she took in the sweet scent of flowers blooming. Canna Lilies and Garden Roses mingling their delicate blooms through the Azaleas.

She loved it in the courtyard behind the shop and below their living quarters. Memories of sharing similar mornings with her mother were always a constant, drawing her back to the small girl in twin braids, sitting and listening to the soft rise and fall of her mother's voice, soaking in every word.

The loss still hit. Always would, she'd come to accept. The ache was less now. A small twinge compared to the grieving, bleeding hole she'd once carried.

Time helped to heal. She learned that.

But, as thoughts of Reed returned, she wondered if there were exceptions. If some wounds would never scab over, no matter the years that passed.

Which left her close to brooding in the short time she had before starting work.

"You've a mind full." She didn't hear her aunt until she settled in the chair beside her. It wasn't a surprise. Rosalie was light of step, always seeming to appear out of nowhere.

"Want to talk about it?" She gazed at her over the rim of her coffee cup.

"Reed's back." It was all that needed to be said.

"Is he now." Worry crept into Rosalie's eyes and lingered. She had images still. Her niece and tears. Plenty of them. Crying out the heartbreak of a young girl hurt by the one she fancied herself in love with.

She'd never been given the full story. But she'd heard enough.

"It doesn't matter." Addie shrugged, not sure if she was trying to convince herself or her aunt. "He doesn't plan on staying long. He has some case he's working on and will be back to where he came from as soon as it's done."

"You're okay with that?"

"Of course. He's the past. Nothing more. I'll admit, I was a bit thrown off to see him again, but it means nothing."

It had to mean nothing. She'd never thought, never allowed herself to believe she'd see him again. She hadn't been prepared for it. She'd handle it now.

He'd once meant so much to her. The source of wonderful dreams for the future. Of love and all that came with it. But now, he meant nothing. She'd only have to be sure to remind herself of that when the weakness came back.

If she was lucky, she wouldn't have to see him again. He'd do his thing, she'd do hers, and neither would cross paths until it was time for him to go again.

He was edgy. This time of waiting wasn't for him. He wanted action. Needed it.

It rubbed against Reed, knowing nothing would be done until he had some hint of what the dubbed Kissing Killer had in mind. It sickened him to think it might come with another dead body.

He'd spent the morning in his hotel room. Searching, always searching, for who he might be. What fueled him. What pushed him on.

He had the reports. The theories by the best of the Bureau. They read like a useless group of words. A white man, mid to late twenties. Troubled childhood. Deep rooted dislike for the opposite sex. A severe need for control.

None of it surprised him. None of it helped him.

By lunch he'd needed out. Couldn't have timed it better when Perry called, inviting him to join him and Jackson for lunch at Mollie Mae's.

They claimed a place on the balcony, enjoying the weather while it was still bearable.

He'd missed this. Scooping up a generous portion of Gumbo, enjoying the spices dancing against his tongue, he savored the moment of sitting in the warm spring weather, eating a dish that couldn't be matched outside New Orleans.

He'd had to go. That he'd never deny. And when the case was over, he'd go again. But some things, the simpler things, he missed. This was home. Always would be. Once New Orleans was in your blood, you didn't let it go.

"So, you grew up here." As if reading the way of his thoughts, Perry looked at him across the table as he wrapped a hand around his glass of sweet tea. "A native like Jackson."

"I did. I am." Shifting in his chair, never one comfortable with talking about himself, Reed glanced down over the busy sidewalk below. "I grew up over in Uptown."

"Where the money is. Old money."

Yes. Old money. Old, suffocating, judgmental money. Strong enough to build empires, destroy lives, and ruin hearts.

An image of Addie came to life. Quickly chasing it away, he went back to his Gumbo, tearing off a chunk of crusty bread from the plate beside him.

"It's old money but it's not mine anymore. I left that behind a long time ago."

"To the Bureau's gain, from what I hear. Not that I'll understand a reason to give it all up for a job pushing at the grindstone."

"It wasn't what I set out to do. I left without having a clue, only knowing I needed out. It was some time, and a whole hell of a lot of mistakes, before figuring out where I belonged."

He hated going back to that time. Barely nineteen, drunk and stupid in an alley. He smelled. Everything around him smelled. A stench so strong it rolled the stomach worse than a crazy night on Bourbon Street.

It had been his bottom. He'd nursed and wallowed in anger and self-contempt for a year, since the day he'd left New Orleans behind. That day had been his turning point. The push he'd needed to figure out what the hell he wanted. To realize the life he was leading would take him nowhere but back to the steps of his parents' home, broken and foolish.

"You're a braver man than me." Perry held up his glass in a mock salute. "There's times I'm tempted to run off and do nothing but perfect being a beach bum."

"You'd bore yourself in no time." Jackson nudged him, speaking the truth.

The conversation shifted then, much to Reed's gratitude. Talk of his past never sat well. Not with the dark still haunting him, reminding him of mistakes made.

Mistakes he could never hope to make up for.

Grabbing a clip from under the counter, Addie bundled thick, red curls to the back of her head.

It had been a long, busy day. And they still had a couple more hours to go before locking the doors.

"Mardi Gras's barely passed and we're already showing numbers better than last year." Rosalie's smile stretched from ear to ear as she waved another customer out the door.

This shop had been her dream. Her's and her sister's. They'd taken the little inheritance given them through their father's will and poured it into a vision of what Magic Moon could be.

In her grief, she'd considered selling it after her sister's death. But Addie needed her, relying on her to step in for the mother she'd lost.

Once the worst of the grief slid on, she'd been grateful she'd kept the shop, continuing their dream.

The bell above the door rang out. Rosalie turned, a welcoming smile on her lips. It quickly faded. "Well, look who dares to grace this space again."

Reed hadn't planned on being welcomed kindly. He was right.

Rosalie's eyes were wary. "What can we do for you, Mr. McReily."

What could she do? He didn't know. Coming back to the shop was a bad idea and yet he was here, unable to stop himself.

Now it was too late to turn back.

Addie came out from behind the counter as he continued to stand just inside the door, silent like a fool. Today her skirt carried the blue of a clear, summer sky, dancing around slender legs as she came closer.

"What do you want, Reed?"

She carried no welcome in her voice. No hint of being anything but weary of seeing him again. He couldn't blame her. He'd broken the trust between them years ago then left instead of trying to earn it back.

"I don't know." He went for honesty. "Except maybe a need to see if the shop was still as I remembered. It's been a long time."

Nothing but doubt met him through Addie's dark gaze. Behind her, Rosalie held the same look. At one time he'd been welcomed by both and spent hours simply watching, enjoying the flow of customers through the doors. He'd made his own sales, realizing he liked the feel of it. The pleasure that came as he bagged their purchases.

That time was gone. The proof of it stared back at him.

"Not much different to see." Addie crossed firm arms around her small breasts and continued to stare hard through those rich, chocolate eyes of hers. "No reason for you to stay."

He dared a step closer, thankful when she stayed rooted where she was. "Unless the store wasn't all I was hoping to see."

He reached for her, wrapping long fingers around her slender wrist as she tried turning away. "I've missed you."

She was silent, so much dancing through her gaze. Gently, slowly, she pulled her wrist free, tucking it safe at her side. "There's nothing about me to miss. You made that clear a long time ago."

It tore through him, the pain whispering beneath her words. He couldn't deny her. Couldn't deny the truth he'd left her with.

It didn't change the urge crawling through him since leaving Perry and Jackson after lunch. He'd considered going back to the hotel and diving back into his computer, searching until his eyes were red for some clue. Some idea where the Kissing Killer had landed in New Orleans and what his next target was.

But something more pressing lodged against him, pushing him the opposite way of his hotel. To the shop where he'd find Addie and have a chance to see her again.

Because, damn, he'd meant it, he missed her. The force of it hit hard after seeing her at Teddy's bar the night before, refusing to let go.

"That was another life." Tempted, as he always was when she was near, he pushed closer, invading her space, enjoying the sudden, sharp rise of her breasts as she sucked in a harsh breath.

Stepping back would only prove a weakness Addie didn't want to admit to. She stayed where she was, fighting off the shock of warmth washing over her.

"It's still my life as I have continued to live it. You may have run off, started over, but I've been here, exactly who I am. Who I have always been."

Behind her, Rosalie cleared her throat, in support or disagreement, she couldn't be sure.

This wasn't the time for this, standing in the middle of the shop, journeying places neither one of them belonged. "I think it's best if you go."

He looked as if he wanted to argue. Addie held her breath.

He pushed closer. For a moment she feared what he might do. Releasing a long, slow breath, he shook his head.

"It was good to see you again." He looked over her toward Rosalie.

He turned back for Addie, a spark in his deep, blue eyes she recognized from years past. One frightening her with the reminder of it. "I wish—"

The echo of the bell above the door cut him off as he turned over his shoulder to watch the man walking through, a vase overflowing with dark red roses held in his beefy hands.

"Adelaide Monrose," he read off the small envelope tucked in the center of the flowers.

Careful, so not a part of her brushed against Reed, she moved for the door. "I'm Adelaide Monrose."

"These are for you." He shoved the roses into her hands, barely waiting long enough for a thank you before repeating his steps out the door and onto the crowded sidewalk.

"Now, who went and sent you such beautiful flowers?" Ignoring Reed as much as her niece was, Rosalie joined her at the door, urging her back to the counter to set the heavy vase down.

He should go. Should follow the delivery man out the door. But a sick need to know who'd sent the flowers kept him there. It wasn't jealousy in the quick, sharp pang against his chest. He had no reason for it. No reason for him to care, one way or another, who might be sending Addie flowers.

Frustration darkened Addie's eyes as they passed over him. She said nothing to encourage him to the door. Instead, she pulled the small envelope from the plastic fork holding it in place and slipped a finger under the delicate fold.

She couldn't imagine who would send her flowers. Couldn't remember the last time she'd had a delivery of them. It had been years ago. Martin, maybe, owner of one of the art galleries on Royal. He'd been sweet, thoughtful enough to send delicate carnations mixed with lilies after their first date.

Unfortunately, she preferred the company of the flowers more than Martin. She'd given in to one more date, as a thank you for the gesture, but had been done after that.

Which didn't matter now. These flowers weren't from Martin or from anyone else she could bring to mind.

Pulling the small card from the envelope, she stared at it.

"That's a bit odd." From behind her Rosalie stared over her shoulder, shaking her head. "Would have been much more helpful to leave a name, unless you have yourself a secret admirer."

Reed couldn't help himself. He had to see. Had to know. The flowers. Suggestions of a secret admirer. He wasn't foolish. He had no hold on Addie any longer, no right to try and claim her as his own. But the old possessive feeling crept back, making him itch to know who sent her flowers and why.

He didn't ask, knowing he'd be turned down if he did. Pinching his fingers around the top of the card, he slid it from Addie's fingers, turning it around for a look.

His heart stopped. Blood drained.

"Don't touch." He swept a hand out, stopping Rosalie as she bent forward and reached out to rub a finger against a smooth, red petal.

Already lifting the phone to his ear, he ignored the angry spark in Addie's gaze.

"What is wrong with you?" She made a reach for the vase.

Reed threw out an arm, stopping her. "Please, trust me. I'll explain as soon as I make a call."

She narrowed her eyes, shook her head, making it clear she wasn't willing to put any trust in him again. Dropping her hand, she hitched a hip against the edge of the counter, watching him.

Reed pulled on every instinct inside to stay calm as he waited for Perry to pick up on the other end. Fear made him want to strike out and hit something.

His gaze fell back to the card still clutched tight between his fingers. A small, simple white card. Plain except for the red lip prints staring back at him.

CHAPTER FIVE

Addie's head was spinning.

One minute she was given flowers. The next, Reed was on the phone and agents flooded the shop.

The roses. That's what they cared about, gathered around. Hushed tones and closed looks drifted from them as Rosalie and Addie watched from the opposite end of the counter.

She had no answers. Reed kept promising later. That, in itself made everything feel so unreal. Strange. How did a simple vase of red roses warrant such a response?

"I'm not standing out here on the sidewalk, you fool." The irritated voice echoed through the shop.

Reed moved before Addie could, a step ahead of her at the door. AnnaBeth's glare shot back at him over Perry's shoulder.

"What have you done?" Accusation rang heavy in her voice.

Reed tapped Perry on the shoulder, making room for her to enter. "I haven't done anything. And I shouldn't be letting you in."

Flipping her blond hair over her shoulder, she flashed him a dark stare. "You're crazy if you believe you can stop me."

Pushing past, she found Addie. "What the hell is going on? Why are a bunch of stuffy suits strutting around, playing bouncer at the door?"

"I wish I knew." Addie turned to Reed, wishing he'd give her answers. Instead, all she got was his back as he turned to talk with another agent.

Shuffling AnnaBeth back to the counter, she passed her aunt cautiously watching the agents move around the delicate inventory, so easy to break if they weren't careful.

"Somebody delivered flowers earlier." Addie waved a hand at the roses sitting at the edge of the counter. "Reed got a sight of them, read the card that came with them, and now this."

AnnaBeth took a closer look at the roses. "I don't understand."

"Neither do I." Addie shook her head as Reed and the other agents came together, lowering their heads in quiet conversation.

They looked at her, at the flowers, and her mind ran with curiosity. What was happening?

She was done waiting to find out. Determined now, three long strides brought her to the group. Ignoring Reed, she centered her attention on the handsome blond standing beside him.

"We still have another hour before we close. I was hoping you might have an idea on how much longer you'll be. We'd really appreciate a chance to do more business before the day is done."

Perry's answering smile was quickly cut off as Reed stepped between them. "We're going now. I don't suggest doing any more business today. Jackson's going to stay with you." He darted a glance at the older lady watching them carefully.

Addie shook her head, but Reed continued on. "I'll be back soon. Once I am, I'll take you to dinner and explain."

"I don't want dinner. Explain now." Stubborn, Addie's chin shot up. Her shoulders squared, ready to battle.

Memories tumbled back. Reed shoved them down, the distraction not what he needed. "Dinner. And I promise to tell you everything I can."

He didn't wait for a response. Perry falling into step beside him, he made his way to the door. The bell above chimed as they found their way out.

"Of all the—"

Addie cut off the angry words as Jackson's gaze weighed heavy on her, a hint of understanding in her eyes.

"Don't let me stop you." Her smile was easy, friendly. "I've been an agent too long to be surprised by anything. I figure, you've got a right to that mad you've got building."

"Do you want a glass of wine? I need a glass of wine." Addie spun on her heels, frustration threatening to boil over. She wanted to strangle Reed. Wanted to take the bottle she was going to fetch and hit him upside the head with it.

AnnaBeth sent her a sympathetic smile as she stormed past but wisely kept her words to herself. She waited until the door in the back slammed behind Addie before turning back to the two other women in the room, shaking her head. "No question about it, Reed's back."

They wanted him to consider it might be nothing more than a coincidence.

The thought made him angry.

Reed didn't believe it was a coincidence. He sure as hell wasn't willing to risk Addie's safety on such a theory.

His gut wrenched. He'd never imagined the ugliness he followed to New Orleans would touch her in any way. The fact he'd led it right to her tore him up. Left him sick and disgusted.

"This is the place." Perry flattened a hand against the glass door and pushed.

They'd walked from the shop to the florist. Traffic inside the Quarter would have made the trip twice as long if they'd crawled into the Bureau issued sedan to make it there.

Baker's Blooms. They'd pulled the name from the logo stamped on the envelope. Located by the Farmer's Market, it sat only a few blocks from Magic Moon. The same delivery man stood behind the counter while another man fussed with an arrangement of carnations beside him.

"How can I help you?" His welcoming voice stretched through the store, mingling with the exotic, heated scent of flowers, overwhelming the senses.

Reed and Perry pulled their badges as one.

"You delivered flowers earlier." Reed took the lead. "To a shop called Magic Moon. To Adelaide Monrose."

Curiosity and a small hint of fear lingered in the grey eyes looking back at him. "Just a bit ago. You were there. I remember."

"Who sent them?" Reed clipped his badge back to his waist.

He hesitated for a moment, looking at the other man arranging flowers at his side. "I don't have a name. Didn't have a reason to get one. He came in. Paid cash."

Reed hadn't figured it would be easy. He swallowed back a frustrated curse. "What about the card with the lip prints?"

"Now that was weird." Behind the counter, he shook his head, a sly, crooked grin stretching his face. "He came in with it already done. When I asked if he was serious, he just stared and waited for me to put it in one of our envelopes."

Perry came up closer, side by side with Reed. "What did he look like?"

The delivery man scratched his head. "He was tall. About your size." He jerked his head at Reed. "A bit on the skinny side. And pale. I remember thinking he desperately needed some sun."

Perry took notes as he talked, glancing up when he stopped. "What about hair color? Eyes?"

"Didn't see either. He had a ball cap on his head. Wore sunglasses. Didn't think much about it. Figured he was trying to hide away a night of too much partying on Bourbon."

Reed wanted more. So much more than a vague description of a tall, skinny, pale man who could have been one of many walking the sidewalks through the Quarter.

He wouldn't get it though. Hated having to accept it.

"If you think of anything else." He pulled a card and pressed it to the counter.

He didn't wait for a response or for Perry. Fear and frustration burning a dangerous streak, he stormed out of the florist, taking a moment to suck in a breath once he reached the crowded sidewalk.

"Didn't figure we'd get much." Perry pushed through the door, joining him. "Still have nothing to connect it."

Except for Reed's gut, screaming at him. "I don't believe in coincidences."

He started down the sidewalk and back for Magic Moon. For Addie.

Perry quickened his step, catching up with him. "I don't like the look of this anymore than you. But I'm not sure I can take the leap yet and believe this is our guy on nothing but blind faith. This could be nothing more than some love sick puppy thinking he's cute by leaving such a card with the flowers."

"It's him."

"The Bureau's not going to take it far until they have more proof." Perry paused outside Magic Moon. "We both know it."

"Then we'll get them proof." Reed shoved on the door and stormed inside, stumbling to a stop at the sight of the four women gathered around the counter.

Wine glasses clutched between their fingers, all four sets of eyes turned, landing hard on where he and Perry stood.

"Are we interrupting?" He dared a few steps closer, noticed, while the others held glasses of red wine, Jackson's glass held a clear, bubbling liquid. Club soda, he guessed, since she was still on duty.

"Of course, you are." More sneer than smile passed over Anna-Beth's face as she looked from him to Perry and back.

"Did you find whatever you were looking for?" Impatience shimmered underneath the tone of Addie's voice.

"Not enough." He took a long, hard look at her and found the worry spearing high.

"Will you tell me what's going on now?" She lifted her glass, staring at him over the rim as she took a sip.

"I promised I would. Are you ready to go?"

"Go?"

"Dinner." He picked up her glass as she set it on the counter, taking a drink for himself.

"I don't think dinner is necessary."

He set the glass back on the counter. "It is if you want answers."

He wasn't playing fair, but didn't care. He wanted time alone with her. Wanted to be close where he could keep an eye on her. If this was the way to get it, he'd take it.

"Fine." She glared at him, yanking her glass out of his reach in case he was tempted for another drink. Deliberate and slow, she lifted it to her mouth, finishing it off.

"Give me ten minutes."

Spinning on her heels, she disappeared through the back door, leaving him staring after her, admiring, as he always had, the delicate sway of her backside.

"You do have a way with her." AnnaBeth held up her own glass in a mock toast.

Yeah. He had a way. One that pushed her to want to stay away while he wanted nothing more than to draw her back.

CHAPTER SIX

I t had been deliberate, the restaurant he took her to.

Claiming the last available table on the balcony, she fought back the memories. The past wasn't what mattered. All she wanted was answers. Once she had them she'd let Reed know it was best if he stayed away for the rest of his time in New Orleans. It was better that way.

Even with the pep talk, images came. Long ago snapshots of a night she'd never forget. Another night on the same balcony at a table not far from where they sat now. A night when she'd been foolishly in love and so naïve to the truth of who Reed really was.

"What can I get you to drink?" Pad in hand, their waitress flashed white teeth, drawing out the age lines around her mouth and eyes.

Wine for her, beer for Reed and Barbecue Shrimp to share then they were alone again. Nerves jumped to life as Addie realized this was the first time they'd been alone since that last fateful night by the river, where he'd made it clear she wasn't good enough for a man of his standing or his family's standing.

The memory nearly had her pushing to her feet, leaving him there. Alone. Dinner with him had been dumb. And far less than what he deserved.

Still, she needed to know. Until she did, she'd stay.

"You don't have any more excuses." Keeping her voice strong, leaving no room for argument, she narrowed her eyes, staring at Reed over the length of the table.

"Tell me what the hell happened today."

He drew in a long breath, waiting a moment while their waitress placed drinks in front of them. "I've been working a case for over a year tracking a man the media calls the Kissing Killer."

A trickle of amusement hit before Addie caught the dark shadow in Reed's blue eyes. "They really call him that? Why?"

Reed didn't want to tell her, wishing he could protect her from the ugly depths of what he faced, day after day. But she had to know. At least some of it. "He leaves a mark on his victims, a red lips kiss."

An image of the card came. Addie sucked in a breath, clearly seeing the single print of red against white.

Reed waited while a plate of Barbecue Shrimp was set between them. "I'm here in New Orleans because this UNSUB, whoever he is, has made it personal. He sent a note. The Bureau received it a few days ago. It was a note for me."

"What do you mean for you? How does he know who you are?"

"Like I said," Reed grabbed a shrimp from the plate, "I've been working this case for over a year. Plenty of time for him to learn my name. And he took it further, learning about my past, where I came from, and deciding to bring his threat of murdering another woman here."

"He's here?" Addie swallowed hard. "In New Orleans?"

Reed made a move to reach for her then thought better of it, tucking his hand beneath the table. "The Bureau doesn't believe we have solid proof yet. But, as far as I'm concerned, the flowers delivered are proof enough."

"You think this killer sent the flowers?" A sick feeling churned through, leaving a bitter taste in her mouth. "Why? I don't understand."

Needing something to do with her hands, to distract from the fear clutching inside, she grabbed a shrimp, peeling away the shell. Part of her wanted to reach for Reed and find in him the strength she'd once known. Use it to stabilize her, keep her steady as she wanted to fall.

She couldn't. Wouldn't.

"It's the timing, the play of it." Reed's blue eyes reached across the table, digging deep. She had to turn away, just for a moment. "He knows my past. Somehow he's learned of your part in it."

"How could he?" She didn't want to go back there. Back to the time she'd spent wrapped in what she'd foolishly believed had been Reed's love. "That was a long time ago. You weren't exactly eager to share our relationship even then."

Reed took the stab. He deserved it. He'd been dumb. Foolish.

"I don't know the answers. I only know he sent those flowers to you."

"Because of the card." Addie thought back to it. "Has he done that before? Sent flowers?"

It was the same question Perry asked. "No. This would be a first. He stalked some of his victims. But he's never taken such a bold step."

"So, there's a chance it's not him." Bolstered by the thought, she grabbed another shrimp. "It isn't that odd, after all, someone signing a card or sealing an envelope with a kiss."

Reed saw the hope and was tempted to leave it alone. But he couldn't. She needed to know. He wasn't sure, yet, if the flowers were a poke at him or a disgusting hint that Addie was in his sights. Either way, it wasn't a risk he was willing to take.

"It's him." He made sure he had her attention. "The Bureau might still need proof, but I don't."

Her heart jumped but she refused to react. Refused to give in to something, in her mind, that was not yet fact. "Well, when the Bureau gets their proof, let me know."

He said nothing as their waitress returned, ready to take their dinner order. Because he needed it, missed it over the years, he ordered the fried catfish and waited while Addie added her order of crab cakes. As the waitress left, he waited, sipping slowly from his beer.

"I want you protected." He again felt the urge to reach for her. Curling his fingers into his palm, he fought it back. "If the Bureau is unwilling to assign an agent, I'll do it myself."

"I don't need protection." Slow, dangerous anger flashing in her eyes, Addie wrapped tight fingers around the stem of her wine glass. "And I certainly don't need it from you."

Reed bit back the first reply jumping to life. Making her madder wouldn't get him anywhere.

"This man kills women." This time he didn't stop himself, reaching across the table he grabbed her hand. "For fun. For his own sick enjoyment."

Heat speared where his fingers curled around hers. The jolt of warmth threatened to knock Addie off balance.

"If this is the same man." She pulled her hand free, tucking it safely below the table.

"The way I see it," her other hand tightened around her wine glass, "you've got your mind set it's him because you desperately want it to be. Need it to be so you can be sure you're on the right path to find him."

Finishing off the last of her wine, she set the glass back on the table. "Chances are, the one who sent the flowers is not the guy you're after. It doesn't make sense for it to be him. He has no way of knowing about me. About us."

The words caught painful in her throat, making her wish for more wine. "The odds of being the one woman he singles out in New Orleans are slim to none."

"Damnit, Addie." His voice barreled over her, catching the attention of those sitting around them. "This isn't some betting game. This is real life."

Thankful to catch sight of their waitress, Addie waved at her empty wine glass. "I know exactly what this is."

She turned back to Reed. Keeping her voice steady, she refused to lose control. "I also know it's my life. You don't get a say in it, not anymore."

Anger rolled back but she refused to react or give in to the heat of it. The waitress returned with another glass of wine, taking the empty one. Addie waited. Silent. Stubborn.

She would not give in. Would not allow Reed to, once more, sweep into her life, set it upside down only to rush out again. Regardless of what he had in his mind, she wasn't going to accept it on his word alone. Those days had passed long ago.

"What do you expect me to do?" He shoved an aggravated hand through his hair, tossing dark strands around his hard-lined face. "Am I supposed to trust you'll be safe? To do nothing to make sure, myself?"

Addie waited to answer as the waitress returned with their dinner. She set the plates in front of them then went off to refill Reed's beer.

"You might be a big, bad agent now. You might have a gun and a badge. But none of that did anything to keep me safe all the time you've been gone. And it won't do it now."

She speared her fork through a crab cake. "I can take care of myself. I've been doing it just fine for years."

Reed wanted to argue. Wanted to shove from his seat, grab her, and shake her until she understood the truth.

She was stubborn. So damn stubborn. For someone so small, she held a mile-long spine of steel. She wouldn't give in no matter how much he pushed or desperately he begged.

Grabbing a fried catfish, he tore in with more force than necessary. "At least promise you'll be more cautious and pay attention to your surroundings. To who's around you."

Her stony stare lasted for only a moment. "Fine. I promise."

It was as good as he was going to get. At least for now.

Letting it drop, he concentrated on his dinner, wishing things were as they once were between them. At one time, she wouldn't have fought or argued with him, but would have trusted him with her whole heart.

He'd been the one to ruin that. The reminder left a bitter taste in his mouth. The waitress set his beer in front of him just in time for him to take a healthy drink, washing it away.

She'd been a vibrant promise of light in his life. So different than the stuffy, rigid upbringing he'd known. He looked up. Addie picked at her crab cake. For a moment, he saw her as she'd been that first day.

Her skirts had been shorter then. Soft, flowing cotton, gliding halfway down her thigh, shimmering around her with every move she made.

Her hair, still the long flow of red curls, had been pulled back in a ponytail, giving him a clear shot of the delicate features of her face. The soft plump of her lips. Dark brown eyes glittering with amusement.

He'd been lost. One look and he was taken.

Her small size and gentle curves fit against him as if she were made for his arms. The delicate flow of her voice had run through his blood, heating his teenage boy desires to levels he'd never known.

She hadn't played games like so many of the girls he'd met. She was open and true, knowing just what she wanted.

"I should be going." The soft sweep of her voice brought him back.

He wasn't ready for dinner to end. Not yet. But he had no excuse to stall without looking like a desperate fool.

"Let me finish this." He held up what was left of his beer. "And I'll pay the check."

That was good enough for Addie, though part of her wanted to stand then and end the night. Long bred manners had her waiting no matter how rapid the urge to flee ran through her veins.

Night started to settle by the time they left the restaurant. Addie turned, more than ready to be home and away from Reed.

He grabbed her, fingers circling around her wrist. "Let's walk back this way." He nodded toward Bourbon, only a few feet away and in the opposite direction than she intended to go.

"Bourbon Street. At night." She shook her head, pulling free from his hold. "Are you crazy?"

"Maybe a little." His smile, so simple, pushed past her barriers. "Humor me. It's been a long time. Never thought I'd miss the craziness, but I do."

She shouldn't. Though the time wouldn't be much longer, she should head back the way she'd planned. Better yet, she should do it alone.

So why she agreed, she couldn't say. Falling into step beside him, she joined the crush of bodies partying their way from one sidewalk to the next. The heavy beat of music poured from open doors, a different song for every club or bar they passed.

Liquor and craziness flowed equally, creating the amazing uniqueness that was the heart of the Quarter. Even as a native, Addie still found joy in it. Still found wonder at what lay at the surface when people truly let go of their expectations, their limitations, and simply enjoyed themselves.

Of course, there was usually payment as well. That came with the glaring light of morning, not during the night when life seemed to be at one's hands, urging them to explore the greatness of it and forget the harshness it could bring.

Working their way through the crowd, Reed slipped his hand through hers. The feel of it had her staggering for a moment, nearly tripping over her own two feet.

A simple touch and old feelings threatened to sweep through. Unwilling to take the risk, she pulled free, tucking her hand safely out of his reach.

He shook his head but didn't say a word, continuing down Bourbon Street with the look and gait of one who knew it in his heart, just as she did.

The more she watched him, the more she realized he wasn't the same boy who'd once taken this very same path with her. Laughing, enjoying it, and taking in all that was around him in a flood of excitement.

Today, the man he was carried a much different way about him. He didn't move with the freedom of letting his cares go, but with the cautious step and awareness of one assessing and judging every possible risk around him.

His gaze moved from side to side, lingering longer when voices raised, liquor spilled from cups, and angry shouts erupted.

He missed nothing. In the chaos that was a night on Bourbon, he saw it all, taking every bit in and determining what might become more. Might become a risk to those who shared the cramped space.

It hit her how much had changed. Not only the harder, more toned shape of him, the deeper ring in his voice, or the clear control of who he was. But it was in the danger he looked for. The threats he sought.

The boy who'd once come to the Quarter to escape the rigid ways of his life, now returned with more rigid demands placed on him. By job and life now rather than family.

She wanted to stop him and urge him to let go. To give himself permission to simply enjoy what had once meant so much to him.

But that would have shown care and an interest she didn't want to admit she had. Didn't want him to know existed.

So they walked in silence. Slow with the masses, moving, stopping, sometimes dancing, around them.

"Do you want to go in?" Reed nodded toward the lively crowd pouring in and out of Teddy's bar. "I'll buy you a drink."

She considered it for a moment. One drink wouldn't hurt anything.

But this was Reed. Every moment with him was a risk. "I need to get back. I promised Rosalie I wouldn't be long. I don't want her to worry."

Not that she would. It was a weak lie. Even when she was a child, Rosalie had never been one to hover over her with worry. She trusted her niece. Gave her freedoms some didn't always agree with when Addie had been younger, raising questions about her ability to step in her sister's shoes and care for a small girl.

Though he was tempted to, Reed didn't argue. Nor did he try reaching for her again, though his hands itched to do so.

He'd done this. He'd made the cut tearing so fierce between them. The blame sat on his shoulders. And though it was a hell of a weight to carry, it was one he couldn't deny.

They walked in silence, turning down Toulouse and away from the constant drum of Bourbon.

Without the push of bodies against them, Addie took advantage, placing much needed space between her and Reed. Close to the shop now, she was eager to get there, ending their time together.

She'd never thought he'd come back. Never prepared herself for the hit of old emotions racing through since seeing him again.

His worry was on the man who'd had the flowers sent. To her, it was nothing compared to the threats her heart gave and her mind recalled.

He was her worry. The one she needed to protect herself from.

Knowing Rosalie would already have the shop turned down and locked up tight for the night, she went behind to the courtyard, stopping at the wrought iron gate leading in.

"Thank you for dinner." Never forgetting the manners she'd been raised with, even for Reed, she stuck out her hand.

He took it, held on while his gaze caught hers.

Realizing her mistake, she tried pulling back. He refused to let go, tugging so she stumbled closer. His deep blue eyes never turned from hers. "Did you miss me?"

His unexpected question catching her off guard, she forgot, for a moment, her need to get away. "I—"

She shook her head, pulling in a harsh breath. "I didn't have anything to miss."

The lie fell sour against her tongue. Disgusted by it, she yanked her hand free and took a step back.

Tears threatened to fall. A hint of the old heartbreak found its way through the barriers. Hurt and loss battled, creating anger bubbling inside. "What the hell would I have to miss from, what did you call it, a crazy fling to scratch an itch?"

"No." She shook her head as he reached for her, backing herself into the gate. He trapped her between him and the wrought iron pressing against her spine.

She couldn't tell what flashed through his eyes. But the force of it frightened her. She fumbled behind her back for the latch to open the gate. His breath brushed against her cheek as he lowered. Hard muscles pressed against her as he left not an inch between them.

Spearing long, rough fingers through her hair, he held her still.

"Reed, please." She hated the desperation in her voice. Hated more that she wasn't sure what she begged for. To be let go or to be taken?

She couldn't find a breath. Couldn't stop the frantic beat of her heart. His spicy scent caught on the air, swirling around her. The feel of him, so close, left her struggling for steady ground.

Time stopped. Seconds passed like hours, Reed's mouth hovering only a breath from hers, promising something forbidden. Unwanted yet so desperately desired.

"Be sure to lock up." Abrupt, leaving only a violent chill in his place, he dropped his hand and stepped back.

Fumbling for stable ground, for rational thought, Addie stared. By the time she found the ability to form a word, he spun on his heels and stormed away.

Disgusted, she heaved in a heavy breath and shoved a hand through her hair, tossing it back from where he'd tugged it loose.

This wasn't right. It wasn't going to work. Only a few days back and Reed was playing his tricks. She wouldn't have it, not now. Not after how hard and long she'd fought to bring to life the woman she'd become after he'd destroyed all she believed in.

He needed to stay away. She needed to keep him away. No more of his excuses to be near her. She was done with him. Just as he'd once made it clear he was done with her.

Reed went to the river, the one place he'd always found relief, no matter the mood.

Even at night, life continued to thrive. Long, thick barges cut through water, darkened by the sky. Brightly lit paddle boats entertained tourists, soulful jazz catching in the wind, brushing back to shore.

Others walked as he did. Couples holding hands. An older woman walking her dog. Teens ducking skateboards around those in their way.

Reed barely noticed any of it, his mind wandering to places better left forgotten.

He shouldn't have come back. A wiser man would have taken the chance to pass on the case, no matter the time he'd put in.

He nearly laughed at that. After all he'd dedicated to getting his hands on the bastard there wasn't a force on earth that could have taken him off the case.

The Kissing Killer was his. In every way. He'd be the one to bring him down.

None of that changed the hell of being back.

Away from New Orleans, away from his past, he almost fooled himself into believing he'd forgotten and moved away from all that happened.

But being back only proved how wrong he was.

To hell with it all. Temper spiking, clashing dangerously with frustration, he stared out over the water, wishing for the same calm it held.

To this day, it still echoed in his head. The demands and expectations that came with being a McReily. Old money, his family was called. A deep, rich heritage spanning back generations, piling higher and higher the responsibilities he'd been expected to carry out.

While McReilys were sure to give to those less fortunate than them, they certainly didn't fraternize with such sorts. They were worthy of their charity but nothing else. Certainly not any kind of true time spent outside of what it took to sign the next donation check.

Even Teddy, blood as he was, was undeserving of much time or effort. He may be family, but he was seen as the product of those who married down, further separating themselves from what it meant to be a McReily.

He hated it, every bit of it. Anger rumbled, threatening to take over.

Years ago, it was that very anger sending him to run off with Teddy every chance he had. To a life so different than the one he had. So vibrant and full of color it was an experience unlike anything he'd known.

Here in the Quarter, where Teddy grew up, was the taste of so much more. He wasn't stuffed into suits and carted off to clubs where he was expected to sit and be silent. To be respectful and boring. The same food. The same drinks. The same talks with the same boring people.

Day after day. Night after night.

He'd loved escaping with Teddy, in the way only a restless teenage boy, on the very edge of manhood, could.

He'd shown him a life worth being part of. Introduced him to the thrill of taking risks. The excitement of never knowing where the night might take you. He'd given him friends so unlike the ones he'd known. True people with blood, rather than ice, running through their veins. AnnaBeth and Clay.

And Addie.

She'd been like a drop of water when he hadn't been aware he was dying of thirst. Catching him from that first look, he'd never had a chance. So soft yet hard in her beliefs. A dreamer. One who took the flash of a star in the black sky and turned it into a story of love, mystery, and romance.

They'd clashed in every way, a challenge for every moment he was near her.

She believed in the good, the romantic, and the overwhelming temptation of what was unknown. She encouraged him at every step to look beyond the static of what he lived and knew. To peer deeper into places he'd never imagined existed.

He remembered her laughter the first day they'd met. Like a song he couldn't free his mind of, he'd taken it with him back home, playing with it through his dreams.

He'd wanted her from that moment. Could think of nothing else. Cringing, he remembered how he'd tried to impress, using money, the importance of his family name, to try and sway her closer and into his arms.

Young and foolish, it never struck him what a waste such efforts were. What worked in the world he'd been raised in meant nothing more than insult in Addie's world.

He'd nearly ruined it all.

"You could have all the money in the world, you still can't buy me." Addie had flipped her long red curls over her slender shoulders, turning her back on him. "Let me know when I can get to know the real Reed you keep hidden behind all that glitz and ego. Maybe then I'll consider giving you a chance."

It had been the slap he needed, finally bringing the understanding that, in her world, it wasn't one's wealth but one's truth that mattered.

The memory of that moment hitting as hard now as it did then, Reed turned away from the river, frustrated steps leading him away.

It was no wonder he faced such a battle with Addie every time they were near. He'd messed up from the start with her. She'd already given him a second chance. Expecting another was too much to hope for.

Because he'd taken that second chance and destroyed it.

Angry now, tempted to stop for a drink to drown it away, he stormed past the tourists filling Jackson's Square, carefully working his way around the fortune tellers, artists, and jewelers set up along the way.

He should have come back and stayed away from Addie. Should have known nothing good would come from it. Now, he didn't have a choice with the threat hanging over her.

Regardless of her hesitance to believe him, of the Bureau's refusal to follow along until they had more proof, he had no doubt she'd fallen into the sight of the killer he hunted. Whether it was with the hope to make her his next victim or a play against Reed, he didn't know. And it didn't matter.

Fear surging again, he hesitated at the corner and thought about turning for Magic Moon. Seriously considered spending the night in the courtyard if it meant keeping her safe.

But she was locked in safe. The Monrose's didn't take their safety lightly, not after the death of Addie's mother.

So tonight, he'd trust it over making a fool of himself. In the morning, he'd find more proof for the Bureau until they had no choice but to see what he did.

It was for the best, since he needed time away from her. Emotions were not his friend. Never had been. And since being around Addie again, they were grasping with a force he found hard to fight back.

Guilt was the worst of them. And regret. They hit with strength as he turned down the block for his hotel, making room for a drunk couple stumbling down the sidewalk.

He'd had everything he could have ever wanted with Addie. She'd given him her heart, trusting him to treasure it.

He'd destroyed it. Because he'd been weak, folding once his parents found out about their relationship.

Hands clenched into fists, he shoved them deep into his pockets as words from so many years ago returned. The start of what was the end for him.

They tried to lower her worth. She wasn't one of them. Never would be. He deserved better. The family name deserved better. He would not lower himself. Would not follow in the path of those before him, becoming a shame to who they were and where they came from.

None of it worked. To him, she was better than the very ones trying to pull her down. For as much as they shoved, he dug in, refusing to be convinced that what he felt for Addie was wrong in any way.

Every day they'd try to convince him. Every night he'd return to Addie, loving her even more for her honesty and acceptance of others just as they were.

It was his grandfather who pulled the right strings.

Reed went back to that hot, summer day sitting in his lush office. Montgomery McReily had been the true Patriarch of the family, ruling with a heavy, but loving, fist. There had been no other like him. Nobody within his blood Reed respected more.

He'd sat at his desk, sipping from his brandy, staring at his grandson with sad, thoughtful eyes. No anger. No judgment or accusation. Only the calm, steady love and guidance he'd always given.

"If you love her as you say, boy, you'll think of her." The grumbling, deep voice echoed in his mind. "Of what a future with a McReily would mean. How it will change her."

Swirling brandy in his glass, he'd come out from behind his desk to sit with Reed in one of the brown leather chairs. "You say you love her free spirit. Her joy in everything she does. Are those also things you are willing to force her to give up in order to spend a future with you? Will you take what you love most about her away from her so that you can make her yours?"

"That's ridiculous." He shook his head. "Why would I have to take anything away from her?"

"Because being a McReily means responsibility. Commitment. You know that, son. You live it every day. It weighs on the shoulders of us all."

Sipping slow from his drink, his grandfather rested a gentle hand over Reed's leg. "Take that girl and all you love about her and put her here. See in your mind what she will face. What will be expected of her. Do you see her able to hold on to who she is under such expectations? Do you still see the same girl you love here in this world?"

Reed didn't want to see it. Didn't want to put Addie here in this life. It was his need to escape that brought her to him. He hadn't thought about what it would be to make her part of anything other than what they had in the separate world he'd created.

"It doesn't have to be that way." With the naivety of youth, he believed it. Was sure a different answer waited somewhere.

"How could it not be?" A hint of regret lingered in his grandfather's voice. He looked hard at his grandson, emotion deep in his blue eyes.

"Being a part of the McReilys demands it. If you choose to walk away, what will you have to offer her for a future other than struggle and need? That, too, will drain away all you love about her."

No. He didn't want to hear it. Didn't want to think it.

It was anger, so strong it nearly took him over, sending him running out of his grandfather's house that day. And loss, though he had yet to admit it, dragging him under as he'd escaped to the Quarter, aimlessly wandering the streets.

No matter how far or long he walked, he couldn't find another answer. His grandfather was right. He'd destroy everything he loved about Addie.

In that understanding came the knowledge of what he would have to do.

With more force than necessary, Reed shoved through the lobby doors. What a fool he'd been. The decisions he'd made held no meaning other than desperation.

The quiet inside the hotel settled over him. He ignored everything but the war of memories battling inside his head.

The Reed he was, the one he never wanted to return to again, saw no other choice but to send Addie running.

If he didn't make sure Addie hated him, he'd never have a chance of breaking away from her, sparing her from what his grandfather made clear was her fate.

So, he'd grabbed on to who he once was before Teddy had shown him different. Before Addie slapped into his face a world so different than the one he'd known.

She'd never take it, never stay away, if he suggested how it would affect her to be part of his life. Addie wasn't that way. She would have dug in her heels, letting her love for him lead her to believe they'd overcome such barriers.

So, he lied. With every sickening bit of who he once was, he poured out the untruths in the worst and harshest ways possible.

Standing in the elevator, waiting for the doors to close, the bile returned to his mouth, as strong and vile as it had ever been.

He'd told her she wasn't good enough for him. That she'd been nothing more than a fling to pass the year.

She'd doubted him. Insisted he was lying.

She'd pressed her palms against his chest, demanding he look her in the eye and say such horrible things.

He couldn't. But he continued on. He had to break her and make her hate him.

He'd succeeded, his biggest triumph and greatest regret rolled into one.

Her tears broke his heart. Her pain a fist still holding tight. He'd destroyed her to save her. A reality with a bitter taste never leaving his mouth.

Then his own anger had come. Resentment so strong, so fierce, he couldn't fight against it.

His family, the responsibility of it, the rigidness of it, had not only cost him so much but had destroyed the one person closest to his heart.

He hated them. Every single one of them. His parents, grandparents. Aunts and Uncles.

Being near them became suffocating, dragging him under with every passing day.

He couldn't go back to the Quarter. Couldn't come close to reclaiming what he had torn to shreds. He hated them for it. Hated the very name McReily for it.

So, he'd run as fast and as far as he could.

Hatred of who he was, where he came from, was his biggest drive. Everything he'd been led to believe meant something in his life had been exactly what took it all away.

He wasn't staying for it. Refused to live with it another day.

So, he ventured on his own.

He worked odd jobs, enough to have the money to buy the booze keeping him numb, day after day, week after week. He slept wherever he could lay his head. Sometimes in a borrowed bed or couch. Other times on the hard ground.

Then he'd met the most interesting, surly, stubborn man of his life.

Mitchell Gray.

He smiled as he stepped off the elevator, the thought of him bringing respect and awe.

After that final dark night when he'd hit bottom, he'd settled in a tiny diner, nothing more than a hole in the wall. He hadn't had a dollar to his name, but it didn't stop him from ordering coffee and toast, hoping to settle his rolling stomach.

Mitchell had been there, sitting in an old cracked booth in the corner. Not that Reed noticed him. All he'd cared about was making sure the waitress wasn't around when he finally stumbled from his seat, leaving without paying his bill and sure he hadn't been seen.

But Mitchell had seen him. He'd caught him barely a block away.

His mind a mess from the dark night before, being confronted opened up gates he'd kept so carefully sealed since leaving home.

Everything Reed held inside for so many months found the permission to spill forth the minute Mitchell confronted him, threatening to yank him back to the diner and face the consequences.

He was an agent with the Bureau. Had seen and heard so much, none of Reed's excuses meant a thing. So the truth came, every ugly bit of it. And with it came a relationship carrying Reed through many years.

Swiping his card against the door, dropping badge and gun on the table, he looked in the long mirror attached to the wall, saw what Mitchell brought to reality.

Someone who started to care again. Who stopped living in self-pity and found a purpose. He was an agent today because of Mitchell.

Digging through the mini bar, grabbing a bottle of cheap scotch, Reed wondered what Mitchell would say, knowing his current case brought him back to the past he'd run from. He'd never get the answer as Mitchell passed away three years earlier. Still he wondered, always finding himself caught in the thought of what his friend and mentor would say about where his life led him.

It said a lot that he hadn't come home for his grandfather's funeral but had put all he had into making sure Mitchell had the goodbye he deserved.

It was his life now. Good and bad. He'd destroyed one, run from it, and started over.

What he faced now was his own doing. His own creation.

He'd deal with it. Just as he'd deal with Addie and everything she challenged in what he'd made for himself. It was no less than what Mitchell would expect.

CHAPTER SEVEN

I t was almost like he was on vacation.

Following the ways of the tourists, he settled at a small table at Café du Monde with a cup of coffee and plate of beignets in front of him.

Oh yes. It was as if he were one of them, taking in the sights. The mystery and intrigue dancing through the French Quarter.

He could almost fool himself into believing he'd come to learn the history. Try the food. Be part of the life pulsing through. Sitting in the morning sun, powdered sugar dusting his fingers, the sound of a river barge horn exploding behind him, he could easily become one here to enjoy it all.

Could, if greater pleasures weren't waiting for him.

The day before had been a wonderful treat. He'd watched from the sidewalk as his flowers had been delivered. Enjoyed great delight to see McReily kick so quickly into action.

He never would have guessed he'd find such a thrill in playing with the agent who shadowed him for so long. There was some justice in it. An ego boost to hold such control. He pulled the strings. It was now his choice to decide when McReily would jump.

He had an itch. Too much time had passed since he'd savored the lush beauty of a woman's body. The tension and fear vibrating through as he trapped her, letting her know how he planned to punish her.

He needed, like an addict, that moment of watching life drain from her. The smooth cool of her breast against his lips as he left his final mark.

Pleasure surged, bringing back the need to know it again.

Yes. It had been too long.

Finishing the last of his coffee, he smiled at a small girl looking at him from the next table. So sweet and innocent they were at that age. If only they stayed that way, he wouldn't need to bring about his punishment.

To make them pay as his mother should have.

Such things didn't matter at the moment. Shaking his head, angry he'd allowed dark imagines to raise their ugly head, he tossed his trash away, mixing into the crowd moving slowly across the busy street.

What mattered now was taking care of the business before him. He could do both, find pleasure in toying with Reed while enjoying the satisfying rush of another kill.

The opportunities were all around him.

He only needed to pick one.

"You've got it running around inside your head, might as well talk about it." Rosalie flicked an errant hand over the shimmering crystals displayed at the end of the counter before coming around to where Addie stood, brooding.

She'd been at it all morning. Tossing around emotions inside her head, wishing she could simply turn them off and forget it all.

"Nothing to talk about." She messed with the credit card receipts, avoiding her aunt's steady gaze. "Everything will be fine as soon as Reed goes back to where he came from."

A tinge of sadness touched Rosalie's heart as she watched her niece. As much as she'd tried over the years to deny it, the pain remained. Reed's coming back had only opened wounds not yet fully scarred over.

Stepping closer, she rested a gentle hand over Addie's. "His leaving the first time didn't solve anything, only took the painful reminders further away."

"No. It solved plenty." Agitated, unable to stand still a second longer, Addie slipped her hand free from her aunt's, moving out from behind the counter.

Fumbling through the Celtic Tapestries hanging from the wall, she nearly tugged them from their place. "He was gone, where I didn't have to see him or be reminded of him every single day. Or hear his words, over and over again, inside my head."

"He tossed me away, Rosalie." Anger and pain mixing dangerously, she folded her arms tight over her middle, chasing off the sudden chill.

His words from that final day were still clear. The dead look in his eyes as he made it clear what they'd had together meant nothing to him. She wasn't good enough, not for someone of his class. Had never had a chance of being good enough for what he'd need when he finally chose to make a commitment to another.

"And then he comes back, acts as if it never happened. As if I'm supposed to suddenly start trusting him now."

And came dangerously close to kissing her.

She fought back the surge of heat tingling against her skin. He hadn't kissed her. That's what mattered. Especially since she couldn't be sure she would have had the strength, or desire, to stop him if he'd tried.

Thankful for the lull in customers, Rosalie came out from behind the counter, dropping a gentle hand over Addie's trembling shoulder. "Do you not wonder why, if he truly cared nothing for you, he would now have it in his heart to worry about you?"

"It's part of his job." Addie shook off any other explanation. "He'd be a disgrace to the badge if he didn't."

"I suppose it is, at least, an easier answer to accept." Shaking her head with a touch of sadness, she dropped a light kiss against Addie's cheek as the bell above the door chimed.

The next round of customers streamed in. Addie shook herself free from the worry and frustration. Rosalie might find it necessary to find excuses, but she knew better.

Once upon a time, she'd given everything she had, everything she was, to Reed. He'd been her first and she'd fallen madly in love, too young and naïve to understand what was in her heart was not in his.

He'd torn her to shreds the day he'd let her know the truth. Searching for reasons why wasn't worth her time. He didn't care then. He certainly didn't care now.

She refused to believe any different.

He spent hours with nothing to show for it. No matter how many questions he asked or how much he dug, nothing led him to who sent the flowers.

Pushing the frustration of it from his mind, Reed concentrated on the information flashing on the monitor. Burke had set him up with a spare office and a computer to use. He'd spent the last of his day searching till his fingers hurt, his eyes blurred.

If he couldn't find a tie in the flowers, he'd continue looking for ties leading to the identity of the Kissing Killer. He'd go back through every little bit of information he had. Every file. Every note. Every observation made.

They had to have missed something. He was determined to find it.

He spent hours lost in the reports from Tennessee, where the first victim had been found. The real answers were there, in the beginning. In that first kill that started it all.

Taking the last swig of cold coffee, he glanced at the clock. Magic Moon would be closing soon. It was time to go.

A few clicks of the mouse and the information was saved for the next day. Tossing the empty cup in the trash, closing up the office, he waved goodbye to Perry and Jackson on his way out.

Addie would fight him if she knew what he was up to. He'd made his way to the shop first thing in the morning, strolling by on the sidewalk, thankful to catch a hint of her long, red curls working behind a display of Tarot cards.

Lunch brought him back. To see, know, she was safe.

She would never agree to him hanging around. And the Bureau continued to refuse protection without further proof. So, he did what he had to, watching without her knowing. Holding back the urge to be her constant shadow while seeing enough, doing enough, to reassure himself she was okay.

Not knowing her plans for the night, he stayed until the shop was dark and locked up before going around to the courtyard.

Hitching against the edge of an old carriage house across the way, he settled in, prepared to watch and wait.

CHAPTER EIGHT

S he hadn't planned to go out. She wanted quiet. A peaceful night of watching old movies and forgetting everything else but the story unfolding in black and white.

The house had been all hers. It was the weekly night for her aunt to meet her friends at the casino. Play the slots, enjoy the free drinks until their pockets were empty—more often than not—and their minds a bit fuzzy.

But it hadn't taken long to realize a night alone wasn't a good idea. Too much time to think and wonder about the past or worry about the present.

Reed's hard, chiseled face was a constant image. His deep voice an echo in her ears no matter how high she turned the volume on the television.

Cursing him, her weakness leaving her unable to chase thoughts of him away, she hit the power button on the remote with more force than necessary, put the bottle of Chardonnay she'd opened back into the fridge.

A quick call to AnnaBeth was all it took to give her a reason to get out. Quick now, nearly desperate with the need to be surrounded by life and noise instead of the quiet, she hurried to her bedroom.

Stripping off the sweats and oversized t-shirt she'd thrown on only an hour earlier, Addie pulled a turquoise skirt and soft ivory shirt with flowers the same shade as the skirt from her closet.

A few minutes in the bathroom, adding a light dusting of make-up, pulling her red curls into a clip at the back of her head, and she was heading for the door.

The night was calm. The heat from the day continued to linger, as it would more and more as spring took its hold. Using the lights of the courtyard to lead her way, she closed the gate behind her, turning away from the quiet she'd hoped for and into the vibrant life she'd discovered she needed instead.

A strange sensation crept as she turned the corner. A tickling at the back of her neck brought an odd feeling of being watched.

Stopping, turning back, she saw nothing more than nameless faces moving along the sidewalk. None seemed interested in her other than to push their way past as she held up the flow moving along.

Shaking her head, she continued on. It was nothing more than further proof Reed put her off her normal self. Not just by his return, but his sudden worry over the flowers that had been delivered.

Now she was frightening herself by doing nothing more than walking down streets she'd known her entire life.

Cursing her ridiculous reaction, she hurried her pace. She wasn't going out to think of Reed or let his worry pull her down.

She was out to forget all of that. To enjoy time with her best friend. A couple drinks and some laughs before calling the day an end.

She pushed through the crowds clogging Bourbon Street and strode through the wide open doors of Teddy's bar with the confidence of a woman who knew what she wanted.

The lively notes of the current night's band surrounded her as she paused a step inside, searching through the dim for the short crop of AnnaBeth's blond hair.

From a table tucked neatly between the two bars, her friend waved, raising her wine glass in salute as Addie headed her way. "Thought I would have to fight a couple of college boys for the table."

She shoved the second glass of wine she'd ordered toward Addie as she took her seat. "I did a bit of a flirt, some eyelash fluttering, and it was as good as ours."

Smiling over the rim of her glass, AnnaBeth waved her fingers at two young men sitting at the edge of the bar, looking back at her with wonder in their eyes.

"Oh, you are evil." Addie nudged her friend, drawing her attention back. The two at the bar continued to stare. "They'll be thinking they have a chance now."

AnnaBeth smiled, shrugged. "Nothing wrong with giving them something to hope for. No need to dash their young, wistful fantasies."

Fantasies were all it would ever be. Ones easily born under the sheer beauty that was her best friend. Before they'd ever left elementary school, AnnaBeth's striking features had taken shape, luring the hearts of many males along the way.

She'd enjoyed her fair share of those males when she'd had a desire to. Always friendly. Always kind. And always knowing nothing would come from it.

As young girls, always the best of friends, they'd done the dreams. The ideas of what their Prince Charming would prove to be. For AnnaBeth, those early childhood visions never wavered.

"A good heart, amazing looks, and a bank account big enough to give me the world." It was, always had been, AnnaBeth's requirements for the right man.

Never in the way of vanity. Only honesty.

"For you lovely ladies." Teddy stepped up to their table, placing two more glasses of wine between them.

"The two over there," he waved a hand toward the end of the bar. "Bought you a round."

"Well, isn't that nice." Lifting her glass, AnnaBeth turned back, lifting her glass in a thankful toast.

Though she was far from the flirt her best friend was, Addie lifted her own glass.

"Give them a wave, Addie Dear." Annabeth's voice was low as she kept her gaze on the two, did another wiggle with her fingers. "A little bit of fun with two handsome men, even the young ones, never hurt anyone."

A step inside, Reed caught Addie raising her hand, waving at the two dreamy-eyed men at the end of the bar.

He didn't figure they were much past the legal age to be in a bar, enjoying the beers held in their hands. They were definitely enjoying themselves and getting their hopes up for two women they didn't stand a chance with.

The innocence of youth.

With a shrug, he cut his way through the many bodies standing and sitting in every free spot available.

If he had to follow Addie, he figured she couldn't do better than Teddy's bar. Here, at least, he'd find some enjoyment for himself while keeping his eye on her.

His cousin was the first to notice him as he approached the table. "There you are." Teddy thumped a firm hand against his back. "You didn't answer my message. Was wondering if I'd see you again."

"Figured you already knew my answer."

Addie's smile faded away as he leaned against the edge of the table beside her. "I have no desire, and no time, to pretend I'm here for any kind of family reunion. As far as I'm concerned, you're the only one I care to see while I'm here."

"I guessed as much. I simply passed on the message given to me."

Reed could say more but wasn't in the mood. He thought of pulling up a chair and joining Addie and AnnaBeth. But a look at Addie made it clear it wouldn't be a wanted stay.

"How about a beer?" He slung an easy arm around Teddy's broad shoulders, leading him toward the bar. "Your treat."

"Yeah. Yeah. Isn't it always." Teddy guided them through the masses, moving behind the bar while Reed found an empty chair beside an older couple sipping their gin and tonics.

"You've got a good thing going here." Reed grabbed his beer as Teddy slid it in front of him, enjoying a long slow drink as he took in the controlled chaos around him. Watched as the band on stage picked up another song.

It wasn't Clay tonight. Those filling the stage had many years over him. Long gray beards and hefty bellies, they were a complete contrast to Clay's band.

"Thanks. I'm pretty proud of it." Teddy collected empty glasses, turning and dumping them in the sink behind the bar. "Always told you I'd find something exciting to do with my life."

He did and he had. Reed wasn't surprised. Teddy had always been the one to shake off the expectations and judgements of others. Living his life how he chose. It was something Reed never understood until he'd finally had the strength to break free and go out on his own.

"I should have come back. To see you." Reed took another slow drink, hoping to chase back the bitter taste of guilt. "I'm sorry for that."

Teddy grabbed a rag, stood with it dangling from his fingers. "I don't need sorry. I don't want sorry. I understand why you went. Why you stayed away."

His gaze drifted, catching Addie as she ducked her head, sharing something private with AnnaBeth. "You trusted me with the truth. I've never forgotten that."

"Maybe it's time you trusted her with the truth." He nudged a head in Addie's direction.

"That chance has come and gone." Reed didn't allow himself the chance to consider it. Some things could never be.

Addie's head fell back in laughter. Those chocolate brown eyes of her shimmering even in the dark of the bar.

Sharing the truth wasn't an option. Not after all this time and the damage caused.

He'd believed walking away would solve the ache deep in his gut and heart. Would cure what he struggled with, taking away the sharp bite of Addie's memory. The painful tug on his heart whenever an image of her came to mind.

He couldn't say, now, if it worked.

He'd never been able to fully forget her. It hadn't been possible. Being away had cleared his mind from the worst of the struggles and given him what he needed to move on. Or so he believed.

Being back now, around her again, he wondered if he'd moved on or had simply been spinning his gears without realizing it. From the moment he'd set eyes on her again, he was back to where he'd been. Able to feel her. To remember the tender push of her slender curves. The delicate brush of her lips passing over his.

He wanted her now as much, if not more, than all those years ago. It tore through him, leaving an awful bite whenever he tried slamming it down.

So, what the truth was, he couldn't be sure anymore. The only thing certain was his need for her wasn't going away anytime soon.

As if sensing his gaze, Addie looked his way, her brown eyes locking with his. Her smile slid away. The amusement, sparking light in her expression only moments before, faded.

The band kicked to life another song. An eighties classic. A moody song of love and betrayal. The deep tempo swirled through the bar, drawing couples to the small worn dance floor in front of the stage.

Reed didn't give himself time to think. Forgetting everything but the redhead beauty looking back at him, he rose to his feet and headed her way.

Addie watched him, unable to turn away. The force of his steady gaze, the heat shimmering in his deep blue eyes, was too much to fight against.

She lost track of what AnnaBeth was saying as Reed drew closer. Forgot everything around her but the sight of him, so strong and viral, coming at her.

"Dance with me." He grabbed her hand, pulling her to her feet before she had a chance to register what was happening.

Shaking her head, she narrowed her eyes, yanking her hand away. "No thank you."

Reed grabbed her. Ignoring AnnaBeth's steely glare, he wrapped long fingers around her slender wrist, turning her back.

"No harm in a dance, unless you're afraid you can't control yourself." He smiled with the challenge in his words. Didn't feel the least bit guilty for them.

"Come on, Addie." He tugged on her, urging her closer to the dance floor. "You used to be fun, once."

"I'm still fun." She shoved away but instead of heading back for the table, she stepped in front of him, working her way through the crowd toward the dance floor.

"I just don't see a reason to prove it to you." She tossed it over her shoulder, waiting for him to catch up. "But I'll give you a dance."

Afraid she'd change her mind if he gave her a second to think about it, Reed slid a firm arm around her slender waist, spinning her onto the dance floor.

She fit into his arms so perfectly. Always had. Her eyes widened as he pulled her close, swaying with her to the music flowing around them.

Yes. This was what he missed. What he hadn't known he craved till he'd come back. For as strong and stubborn as she was, she had a softness, a delicate part of her whenever he held her, teasing him. Leaving him hungry to pull her closer until nothing was between them.

"Hold on." Reed's whispered words fanned against Addie's neck, sending chills as he spun her away then pulled her back against his hard chest.

This was a bad idea. What had she been thinking? He'd challenged her, and like a fool she'd fallen for it. Just a dance. Nothing more. Nothing dangerous. She could handle it.

She'd been wrong.

To be held by him again, so close her heart matched his beat, her skin burning where his brushed with hers. It was more than she was prepared for, bringing back so many buried memories, feelings, she wasn't ready, or willing, to face.

The tempo of the song throbbed around them. Bodies added to the floor, forcing them closer. Reed held her tight. The press of his hand against the small of her back, the brush of hard lines rubbing against soft curves reminded her of everything she only wanted to forget.

He was the only one who captured her heart. Led her to that first realization of what love truly was. In all the years he'd been gone, she'd done her best to deny everything he'd once been.

But here and now he brought the doubts. The worry that what she thought she'd long been done with was nothing more than an evil joke. A teasing at her heart of what she'd wanted to let go but never had.

Again, he spun her out, brought her back. The others faded as she came back against him. She became lost in only the two of them.

The feel of his arms holding her close. His spicy scent surrounding her, the warmth of him was like a drug taking her under.

Glancing up, she caught the heat in his deep, blue eyes, felt it pour through her. She couldn't look away. Couldn't do anything but sway with him. Caught in his heavy gaze, she was struck by the need spiraling through.

It would be so easy to push on her toes and lay her lips to his. To find that dark forbidden place still craving for the feel of him.

He brought fire from nothing more than a kiss, igniting wants and needs inside she was helpless to fight.

Would it be so bad, finding that thrill again, experiencing what it was like to be so lost and desperate with desire?

The questions, the realization she was actually considering it, jolted her back. She tore her gaze away, stepping out of his arms as the song ended.

He went to pull her back, but she shook her head and took another step back.

"One dance." She prayed her voice gave no hint to what tumbled inside. "That was the deal."

Without another word, she turned on her heels, thankful when the echo of Reed's steps didn't follow. She'd needed a night out to prevent thinking of him. Instead, she'd only accomplished guaranteeing thoughts of him would continue to haunt her for days to come.

He'd left her alone.

Addie was thankful for it as he went back to his place at the bar, sparing her only one quick glance.

The hours left passed uneventfully. Finishing off her final glass of wine, she stepped up to the bar to pay off their tab.

"Already taken care of." Teddy glanced at Reed pushing to his feet as he shoved her credit card back at her.

It was the last thing she wanted. But arguing would be useless.

Manners, long bred into her, insisted she say something, though she hated to. "Thank you for that."

"He gave me the family discount. And your young friends at the other bar had already taken care of another round so the damage wasn't bad."

"Well, thank you again." The polite words felt so strange falling from her lips. Shaking it off, she returned to the table, waiting for AnnaBeth.

Side by side, they made their way through the crowd to the busy sidewalk outside.

"We'll both be dragging our butts tomorrow, but it was worth it." AnnaBeth wrapped Addie in a hug before stepping back and waving her way down the sidewalk.

Turning the opposite way, Addie headed for home, knowing AnnaBeth was right, she would be dragging in the morning. Not that it would be the first time.

"You really should pay more attention to who's around you." Reed materialized at her side, causing her to jolt. "Your two young friends from the bar followed you out, seemed to give up when you and AnnaBeth split ways."

Shooting him an ugly look over her shoulder, she quickened her step. "Go away, Reed. The night is over."

Matching her pace, he merely smiled at her. "So, I'm guessing I won't be getting another dance."

"I'm going home. You should do the same."

"I'll be back in my hotel room as soon as I know you're home and locked in safe and sound." He stepped off the curb, letting another couple pass between them. Stepped back up to hug her side again.

"You don't need to make sure of anything. I can make it home fine. Just as I have done every night I've been out."

"Either I walk with you, or I follow you." He shrugged. "Your choice."

The memory of feeling as if she was being followed on the way to the bar swept back.

"Have you been following me?" She stopped, fighting back the first hints of anger.

"I've done what needs to be done." Wrapping long fingers around her arm, he urged her forward. "In case you've forgotten, you have a killer sending you flowers."

"No." Pulling free, she quickened her step. "I had flowers sent by someone you are assuming is a killer."

She didn't bother looking back. He'd catch up. His shoulder brushed hers as he came up beside her, proving her right.

"I'm not assuming anything. And until I figure out what he's up to, you're going to have to get used to me being around."

"So, I get to pay for your paranoia?" She cut the corner short, happy when it was enough to push him a step behind.

She was almost to the gate for the courtyard when he grabbed her and spun her around. "You can call it what you please. I'm not willing to take the risk."

Suddenly, so weary of it all, Addie gave a gentle shake to her arm, tossing off his hold. "I don't want this, Reed. Any of it."

She swept out her hand, encircling them both. Looked up at him through the shadow of light shimmering out from the courtyard at their side.

The sadness in her eyes tugged at Reed. He could handle the anger, sometimes craved it. But the sadness tore at him, leaving him feeling clumsy. Desperate.

"The last thing I want to do is hurt you." He wrapped gentle fingers around her arms, holding her where she was. "Lord knows I did enough of that in the past. But damnit, I don't like this. I don't like the feel of it."

Addie stumbled over emotions. Couldn't find the strength to pull away. "I don't want to think about it now. None of it. Not the killer, the flowers. Not you."

She cursed silently as tears threatened. This was not how she wanted to end the night. "I just want to lock myself inside and go to sleep."

She pulled away, turning for the latch on the gate. Reed was right behind her as she swung it open, stepping onto the cobblestone path cutting through the lush plants and vibrant flowers.

She tried ignoring him. She'd never let him inside the house, so he'd have no choice but to turn back sooner or later. His spicy scent caught on the breeze, swirling around her. The warmth of him pushed against her from behind, leaving her too aware of how close he was.

The water in the fountain trickled behind her as she spun around. "Please. Just go."

He should. Was prepared to. Something in the look of her stopped him. For all her strength, all her courage, she looked so vulnerable. The shadow of light and dark played over her delicate features. The breeze tossed long red curls around her gentle face.

He moved closer, watching her eyes widen. Her full lips pulled into a tight line. A mix of fear and defiance flashed in her dark gaze.

"I can't." The honesty of it burned. "I know I should. But I can't find the strength to."

He hovered close, his breath a mix with hers with only a slice of space between them. "I've spent so long trying to deny it, but I've missed you."

"Don't." Addie pressed her hand against his chest, wanting to push him away. Instead, she lingered, fingers molding over hard muscles through the thin cotton of his shirt.

She didn't want this. Didn't want any of it. Long ago she'd chased away her feelings for Reed. Buried them where they belonged. It was weakness now, the very thing she hated, allowing them a chance to return, reminding her of everything she'd once had.

She never should have agreed to a dance with him. Never should have allowed him to walk home with her. Every time she wanted him to go away, she did something to invite him closer.

"I have to." He closed fingers around where hers lingered on his chest. Pressed until his body molded with hers. "I've wanted to know this since the minute I saw you again."

Time stopped. The breeze stilled as he lowered, his blue gaze holding hers, refusing to let go as he brushed his lips over hers.

It was light. So simple. Yet heat exploded and simmered through. She wanted more. Hated herself for it.

With a growl, Reed twisted his arms behind her back, finding her lips again. What started slow, built. Nibbling on her bottom lip, he took, demanded, until she opened for him.

She should push him away, ending the kiss before it got out of hand. But she couldn't. She could only feel, sensation grabbing her, dragging her under.

His mouth fitted to hers, took as it teased. She wanted this. The realization terrified her even as she pushed closer, searching for more.

Here was everything. Everything she'd lost and fought so hard to deny. It was in the familiar warmth of being held in Reed's arms. In the taste of him. In the fire quickly finding life inside, sparking a burn through her limbs.

A moan escaped as he pulled away.

Cupping a hand on each side of her face, he held her, blue eyes searching, looking deep to whatever she hid inside.

"Damnit, Addie." Spearing long fingers through her hair, he rested only a breath from her trembling lips. "You've always had a way to drive me crazy."

Angry with it, he took again, frustration now guiding him. His hands curled in her hair, holding her where he wanted her as his mouth took, pushing at her without relief until she surrendered.

She was his. In every way she'd vowed she would never be again. He could take her, right there, and she'd go without hesitation, seeking desperately all he offered with his heated touch. His desperate need to have her.

No. She fought desperately for control. This was dangerous. It was wrong. She couldn't follow the path her body screamed for. Not when the risks were so great.

Though everything inside screamed in protest, she found the strength to push her hands against his chest and step away. A chill raced up her spine as the kiss broke. Wrapping arms around her middle, she fought it off.

He reached for her. Shaking her head, she took another step back. "No. Please."

His head cloudy with desire, it took a moment for Reed to understand her words. He wanted to draw her back. The pleading in her dark eyes, the sadness shimmering through, warned him against it.

He had nothing to say. Nothing more he could do that wouldn't cause her more pain. With one last hard look, he turned on his heels and left her standing in the courtyard as he closed the gate quietly behind him.

CHAPTER NINE

H e liked the life here. It called to him. Thrived in him.

They were getting lively now, with the hour past midnight. He'd nursed through two beers, watching them. From the ones he was sure were not yet of age to the older women enjoying a brief slice of freedom from their responsibilities of home, husband, and kids.

So many choices. The breeding ground was the best of his dreams. He couldn't have asked for better.

He'd watched Addie earlier, intrigued when McReily pulled her to the dance floor. He'd been tempted then to take her.

He imagined what it would be like, enjoying what McReily had taken only hours before. Savoring the sweet knowledge of how he'd make them both suffer.

But the excitement of the game was more pleasing than a quick solution. Thinking how he'd have McReily jumping when he was done was almost enough to convince him to put off his plans for the night.

But the urge was too strong to deny. He'd gone too long without. It was time for another. Time to find the sweet pleasure only the supple softness of a woman's body gave. The sense of amazing power as her life poured into his hands, that last flicker in her eyes meant only for him.

She was here, in all this marvelous mix of bodies. Waiting for him. Ready for all he had to offer.

Hands shoved in the front pockets of his worn jeans, he drew no attention as he worked his way with the crowds bursting along Bourbon Street. The music was a constant, rapid beat. The laughter and drunken calls added their own rhythm to the chaos.

A group of them caught his eye. Long legs, long hair, and beauty caught in between. They stood as three outside one of the more crowded bars. The strobing lights from inside rained over them in a muted mix of color.

The redhead drew him in. How fitting it seemed, almost as if planned for. Though she stood taller and carried nothing else close to Addie's features, the long red curls were enough to convince him he'd found the one.

He hung back, close enough to follow but far enough not to give them reason to worry. They were younger. College aged, he guessed. Probably here celebrating Spring Break, seeking a week of craziness before going back to their studies.

They spent another hour moving from one bar to the next. Taking shots. Dancing. Laughing until the early hours of morning. They were feeling their fun by the time they turned off Bourbon.

Here, on a quieter street, it was harder to remain unseen. He lingered in shadows, keeping his steps slow and silent behind them. Not that he figured there was much of a threat of being noticed with the way they swayed happily down the sidewalk.

If they had, he had a feeling their senses were so long ago dulled it wouldn't register to have a reason to fear him.

The redhead stopped at the glass doors leading into a hotel and glanced over her shoulder. He stepped back, out of sight.

The tall, lanky blond beside her threw an arm over her shoulders, tugging her along as they stumbled into the hotel lobby.

He was quick, making his way inside in time to catch them heading for the elevators. He didn't know what his next step would be, but he couldn't let this chance pass him by. Pasting a charming smile to his lips, he hurried toward them, shoving a hand between the doors before they slid closed.

Caught in their happy buzz, they barely noticed him as he joined them on the elevator. Seconds later, it began to climb, ringing to a stop one floor up.

"That's me." The brunette untangled from the other two, tossing them a smile over her shoulder as she headed out.

Picking up the role of a gentleman, he held the elevator door for her. Nodded at her quick thanks before she stepped out into the long hallway.

And then they headed up again. Another floor. Another stop. It was the blond who stepped out this time after a quick, sloppy kiss on the redhead's cheek. She wiggled her fingers as he held the door for her, blowing one final kiss at her friend before disappearing down the hallway.

Then it was just them. He couldn't have planned it better if he'd tried. He gave away nothing. Facing forward, he pretended he couldn't feel her warmth behind him or smell her alluring scent drift around him.

The elevator stopped again on the next floor. He didn't make a move, only held the doors open one more time as she slid past, a polite smile on her red lips. A spark of the night still lingered in her crystal blue eyes.

She never looked back. Never thought to check on him as she headed toward her room. He slid quietly from the elevator and followed her down the hall, past the rumbling ice machine, and the glowing red from the pop machine.

Her shoulder hit against the wall as she fumbled in her purse. She had no clue he waited behind her. Pulling out her key card, she slid it into the door, pushing it open.

He was right behind her, shoving as she moved inside. Shock froze her for a moment, but he continued her forward, closing the door behind them.

She opened her mouth, and he knew the scream was coming. Had it not been for the drag of alcohol she might have been successful before he clamped his hand over her mouth, yanking her away from the door.

"Hello, Sweetheart." His whisper was low in her ear. Digging into his pocket, he pulled out a cloth, replacing his hand over her mouth with it. "We're about to have some fun together."

Her fear surrounded him a moment before she went still and soft in his arms.

Sleep wasn't going to come, no matter how desperately Addie wished for it.

Giving up, she rolled out of bed. Grabbing an old, ratted sweater, she pulled it over the tank and shorts she wore before quietly opening her bedroom door.

Her aunt stumbled in an hour ago and headed straight for her bed, sleeping off her fun for the night. She didn't want to wake her. Didn't want to explain why she was up at such a terrible hour.

Growing up in this house with her mother, before her death, and her aunt, she knew where the creaks were that would give her late-night movements away.

As a teenager she'd perfected it. Sneaking out with AnnaBeth after Rosalie had fallen asleep, stumbling back in before she was up and preparing for the day, none the wiser of her niece's activities.

Now it wasn't getting caught worrying her, only having to supply answers she didn't want to give.

Safer in the kitchen, she turned on the light, waiting a moment for her eyes to adjust. Making her way to the kettle, she set it to fill in the sink while shuffling through her collection of tea.

For whatever one needed, she had the tea for it. While her aunt was more of a coffee drinker, Addie learned the pleasure of tea through her mother.

When she allowed it, she'd go back to the young girl she was, so confused and heartbroken after losing her mom. She'd feared, for so long, the tears would never stop, the pain would never ease.

Losing her mother had taken her life and turned it upside down. It left her raw and broken inside.

And yet, somehow, tea helped. She'd make a cup, sip, and think of her mother. Feel her beside her, enjoying her own while giving Addie the knowledge to what kind was best for whatever situation.

It was a connection to her mom she'd never lost. One she carried into her adult years.

Shaking away the memories, knowing they were the last thing she needed on top of what she already struggled with, she pulled a lavender tea from its place, setting the kettle to boil on the stove.

Minutes later, a steaming mug of tea cradled in her hands, she slipped out onto the balcony edging the front room. She stood for a moment at the wrought-iron rail, looking down on the empty street.

Life in this part of the Quarter had died down long ago. It was quiet and peaceful, just what she needed to sit with her tea and fumble through the thoughts clouding her mind.

The feel of Reed's kiss still warmed her lips, even all these hours later. It teased at her while she battled sleep, bringing temptations that had no right to exist.

For all the years she'd thought of seeing him again, dancing and a bone-melting kiss had never been part of the scenario. She'd always imagined slapping him then turning her back on him and storming away as he had done to her so many years ago.

But the truth wasn't even close. Seeing him again hadn't turned out to be anything like she imagined. The worst proof of it continued to linger on her lips.

He'd broken something in her. In a way no one ever had. In the beginning, every time she'd closed her eyes, she'd been back to that moment. The tears streaming, unable to stop them. The slice of pain for every word, letting her know he didn't love her, had never loved her. And she could never hope to be good enough for someone like him. A McReily. The name and the money meaning more than she could ever imagine.

It was the shock, that's what she remembered most after the tears slid away and the pain ebbed to a low roar. How did she not see who he truly was? How could she have ever put her trust in someone so cold? So cruel?

For so long afterward, she searched for signs. Something she missed in the time they'd been together. A hint of the true man hiding beneath the one she thought she'd known.

She'd found nothing. No matter how desperately she ran back through every moment they spent together. The long, passionate kisses. Stolen nights wrapped tight to one another. The laughter. The fun. The need to be together, no matter what they were doing.

What did she miss? For every moment, every second they spent together, nothing warned her of what was to come. It was as if he'd been two different people. The one she'd loved for so long and the one she'd met on that final day when he'd destroyed her before walking away.

Irritated with it all, she shoved up from her chair to pace from one end of the balcony to the other. This was why she couldn't sleep. Why she feared the dreams if allowed to come.

Because every time she closed her eyes, it wasn't the Reed who destroyed her that she saw. It was the Reed who loved her. Made her feel cherished. Kissed her in the courtyard as if he'd actually missed the time they'd been apart, wanting her in the way he once had.

And that only made her pitiful. Stopping again, running a frustrated hand through her hair, she looked back over the quiet street, almost wished for the rowdiness on Bourbon. It would be a distraction, something she desperately needed.

Because this wasn't going to work, brooding over Reed, feeling and missing his kiss while tempted to forget how he'd hurt her.

No. It wasn't going to work at all.

She swore a thousand tiny needles pierced her brain.

Fighting the pain, Mandy forced her eyes open. Dim, dusty light greeted her, a single dull bulb hanging from above providing the only source.

Where was she? What was going on?

She tried to turn and figure out where she was, but nothing happened. Hard as she tried, she couldn't move, as if her brain and the rest of her were missing a connection.

Fear struck, hard and fierce. She couldn't scream. Couldn't do anything.

"Odd sensation isn't it." The low, grumbling voice shifted around her. She sensed him, his warmth at her side. But she couldn't see him or move to find him.

"The drug is effective but temporary." Then he was there, pale blue eyes staring down on her under a crop of hair so blond it was almost white. Recognition flashed for a second then slipped away. He traced a finger down her cheek then lifted it to his lips.

"You and I." He was gone from sight again. "We're going to have some fun."

A smooth, silver blade flashed in front of her. She fought desperately to move. To escape.

No amount of fear was strong enough to battle against whatever he drugged her with. She was trapped. A prisoner to him and her own body.

Panic soared as he grazed the tip of the knife along the sensitive skin between her ear and shoulder. She waited for the sharp puncture of skin. The slicing pain she was sure would come.

His face again came into view, the slow smile on his lips bringing the vile taste of nausea to her throat. "Soon, you'll move again, and I'll enjoy taking advantage of that."

The knife slid lower, pressing between her breasts as the sound of fabric tearing echoed in the air. He continued down, cutting her clothes away, slowly drawing it out so she was aware of every inch of her body being exposed with the constant threat of the blade sliding so close to skin.

She couldn't see but knew when he had her clothes completely stripped. His hungry gaze passed over her, chilling her to the bone.

"Oh yes. We will certainly enjoy ourselves." He hovered close, the acrid warmth of his breath washing over her in sickening waves.

His mouth slid, slick and cold, over hers. He moaned, deep in his throat, pressing her deeper into the cot where she was trapped.

This was power. The ultimate taste of ecstasy. In these moments, before the paralysis wore off, he fought for control. Wanting it right then, severe pleasure raced through, shoving him desperately toward the edge.

He could take her now, bury deep and find that sweet, painful release he craved. It was all him. His control. His choice to do as he pleased.

With one more taste of her, a slow, deliberate run of his rough finger against the long length of creamy skin, he shoved away. He had, in the past, lost grip on his control, ending things before he was ready.

Time had taught him better. For as much as he craved satisfaction now, what was still to come was worth the wait, no matter how painful it proved to be.

All those beatings. All the times his mother sought out something harder, greater, in her quest to cause more pain. The ugly whisper of how he was weak and simple minded, unable to resist the smallest temptation.

She'd declared he'd be nothing. Would never experience hard-earned restraint or know self-control and the ability to resist.

He'd proved her wrong. Continued to prove her wrong. For everyone he found and enjoyed he became stronger, more able to resist the sweet temptation of taking on his first needs, drawing it out until the right time came to him.

Not only was this sweet beauty, lying so still and ready, proving his mother wrong. But Addie played into the mix, too.

His desire for her grew by the day. Every moment he thought of her, a greater need built inside.

But instead of taking her he held it back, knowing, for every moment time stretched, he'd find a greater pleasure waiting for him.

CHAPTER TEN

"Well, hello beautiful."

In all his flash and flair, Clay burst through the door of Magic Moon. He'd chosen the shock of Sapphire for the day. His blazer, rich in color, hung over a red paisley shirt tucked loosely into baggy black pants.

Thumbs tucked into his trademark suspenders, his bright smile a blast of brilliant white, he edged around the group of customers hovered around the handmade jewelry, grabbing Addie's hands as soon as he reached the counter.

"I'm bored." He tugged on her, urging her out from behind the cash register. "Entertain me."

She smiled. They'd played the same game for years. As Anna-Beth's younger brother, he'd always held a special place in her heart.

"I'm stuck here till closing." Pushing to her toes, she dropped a quick kiss against his rough cheek. "Rosalie's away mixing business with pleasure in Baton Rouge. It's just me here for the next few days."

His smile didn't fade as he checked the bulky silver watch around his wrist. "That gives me enough time to go down to Willie's, get our favorite pizza, and be back as you're locking the doors."

She couldn't deny him. Wouldn't, even if she could.

"You do that." She stepped back behind the counter as the group of customers approached, jewelry dangling from their hands. "I'll toss a salad, open a bottle of wine, and we'll make a night of it."

"You would have fallen into the river if I hadn't caught you." Clay threw back his head, laughter, rich and thick, filling the courtyard.

Addie scowled at him. Old friends never forgot your most embarrassing moments. "It was Mardi Gras. I was in ridiculously high heels. And I'd had a bit more than my fair share of champagne."

As far as she was concerned, it was the only explanation needed.

"You were still holding the bottle." Grabbing another piece of pizza, Clay shook his head. "If I remember right, you were using it as a microphone to serenade Reed."

She remembered. She may have had a few too many drinks, but the memories remained, even the ones she preferred to forget.

That year had been filled with so much fun. So much laughter and love. She'd soared on it, floating high with a heart full of Reed and everything she believed he offered. Everything he yanked away the night he'd told her the truth.

"I've grown out of that now." She wasn't sure if she was talking about getting drunk on champagne or losing her heart to Reed. "I prefer a quiet night of pizza and wine with a good friend these days."

To prove her point, she grabbed the bottle of wine, topped off her glass, raising it in a toast.

"You don't like talking about him, do you?" Knowledge settled in Clay's bright, blue eyes. Knowledge she wished she could deny but it would be useless.

Deciding she deserved it, she grabbed another piece of pizza, refusing to think of the calories. "I don't see a need to. I've been fine all these years without his name coming up."

"We did that for you." Seeing the proof of the pain lingering in Addie's dark eyes, Clay reached over the small round table between them, resting a hand over hers.

"We still talked. Still wondered."

"Wondered about what?"

"He up and left only a month after ending things with you, cutting off all ties with his family. You were never curious why?"

"No." She washed down the lie with a sip of wine. "Why should I have been?"

She didn't want to go down the road he was leading them. Reed being back seemed to push everyone for a trip down memory lane, one she preferred not to take but couldn't seem to avoid.

"Well, I've always wondered." Finishing off the last of his pizza, he rested back in his chair. "I can't place the Reed we knew for that year with the one he became on that final night."

"Maybe it was because he was really good at fooling all of us."

"Maybe."

Wrapping long fingers around the stem of his wine glass, he stared at her over the rim. "Teddy says his parents have been trying to reach him since he's been back, but he's refusing to talk to them."

So maybe she was a little curious, though she wasn't about to admit it. "Maybe he doesn't have the time."

Picking at the olives on her pizza, she cursed Clay for making her wonder. She'd been so hurt, so angry, when Reed had left. She hadn't thought about what happened between him and his family. He was gone. That's all that mattered. He'd broken her heart and left. Nothing else, at that point in time, made an impact.

"Do you think Teddy knows what happened?" She pushed her plate out of the way.

"I'm guessing he's always known more than he's shared." Stretching out his long legs, he looked out over the slow drip of the fountain.

"You won't get more out of him than he's willing to give. Trust me, I've tried. Reed's always been his first loyalty."

She remembered. They'd acted more like brothers than distant cousins whenever they were together. If there were secrets to hold, he'd be the one to have them.

What did she care? Reed could have all the secrets he wanted. It no longer mattered to her. His reasons for not talking to his family were no concern of hers. What Teddy knew, what happened all those years ago, didn't change anything.

Her life, her care, was in today where Reed no longer had a place.

He mourned the end, as any lover would.

For days he'd enjoyed all her beauty had to offer, bringing her to the edge only to allow another breath, another beat of her heart.

Like the others, her fight had finally faded. She'd been a stubborn one, exciting him that much more. It had taken more to break her, show her that her destiny was his, controlled by his hands.

Her screams echoed inside the close walls, feeding on his arousal. His need to take. And he had. Over and over again. Mixing pain with pleasure. Punishment with passion.

Until she'd become his completely, breaking into the true weakness she held inside.

He knew then, it was time to let her go.

He no longer had a reason to bound her with the rope edging the bed. Her gaze already held the knowledge of death. The acceptance her life would end.

For one last time he took. She no longer struggled as the blade of his knife cut thin into her skin. Didn't react as his knees shoved hard against her thighs, forcing her open.

He sunk deep, taking what was his. Head thrown back, eyes closed, he heard the snarl of his mother, as he always did. Claiming him worthless. Nothing in strength or might. A mere object for her to do as she pleased.

With each hard thrust he burned in the anger of it. Reveled in the violation he held over her as he took and proved who deserved the pain. The torture.

He took because he could. Ravaged because it gave him strength. Every woman he conquered was proof to his mother's failings. Her belief of his worth. Someday he'd pound her voice from his head, finding true freedom in those he took as his own.

He filled her, taking a moment to catch his breath before swinging off.

"It will be a shame to let you go." He trailed a light finger down her cheek. "But the time has come."

There was still enough inside her for a flicker of fear to flash in her gaze. He made his way to the small shelf shoved against the opposite wall. He dropped the knife, picking up the small, silver tube, rough and worn from age.

Pulling off the top, he dropped it then twisted the slender column hidden inside. It was his mother's lipstick. Vicious Red. She'd worn it every day, religiously, swiping it carefully over her lips, over and over again.

Those lips, always stained a dark, blood red, snarling at him. Attacking him. Dripping with spit when she'd finally lost control.

It was the color of his nightmares. His validation. His revenge.

Slow, he applied it to his lips, taking care as he always did. The time was close. He'd mark and he'd take.

He didn't have a need for weapons now. Nothing to create further pain. Only him and his need to end the life he'd savored and taken as his own.

Lips stained blood red, he found that last jolt of excitement as he curled long fingers around her neck, the pulse of her last moments hitting weak against his palm. He tightened, heard her fight for breath, then released.

"You are mine. Completely mine. You will die, knowing only me." With his hand still curved around her neck, he lowered, pressing his lips hard against her right breast, forever marking her with his kiss.

He didn't see her face again. Concentrated on nothing but the red stain against her pale skin as he tightened his hands around her neck, strangling away the last of her life.

CHAPTER ELEVEN

The more days gone, the more frustrated Reed became.

After almost a week, not only did he have nothing to prove a connection between the flowers sent to Addie and the Kissing Killer, there was no sign he was even in New Orleans.

"Some are questioning whether we should bring you back." Marshall's deep voice was a low hum through the phone. "Thoughts are this might be nothing more than a distraction, meant to send you away from the next target."

He didn't want to hear it. Staring out the window of his hotel, Reed looked down on the tourists bustling along the sidewalks, wondering if it was too early to enjoy the scotch tucked away in the mini bar.

"He's here."

"Because of the flowers."

It was about the same as he was getting from Burke and his agents. As time passed, they became more and more convinced the flowers meant nothing.

"Because I know it." No longer caring about the time, he shoved up from his seat, yanking open the small door on the mini bar.

"Because my gut tells me he's here. I don't give a damn if others want to take the flowers as the same risk. I know him, better than anyone. I've spent the last year inside his sick head, trying to wrap my mind around his twisted thoughts. He's here. And for whatever reason, he has Addie in his sights."

Not bothering to fetch ice, he poured the small bottle of scotch into a glass. "I need you to trust me on this."

He didn't sit again, choosing to stand, stare out the window, and sip from his scotch.

"I want to. Hell, it's not hard to admit you're one of my best. Your gut hasn't done me wrong yet."

"But?"

"But the doubt is coming from higher than my control. I'll do what I can. But much more of nothing and I won't be able to convince anyone, no matter how trustworthy your gut is."

He didn't like it. Didn't like the Bureau was already getting itchy for results. Results he couldn't yet provide. "They can try pulling me back before it's done, but I won't be making promises I'll be going."

"Then let's hope it doesn't come to that."

Reed was hoping for plenty of things. That was just one on a long list. Ending the call, he finished off the last of his scotch while staring blindly out the window.

For all he'd hated coming back, the last thing he wanted now was to leave. Not while he still had no answers and was convinced Addie somehow played into the plans of a sick man.

He'd once run from her. Now he was trapped to her until she was safe.

Not that she'd enjoy such thoughts. Hell, he didn't enjoy them.

Images from the night in the courtyard haunted him for days. He still tasted her. Yearned for her. Like the lovesick boy he'd once been, she darted through every thought he carried, teasing and taunting no matter how hard he fought.

Though he continued his vigils, making sure she was safe, he'd kept his distance. Careful not to let her know of his presence, he'd hovered in the alley, watching her pass through the lighted windows, her soft delicate shape a shadow as she moved.

But tonight, he had an urge for more. The frustration of so many days of nothing, the desire only growing stronger with every day, played into the restlessness seeping through his bones, pushing him to escape. To distract his thoughts from murder and the past.

And though Addie was his past, she was his present, as well. That's what he needed.

It had been a long, busy day.

Watching the clock and counting down the minutes, Addie was more than ready to close the shop. It had been only her again, her aunt still away in Baton Rouge.

The day had been nice, drawing out the tourists in large crowds. They came in pairs and groups. Some buying. Some browsing. Keeping her busy and on her feet from the moment she opened.

She hadn't had time to do more than snack her way through the bag of Trail Mix she kept under the counter for lunch. Her stomach growled at her now, letting her know it wasn't enough.

Five more minutes then she'd lock up, head upstairs, make dinner, and settle in with a movie for the night. The idea of it making her anxious, she stared at the minute hand, urging it forward.

"Close enough," she decided with only a couple minutes left.

Grabbing the keys, she headed for the door, stopped when the bell above it rang before she reached it.

Plastering a welcoming smile on her lips, she cursed it away when her eyes landed on Reed. "We're closed."

Ignoring the extra beat her heart took at the sight of him, she formed a frustrated fist around the keys in her hand, metal biting into soft flesh as she approached.

"Then I have better timing then I'd hoped." He made no attempt to move. His smug smile grated against her nerves as he stood between her and the door.

She didn't want to respond to him. Didn't want the flicker of heat in her blood or the memory of his kiss on her lips. "What do you want?"

Knowing he wouldn't be going away easily and not wanting to risk another customer coming in, she shoved past to lock the door.

"You." Reed laughed at the dirty look she shot him. Falling into step behind her as she headed back for the counter, he resisted the urge to reach out and run his fingers through the red curls bouncing from the force of her angry steps.

"I was thinking dinner. A nice walk along the river." He grabbed her hand as she continued to walk away, spinning her around to face him. "I've missed you these last few days."

Warmth spread where his fingers tangled with hers. Addie was trapped under the hard hold of his blue eyes, the need in them.

"Well, that makes one of us." She pulled free, continuing on until she had the safety of the counter between them. "I already have plans for the night."

Ignoring the barrier, he came around behind the counter. "Cancel them."

He pressed her in close. His spicy scent surrounded her. Teased her.

Fighting to catch her breath, she flattened against the wall behind her, needing space. "Why should I do that? Because you tell me to?"

"No." His gaze shimmered with the knowledge of what he was doing to her. He stepped closer, sliding a slow finger down her cheek. "Because you know you want to spend the evening with me, no matter how hard you're trying to deny it."

He set her off balance, leaving her struggling to remember why she didn't want him around. Why it was dangerous to be with him. "You're a bit too sure of yourself."

She tried ducking around him. He put an arm at the wall at her side, stopping her. "Only about what's important."

He leaned low, his lips a breathing tease against hers.

She wanted him to kiss her. The truth frightened her as much as it excited her. "Why?"

She wasn't sure what she asked. What answer she wanted. Thoughts tangled. He was waiting for her response. Something he wanted her to say. She couldn't think of it. Couldn't concentrate on anything but her desperate need to feel his mouth against hers, finding that instant shock as he first took her and drew her in.

He nibbled on her bottom lip. "Dinner. With me. Say yes."

Trapped between hard muscle and the wall at her back, she stared. The ability to speak suddenly became something she couldn't grasp.

"Dinner, Addie." He took again. A soft, slow kiss, drawing her up and into him.

When he drew away, she was lost. Words were impossible. She could only nod, agreeing to dinner.

His flash of smile lasted only a moment before he took her again. Lips clashing with hers, he drug her in, urging, teasing, until she responded. Opening to him. Allowing him to taste more.

She didn't want it to end. Wanted to stay in that moment forever. But she needed to break away. Needed a breath before she was completely lost and unable to turn back from the dangerous path they traveled.

It took all her strength to lift her arms between them, softly push against his chest. "I need—"

She sucked in a breath, willing her heart to slow. "I need some time to get ready."

It took everything for Reed not to reach for her again. She felt so right and perfect in his arms. He'd forgotten, or forced himself to forget, how she fit against him. As if her slender delicate curves were made just for him, carved to find their place within his hold.

Reaching for her again would mean not being able to let go. "Got a beer? I'll wait."

She was shaken. It helped his ego, knowing he still had that ability over her. Unable to stop himself, he reached for her, wrapping fingers around her slender wrist and tugging her back.

He nibbled a moment then drug her in for one more kiss, loving the feel of her shuddering in his arms. "Later, we'll have to try this again."

Without giving her a chance to respond, he turned her for the door. She shot a look at him over her shoulder, in anger or anticipation, he couldn't be sure.

It was going to be interesting to try and figure it out before the night was done.

She was a fool. It was as simple as that.

Standing under the hot stream from the shower, Addie did her best not to think of Reed sitting in the front room, sipping his beer while he waited for her.

What was she thinking, agreeing to go out to dinner with him? What had she been thinking allowing him to kiss her crazy when she'd sworn she wouldn't let it happen again?

He'd hurt her, deeper than any other person had. She had to remember that, holding it as her protection when he was around. Risking herself to him again was not a path she cared to travel.

But, damn, it was so hard when he was close, sweeping her up into the warmth of him. The feel of him. Reminding her of everything she'd denied she'd missed until he'd rushed back into her life.

Turning off the water and wrapping a towel around her, she swiped her hand over the mirror. Staring at the woman looking back at her, she swore she'd do better. Promised to have more strength, more determination, when it came to dealing with Reed.

Ignoring the doubt reflected back through her eyes, she stepped into her bedroom, a wave of sweetly scented steam following behind. Refusing to fuss for dinner with Reed, she grabbed a maroon skirt and matching shirt from the closet and hurried into them. Slipping small, gold studs into her ears, she returned to the bathroom.

A quick blow dry of her long hair, sweeping it up at the back of her head, curls tumbling down, and a touch of lipstick and mascara, was enough. Walking through a puff of her favorite perfume, she paused at the bedroom door, her hand resting on the smooth knob.

She could do this. For all that Reed was, all that he tempted her, she was stronger. She could fight it. Fight him and the desire he threatened to bring back to life.

Sucking in a hard, determined breath, she opened the door and stepped into the front room. Shoulders squared. Spine stiff.

He stood, staring out the long row of windows, turning when he heard her behind him. Shadowed by the setting sun, dark hair tousled, deep blue eyes full of an emotion she was afraid to name, her heart kicked up a beat. Her mind washed clear of everything she'd just sworn to.

It took everything not to cross to him and throw her arms around him, begging for his lips on hers. His hands running over her, lighting the fire he was so good at sparking to life.

"I'm ready." She fought to keep the shiver of need from her voice.

Reed's steps were slow, lazy, a complete lie to what ran through him. Everything inside screamed to grab her, forget about dinner, and drag her back into her bedroom. He wanted to taste her. Know her in a way he hadn't for far too long.

Damn. What swelled in his heart was not what he wanted. It slid him right back to the boy he used to be. The one who existed before he tore out Addie's heart, leaving it shattered at her feet.

He bit it all back. Taking her hand in his, he led her toward the back stairway, down to the kitchen, and out the door to the courtyard.

They didn't speak, both lost in their own thoughts through the courtyard and into the alley. It wasn't until they reached the busy sidewalk that Addie carefully slipped her hand free and found the ability to talk.

"Where are we going?" She took a safe step away, putting some much-needed distance between them.

"Gumbo house. I remember it was once a favorite of yours."

It still was though she wasn't going to admit it. Keeping her hand safely tucked away from his reach, she turned her concentration to those they passed along the way, desperately needing to divert it from the man at her side.

She was thankful the restaurant was busy. Close and intimate was the last thing she wanted. It was hard enough ignoring the warmth of Reed behind her as they were led to their table. To fight off her awareness of him as his shoulder brushed hers while he pulled out her chair.

He ordered Oysters and a bottle of wine without giving her a chance to order for herself. "What if I wanted Jambalaya and an iced tea?"

"Do you?" He tested her, the look on his face too knowing for her own comfort.

She didn't. The fact that he knew it rubbed hard. She loved the oysters here. Reed remembering that, though, didn't sit well. He was supposed to move on and forget everything about her.

Instead of answering, she smiled at the waitress returning with their wine, waiting for Reed to get through the customary sniff and taste before wrapping her fingers around the stem of her glass, enjoying a long, slow sip.

"You're more irritating than I remember."

"I've been practicing over the years."

She couldn't help the laugh. Damned him for it as soon as it escaped. She didn't want to like him. Didn't want to be reminded why she'd once loved him. "Why are you doing this?"

He could play the game and pretend he didn't know what she was talking about. But what good would it do? "Because I've missed you."

"How can you miss someone you never cared about?"

And there it was. The question asking for truth. He wasn't prepared for it. Wasn't ready to tell it. Sipping slowly from his wine, he stared at her and considered lying to her again.

But what good would it do now? What purpose would it serve?

He couldn't find an answer to that. Not one that settled without resistance. "I never stopped caring about you."

He didn't expect her reaction. Wasn't prepared for her to slam her glass on the table and push up from her seat.

"Where are you going?" He reached for her, wrapped tight fingers around her wrist, stopping her.

Her anger washed over him as she glared at him.

"Do you think I've forgotten," Addie hissed under her breath, aware of the attention she'd grabbed shoving up from her chair. "Every painful word you told me is a script forever imprinted in my mind? You didn't care. You never cared. You made that clear."

The painful emotions tumbling through were so great she feared she'd get lost under the force of them.

"How dare you sit here now and try to lie to me." She tried pulling free, but he held tight.

"I didn't lie." His voice was calm, only helping to irritate her more. "Sit down, Addie, and I'll explain."

She didn't want to. Didn't want to hear it. Nothing he said now would change the past. No words would make the pain disappear. Still, she sank back into her chair.

She stared at him with silent anger as their waitress returned, setting a plate overflowing with oysters in front of them.

"I don't know what you could explain." She waited for their waitress to leave before flattening her hands against the table, leaning forward. "You made your feelings more than clear years ago."

Reed didn't answer at first, making a point of grabbing an oyster and dropping it on the small plate in front of him. "They weren't my feelings. They were what you needed to hear."

"What does that mean?" She couldn't be more confused if he was talking a foreign language. "You think I needed to hear that you never loved me? That I wasn't, and never would be, good enough for you?"

"It was a lie." He looked so defeated as he reached for his wine glass. "I needed you to hate me. It was the only way."

She wished he would make sense. Wished she could go back to a few minutes ago, before this conversation ever began. Needing it desperately, she grabbed her glass and took a long slow sip of wine. "I don't understand. None of this."

She wasn't sure she wanted to. What good would it do to go back and dig up things better left buried in the past? Not knowing could be a blessing she wasn't aware she'd been granted.

"My family would have destroyed you." Reed made a reach for her hand.

She couldn't handle it, not even the simplest touch from him. Pulling away, she buried her hand safely in her lap. "I don't care about your family. I never did. Putting so much importance in nothing more than a last name is ridiculous, if you ask me."

Old anger caught a new flame. He'd tried in the beginning, using the McReily name as some sort of influence over her. It had been pitiful. If she hadn't struggled with an overwhelming attraction for him from the moment she set eyes on him, she would have walked away then.

There had been more to him. She'd seen it underneath the carefully polished rich boy. For a year he'd had her fooled, believing underneath all his wealth and prestige he actually had a heart.

A heart that turned out to be nothing more than a cold stone.

"It is ridiculous. It doesn't change the reality of who I was, who my family was...is."

"I didn't want to see it at first." Sensing they both needed it, he grabbed the wine bottle, topping off their glasses.

"Being down here in the Quarter, away from all the reality of the boredom and responsibilities that came with being a McReily, it was easy to convince myself that none of that life would touch the new one I had discovered."

"But, it would have touched you." He stared hard into her dark brown eyes, saw the spark of the young girl she'd been, the woman she'd become. How could he ever get her to understand it was that he hadn't wanted to destroy?

"How could it have touched me?" She grabbed for an oyster and dropped it on her plate. "The only member of your family I ever met was Teddy. In all that time we were together, I never knew anyone else."

She'd brought her hand up from her lap. He wanted to reach for it again but knew better. "I wanted it that way. I didn't want the life I'd found here with you, with the others, to have anything to do with the life I was trying to escape. I hated that part of who I was. I couldn't run far enough from it."

"I knew that." Addie sucked the meat from her oyster without tasting it then reached for another, needing to keep her hands busy. "I believed you when you told me what it was like growing up in your family."

"You don't believe me anymore?"

"No." He shook his head, dark hair tumbling over his forehead. "Don't answer that."

Silence fell. They had been heading somewhere, but Addie wondered if they'd lost track along the way, caught up in old hurts and losing the present in the past they shared. "It doesn't matter. None of this matters. What happened is done. There's no reason to talk about it now."

"Except that I hurt you. And you deserve to know why."

She shook her head before he finished but Reed ignored her.

"We couldn't have gone forward from where we were. Or, at least, that's what I believed."

She didn't want to hear anymore. Hating him was her barrier, her ability to exist with the hurt he'd caused. "I really don't need to know. I don't care enough."

It was a lie. They both knew it.

Reed's gaze was heavy, full of emotions she didn't want to know, as their waitress returned. They ordered Seafood Gumbo, pasting smiles on their faces as they did. Noticing nothing, or choosing not to see it, their waitress nodded, tucked her pad back into the black apron around her waist, and left them to themselves once again.

She'd hoped that would be the end of it. They'd finish their oysters, enjoy another glass of wine with their dinner and be done with it all.

Hopeful with it, she grabbed another oyster while Reed did the same.

"If we'd kept going as we were that year," he dropped it on his plate, looked at her over the length of the table. "Do you ever wonder where we'd be today?"

"No." The lie was quick but sour on her lips. Grabbing her wine, she washed down the taste of it.

He shrugged, knowing better but choosing to say nothing. "I could have brought you into the McReily family and watched while they shattered everything I loved about you. Or I could have walked away from them and been left with nothing to offer you."

"Because I cared so much about what you could give me." She couldn't hide the sarcasm.

"I cared." He bunched his long fingers into a fist against the table. "That was the hell of it. I never put thought to it until my family shoved the truth at me. I could either let them take away everything you were, or I could do it myself."

A hint of anger began to threaten. Addie sucked in a harsh breath, willing it back. "I would say you did a pretty good job of doing it yourself." The ugly words came back again, leaving her to wonder if she'd ever truly be free of them.

"I needed you to hate me. It was the only way."

"The only way for what?" Losing her grasp on her temper, her voice rose. She was tempted to shove from her seat and walk out without giving him a chance to stop her this time.

"To stay away from you. Had there remained the slightest chance, I never would have been able to turn away. I would have kept coming back, making it worse. I had to make sure you hated me. Would never let me back into your life."

She didn't want to hear anymore. She had hated him. Still did, in some ways. How could he think such cruelty would have solved anything? Where were the lines between the lies he claimed he told and the truth of what he felt?

She had too many questions with answers she wasn't sure she wanted to know. "I can't do this. Not now."

Though need was in his eyes, he didn't push. The tension was thick around the table as they finished up the oysters and waited for their Gumbo.

She couldn't do this. Couldn't go back to the past she'd been trying to forget for so many years, believing she was close to doing just that until Reed sauntered back into her life, threatening to change everything she once held as truth.

CHAPTER TWELVE

Her mother was sure to be having a fit by now.

Sixteen year old, Crystal Amers giggled at the thought, caring nothing about the trouble she might be in.

Who cared about punishment and consequences when you were on the arm of Cameron Michaels. The most popular boy in school. The football star every girl wished for, smiled at wistfully when he passed them in the halls.

The past couple weeks, they'd been an item. Her, a sophomore, dating a Senior. And not just any Senior. One that had her friends drooling with envy. Pushed her up the ever-important ladder of popularity.

She wasn't about to say no when he'd asked her to break curfew. Only a fool would think otherwise. He'd taken her to a party with his football friends. Encouraged her to try their concoction of Jungle Juice.

It had been good. Too good. It didn't take long to figure out, though she couldn't taste it, a dangerous amount of alcohol was in the sweet drink.

Her parents didn't allow drinking of any kind. They still chose to see her as a little girl. Refused to acknowledge the woman she was becoming, so sure they could keep her under the strict rules they claimed was for her own good.

This was what was good, Cameron's arm slung around her shoulders, holding her tight. He'd suggested a romantic walk after the party, and she'd been eager to accept. Didn't care about the fact her parents would worry when she didn't come through the front door on time.

"Here." Cameron waved at the open gates of the cemetery. "They haven't closed them yet."

For the first time she hesitated. It wasn't that she was afraid. She'd been born and raised in New Orleans. The stories of ghosts and spirits hovering had been part of her upbringing.

But, even the most rational person had to know the discomfort of entering a cemetery after the sun set, leaving only dark shadows to lead the way. Tease at what waited inside the many crumbling tombs.

Sensing her hesitation, he drew her around to face him, dropping a long, heated kiss against her lips. "I'll protect you."

His smile was teasing as he cupped her breast, squeezing with anticipation heavy in his dark gaze.

The first sliver of doubt surfaced. She quickly chased it away. There was nothing to fear, from him or the cemetery. It had been such a great night. She wasn't going to ruin it now.

"I know you will." She smiled at him, sliding her hand through his as he led her through the gate.

Nuzzling her neck, he stumbled along, tugging her with him. She tripped over a stray rock, fell into him. Keeping her steady, he wrapped tight arms around her, curving firm hands over her backside.

"This is good." He pushed her flush against him, leaving no doubt what ran through his mind. His tongue gliding beneath her col-lar-bone, he half-blindly led her deeper through the tombs, search-ing for the perfect spot.

They stumbled, laughed, kept going, swaying down the pebble grey path cutting between old stone and brick.

Crystal no longer cared about the fear of walking through the cemetery at night. Any apprehension she had slid away as Cameron's hands and mouth roamed over her, heating her blood until she was sure it would boil over.

"You taste so good." His mouth found hers again as he backed her down the skinny path. She trusted him. Didn't need to see where he was leading her. It didn't matter. Nothing mattered but the way he made her feel. The promise of what was yet to come.

"So good." He pulled away from her mouth to nibble on her ear.

She felt the change only a second later. Suddenly stiff under her hands, he froze in place, his attention focused over her shoulder.

"What happened?" She pressed her palms against his chest, push-ing to her toes and dropping a kiss against his lips. "Did you see a ghost?"

He didn't answer, only stared.

Something wasn't right. Stepping back, out of his hold, she turned, following the line of his heavy gaze.

Her next breath caught in her lungs, nearly choking her. Stum-bling back, she fell into Cameron. "Is she—"

She sucked air through her lungs. "Is she dead?"

It was a stupid question. Propped against a gray tomb, the woman was naked, red hair tumbling over her shoulders and brushing against her breasts.

Something was on the inside curve of her right breast. She needed to see. Needed to know.

Daring a step closer, she peered hard through the dark. Took another step until she was close enough to stare into the empty, death-ridden eyes. Cold wrapped around her. A chill raced up her spine.

Shock held then exploded inside as she saw the lip prints against the breast. As if she'd been kissed. The red a harsh contrast against pale skin.

Unable to take a second more, she turned and screamed.

Addie wished she had never brought up the past.

It was no use trying to talk Reed out of walking her home once they left the restaurant. Resigned to it, she stepped onto the side-walk, waiting for him to come out behind her.

Here, a block from Bourbon, the chaotic life drifted through the air, surrounding them. She was tempted to turn that way. To spend the rest of the night in loud music and flowing drinks. Whatever it took to stay away from thoughts of what she'd learned.

But she wasn't up for it. And didn't really believe it would help, anyhow.

She couldn't shift through what he'd told her. Couldn't get her mind to work around it to figure out how she felt about what she'd learned.

So, she chose to avoid it. Which would be much easier as soon as she was away from Reed.

"Thank you for dinner." She refused to touch the latch.

He did it for her. Reaching behind her, he opened the gate. He said nothing, only stared at her until, with a heavy sigh, she stepped through, into the courtyard.

She'd let him walk her to the door as that was what he was pushing for. That would be the line. She wanted to be inside. Alone.

"I can make it from here." She stood at the closed door, wishing him away.

"You want me to go. But I can't seem to do it."

"Please." She fumbled in her pocket, grabbing her keys, unlock-ing the door but refusing the invitation of opening it, instead flattening her back against the hard wood. She'd had enough for the evening. Just wanted time to forget it all.

For a moment, she thought he'd give her that chance. Thought he'd turn and go as she hoped.

His gaze darkened. Instead of turning away, he took a step closer, trapping her between the hard lines sculpting his chest and the door at her back. "I need this first."

She was mad at him. She was hurt, confused. Yet none of that stopped the quick twist in her gut as his lips brushed against hers. He cupped gentle hands around the sides of her face, spearing long fingers through her hair and holding her trapped under the intensity in his deep blue eyes.

"I've never stopped needing this." Finding her mouth again, he drew her up and into him while keeping his hold on her face, leaving her trapped.

He strayed, nibbling at the sensitive skin in the curve of her neck, hands sliding down, skimming gently over her sides.

She should tell him to go. Make it clear she didn't want this. But her body proved otherwise. The heat in her blood made it impossible to lie. She did want this. Even after all these years, her need for Reed was still strong.

His lips slid slowly over her collar bone. He fumbled behind her to turn the knob. It took nothing for him to encourage her over the threshold, closing the door behind them.

He was back, claiming her mouth and pulling her under. Gentle hardened as need grew. Slow caught speed until she was desperate for a breath.

Her spine pressed against the kitchen counter, she reached for him, molding her hands over the muscles sculpting his chest. Wanting to feel even as she called herself a fool for doing so.

"God, Addie." Reed pulled his mouth away, desperately needing a breath. His hands still roamed. Over the slender curve of her shoulders. The firm swell of her breasts. "I can't think of anything but having you."

It was the hard truth slapping at him. His desire for her was as strong, if not stronger, than it had been. Opening the gates, telling her the truth, brought forth a strange permission to give in to the need raging inside. To satisfy what he'd craved since the moment he'd turned his back on everything.

She pressed into him, nearly breaking the last bit of control. Sucking it in, holding on to what he had, he wrapped tight arms around her, holding them both up.

She'd been his from the beginning. Every emotion, every feeling he'd once had surged forth. Needing more, he tugged on the edges of her shirt, easing it up and over her head.

Covered in soft, pink lace, her breasts heaved with the breath she sucked through her lungs. "Reed, I—"

So much tumbled through her dark gaze. Desire clashed with fear. Need battled against doubt.

Watching her, he circled his thumb over the hardened nipple pushing against delicate fabric. Her eyes widened but she didn't turn away. She kept him with her. Let him see the heat building, clouding her vision, as he teased.

He found his way under the lace. Skin meeting skin. This was what he missed. Touching her, without restrictions. Without guilt.

Her eyes locked with his. He cupped a gentle hand over her breast, his own blood boiling as her gaze clouded over.

For those he'd known since Addie, none came close to what she did to him. What she drew forth from deep inside. She controlled him, always making him want for more.

He'd once believed it was just age or the innocence of youth, playing into what surged inside. He'd been wrong. So wrong.

It was Addie. Who she was. What she did to him. She was so unlike anyone he'd ever had in his life. Even now, she continued to be that brief wash of fresh air, reminding him of goodness. Of a light in all that seemed so dark.

He stroked lower, down the slender curve of her waist, playing with the soft band of her skirt. And still she watched, holding him in all that shadowed her dark brown eyes.

He had to taste her, desperately needing the connection. Lowering his mouth to hers, fingers teasing along the edge of her skirt, he drew in everything she was.

She fed in to him, giving as only she could. It took everything inside not to take her there, on the kitchen counter. Losing himself inside her in a frantic, desperate tumble.

He eased her away and towards the door leading from the kitchen to the stairs, lips still heavy against hers. Fingers roaming over her.

He stumbled then cursed at the distinctive sound of his ringtone. Temptation was strong to ignore it. To continue to take all he could from Addie while denying the interruption.

But he couldn't. The first and second ring slid into a third. He growled rough against her mouth before yanking his phone from his pocket.

Her mind clouded with desire, every inch of her body on fire, Addie could only stare as Reed shoved the phone to his ear.

She needed this, she realized. This moment to suck in a breath. To search frantically for clear thought under the thick fog of arousal.

Where they were headed terrified her even as it excited her.

"Damn. Where?" The hard rush of his voice broke through her thoughts. He changed from the man who'd just had his hands on her, igniting a fire, to the spine-stiff, serious agent he was.

Anger flashed where desire had only moments ago lingered as he ended the call. "I have to go."

He was brisk, wrapping long fingers around her arms and staring for a moment. Dropping a kiss on her lips, he lingered.

"We will finish this," he promised, disappearing out the door, leaving her alone in the kitchen. She stood there, lost in all that had happened. Her mind and heart continuing to race.

She'd have gone with him. She didn't bother to deny it. If he'd succeeded in leading her from the kitchen to her room she wouldn't have put up a fight.

The knowledge of it didn't sit well. Left her jumpy and restless.

She flipped the locks on the door and turned out the lights for the kitchen on her way out. She wouldn't be able to sleep, that much she knew. Opening the balcony doors, she stepped out into the warm night air, inhaling deep.

A month ago, she would have told anyone who asked that her life was in order and exactly where she wanted. She loved what she did. Where she lived. Had great friends and a social life that never left her wanting for more.

But since Reed had come back—

Curling hard fingers around the edge of the banister, Addie stared, unseeing, at the quiet street below. Since he'd come back she spent more nights than not fighting for sleep. Her mind wandering, worrying. Dragging up a past she would have sworn she'd buried away.

And now, learning everything she'd held as truth had been a lie.

Groaning, pinching a finger to the bridge of her nose, she fought off the headache threatening. Anger came, along with hurt and confusion.

So many emotions. So many things she didn't have the strength or patience to work through at the moment.

Maybe in the morning, she decided with a soft sigh, finding her way back inside and closing the door, and her thoughts, behind her.

"Looks like you were right. Your guy made it to New Orleans." Waiting at the gates of the cemetery, Perry waved a hand at the eerie circle of lights hovering near the back. "Or we're assuming it's him. Waiting on you to make the final call."

Reed felt the same tightening in his gut. The hint of adrenaline shooting through his veins. It was the same for every body they'd found. Instincts kicking in. Personal feelings carefully kept away.

Keeping in step with Perry, he followed the shine of spotlights illuminating the scene. The buzz of controlled chaos drifted back, floating over crypts and circling around him.

Surrounded by the local badges, Jackson flashed a quick smile, breaking away from the heavy group. "They're hovering on the edge. Orders are they aren't to touch a thing until you're here. We don't want any mistakes on this."

He looked past her to the body propped against an old tomb. He didn't have to see the mark to know it was already there. They wouldn't have called him in if it hadn't been.

A breeze caught as he edged around Jackson, a dark whisper of sound and motion, moving through the cemetery. The officers in their crisp, blue uniforms shifted away, making a path as he approached, their eyes heavy on his back as he knelt in front of the woman no longer with a life to claim.

Blank eyes stared back at him under a thick fold of red curls. She was so young. Early twenties, if he had to guess. Like the others. Taken before they'd ever had a chance to fully live.

His gaze dropped to her breasts. It was there. Red lipstick, bold and telling, against pale skin. A final kiss, leaving no doubt he'd taken another.

"It's your guy." Perry's words were statement, not question, as he came to stand beside Reed. Even with all the years he'd been part of the Bureau, his gut tightened at the sight of the dead woman. Death had never been an easy one for him.

"It's him." Reed straightened. He'd seen the dim finger-size bruises around her slender neck. She'd been strangled like the others.

And tortured. More bruising along her torso, thighs and arms, showed proof to it.

Damn. Shaking his head in anger, he turned away.

Was this one his fault? Had he been so busy trying to prove the killer was after Addie he'd missed something that might have prevented this?

He didn't like the answers coming to mind. He'd been so sure. Hadn't had a single doubt it was Addie he was after.

Because he'd let personal feelings get in the way. The truth kicked hard. He'd seen that card with the flowers and had slipped so easily into the need to protect Addie. His feelings for her clouding any chance at considering he might be wrong.

And another innocent woman paid the price because of it.

"The locals will process the scene." Jackson was back at his side. "They'll let us know what, if any, evidence they find."

Reed's nod was weak. They wouldn't find anything of use.

Another body. Another useless death. And this time, more than ever before, the horror of it weighed heavy on his shoulders.

CHAPTER THIRTEEN

G uilt played a nasty game.

Inside the New Orleans office, Reed stared out the tiny window looking over the glaring afternoon sun. It had been a long night and an even longer day.

No identification was found on the dead woman. But the start of the day led them to a name. Amanda Roberts. A student at the University of Texas, she'd headed to New Orleans with her college friends for a much-needed escape after a long week of finals.

They'd spent their second night in the Quarter in the same manner they did their first. Every bar, every dance floor, a new adventure to be discovered.

It was late afternoon the next day before her friends started to worry, figuring she was sleeping off the wild times from the night before. By five in the evening, they were knocking on her door. Just before midnight they were at the police station, filing a missing person report.

That was days ago. Her friends returned home, leaving a string of long-distance phone calls in an attempt to gain more information. Her parents were on their way to New Orleans to identify her body. The media was starting to gather as they caught hint of a serial killer in their midst.

Yeah, one hell of a day.

"You look like hell."

Reed's head shot up at the sound of the familiar voice. Standing in the door of the office, Branson flashed bright white teeth through his smile.

Dressed in a Hawaiian shirt and khaki shorts, skin darkened by plenty of time in the sun, he looked like the ultimate tourist standing in the darkened hall of the Bureau office.

"What did you do, decide the whole cruise and marriage thing wasn't for you?" Shoving back from his desk, Reed pushed to his feet.

"Hell, no." Stepping into the tiny office, Branson ran a slow eye over his partner, taking in the exhaustion ringing dark circles under his eyes. "If I had my way, I'd still be sailing the seas."

He hooked a hip against the corner of the desk as he shook his partner's hand while taking a look at the spread of papers he'd been going through and the flash of information on the monitor he'd stared at.

"You know what they say," he shrugged. "All good things must come to an end. We were getting off the plane in D.C. when Marshall called to fill me in on what was going on. I didn't bother going to the office. I took my beautiful new wife home, kissed her goodbye, and headed back for the airport to join you."

"I appreciate it." He dropped a friendly smack to his back. "But I hate being the reason you had to leave that beautiful wife of yours so soon after taking your vows."

"We'll add it up to you owing me one." Leaning over the desk, Branson shifted through the papers. "So, what have we got so far?"

"Absolutely nothing." Frustration returning, Reed reclaimed his chair. "Like every other time."

"Well, hell." Branson fell into the chair across from the desk. "We hoped but knew we might get the same results."

Yeah. He knew. Didn't mean he liked it. "I thought, for a moment, he was setting his sights on someone else."

"He's never given us a clue who he's been after before. Why the change to think he was now?"

"Because flowers were sent. To someone I know."

Reed sucked in a deep breath, fighting back the memories of the night before with Addie, so ready to take her right there in her kitchen. "Someone I've known for a long time. A card came with them. It had the same mark, that red kiss. And nothing else."

Branson's stare was hard, searching, as it reached Reed on the opposite end of the desk. "Makes sense. He sent that letter to the D.C. office, making it clear he was out to make it personal with you. If I was in your shoes, I would have suspected the same."

"Yeah well, my suspecting it might have cost another woman her life."

"You thinking of taking the blame for this?" He tapped a finger against the picture of the dead woman resting on top of the desk.

Reed shrugged, hating that he took it where he did. "It's a possibility. I was so busy trying to prove he was after Addie, who knows what I missed in the meantime."

"How often have you been able to stop him in the past?" Branson's dark gaze peered straight through him, pushing him to things he didn't' want to admit.

"Doesn't mean there wasn't something to be found this time."

"You searching for a reason to blame yourself?"

He wasn't. But damn, now that Branson had shown up, he was quickly making it seem that way.

Branson leaned forward, hovering over the desk. "If I'd been in your shoes, I would have followed through on the same assumption. How could you not?"

He was trying hard, Reed would give him that. It couldn't be said it was working, though. Not with the dark path his thoughts were taking.

It did no good to waste time on things that couldn't be changed. "Have I mentioned I'm glad you're here?"

Gathering the papers littering the desk in front of him, Reed tucked them carefully into line. "Perry and Jackson are good agents. But it's nice to have someone who knows this case as deep as I do. Plus, I kind of missed your ugly mug."

"I knew, deep down inside, you loved me. So," Branson stuck a foot on the edge of the desk, resting the other over it. "Tell me what you've got."

"Oh, thank goodness you're all right." Rosalie hurried into the shop, bringing the hot, sticky air from outside with her. Hurrying past the customers gathered at the tapestries, she reached the counter in four large strides, grabbing Addie's hands in hers.

"Of course, I am." Surprised to see her aunt back early from Baton Rouge, Addie gave her fingers a quick squeeze before slowly working her hands free. "Why wouldn't I be?"

"Because, I saw on the news—"

The worry easing now that she'd seen with her own eyes that her niece was okay, Rosalie sucked in a slow breath, became aware of the others inside the shop. "I saw the story about that poor girl they found at the cemetery."

Addie heard the same story. It was hard to miss as the whispers of it filtered through the streets and into the store. She hadn't heard from Reed since he'd taken the call. But she had no doubt it had been for the murdered woman.

"What reason would you have to worry about me?" She smiled at the older woman approaching the counter.

Her blue eyes sparkling, she set a fairy laced tapestry on the counter. "My granddaughter is going to love this."

She beamed at Addie while running a soft finger over the stitched edge. "I thought, perhaps, I could look at some of your charms as well."

"Of course."

Rosalie moved out of the way, finding a place behind the counter. Addie pulled the padded display from the glass shelves, arranging them in clear view of the older woman.

"Each charm has its own description." She pointed a finger to the small labels beneath each one. "And explanations for its uses and cures. Take your time. Let me know if you have any questions."

She stepped away, giving the other woman space.

"I'm perfectly fine." She edged up close to her aunt, keeping her voice low. "I don't know why you worried."

"Because," Rosalie shoved her travel bag under the counter then fluffed at her hair. The long frantic drive had taken its toll which wouldn't do with customers around. "The news reported a serial killer, just like Reed said. I remember him thinking he was after you. Couldn't get it out of my mind."

Addie wanted to shake her head at her aunt's words but couldn't. She'd thought of the same.

It hadn't hit, not really, the true horror of what he'd told her. It hovered in some sort of abstract idea she couldn't grasp. Wasn't completely sure she believed.

Not when she'd been so busy pushing back against Reed's insistence the killer was after her. Relief came with the knowledge he'd been wrong. Guilt came after that. A woman had been strangled and left naked in a cemetery. She had a sick twist in her stomach knowing that, leaving her hating the fact a small dose of comfort came that it hadn't been her as Reed first predicted.

"Well, it wasn't me. I'm just sorry it cut your trip short."

Smiling as a young couple approached the counter, Rosalie dropped a quick kiss against Addie's cheek. "I was getting close to being ready to come home, anyhow, so nothing to be sorry for."

She moved around her to greet the couple, leaving Addie to tend to the older woman still going through the crystals.

It was just another usual day in the Quarter. Yet, to Addie, it suddenly felt so different.

"Clay's playing and you need a night out."

Sprawled over Addie's bed, Annabeth sipped from the glass of wine she'd insisted she needed the moment she'd walked through the door. "So do I. It's been a hell of a week with all those stuffy men in their crisp and boring suits filing through the hotel."

"My true talents are wasted," her friend smiled over the rim of her glass, "when it comes to planning for a bunch of boring account executives. Though some of them did have some great money potential."

Addie picked up the pillow beside Annabeth and threw it at her. "You're pitiful."

"Nah." She shrugged while taking another sip of wine. "Just honest. I'm one girl who will need dollar signs, plenty of them, before ever saying, I do."

Laughing, Addie eased on to the edge of the bed beside her, grabbing AnnaBeth's glass for a sip of her own. "Sometimes those dollar signs aren't all they're made out to be. They can have a pretty terrible bite if you aren't careful."

In the way only a best friend could, AnnaBeth sensed exactly what was under Addie's words.

"Come on." She rolled from the bed and held out a hand.

"Where are we going?" Addie rested her hand in AnnaBeth's, allowing her to pull her to her feet.

"To the kitchen to get the bottle of wine and another glass. We need some girl talk and that calls for more than sharing one glass of wine between us."

She didn't protest as AnnaBeth led her out of the bedroom and down the stairs to the kitchen. Wrapping long fingers around the neck of the wine bottle, she grabbed the stem of another wine glass in her other hand then led them out the back door into the courtyard.

"It's hot but manageable." She waved Addie to one of the chairs around the small, wrought-iron table by the fountain, claiming the other as she set both bottle and glass down in front of her.

Topping off the glass Addie still held in her hand, she filled the other one for herself. "So, spill it."

Addie could play dumb. She could pretend she didn't know what AnnaBeth was talking about. But it would be worthless.

"Reed's decided what happened all those years ago was nothing but a lie." She heard it, the child-like whining in her voice. Taking a sip of wine, she tried washing it away. "He claims he always loved me but lied to me, destroyed me. "

She took another sip, needing it desperately. "He did all of it to protect me. Because, somehow, in his twisted way of thinking, that made it better. Made it okay."

All the emotions she'd pushed down threatened to return with a force she couldn't control. She'd thought it had been easy, stuffing it all away after learning about the horrible death of the woman they'd found in the cemetery. It had been like a trickle. A leak she hadn't had control over.

As she'd tried concentrating on something else, bits and scraps of emotions found their way through, threatening to make her think of something she only wanted to forget. Face emotions she wasn't sure of, refusing to give herself the time to admit to them, much less work through them.

They were there now. The trickle turning into an overflow as she sat with AnnaBeth, sipping on wine in the sultry, evening heat.

"He's decided to change the rules on you." AnnaBeth rested a hand over hers on the table.

"What rules?"

"The ones carefully keeping you hating him."

"I still hate him. Just for different reasons, now. *If* he's telling the truth now, which how the hell do I know."

"He could be lying now." She shrugged as she took a long, slow drink of her wine. "It doesn't change the fact he either told the truth and hurt me, or he lied and hurt me."

Oh, yes, so much was brewing there. The heat of it wrapped around AnnaBeth where she sat on the opposite side of the table. "So, tell me about it."

For all the emotions churning inside, Addie was still hesitant to try and put it into words. "I'm not sure what to tell."

She dropped her hands to her lap, fumbling with them. "I've gone years believing I was nothing more than a fling to Reed. Someone who was never going to be good enough for him. Now, after all this time, he wants me to think different."

She was going to talk around it the best she could. AnnaBeth expected no less from her best friend. So, she'd wait her out. Let her get around to it. "Different, how?"

"He wants me believing now it was about his family and his need to protect me from them." Addie shook her head, disgust and doubt a dangerous mix. "Suddenly, I wasn't the problem. They were. He claims he tore me apart like he did because he needed me to hate him in order to protect me."

Saying it only made her angrier, more desperate to dismiss every word he'd given. "Who thinks like that?"

"Apparently, Reed does. Or, at least, he did."

AnnaBeth picked up her glass, sipping slowly while staring at Addie over the rim. "It never did seem to fit the way Reed treated you, what he said in the end. I've always wondered if there was more to it."

"You believe him?" Defiance flashed in Addie's gaze catching hers from across the table. AnnaBeth didn't let it deter her. She was a friend who believed in honesty, even when it wasn't always so easy to hear.

"It makes more sense than the crap he fed you all those years ago." Grabbing the wine bottle, she refilled their glasses, figuring they needed it.

"His family was crap. We know that. Doesn't really surprise me if he had some twisted belief he needed to keep you away from them." Her eyes were kind as they met Addie's, though she wasn't sure it did much good compared to the fire burning in hers. "But obviously, if this is his truth now, you're as angry as you were when you believed him before."

"I deserve to be angry, don't I?"

"You deserve to feel whatever it is you feel. But, I have to say, I'm more prone to believe him now over what he told you back then. It makes more sense."

It was the same direction Addie followed more than once. It didn't make it better. The hurt still existed. "He could have told me the truth back then."

"He *should* have told you the truth," AnnaBeth agreed, her smooth voice full of conviction. "You deserved it."

"Yes. I did."

And there it was, what had bothered her since Reed told her the reasons behind the hurt he'd caused all those years ago. No matter how much he justified it or tried to make it seem right, he'd still hurt her. Through deception or truth, the outcome was the same. Her heart had been broken. Her trust had been shattered.

"What are you going to do about it?"

The question catching her off guard, Addie only stared. "Do about what?"

"About you and Reed."

"There is no Reed and I so there's not a damn thing to do about it."

The anger she'd finally admitted to taking root, Addie shoved from her chair, taking her wine glass with her. "The past, regardless of what it was, means nothing now. Before long, he'll go back to whatever life he left, and I'll keep living my life here without him."

She finished the last of her wine, setting the empty glass on the table with a forceful snap. "Let's go out, like you said."

She had a need now to escape, get away from the emotions quickly pushing forth, demanding attention.

"Seems sad to me." Shrugging, Annabeth grabbed the bottle, the glasses, and pushed to her feet. "The two of you going back to your corners and pretending all over again you can forget about each other."

Addie bit back her angry response. It wasn't worth it.

"Give me that." She took the bottle from her friend's hands and turned for the door. "We'll finish this off while I get ready."

With that, she hoped, she put an end to any more talk of her and Reed.

CHAPTER FOURTEEN

H e was worn. He was weary. And he was cranky.

None of it proved to be a good combination.

Inside his hotel room, Reed stood at the window, staring out over the Quarter. The day had been long. Too long. He wanted to pour himself a drink, maybe two or three, and forget everything until he tumbled, unknowing and uncaring, into bed.

That would have to wait. Drawing in a long deep breath, he answered the hard knock on his door. Branson waited on the other side.

"I'm ready." His smile was a bit too enthusiastic, considering what hung over their heads. "I'm in your hands now, ready to see this New Orleans of yours."

Reed turned away without answering, wishing again for that night of drinking and oblivion. "Don't get your hopes up. I'm just taking you to my cousin's bar. You want more than that, you'll have to go exploring on your own.

Branson didn't miss the tension in his partner's voice. He could ignore it or push it. With a hard look at Reed, and the knowledge he'd gained after so many years working at his side, he figured ignoring it was the best solution for the moment.

"Fine, I'm ready to see this cousin's bar. It's got to be better than sitting in my room, missing my wife."

Reed didn't argue. He'd promised the night out, he reminded himself as he grabbed his wallet from the dresser. It was, he figured, a needed distraction, keeping his mind off what it was he really wanted...Addie.

Leading the way out of his room, locking the door behind him, he did his best to push away his need for her. It wasn't the time for it.

He'd seen death and horror, the terrible workings of the crazy, and he'd always made it through by his own will. Somehow, this one was different, hitting harder than the others. He knew the way of the killer, always expecting clearly what he'd find. But that young woman, bared and vulnerable in the cemetery stuck right in the back yard of where he'd grown up changed things.

Not a bit of it was good.

Biting down a frustrated growl, he hit the button for the elevator harder than necessary, ignoring Branson's curious gaze.

Stepping on to the elevator when the heavy doors slid open, he waited for his partner to join him before hitting the button that would lower them to the lobby.

It was time to suck it up. He'd made a promise to his partner. He'd keep it and do his best not to be a surly grouch about it.

Shuffling with the other hotel guests out of the elevator and into the streets, he waited for Branson to fall into step beside him before turning the corner for Bourbon.

"You've talked about it, but I have to admit, I've never truly grasped the reality of this place." Taking in his surroundings, agent instincts making him aware of everything and everyone around him, he shot a grin Reed's way before moving into the midst of the crowds.

It was a strange world to those who'd never experienced it before. Especially the life vibrating so strong along Bourbon Street once the night set and the many bars kicked up.

They dodged around a stumbling group coming at them with beer cans clenched in their hands. Side-stepped an older couple, slowly moving, arm in arm, in the opposite direction.

"Funny," Branson glanced at Reed as they found a place in the middle of the street, "though I know this is your place, your roots, it doesn't exactly fit. You have an edge that doesn't exactly match all this."

Reed could tell him about the fact his upbringing had actually been in another part of the city. In a life where such careless celebration of life was strictly denied. In a place where such public displays of true enjoyment were never embraced but, instead, looked down upon.

He didn't bother. Branson knew enough about his background. More than he usually shared. That was enough. He had no reason to share more when it wouldn't make a difference in the here and now.

"The edge is because I need a drink." He pushed through the bodies so close, stepping onto the sidewalk in front of Teddy's bar. "It's been one hell of a day."

With his first step inside, he knew.

He didn't have to see or hear her. The awareness was there without such things. His eyes searched in the dim light, finding the gentle tumble of red curls over slender shoulders.

Her head was bent low with AnnaBeth's. She stiffened and lifted her gaze, finding him standing just inside the door.

A hint of need flashed in her dark brown gaze before quickly giving way to a flash of anger.

So, they were back there again. He shook his head, shoving down the disappointment. He'd hoped, after their last night together, things would be different.

He'd obviously been wrong. Even with the truth now between them, it seemed he was destined to live with her anger.

Purposely arching around her with nothing more than a quick nod of the head, he led Branson to the bar, snagging two stools as the couple occupying them tossed down money for their drinks and moved on.

The heavy rise and fall of a classical Rock ballad shifted through the crowd. Stealing a quick glance at the stage, a smile tugged on the corners of his mouth as Clay's voice drew people to the dance floor.

Waving away the approaching bartender, Teddy edged along the opposite side of the bar. "Didn't figure I'd be seeing you in here."

He grabbed a rag, wiping away the bottle marks left by the last customers. "Not with what's been going on with that woman that was found."

"It was time for a break." Reed shrugged, not wanting to talk about the woman who's pale, lifeless face continued to haunt his thoughts.

"And my partner here," he tossed his head to the side, "is an Orleans virgin. I thought I'd get him out to see what all the fuss is about."

"Mitch." Beside him, Branson stuck out a thick, beefy hand. "I'm guessing you must be the cousin I've heard about."

"That would be me. It's nice to finally meet somebody from Reed's other life."

Winking at Reed, he tossed the rag back under the bar. "What can I get you two?"

They ordered beers and waited for Teddy to place the bottles in front of them.

"So, I hear they identified the woman they found in the cemetery." Teddy looked between his cousin and his partner, seeking answers just as, it seemed, everyone was doing.

New Orleans wasn't new to crime, or even death. But something like this, it hit harder. Made everyone a bit more uncomfortable.

"I'm guessing this means we don't have to worry about him coming after Addie anymore."

Reed wished he could agree. He should with all the facts now in place. What he'd refused to believe was coincidence, now seemed to be exactly that.

"I'm not dismissing anything right now. Not until we have more answers."

Teddy's surprised gaze met his, matching the same one he felt from Branson, burning against his side. "You can't believe she's still in any danger. It's obvious, now, she wasn't the one your killer was after."

Except for the card that came with the flowers. It still didn't sit right with Reed, not even with the latest victim.

As his earlier guilt eased, the feeling that something still wasn't right returned. He couldn't put a finger on it, but he felt it just the same. "I've been at this too long to know what's obvious and what's truth isn't always the same."

Teddy's gaze, unsettled now, looked over him to where Addie and AnnaBeth sat. "No offense, but I'm going to hope like hell you're wrong."

So was he, Reed agreed silently as he took a drink.

If his goal was to drive her crazy, he was doing a damn good job at it.

Refusing to look back to where Reed sat at the bar, she clapped hard as Clay finished up his latest song before announcing they were taking a short break.

"And my ladies wait for me." Sweeping between her and Anna-Beth he dropped a kiss on their cheeks. He smelled of smoke and sweat and the energized adrenaline only a musician understood. "I need to fetch a drink and I'll be back."

Though it was only asking for trouble, she watched him head for the bar. Waited the few seconds it took him before he realized Reed was there.

Cutting through the crowd, his booming voice echoed back as he threw a friendly arm around Reed's shoulders. She couldn't hear their muted conversation over the roar of voices as Clay turned and threw another arm around the man at Reed's side.

Laughter boomed and she turned away, refusing to wonder what brought it. It was better to sit with AnnaBeth and keep her thoughts far away from the tempting, dark male seated at the end of the bar.

"He's not going to go away." AnnaBeth hooked a comforting arm around Addie, leaned in close. She heard her baby brother inviting Reed to the table.

Before she could warn Addie, Clay was back, a smile beaming as he snagged the two empty chairs from the table beside them. "Pucker up girls, I've got shots on the way. Need to wet the whistle before the next set."

Addie was ready to ask how the extra chairs had anything to do with the shots he'd ordered when she sensed movement behind her.

She didn't bother turning. Refused to acknowledge Reed as his warm, spicy scent reached her, teasing with thoughts better left forgotten.

She braced as he passed over the two chairs Clay drug over, grabbing the empty chair beside her instead. More than anything she wanted to ignore him and pretend he wasn't there. But, as the man who'd come into the bar with him claimed the chair next to Reed, manners insisted she turn to acknowledge them.

"Thought you'd be busy."

"I have been." He set his beer bottle on the table, leaning in closer. "Did you miss me?"

The heat of him waving over her was almost her undoing. Needing to wash down the sudden knot in her throat, she took a slow sip of her wine. "Didn't realize you were away."

Her answering smile was anything but friendly.

A few nights ago, Reed believed finally bringing out the truth would be a good thing. Tonight, he realized he was wrong. So very wrong.

"Who's your friend?" Dropping a comforting hand over Addie's leg underneath the table, AnnaBeth pulled the attention her way.

"Mitch Branson." The other man answered before Reed had a chance. "I'm Reed's partner."

He stuck out a hand, first for AnnaBeth then Addie.

He had a nice look to him. AnnaBeth was intrigued until she saw the simple gold band on his left hand. She didn't do married. Even for her, she had lines she wouldn't cross.

"This is my sister, AnnaBeth," Clay picked up where both women fell silent. "And her best friend, Addie."

He beamed at Teddy as he approached with a loaded tray. "And we're all going to enjoy a shot before I get back to singing."

It was the last thing she needed. After the wine shared with Anna-Beth back at the house, and what she'd enjoyed since they reached the bar, more alcohol was only asking for trouble.

But the press of Reed against her side, the feel of him reminding her of entirely too much, was enough to have her reaching eagerly for the small glass Teddy set in front of her.

"What are we toasting?" She held hers up, waiting for the others to do the same.

"To old friends and new." Clay winked at Mitch as he held his own glass above his head. "And to your great taste that brought you here to hear me sing."

They laughed as they downed the amber liquid. Smooth cinnamon, carrying a slight burn, streamed down Addie's throat, calming the nerves set uneasy by Reed's nearness.

She was tempted to ask for another but knew better than to risk it. Already, her head was a bit light. Much more and she'd be paying the price.

"You'll stay for my next set." Clay set down his empty glass.

He widened his bright blue eyes at the hesitation coming back at him. Smiled wide when the hint was taken and everyone nodded.

"Great." He pushed back from the table. "Get your requests in and I'll sing some songs for you."

Flashing a smile, he was gone, hurrying to the bar to grab a water bottle before returning to the stage.

Addie cursed silently as Reed settled in beside her, obviously having no intention of returning to his place at the bar. Not that he could have, she realized with a glance over her shoulder, as the seats they left were already occupied by another couple putting in their orders with the bartender.

Knowing she shouldn't, but doing it anyway, she accepted Anna-Beth's suggestion for another glass of wine. If she was going to swallow the bitter fact she couldn't seem to get away from Reed, she was at least going to need something to wash it down with.

CHAPTER FIFTEEN

It was close, but Addie stopped herself from stumbling on her way out the door. It was that last glass of wine. She cursed her decision as she hooked an arm through AnnaBeth's, using her to stay steady as they stepped onto the sidewalk.

"I've got her." Reed grabbed her arm, holding her from the other side.

"Why don't you make sure Mitch gets back to the hotel." He shot a look over Addie's head. "I'll make sure she gets back in one piece."

Reluctance lingered in AnnaBeth's returning gaze. Reed waited it out. Shooting him her own warning look, leaving little doubt to the pain she'd cause if he screwed up this small bit of trust she was giving him, she stepped away from Addie.

She slid her arm through Mitch's.

"If we get lost for a while, don't bother coming to look for us." She winked back at Addie's hesitant stare, hoped she was doing the right thing.

"I suppose it's a waste to tell you I can make it home on my own." Addie took an unsteady step away from Reed, needing the distance.

He didn't bother answering. Wrapping a tight hand around her arm, he moved them out of the direct route of a group tumbling toward them before making the turn onto Toulouse, getting them out of the crush of bodies filling Bourbon.

"How about you tell me, instead, what has you so mad." His hand slid down her arm, catching her hand in his.

She didn't pull away, though she had the urge to. "There's nothing to tell. I've been mad at you for a long time. Tonight is no different."

He stopped, quick and sudden, pulling her against him. "You didn't seem too mad the other night."

The flicker of memory caught her, leaving her more unsteady.

She'd still been mad, but it hadn't mattered. Not in that moment. Not while just a touch from Reed heated her blood, left her wanting more.

She'd had time to cool down. Time to process all he'd told her. And she was mad. More than she liked to admit.

His truth hadn't eased the pain he'd caused, only brought more questions and confusion. More need to understand why. "You distracted me."

She edged out of his hold, gaining a foot ahead of him along the sidewalk.

He caught up with her quickly. She turned the corner, into the alley, thankful the gate into the courtyard was close.

"Maybe I should try again." He stopped her before she grabbed the latch. Turning her, he clasped steady hands around her arms, holding her still under his moody gaze. "I tend to like you hot and bothered over angry."

"It's not a switch you can flip." She refused to let him know how much his body, so close to hers, was affecting her.

"Isn't it?" He caught her mouth with his.

The sensible part of her told her to break away. To escape through the gate and not look back. But, as it always seemed to be with Reed, what was sensible didn't matter when it came up against how he made her feel.

She'd never been able to fight it. Never had a defense against what he aroused with nothing more than a simple touch. It didn't matter how long he'd been gone. Didn't matter the anger she carried. None of it prevented what he brought to life inside.

Even as it frightened her, it excited her. Made her want for everything he offered.

His arms came around behind her, pulling her tighter. His mouth took without hesitation, drawing her in and shoving back all the doubt and anger.

Maybe it was the alcohol. Maybe it was the simple fact she was exhausted from fighting back all that simmered inside. She didn't know the truth of it, but she knew what she wanted.

Pulling back, just enough to find herself lost in the heat of his deep, blue eyes, she pressed her hands against the rough crease of muscles lining his chest.

"My aunt is home. She came back early when she heard about what happened."

Her words didn't register with Reed. Not when he was caught up in the feel of her soft curves molding against him. She'd always fit so perfectly, as if they'd been created for one another.

He tried finding her mouth again, growling when she turned away.

"I'm not much for this alley." She gave a shove against his chest, slowly bringing him back to what was being said. "And I'm certainly not taking this inside."

She allowed his kiss then, a tease before moving back. "Don't you have a hotel room?"

Forcing his mind to come back, he fought the need to take her again, concentrating, instead, on what she was saying. Hope spiked as her words settled. Still, with Addie, he could be wrong.

"I do." He twisted a red curl around his finger and tucked it behind her ear. "What did you have in mind?"

He held his breath, waiting. The struggle was clear in those chocolate eyes of hers, battling between reason and need.

She hesitated for only a moment before pushing on to her toes, brushing her lips against his. "I don't know what I have in mind, exactly. I'm guessing we could figure it out."

His heart leapt, picking up an extra beat as it drummed against his chest. He didn't bother letting go as he backed her out of the alley, turning in the direction of his hotel.

Need tore through him. He feared if he didn't get her to his hotel room in time, she'd change her mind, ripping away all the erotic thoughts currently tumbling through his head.

He'd wanted her since the moment he'd set eyes on her again. Now, the hope of finally being able to rediscover all that had once excited him, fueled more through his veins, left him with a desperation he couldn't begin to fight.

Pushing out from the shadows, he fell in step behind the two stumbling down the alley, unable to keep their hands off one another.

His day had been all about Addie. From her working in the shop to leaving for the bar on Bourbon, he'd watched and followed.

McReily had been at the bar with that partner of his who was as irritating in his belief he could actually stop him. It didn't matter. He may have come for the agent who stalked him, tracked him for so long, but everything was different now.

He slipped behind a group of what he guessed were football fans by the shirts they wore. Following right on their heels, he kept a careful eye on the other two as they moved their way along the sidewalk, seemingly oblivious to those around them.

The tumble of red curls shifted through his vision, tempting him. He'd thought taking another would give him the patience needed, satisfying the itch burning since he'd left the cabin in Tennessee.

He'd been wrong.

Not even a day had passed after laying his latest beauty to rest before he was drawn to Addie again. Wanting to see her, needing it with a desperation he'd not known before.

He'd fought it, refusing to give in to temptation and lose control. Being weak, teased by a woman, wasn't an option. The idea it was a risk angered him. Tempted him to simply do away with the one causing it, forgetting the plans he had in place.

They turned the corner and stepped into the hotel claiming it. He went with them, careful to stay back, unseen.

Not that he worried about being recognized. McReily still had no clue who he was. It was quickly becoming no longer about him or the original need to make him pay. It was about her. About the beautiful redheaded beauty who'd captured his attention and refused to let go.

He didn't want her to know his face. Not yet. Not until everything was in place and he was truly prepared for all he had planned for her.

He barely heard the ding of the elevator. Mouth trapped with Addie's, it took everything Reed had to pay enough attention to move them out into the hall.

He wanted this. Oh hell, how he wanted this. But a nagging thought lingered in the back of his head as they stumbled toward his room. One he couldn't rid himself of, no matter how desperately he tried.

At the door, he forced reason to take over. Curling firm fingers around Addie's slender shoulders, he pulled her away, hating every second of it. "Tell me this isn't alcohol making the choice."

Unable to help himself, he bent down to steal another kiss, needing it as desperately as he needed his next breath. "Tell me you aren't going to regret this once you sober up."

With a considering tilt to her eyebrows, she looked at him. "Is that what you think, that's it's the liquor making me want you?"

He looked so uncertain about how to respond, Addie almost felt sorry for him.

"Don't you worry about me." She slid slow, seductive hands over the muscles carving his chest, rounding them over his broad shoulders. "I haven't drunk that much. I'm still fully in control of my desires."

"And you," she pushed to her toes, nipping at his bottom lip, "are definitely one of those desires."

It's what he needed to hear. More than he was willing to admit. On a growl, Reed wrapped strong arms around her, trapping her against him.

Fumbling for his key card, he tapped it to the door, never taking his hands or mouth from hers. Kicking back, he pushed the door open and brought her with him as he blindly found his way over the threshold.

He barely had the door closed before spearing fingers through the long fall of her red curls, pushing her until her back flattened against the wall. "No turning back, Addie."

He caught her bottom lip and took a quick nip. She pulled away, staring at him through her dark eyes. "No turning back."

Rising on her toes, she took her own nip at him, drawing him in until all other thoughts disappeared.

He was there again. Back to all those moments and stolen nights when all he knew, all he could grasp, was his time with Addie. Learning, discovering, every inch of her luscious body. Making her his, in every way, so that no other could claim her in the way he did.

He pushed closer until she was pinned between him and the wall. He didn't give an inch, holding her, enjoying the soft press of her curves against him as he teased every sense burning inside.

He couldn't get enough. Taking over control of the kiss, he demanded more as his hands slid, down her slender shoulders, over the delicate curves of her breasts.

He needed to feel every glorious inch of her. Needed to take all that was once his. Cupping his palms under the bottom swell of her breasts, he ran the pad of his thumb over the already hardened nipples, earning a gasp of pleasure.

Addie pulled back, desperately needing a breath. He was bringing to life sensations she hadn't experienced in a very long time.

Caught between him and the hard wall at her back, she arched her neck, staring into blue eyes as deep and stormy as the ocean. He watched her as he took, his hands moving from her breasts, caressing down, catching the curve in her waist before tracing over her hips, drawing her closer.

She wanted. She needed. Desperate to feel and know every inch of him as he was knowing her, she reached for him. He stopped her. Grabbing her wrists, cradling them in one hand, he pinned them above her head, pressed her against the wall as he took her mouth again.

"Not yet." Hunger burned in his eyes as his free hand slid, slow and seductive, over the curve of her thigh, teasing so close to where she throbbed.

"I want to see you." He tugged on the waist of her skirt, encouraging it down and over her legs until it rested in a pool at her feet.

Letting go of her wrists, he stepped back, his heated gaze flowing over her from head to toe. "Just like this."

Reaching out, he yanked on the simple tank she wore, pulling it slowly over her head and tossing it to the ground with her skirt. She stood in nothing more than her matching sapphire panties and bra, fighting the urge to fold her arms over her middle as Reed's heavy stare burned against all that he'd bared.

The heat in his deep, blue eyes was almost more than she could take as he came at her again. "Yes. Just like this."

He cupped rough palms around her cheeks, holding her, unable to do anything but meet his heated gaze. His lips tasted, drawing her up and into him. She was lost again as he pressed so close, his spicy scent surrounding her, reminding her of all she'd tried so hard to forget.

He slid his hands between her and the wall, working on the clasp of her bra until it fell free.

"So beautiful."

His voice was nothing more than a whisper as he caught her breasts in his hands, trailed his mouth down, circling his tongue around a hardened nipple.

She arched into him, heat spiraling through. He'd always been able to ignite the most primitive of desires. Drawing her up and into him until she no longer knew where he ended and she began.

It frightened her that first night they had. Frightened her still as he took her in, his hands and mouth taking everything she had, making it his.

She was a prisoner under his touch. Caught against the wall as his mouth took and his hands roamed. Fire licked under her skin, quickening the beat of her heart, mixing with the continued alcohol buzz so she felt like she was floating with every sensation on overdrive.

His fingers skimmed over her waist, dipping until they played at the edge of her panties. Again, he teased, drawing her up with hope only to drift away again.

"Reed." His name was a slow sigh escaping from her lips. She pushed into him as his touch traveled again, needing more than she could ever describe.

His heated gaze came back to her, watching, holding as his fingers slipped beneath the silk fabric between her legs, finding the core of everything burning inside.

She arched, nearly lost her stand. If it hadn't been for Reed's body pressed against hers, she would have been a pool at his feet. Shifting his knee between her legs, opening her to his touch, he watched. His heated stare never strayed as her eye's widened and a gasp escaped her lips.

"I always loved to watch you." Reed's voice was a low grumble, full of desire and something even stronger, hitting him hard, taking control he wasn't sure he was ready to give up.

He wanted to take from her until she had no resistance left. Draw her into him until she remembered, with the same ache holding him hostage, what once ruled them whenever they came together.

She was his, unable to look away as he teased her higher and higher, never allowing her to reach the release she so desperately sought.

That was how he wanted her, belonging to him, completely. It was selfish. It was greedy. But he couldn't stop the need barreling through.

"Reed, I—"

On a harsh breath that was almost painful, her head fell back. She shuddered under the cup of his palm against her.

Lowering his mouth to hers, he curled an arm beneath her shoulders and another under her legs. Lifting her, never breaking the kiss, he stumbled toward the bed. The need raging inside demanded satisfaction with a loud, angry roar.

Never before had he been so possessive, so desperate, to claim her as his, in every way. Never before had he battled to keep some sort of control as the hunger rumbled through.

Though urgency ruled, he lowered her slowly to the soft mattress. He wouldn't rush. Not when he wanted to savor every moment of Addie back in his arms, caught underneath his weight as he took her, burying deep inside.

Slipping away the last of her clothes, he stood above her. The heat of her stare fueled the fire inside as he quickly stripped away his own.

For a moment, he couldn't come back to her, trapped as he took in every sensual curve as her own eyes slid over him.

So much was there. So much neither had the courage to say. Refusing to give it a chance to grow and douse the heat burning between them, he came back, dropping his weight over her delicate body.

She reached for him, and he stopped her, needing this moment to be the one in control.

"No. Let me." He brushed gentle fingers over her arms, lifting them above her head.

She didn't fight as he nipped at her bottom lip, trailing his tongue over the delicate curve of her chin to the sensitive, throbbing line gracing her slender neck.

She gave all he wanted. Surrendered so that she was his.

He took. He needed the taste of her. The feel of her as he trailed his heated touch down the slope of her shoulders, cupping her breasts, taking them as he rubbed the rough pad of his thumb over a hardened nipple.

Addie gasped, the force of it ripping from deep inside. She needed. Wanted. Clear thought was impossible. Sensation after sensation waved over her, leaving her helpless to Reed's demands.

"Look at me." Hovering over her, his hand pushed between her legs, closing around her.

She couldn't focus. Couldn't do anything but arch into him, begging for more. Needing it desperately.

"Addie." He slipped a finger inside, driving her close to the edge. "Look at me."

She fought for it, battling back the need to tumble over and give in to everything raging through as he slid inside then slowly back, taking her to a point of no return.

Forcing her eyes open, she stared into his.

"Yes." His voice was slow and rich, sliding over her. He pulled his hand away, moving over her. "Stay with me, sweetheart."

She didn't know if she could. It was too much.

He cupped his hands around her hips, lifting her to him. For a moment, he stayed where he teased. As much as she wanted, as desperately as she needed, it felt like an eternity before he slowly slid inside.

It was almost enough to tumble her over the edge. Sucking in a harsh breath, her gaze still trapped under his deep blue eyes, she arched into him, drawing him deep inside.

She found satisfaction as his own gaze clouded over. He stumbled for control, just as she did, his fingers digging hard into her hips as he fought for a breath.

"Addie." Her name was barely a whisper, falling soft from his lips as he began to move. Slow and seductive, lifting her an inch at a time. Taking as he was giving until she was sure she'd reach the crest eagerly waiting for her.

"Not yet." He buried deep inside her. His arms shook, holding him over her. His chest heaved heavy with each breath tearing through his lungs.

Urging her up until she was propped against the pillows bunched against the headboard, he rose over her. Curling long fingers around her waist, he held her to him, moving her as he chose with every thrust.

She had no choice. No ability to do anything other than what his hold demanded as he took her. He pushed hard inside, leaving her breathless, desperate for release. Her heart pounding, she stared up at him with pleading eyes. It was too much.

"Please, Reed." She tried reaching for him, bringing him back down where she could gain some control.

"No, sweetheart." He dropped for only a second, brushing a quick frantic kiss across her trembling lips. "Tonight, you're mine, in every way."

Proving his point, he shoved on her shoulders, pinning her back to the pillows. And he took. Over and over again. She shook from the force, unable to know anything but the need running raw through her veins.

There was nothing slow, now. It was fierce and desperate. Addie rode on it, higher and higher until the edge lingered, encouraging her to tumble over.

Needing something to hold on to, she fisted her hands into the sheets beneath her. Reed fell over her as she exploded, every inch of her body rocking with wave after wave of release.

He curved strong arms around her, yanking her close. She shuddered around him. He sunk deep, joining her over the edge as her name fell in a harsh plea before he collapsed on top of her.

CHAPTER SIXTEEN

What had she done?

It took only a few minutes after waking up tucked into Reed's side, his arm slung heavy over her, for the question to hit.

His warm, even breaths washed over her as Addie stared out the window at the start of the rising sun. She didn't regret. That wasn't what bothered her. But she questioned, wondered, at the memories from the night before.

It was not what she expected. In fact, such a claim was an understatement to the feelings rushing through.

A few too many glasses of wine didn't change what she promised Reed. It wasn't the alcohol speaking, though it did have its place in weakening her defenses. She knew what it was she wanted. Had no questions about her need to know, again, all that she and Reed once shared.

It had been like an itch she desperately needed scratched. Since the moment she'd seen him at Teddy's bar, she'd had a wonder and need to know. Last night had been her chance to finally satisfy what weighed on her.

She hadn't expected the force of it.

Being with Reed again—

No. She was afraid to allow herself the memory of it. Later, when she wasn't surrounded by his tempting, rich scent, fighting memories in the very bed they were made, she'd put more thought into it.

Carefully, she lifted his arm draped over her, easing it to his side.

"Going somewhere?" His voice, heavy with sleep, stopped her as she tried slipping from the edge of the bed.

"I need to get home and get ready to open the shop for the day."

With one eye open, he looked around her to the window. "Still early." He reached for her, drawing her back. "No reason to leave yet."

"But, I—"

"Oh." Her head fell back against the pillow as his tongue trailed the sensitive line between her ear and shoulder.

It would be so easy to fall back into him again, finding what they'd shared the night before. So much of her wanted that. Wanted to forget and simply enjoy what she hadn't in a long time.

But the early start of morning brought not only the rising sun, but the return of what she'd allowed herself to forget the night before.

It wasn't easy, sliding out from Reed's enticing touch. "I need to go."

She didn't make a quick break from the bed, staying on the edge, looking down at him where he remained stretched out with his head resting against the pillow she'd abandoned.

"I didn't think there would be regrets." He didn't reach for her, but his probing gaze held her captive, keeping her where she was.

"I don't have any." To prove her point, she lowered, pressing her lips to his and lingering a moment, taking in all that she was about to walk away from. "But I don't think a repeat is for the best right now."

He reached for her, fingers sliding through hers as she finally found the strength to rise from the bed. Underneath the messy tumble of dark hair, he stared at her, deep blue eyes encouraging her back.

It took everything she had to fight against it. "It's best if I go."

He was up, wrapping a tight hold around her wrist before she could step away. "Tell me why."

She didn't want to. Everything inside screamed for her to pull free and walk away. She sucked in a deep breath and settled on the edge of the bed, careful to make sure she could escape quickly if she needed to.

"You lied." The words were so simple and yet not where she wanted to go.

She was leaving because the night before had been more than she expected. The feelings too great for her to work through.

That's what she told herself. Had insisted on since the moment she opened her eyes. And it was the truth.

Those two words—they held the underlying truth she hadn't been able to admit to herself.

"Last night was what I wanted. Wine-encouraged, or not, I wanted you and I don't regret it."

She sucked in a harsh breath, lifting her shoulders, letting them drop. "It doesn't change the fact, if I believe what you told me the other night, you lied to me. And worse, your lie destroyed me."

Unable to continue sitting so close to him while the hurt wound its way back in, she punched her hands into the mattress at her sides, shoving away from the bed.

Reed wasn't sure what to say. He wanted to grab her and pull her back down so that they could only feel and not talk. It was better that way, as far as he was concerned.

He didn't figure she'd be willing.

"I did it for you." Preparing to settle in for whatever ran through her mind, he piled pillows against the headboard and settled back.

"No." The single word cut through, quick and sharp. From a few steps away, Addie stared at him through eyes heated by anger. "You did it for yourself. It was the easy way out and you took it."

"Easy." The pillows behind him forgotten, Reed shot to his feet, reaching her in one angry stride. He hovered over her but she didn't retreat.

"You think it was easy, walking away from you? Needing you to believe I didn't care about you?"

"No." She shook her head. Where he expected a responding anger, he found only sad acceptance.

"I think it was easier for you to convince yourself you'd done the right thing by lying to me and hurting me than to admit you should have trusted me enough to tell me the truth."

Damn. This was not what he needed.

She moved around him, grabbing her clothes scattered over the floor.

"Addie." He wanted to reach for her but couldn't do it.

She looked at him, her bra dangling from her fingers. "It's okay. I don't expect you to say anything."

Slipping her arms through, she hooked it behind her back. She came back to him, standing so close yet not touching. "We both needed what happened. Now we can move on."

"Move on, how?" He didn't like the resigned acceptance in her voice.

"You should have trusted me enough to tell me the truth." Pushing to her toes, she dropped a quick, soft kiss to his mouth.

Before he could reach for her and hold her close a moment longer, she backed away.

It seemed so fast, one minute she'd been within his reach, and the next, she was fully dressed, looking at him from the opposite side of the bed.

"I really do need to go." She looked from him to the door. "If I'm lucky, I'll get back before Rosalie wakes up and I won't have to explain where I've been."

She was so distant, so casual. It wasn't anything like what he expected. With Addie, it never was.

He had visions of spending the morning in bed, exploring every inch of her all over again. Of breakfast shared together before sending her off with a long, drawn-out kiss, sure to force her to think of him the rest of the day.

Instead, she came back to him, brushing her lips across his cheek before finding her way to the door.

"I'll call you." She looked at him one last time before slipping out, leaving him alone, confused, and lost inside the room.

I'll call you.

Addie didn't know whether to laugh or cry at her final words to Reed. They'd repeated inside her head since the moment she'd left the hotel.

She'd wanted out, needed it desperately, but never did she think she'd be able to handle it all so casually, as if every moment wasn't pulling her back to him, begging to be caught in his arms again.

"Oh, that smells heavenly." Sleep-tangled hair falling over her shoulders, Rosalie stumbled into the kitchen and took a long, slow sniff of the fresh pot of coffee Addie brewed.

Pouring a cup, holding it between her hands, she joined her niece at the table. "You're up early."

She chose not to mention that Addie still wore the same clothes from the night before. Or that, when she'd woken in the middle of the night for a glass of water, she had definitely been alone.

It was on the tip of her tongue to lie, but Addie couldn't do it, not to her aunt. "I just got home."

She sighed, heavy and slow. Unable to meet Rosalie's gaze, she turned and stared out the window overlooking the courtyard.

"Something to talk about?" Rosalie's hand was gentle as it curved over her shoulder.

She shook her head, watching as a Robin took a morning bath in the fountain. "Nothing that would be worth it."

"I'll toast us up some bagels." Unable to look at her aunt, she pushed up from the table, empty mug in her hand.

Rosalie watched as she dropped a tea bag in her mug, hands not quite steady. She poured hot water over it then grabbed the bagels out of the bread box on the counter, lost somewhere in her thoughts. Though she wasn't yet awake for the day or ready to face something as simple as throwing together a quick breakfast, she pushed to her feet, coming up behind where her niece fumbled with the toaster.

"Did you know I was once madly in love?" She took the bagels from Addie's hands, sliding them into the slots of the toaster. "Back before you were a thought in your Momma's mind."

Left with nothing to do with her hands, Addie clasped them behind her back. She didn't know what she was supposed to say. She'd heard the talk, way back when. Had memories of her mother mentioning a love that had forever caught Rosalie's heart.

She'd been young when those words had spread. "I heard a little, but I don't remember much of it."

She wasn't sure she wanted to hear it now.

Hesitation sparked in her niece's eyes. Hoping to ease it, Rosalie offered a light smile before ducking into the fridge, moving jars and containers aside until she found the cream cheese.

"His name was Ethan." She set the tub on the counter by the toaster, pulled two plates from the cupboard above her head. "I thought he was the most handsome man who ever walked this earth."

She didn't want to know where this was going, Addie was sure of it.

"What happened?" She pulled a knife from the drawer, setting it on the tub of cream cheese as the toaster popped. Pulling a slice from each, she handed one to her aunt before taking her own.

"My dad, your grandpa, would tell you, if he was still alive," she picked up the knife, waving it at Addie, "the problem was, he was a Yankee. And we had no use for him."

A hint of loss darkened her gaze as it passed over Addie. "His home was New York, but he'd come here for college. I met him during my senior year of high school."

Lost for a moment in the memories, she grabbed her plate and settled back at the table, waiting for Addie to join her.

Finishing up smearing her bagel, Addie grabbed her tea and reclaimed her chair. She didn't say anything, waiting for Rosalie to continue.

"Though I loved him, your grandfather could be a hard man at times. Very set and old fashioned in his ways."

It was all new to Addie, learning this. Both of her grandparents died before she ever had a chance to know them. It had always been just her mom, her aunt and her. And then, just her and her aunt. The two of them the only family left.

"He did everything possible to keep me from seeing Ethan. If it wasn't for your mom, always so good at coming up with diversions, I don't think I ever would have seen him."

She sighed, long and slow, and Addie wondered what it was Rosalie saw as she stared past her shoulder, lost in her memories.

"He wanted us to run away together. We'd get married, he promised, and start our own family."

Addie couldn't find the words to respond. For the first time, she was being given a glimpse at her aunt's past she'd never had before.

"Your mom," Rosalie's gaze came back to her, "she told me I should go. Should follow my heart and run away with him. She always used to swear you only met your one true love once in your life, and she was convinced Ethan was mine."

"But you weren't?" Addie took a slow sip from her coffee, watching her aunt over the rim. Sadness darkened her emerald eyes.

Picking at her bagel, Rosalie shook her head. "I believed I loved him, and he loved me. There was something between us that I had never known before. Had never imagined I would ever know. But I wasn't sure it would be enough. I was so afraid of what the future held and couldn't see past all the reasons why I was convinced it would never work."

Addie knew why her aunt told her the story, but it wasn't in her to put a stop to it.

She'd never seen the sadness, giving a glimpse at the heartache her aunt suffered. Though it would have been better, wiser, to walk away before she went any further, she couldn't do it. Instead, she pulled off a bite from her bagel and waited for the rest.

"So." Sighing, deep and slow, Rosalie picked up her coffee cup, but never took a sip. "Instead of running off with him, I ended things between us. I let my fear rule and made up excuses for why it was best that we didn't see each other anymore."

Just like Reed had done to her. Her aunt didn't need to say it. It was the truth she was sharing. She'd lied to Ethan as Reed had lied to her, with the same belief it was for the best.

"What happened to him? What happened to Ethan?"

"Last I heard, he was back in New York, married with a kid." Rosalie's gaze drifted again, staring out into a place Addie could never reach. "We didn't have a second chance. I lied, I sent him away, and that, sadly, is the end of our story."

The tears came. Not for herself, but for her aunt. For what she lost and never found again.

The rest of the story she didn't need to tell. The one of Rosalie still single, finding companionship but no true commitment with any man.

It wasn't something Addie wanted to consider when she put her aunt's experience against her own. So, she wouldn't. It was just that simple.

"The bastard may have made his first mistake." Branson stuck his head through the open door of the office Reed borrowed inside the New Orleans office, flashing a mouthful of teeth at him. "The lab has a hair left on the body that doesn't belong to our victim."

Reed knew better than to get his hopes up. Still, it was the kind of news he liked to hear, even with the likely risk it would mean nothing in the end. "They running it for DNA?"

"As we speak." Branson stepped further into the office, settling in the chair across from where Reed sat behind the desk.

"If they don't find a match here, they'll send it to D.C. for a familial DNA. We might get lucky."

It would still take time, with no guarantee. There was no way to know if the hair belonged to their killer, or not. Broadening the scope to include family members who might be in the system was just as much of a long shot. Especially if the hair had nothing to do with who they were looking for.

"We don't count on anything until we know for sure." Reed repeated what his partner already knew. "We've got time here. We need to do some searching."

"You have something on your mind?"

"He made a mistake coming to my backyard. All we've had is the belief his roots are in Tennessee. Every other state, every murder, leaves us with nothing but more questions."

He picked up his cup of coffee, sipping slowly from the cold dredges lining the bottom. "We know what he does to his victims takes privacy. This is my territory. I know what's here. What surrounds us."

On the opposite end of the desk, his partner's interest peeked. "You suggesting some old-fashioned foot patrol? The kind that used to work just fine before computers took over."

Reed nodded, setting his empty cup down. It was exactly what he was talking about. There wasn't a single thing the best computer program could tell him that had more accuracy than his own knowledge. Not here. Not within the boundaries of the one place he knew better than anywhere.

"I think it's time I take you sight-seeing in some of the less-known areas around here." Curling long fingers around the edge of the desk, he pushed back.

Branson did the same, joining him at the door. "I'm always up for some sight-seeing."

It was a longshot. Still, it was doing something, especially as he felt so helpless lately. With both the killer and Addie.

Their tie together was enough to leave him itching more to get out of the office and do some searching. Because, having Addie on his mind, in any way, wasn't doing him a bit of good.

Their little bout that morning left him stumbling, desperate for stable ground. He refused to think about it. Refused to put his mind on what she'd said or might have meant by it. It hadn't been easy to find another means of distraction.

Work always helped. Finding and hunting down the bad guy never failed him before in shoving unwanted thoughts from his mind.

A step in front of his partner, he pushed out into the heavy, humid heat. He couldn't avoid thoughts of Addie forever. But, for now, he was going to give it his best shot.

CHAPTER SEVENTEEN

It was time they met.

Standing on the crowded sidewalk across from Magic Moon, caring nothing about the others forced to move around him, he watched the front door.

With the glare of the sun against newly washed windows, he couldn't see inside. He stood, watched and hoped, waiting for a quick glimpse of long, red hair. The soft, delicate sway of a skirt gracing shapely legs. A glimmer of jewelry around a slender neck.

Stepping from the curb, he looked around. Though he'd love for another excuse to taunt McReily, this was not the time. He wanted the lovely Addie's attention all to himself. He'd never get it if the annoying agent sauntered his way in and caught her eye as he always seemed to do.

But there was no sign of him as he worked his way to the opposite sidewalk. Pushing on the door, the bell above rung out his arrival, calling to the older woman behind the counter.

She wasn't who he wanted, but he smiled as she approached. "Welcome to Magic Moon, if there's anything I can help you with, let me know."

"I thought I'd take a look around." He caught sight of Addie out of the corner of his eye, red tumbles of hair drawing him in. Starting with a display of cards, he did his best to act like nothing more than the casual tourist, taking in all the store had to offer.

The older woman flashed a smile. "You let me know if there is anything I can help you with."

He didn't answer, too caught in the temptation of getting closer to the one he wanted.

Her attention caught by two younger women showing gleeful excitement in a long row of handmade skirts, she didn't notice his slow, careful approach.

He had no care for what was around him, didn't care anything about it, still he lingered over some thick material stretched along the wall beside where Addie stood.

The soft timber of her voice washed over him. Her scent, a sweet flowery mix, reached him as he drew closer. She looked away from the two she helped, dark brown eyes, so deep and rich, meeting his.

Oh yes, she was going to be worth it. So worth it. Baiting McReily had done him good. Better than he'd ever imagined. In his need to tease the irritating agent, he'd found the most perfect answer to every desire he'd carried inside. The reason, finally, for what he'd been so driven to do. To prove.

Without thought, he moved closer. It would take nothing to reach out, feel the warmth of her under his touch, enjoy the vibrant beat of her pulse. Everything she was surrounded him, leaving him wanting for more.

"Can I help you?"

Caught by the sudden intrusion of her voice, he stumbled for a moment, fighting to pull back the desire running through his veins. "I—"

Damn. He'd blow it if he didn't pull it together. To lose it now was unacceptable.

"I'm sorry." Chasing away the need burning through, he flashed a smile and took a step back. "I was carried away in admiring what you have here."

She wasn't convinced. Doubt lingered in her gaze.

"I'll be happy to help you as soon as I'm done here." Addie forced a smile she didn't feel. Something about him set her off, making her uncomfortable.

"No rush." His teeth flashed bright underneath thin lips. "I'm still browsing."

He moved away and she released the breath she hadn't been aware she was holding. Thankful for the space, she turned back to the two she'd been helping, hoping they'd take their time in deciding what they wanted.

His unsettling gaze burned into her back as the two women flipped through the skirts. She shifted uncomfortably.

She had no reason for her unease. She had to be overreacting. He was just another customer. One who obviously didn't understand the importance of personal space. But still a customer like the many others who passed through the door, day after day.

"Which one do you think is best?"

Drawn back to the ones she was currently helping, Addie chased away the discomfort sliding down her spine, forcing her mind back to the customers currently needing her attention.

"I think," she took a long, slow look at the two skirts the petite blond held in front of her. "The sapphire one draws out the color of your eyes."

She beamed. "You think so?"

Turning back for the skinny mirror hanging from the wall, she held the skirt to her waist, turning with it so it flared around her.

"I do." Shaking off the strange moment, Addie stepped up behind her at the mirror. Gently pulling on a corner of the delicate fabric, she smiled back at the woman through their reflection. "Look how it pulls out the blue in your eyes."

"She's right." Her friend stepped up behind them, nodded. "That one is definitely right for you."

Slinging the skirt over her arm, she beamed at Addie. "I'll take it."

Leading the way back to the counter, Addie refused to acknowledge the extra echo of steps from behind. The two women chatted happily about their plans for the night while she found her way behind the cash register to ring up their sales.

He was just out of the corner of her eye, waiting for her to finish. She wanted to make the sale last longer, extend it in some way, but the two across from her were too excited to get going for her to feel right about doing so.

He was just another customer, she reminded herself again. She had no reason to make it more than it was.

"Here you go." She held out their bags, fighting back the urge to hold on to them a bit longer.

Just a customer. She repeated it, over and over, as they thanked her and headed for the door. Looking for her aunt, she found her heading for a couple walking through the door. That left only her.

Forcing what she hoped was a friendly smile, she turned to where he'd hovered only a few feet away from the counter. Blond hair, so light it was nearly white, fell in a slight mess over his forehead as he smiled back at her.

Instead of comforting her, it only added more unease, especially when it failed to reach his pale, blue eyes.

"Okay." Needing it more than she realized, she sucked in a long harsh breath, steadying herself. "What can I help you with?"

He only stared. Stepping back, she glanced at her aunt again, thankful she wasn't alone.

"I'm looking for a gift. For my mother." He ran a slow finger over one of the silk scarves hanging beside him. "I promised I'd bring her back something."

A son buying a gift for his mother would have usually eased whatever tension she carried. From him it only made it greater.

Something—the tone of his voice, the cold echo in his words—made her more uncomfortable.

"Okay." She moved away from the counter, daring to get closer. "Is there anything, in particular, you're looking for?"

"Not really." He took a step forward and she fought back the desperate need to withdraw. "I was hoping you'd help me with that."

Under the guise of giving him more space to look around, she inched away. "Okay. Tell me about her. Maybe I can help."

Anger flashed in his pale gaze, enough to force her back further. He quickly covered it, smiling once more as he moved away from the scarves.

"She's very simple. Has never even ventured outside the Tennessee town she was born and raised in."

He turned for a row of bracelets, carved from ritual stones. "And she's not easy to impress, no matter how you might try. Nothing is ever good enough for her."

Addie didn't know how to respond or what to suggest. Still, she had a job to do, regardless of personal feelings. "Perhaps something original and unique, then. Something she'd never expect and might surprise her enough to be thankful."

It was there again, the anger chased away by another smile still not reaching the cold sheen shadowing his eyes. "What did you have in mind?"

Flipping through, in her mind, the variety of inventory they carried, she considered what to get the never happy mother he spoke of. Though she'd never been there, she tried to imagine life in Tennessee. What might be important to a woman living there, raising a family there.

"What about this?" Careful to keep her distance, she led him back toward the right corner of the shop where they featured their local artists.

"These frames are created by a wonderful man who lives just outside the Quarter." She moved aside so he could look at the display. "He does each one individually, depending on his mood, and includes a blessing stone for each."

She picked up one carved delicately from oak with the twist and turns of a tree climbing over its slender sides. "This one has the stone for family carefully embedded into the carving. It's meant to bring love and luck to those portrayed within its frame."

He took it, his fingers brushing hers, sending an icy chill up her spine.

"What if there is no love or luck inside the family?" His pale gaze caught hers over the top of the frame.

"Then there are others." Her words were rushed, almost desperate, as she reached for another frame. "This one has a blessing stone for the home."

She nearly shoved it into his hands, desperate to find what he wanted and get him on his way. "It's in Pewter and meant to hold protection for those who live within the house."

He still didn't look pleased. Under normal situations, Addie would have thrived with the challenge, enjoying the pressure of finding the right gift for the right person. She could see, inside her head, every bit of merchandise they stocked. Took great pride in trying to match the right item with the customer seeking it.

With him, desperation left her struggling to satisfy him and move him along. "If the frames aren't what you're looking for, we have other choices."

She hated having to say it, wished the words never left her mouth. But she couldn't let her unease take away from what she was there for. What the store existed for.

"What about this one?" He set down the Pewter frame, pushed aside another to get to the one he asked about. It was wood, like the first, but made from the rough bark of a Hickory tree.

"That blessing stone is for prosperity. It's meant to guide along the path of success and riches."

He ran a thoughtful thumb along the edges. Deep thought shadowed his hard gaze. Addie didn't want to think about what ran through his head. "I'll take it."

Relieved, her steps quick, she returned to the counter, thankful to put it between them.

Wrapping the frame in tissue paper, she was careful not to meet his eyes, having no desire for the discomfort to return. She rang up the sale, took the cash he handed over, made change, and held out his plastic bag holding his purchase.

She'd done it all in record time, more than ready for him to go.

He reached for it, his cold, hard touch passing against her fingers. She drew back so quick she nearly dropped the bag before he had a grip on it.

"Sorry." She forced a smile while wishing him away. He stared at her over the counter, the bag clutched between long, skinny fingers. A dark shadow haunted his pale, blue eyes. His lips, no longer smiling, formed a tight, fierce line as he took her in.

"Addie." Her aunt stepped up beside her behind the counter. "Is everything okay?"

Swallowing hard over the knot in her throat, thankful for her aunt's timing, she tore her eyes away from the man on the other side of the counter. "Yes. Of course. I was just finishing up a purchase."

Rosalie knew there was more but chose to remain silent. The man across the counter continued to stand and stare. A slice of anger heated his gaze as it swept over her.

It was gone by the time he looked back at Addie.

"Thank you for the help. I appreciate it." He flashed them his back, finding his way out the door.

Addie had never been so thankful to watch a customer leave.

"Thank goodness he's gone." She leaned onto the counter, needing the stability for legs suddenly weak and shaky.

"What was that all about?" Glancing at the door, Rosalie watched him turn down the sidewalk. "You're as white as a ghost."

She dropped a gentle hand over her niece's shoulder. "Did he say something to you?"

"No." Addie sucked in a breath and took one last sag against the counter before pushing back.

"Nothing like that. He just made me uncomfortable. Something about him didn't sit right with me. And in the end, I wasn't sure he'd leave until you came up."

She was making more out of it than it was, she was sure of it, but the uneasiness remained. The ringing of the bell above the door didn't help. She nearly stumbled back into her aunt as the sound echoed through the shop.

And then she saw him and was tempted to run and hide for the rest of the day.

Reed expected the anger, but not the fear reflecting in Addie's dark brown eyes.

He was quick, moving past the displays to get to her. "What's going on?"

"Nothing." The single word was a snap of frustration.

He waited, knowing better.

He was sure she would lash out, instead she sucked in a harsh breath and shook her head. "You caught me at a bad moment, that's all."

"I think," Rosalie draped a gentle arm over her shoulders, "a break from here might be just what she needs."

"I can close up," she quickly added as Addie turned to argue. "You go take a nice walk, get some fresh air, and enjoy what's left of the day."

Reed wasn't sure if he should be insulted or amused by the reluctance Addie shot at her aunt. He'd just enjoyed her in his bed, rediscovering every beautiful, luscious inch of her. He obviously couldn't be that repulsive.

"A walk sounds like the perfect answer." He grabbed her hand, tightening his hold when she made a move to pull away. "I'll splurge for a couple sweet teas along the way."

Addie wanted to refuse. She should simply say no, but she didn't have enough energy left to argue.

"Fine." Grabbing her purse, she came out from behind the counter. "But it better be Oscar's tea you're making promises of."

It might still be afternoon, but she figured she more than deserved the indulgence of their vodka sweet tea. And since Reed was making the offer.

"It will be our first stop." He took her arm, waved goodbye to Rosalie while ushering her out the door before she had a chance to change her mind.

He hadn't planned on spending the rest of the day with her. His plans had been to see her again, for just a moment, as his mind hadn't stopped buzzing with the night they'd spent together. He thought he'd convince her to have dinner with him later and then maybe urge her back to his hotel room for a repeat of the night before.

But this worked, too. He only had to let Branson know he wouldn't be coming back to the office. They'd spent the day doing enough old-fashioned leg work, he figured he earned the early call to his day.

He elbowed them past the crowds until there was a big enough break along the sidewalk for them to walk comfortably. "So, tell me what caused your bad moment?"

"It's nothing, really. I'm sure it was just me over-reacting."

"How about you tell me, and I'll let you know what I think." He slipped his fingers through hers, happy when she didn't pull away. The things she said before leaving him that morning had him wondering and worrying. He wasn't sure what to expect at this point. The fact she was with him was enough to be thankful for.

"It was a customer who came in before you showed up." She stayed in step with him as he turned at Jackson Square, keeping his promise and heading for Oscar's. "Something about him didn't sit well with me. I couldn't get him out fast enough."

He wondered about that, somebody getting to her in such a way. It wasn't like her. Wasn't the kind of person he'd always known her to be. Judging others, no matter who they might or might not be, wasn't who she was. The way she'd reacted to him when they first met was proof of that. "Tell me about him."

"There's not much to tell." She shrugged as she stepped off the curb, letting a rowdy group of men pass by, beer sloshing over the edges of their plastic cups.

Reed took her hand again, leading her around the corner to the small door leading into Oscar's. Knowing exactly what she wanted, she led the way to the bar, placing her order before he put in his own for one of their beers on tap.

She turned, leaning her back against the bar to wait. "He came in claiming he was looking for a gift for his mother. There was something dark about him. Whenever he smiled, it never reached his eyes. And the way he carried himself, it was almost as if he was barely holding down a whole burst of anger."

"I don't know." Her dark eyes met his, doubt reflecting in their depths. "I know something wasn't right about him. But honestly, all he wanted was to buy something for his mother back in Tennessee."

Reed caught on her last word. "He said Tennessee?"

Catching the different tone in his voice, Addie looked at him in surprise. "Yes. To me, it sounded like that was where he was visiting from, and he wanted to take back something for his mom."

He couldn't explain it. Wasn't going to try. Something deep in his gut screamed something was very wrong with Addie's uncomfortable visitor. Something that led to tortured and murdered women and a trip to New Orleans to taunt him.

"What else can you remember about him or what he might have said?"

Addie didn't understand the sudden shift in his mood. She'd expected him to agree she'd over-reacted and had nothing to worry about. Instead, he seemed more worried than she had been.

"I don't know." She grabbed her tea as the bartender slid it over the bar at her.

"He really didn't have much to say other than to make it clear his mother was hard to impress. I showed him some frames. He didn't care for the first two but, at the end, picked the one meant for prosperity."

Reed grabbed his beer and urged her out the door, needing to move, to think. "So, you got a good look at him. Could you describe him to a sketch artist?"

"Of course." She stopped at the corner of Jackson's Square, curiosity brewing in those dark eyes of hers. "But why would I?"

It was such a long shot. But his gut told him he needed to act. Couldn't afford to believe it was a coincidence that the stranger who'd been in the shop, made Addie so uncomfortable, happened to be from Tennessee. It was the one solid lead they believed in. He'd been doubted for the flowers, and he'd be doubted for this as well, but he couldn't afford to let it stop him.

"I think your visitor might be the same one who sent you those flowers."

He took her arm and tried to keep her going, but she stood firm where she was. "Oh no. I'm not going there again."

She broke away from him, starting off a step ahead. He caught up quickly, grabbing her hand, slowing her down to his pace. He didn't want her upset. Staying calm was important, especially if he wanted her to work with him.

Walking through the local artists setting up for the evening along the outer edge of the wrought-iron fence circling the gardens, he moved her toward the steps in front of St. Louis.

Musicians with their well-used instruments played Jazz for the tourists who passed. It was a good distraction. One he was going to need. Settling them between the music and the Cathedral, he took her hand, holding it steady in his grasp.

"I need you to listen to me." He caught her gaze, refusing to let it go. She wasn't happy, he could see as much. But she didn't refuse, waiting silently for him to continue.

"I know it doesn't make sense but I'm asking you to trust me."

He didn't miss the pained look sneaking over her face, but she remained silent. "My gut is telling me the man you saw today and the one who sent you those flowers is the one we are after. The one who has been killing innocent women."

Addie shifted, uncomfortable with the fear he drew forth. She didn't want to believe it. Such a reality was more than she could wrap her head around.

"Until now, he's been elusive. The most we've been able to determine about him is that he is, more than likely, from Tennessee, where he took his first victim."

Reed's hand tightened around hers as he paused long enough to look out at those passing by in front of them. "His coming to New Orleans changed things."

She heard the strength in his words, the need for her to accept what he was telling her. It wasn't where she wanted to go, but she had to admit, after the experience she'd had, it was easier to accept what he was saying as truth.

"He made his first mistake, bating me and bringing me here." He wasn't talking directly to her anymore. His attention drifted to a place she couldn't see. A place where he was making his own reasons for his own beliefs.

"And then he made himself known by sending those flowers, something he's never done. Now he's allowed you to see him, identify him. We've never had someone able to do that. Anyone who has seen him has ended up dead."

An ice-cold shiver ran up her spine. "You still don't know if it's him. There's a chance your gut is wrong."

"There's always that chance, but if I'm not, we've got a huge break in the case. One we only hoped for until now."

The rise and fall of the music surrounded her, mixing with the constant chatter of those walking by. Addie focused on it, needing it to ground her as she ran through her mind all Reed told her.

"What is it you want me to do?"

A relieved smile stretched over the hard-carved lines of his face, drawing her in even as she fought against it. "I want to set up a time, hopefully tomorrow, for you to meet with one of the Bureau's sketch artists. Every little detail you can remember about him will help."

She could do that, even if it turned out to mean nothing. "Okay. Just let me know when."

He bent down and brushed a quick kiss over her lips, catching her by surprise.

"I'll get your protection ordered right away. I'm thinking at least one, if not two, agents with you at all times."

"What?" Flattening a hand to his chest, she pushed away. "I don't need protection. I didn't agree to that."

Reed bit back the flash of frustration threatening to burst through. "This man kills women for his own enjoyment. I'm not willing to let you become his next victim."

Anger built inside. She wasn't his to protect, hadn't been for a long time. He didn't get to dictate her life to the point of sticking a couple stuffy agents on her.

"I agreed to the sketch artist, but I'm not agreeing to anything else." Rising to her feet, she turned away from him, walking off to drop money in the bucket for the musicians.

He caught her before she made it more than a few feet. Grabbing her arm, he spun her around. "He came into the store. Don't think for a minute there wasn't a very calculated reason for it. Are you really willing to risk your life because of your own stubbornness?"

She didn't want this. Had no desire to fall back into the same argument. Easing her arm free from his grasp, she sucked in a hard breath.

"I'm not as convinced as you. I'll meet with your sketch artist because I don't see any harm in it. But I'm not willing to jump on your belief that he's the same one murdering all those innocent women."

Reed wanted to grab her and shake her until she saw reason. But it would be useless. Her stubborn streak was hard to break. Pushing at her, testing it, would only force her to dig in deeper and refuse any reasons he offered.

So, like before, he'd take care of it on his own. It might be going against her wishes, but he didn't doubt it was for her own good.

CHAPTER EIGHTEEN

Addie was suspicious.

It wasn't like Reed, stepping away from an argument like he did. It was like flipping a switch, how easily he turned it off, changing his attention from demanding protection to convincing her to have dinner with him.

Caught off guard, she stumbled through a denial that went nowhere. Reed knew he'd won before she ever finished. So now she sat on a balcony overlooking Bourbon, sharing oysters and a bottle of wine with him.

And silently kicking herself for giving in again.

The Friday night crowd shuffling along the street below was thick. Sipping from her glass of wine, she watched over the short level of the banister as they moved in groups, from two to many, filling the space from sidewalk to sidewalk.

She was watching for him, she realized, as her eyes caught on another pale blond head poking out from the others. As much as she wanted to forget, part of her wanted another look at him.

"You okay?" The deep timber of Reed's voice drew her back.

Shoving thoughts of her strange visitor aside, she turned back to the table, grabbing an oyster from the center of the table and dropping it on the small plate in front of her.

"Yes. Just watching what's happening below. I have a feeling tonight is going to be a wild one. The bars have barely kicked up for the night and already a few crazies are carrying on."

"Such is life in the Quarter."

"Do you miss it?"

Addie had wondered since he'd been back. She couldn't imagine leaving this place she loved. Reed wasn't a Quarter native, but he was a New Orleans native, with roots that went further back than most. She tried imagining what it would be like, leaving all that behind.

She thought he wouldn't answer as his gaze broke from hers, drifting over her shoulder.

"At first I didn't. I wanted out and I didn't care to look back. I couldn't get away fast enough, or far enough."

Harsh lines pulled tight over the chiseled features of his face. Angry shadows darkened his blue eyes.

For so long, she'd believed he happily left New Orleans. In her head, she'd created a story of the spoiled, rich boy who put so little depth into where he came from, and the relationships he'd formed, he easily tossed it aside to search for his next adventure.

In her vision, he hadn't struggled. Hadn't been angry or burdened with a desperate need to get away. He'd had only a simple, self-absorbed need leading the way.

"After some years, it would start to leak back. A memory here and there. A craving for what I couldn't find anywhere but here."

"And memories of you." He picked up his wine glass. "Of all things I started to miss, you were the one holding the greatest pull."

"Don't do that. Don't tell me those things."

He grabbed her hand, closing it between his large palms. "It's the truth. You'll have to find a way to live with that. I spent more than my fair share of nights trying to drink you away, only succeeding in suffering the next morning. I don't always like the truth of it either, but it's there, regardless."

She wanted to get up and walk away. She pulled her hand away, hiding it under the table. Her defense against him had always been the belief in what he'd told her that long-ago day. Changing it, changing the story she'd clung to, wasn't something she was ready to accept with the same conviction Reed demanded from her.

It beat against her defenses, even as the anger held for the lies he told. When he talked like this, when he created the idea the feelings still lingered, she couldn't deny them as she once had. Couldn't brush him off with the echo of his past painful words like she'd had in the past.

The fear of it settling in her gut, she curled her fingers around the arms of the chair. She'd make excuses and go. It was for the best.

"You're here." The familiar voice erupted behind her. Turning, she watched AnnaBeth hook her arm through Clay's, hurrying his steps to match hers.

She pulled Addie to her feet, wrapping her in a quick hug. "Clay and I were going to get a table and call you to join us. You saved me a step."

"Your phone should be ringing soon, too." Letting go of Addie, she looked at Reed. "Teddy's joining us, said he'd see if you wanted to do the same."

"Like old times." Dressed in his usual flair, choosing shocking red suspenders over a dark blue shirt for his only night off from playing, Clay pinched the wire-rimmed nose of his sunglasses. He pulled them off as he searched the balcony for empty chairs.

As predicted, Reed's phone rang. Realizing she wouldn't be leaving after all, Addie helped AnnaBeth and Clay pull over extra chairs as he took his cousin's call.

It would be like old times, just as Clay predicted. But she wasn't sure she'd enjoy it the same.

"You came running out of that cemetery like you'd seen a ghost." Teddy slapped a hard hand to Reed's back, rumbling with laughter.

"I thought I had." Reed forced a scowl for his cousin, remembering the night. "You and Clay and your little prank about scared the life out of me."

Clay's laughter echoed around the table. "Just a flashlight and the right sort of shade is all it took. You saw those shadows on the tomb and ran like a baby. Don't suppose you want the big tough agents you work with knowing that."

"In his defense," AnnaBeth winked at him. "We didn't quite have him broken in yet. It didn't take much to have him believing in ghosts."

He'd have argued if it wasn't the truth. He'd been, so much, the pampered, spoiled rich boy, coming into their territory. They'd let him know it, too. In the way of friends. The easy teasing, the ribbing when he showed his streak of green against their more seasoned ways.

He'd come around. Looking at the faces from his past gathered around the table, he was struck with how much he'd missed them. He'd hid it, denied it, for so many years. It was easier that way. Not just with Addie, but with all of them.

"I'm wiser to your ways now." Because AnnaBeth had taken over sharing the wine with Addie, Reed waved down their waitress to order a beer. "There won't be any repeats."

Teddy gave his back another hard pat. "You keep telling yourself that."

And in that moment, it felt like he'd never left.

They ordered more oysters, beer, and wine. Daylight slipped away as the excited roar from Bourbon below grew louder.

AnnaBeth topped off her glass. Addie found herself drawn in, caught by the reminder of what it had once been like for her and

Reed. His deep blue gaze came back to her as he wrapped long fingers around his beer bottle. For a moment he just looked, sending away everyone else around the table. Then he winked, a slow, smooth motion, making her feel as if they held some secret the others would never know.

And those old feelings crept back, no matter how hard she fought against them.

He'd once been her world. If she wasn't careful, he'd be there again.

"Got a call this afternoon." Teddy took a slow sip from his beer. "The family is getting itchy and cranky that they haven't seen you since you've been back."

Addie caught the small slash of anger in Reed's eyes before he shrugged it away. "Don't see a reason to go back there. The Quarter's fine for me."

Wrapping her fingers around the stem of her wine glass, she studied him from across the table. He wanted to look unaffected, grabbing an oyster from the center plate and washing it down with a long draw from his beer. But emotions darkened his gaze and he shifted restlessly in his seat.

She thought of what he'd told her. Of his claim that his family would destroy her. He'd left them behind as he had her. And, it seemed, continued to leave them cut out of his life, even now.

It made her curious, though she wouldn't ask questions now. Not when it was clear he hoped only to forget the topic of family ever came up.

Teddy seemed to carry the same thoughts.

"No problem with me." He brushed it off with an absent wave of his hand. "Just figured I'd let you know."

And there it ended, the conversation again turning to light and easy.

"I think it's time for a bathroom break." AnnaBeth set down her wine glass, nudging Addie with her elbow. "Come with me."

Questions burned in her friend's bright blue eyes. Addie pushed up from her seat, following AnnaBeth through the doors leading inside.

"So," AnnaBeth drew out the single word as she pushed on the heavy wooden door leading into the bathroom. "I'm finding you with Reed, more and more, lately."

She passed the empty stalls, finding her way to the counter and small sink pressed into the far corner. Staring into the mirror, she fluffed at the ends of her short blond hair. Addie came up behind her.

"He doesn't make it easy to avoid him." Tugging on AnnaBeth's purse, knowing she always carried a full make-up counter in its depths, she dug through until she found the color lipstick she wanted. "He can be irritating that way."

Leaning closer to the mirror, she stroked a light coat over her lips. "I slept with him."

She said it so casually, matter-of-fact, it took AnnaBeth a moment to respond. Her hands falling to her sides, she stared for a long, slow second through the mirror before her bright eyes widened and she turned in one quick sweep.

Catching Addie off guard, she threw her arms around her, yanking her into a hug. "It's about time."

Stepping back, she held her out, fingers curled over her shoulders. "I'd hoped you'd get that taken care of it. You needed it."

"I needed to have sex with Reed?"

"You needed to have sex...period." AnnaBeth's laugh filled the bathroom. "I was beginning to wonder if you were going celibate on me."

Addie opened her mouth to argue, snapping it shut when she realized it had been over a year since she'd last enjoyed any kind of private, intimate time with a member of the opposite sex.

"Some of us don't need sex to survive."

"Oh, please." AnnaBeth flung that away with a simple wave of her hand, resting back against the counter. "I won't waste time asking how it was. I already know the answer."

She took the lipstick Addie held out, dumping it back in her purse. "But how are you doing?"

Unable to stop them, images from the night before came flooding back. Shaking her head, she chased them away.

"I'm fine," she lied, catching AnnaBeth's doubt as soon as the words escaped.

Sighing, she leaned back against the counter next to her friend. "I didn't exactly leave him on a happy note this morning.

"It's not anger, anymore. Not really. It's more hurt now. Hurt that he didn't tell me what was happening with his family. That he chose to lie to me instead of trusting me enough to tell me the truth. And hurt that he's swept back into my life and wants to pick it all back up without a single thing changing."

She released a slow breath, shook her head. "It doesn't matter. Once he finishes up his case, he'll be gone again, and I can get back to my life free of him."

AnnaBeth didn't look convinced but let it go. "Is he getting anywhere with what happened to that poor woman?"

"He seems to think I might have met the one who killed her."

"What?" The high shrill of AnnaBeth's voice tore through the bathroom as she grabbed her. "Why does he think that?"

"I had," she eased away from AnnaBeth's tight hold, "a bit of a weird encounter today with a man who came into the shop. Reed seems to believe he's the one they're after. He convinced me to meet with a sketch artist tomorrow."

"I don't like this. Maybe we should take a girl's trip somewhere. Get you away from all this."

"I'm always up for a girl's trip, but not for this reason. I'm fine. Reed is overreacting. That's all."

"And if he's not?"

The question hung in the air. Addie couldn't answer it. Didn't want to think about it. She had to believe he was wrong to keep her sanity. Considering anything else brought a fear she wasn't willing to accept.

CHAPTER NINETEEN

"**W**here are you going?"

Addie barely made it a step down the sidewalk before Reed's fingers wrapped around her arm, pulling her back. It was just the two of them fighting for space among the crowds filling Bourbon. Annabeth and Clay headed home while Teddy returned to his bar.

"I'm tired." She eased from his hold. "I'm ready to go home. To my own bed."

"You don't think that would be a bit awkward?" Reed pushed her back against the outer wall of the restaurant. Even with the mixture of smells around them, his spicy scent surrounded her, reminding her of things better left forgotten.

She drug a breath through her lungs, concentrating on what he'd said and not on the temptations he drew forth. "What would be awkward?"

"The two of us in your bed with your aunt so close by."

"You know that's not what I meant." She shoved at him, desperately needing space. "I'm going home to my bed...alone."

She made a move to continue down the sidewalk, but he grabbed her again. "I want you. In my bed."

To prove his point, he bent and nipped at her bottom lip.

She should fight him. Should let him know they'd had a night they'd never forget and should leave it at that. It was the wisest path. The one promising less pain and regrets.

Yet, the need to give in to what he promised was too great to resist. Maybe she was weak. Maybe she didn't have the spine of steel she'd prided herself on when Reed first showed his face again.

Whatever it was, whatever the reason, she accepted she wouldn't be going home as she planned. It didn't mean, though, she'd let him off the hook yet. Not when the press of his lips traveling over her skin felt so good. When the hard curve of his muscles fit so right, pressed so close.

"Rosalie will worry." She looked at him, hoping she hid the desire blazing through.

"You can text her." Wrapping his fingers with hers, he urged her away from the wall, turning her in the opposite direction from home. "Let her know you'll be safe and sound with me."

"I'm not sure she'll believe I'm safe with you." This time, she let him see what burned inside. "I'm not sure I believe it."

He stopped again, forcing the crowds to split around them. "Is that what you want? Safety?"

The heated spark in his deep blue eyes left her breathless. Though his tone had been light, challenge lingered in his voice.

At the moment, safety was far from what she felt or wanted. Surrounded by the constant push of strangers, the tainted scents filling the Quarter, all she knew, recognized, was the need drumming through as Reed kept them in the middle of it all, staring down on her with an expression that frightened even as it aroused.

"I want you." She couldn't stop the words, didn't even try. Pushing to her toes, she caught his inviting mouth with hers, dragging him under with her.

He needed nothing more. Groaning, he let the kiss linger before grabbing her hand and hurrying her the couple blocks left to his hotel.

Reed needed to get it out of him. This desperation he carried for Addie wasn't good. It controlled too much. Ruled where it had no place.

He'd thought she'd tempted him when she was the beautiful, confident young girl he'd first laid eyes on. It didn't compare to what she did to him now as the alluring, tantalizing woman she'd become.

He was ready to take. Didn't have the patience to wait.

Curling his arms under her legs, he swept her from her feet before she could make another move. The dim light coming through the window guiding him through the room, he found his way to the bed.

He wasn't gentle or kind as he dropped her on the mattress, standing above and staring down at the beauty that was his for the taking. Shock mixed with desire as she looked up at him, so much a contrast of the innocence she'd once held and the woman she'd become.

Her skirt caught when he dropped her, riding high over her thigh. Unable to resist, he bent down, running slow fingers over the smooth, creamy skin. Her dark brown eyes widened as he wedged a knee against the mattress, coming down over her as his touch continued to roam.

"You've always been able to drive me crazy. Even when I've foolishly believed I had a strength against you, I've fallen." His weight pinned her down, held her where he wanted her. She shuddered. Her chest rose and fell heavy as she sucked in air. He took her with his mouth, the roaming of his hands.

Addie tried lifting her arms, to touch as he was, but found them trapped under his weight. She could do nothing. His lips claiming hers dragged her under. His fingers slowly worked close to the core of her need only to drift away.

She couldn't have it. Couldn't give in to the need raging through, the emotions it brought with it. She needed control. Craved it as much as the feel of Reed washing over her.

It took every ounce of strength to pull her mouth from his, breaking free from the hold he had over her. She shifted beneath him, freeing her hands locked under his hold.

"Let me." She hooked her heels into the mattress, pushing against him. He moved and she hurried out from under the pressure of his weight, fumbling to her knees at the edge of the bed.

He looked up at her. What simmered in his deep blue eyes was almost enough to send her tumbling over the edge. She held on. Wanting this. Desperately needing the control.

She inched her hands up her sides, stopping under the curve of her breasts.

"This is what you want," she teased with the slow drawl of her voice.

He didn't answer, his gaze ignited by so much heat it burned against her.

Pushed by the power of it, she gathered her shirt into her hands, slowly eased it away. Tossing it carelessly to the floor she kept her gaze locked with his, drawing more strength from what sparked in the heated depths.

He didn't try to reach for her, touching her only with his eyes as they slid over her kneeling before him. Using it, slow with it, she grazed her fingers up the gentle slope of her sides. Never looking away. Watching him as he watched her.

She eased around to her back, grasping for the clasps holding her bra together. His breath caught. Fire burned in his gaze. It gave her a strength she never imagined. A boost to her ego knowing how she could hold him in his desire for her.

Bending over, she caught his mouth with the same possession he had claimed hers. Making him want. Making him need. She took it all before tearing away and pushing back to her knees, raising over him again.

"Damnit, Addie," he hissed, reaching for her. She moved out of his reach, hovering at the edge of the bed. If he wanted to, he could easily grab her and pull her down, ending the tease she was finding so much power in. He didn't, giving her the moment she needed to be the one in control. The one to make him feel what it was like to need so desperately.

She went back to the clasps holding her bra over her breasts, unhooking one and then, slowly, the other. Under Reed's heavy stare, the lace slipped free into her hands. She held it for a moment before tossing it to the floor.

And Reed suffered.

Trapped, though nothing held him down, he ached deep in his bones as Addie's hands lingered beneath her breasts before sliding lower, teasing at the waist of her skirt.

She had him in every way. Held in a spell he couldn't break free from, watching those lovely hands glide over soft, silky skin, stripping away the barriers.

A teasing smile spread over her luscious lips as her fingers slipped lower, pulling her skirt with her. Inch by painful inch, she slid it down, killing him.

It caught at her knees pushed into the mattress and she stopped.

Unable to take it a second more, Reed pushed up, grabbing her before she had a chance to move away. Shoving rough fingers through the long strands of her red hair, he brought her mouth to his, claiming everything she had just promised. The desperate need for it burning painfully through his limbs.

Her hands fumbled, grabbing onto his shoulders for stability. Pushing into him, she let him feel the same desperation heating her skin as it forced trembles to take her.

"No more teasing," he demanded, tearing his mouth away and arching her back until she was vulnerable in his hold. He didn't bother with finishing what she'd done with her skirt, cupping his hand over the peach lace she'd bared between her legs.

It was too much. Her breath caught and her eyes darkened with what tore between them. Her delicate scent swarmed around him. The warmth of her burned against him. He had to take before he was torn apart with the desire tearing through.

He took her mouth again as his fingers slipped beneath the lace.

"Oh Reed...no." Even as Addie pushed the words past his probing lips, she rose into his touch, seeking more.

Holding her, back arched over his arm, he pulled back. "Do you want me to stop?"

She didn't. She feared what would happen if he did. Feared what would happen if they continued.

This wasn't right. It couldn't be right. She was helpless to it. Lost without any control over what was happening to her.

"Don't stop."

Reed growled, pushing her down to the mattress and coming down on top of her. He had the rest of her clothes stripped away in only seconds before quickly taking care of his own.

His weight holding her down, he brushed a gentle hand over the inside of her legs, slowly working higher until he found his way again to the core of where she ached.

"This isn't right." Her words were nothing but a hiss of air as he slipped his fingers inside, drawing her hips off the mattress in a quick, frantic jolt.

He pushed deeper, watching her. "It feels right."

She shook her head as he came down, nibbling at the sensitive skin between her ear and shoulder. He had her a mess, unable to think of anything other than what he was doing to her.

His mouth trailed lower, circling his tongue slow over a hardened nipple.

"I shouldn't want this, want you." She rose into him, wrapping her arms around him, holding on desperately.

"But you do." To prove his point, he drove her higher, over and over until she hovered at the edge before he pulled away.

She cried out and he muffled it with a hard kiss, taking more. Showing her how desperately she did want him.

Tearing away, he shoved his hands through her hair fanned over the mattress, holding her gaze locked with his.

"You'll never stop wanting me." He pushed his knees between her legs, opening her to him.

She couldn't respond, couldn't find the ability to utter a single word as he grabbed her hips, held her still while he buried deep inside.

They both gasped for breath, caught under the force of what raged between them. Frightened them as it pleasured them. Drawing them to a place they both feared yet needed with every ounce of their bodies, their souls.

"Damnit, Addie." Reed fell over her, claiming her with a kiss full of the dark desires racing through. He couldn't fight the need. Where he wanted to savor, to take her slowly until she writhed beneath him, he had no control left.

He was quick. He was hard. She rose into him, taking and return-ing the same desperation. He knew only her—the sight, the feel, the smell of her—as he took, and then took some more.

It wasn't enough. It would never be enough. He had to have more. Needed it like he did the next breath fighting through his lungs.

Wrapping tight fingers around her slender waist, digging into delicate skin, he turned, taking her with him. With his back on the mattress, he held her above him for a moment, sucking in a painful breath before he shoved her down over him, filling her in one violent streak of need and want.

Addie shuddered, sure she would explode. She fought it back, not wanting it to end.

Falling over him so they became one in every way, soft curves against hard lines, held tight as his arms came around her, holding her.

"I'll never stop wanting you." His voice was a harsh whisper against her ear. He clung to her as if she were his lifeline, driving into her, over and over again.

Trapped by the force of his hold as well as her own desire, she moved with him, matching every thrust, every desperate gasp of need.

It wasn't right. But, the way he made her feel, it didn't matter what was right and what wasn't. Only this. Only the spiraling heat taking over mattered as she clung to him. As wrong as it was, it felt so right. So much a part of what she was. What she had been since the moment Reed stepped into her life

His hold around her tightened. The heat sparking through be-came more than she could handle.

"It's always been you." The soft whisper of Reed's words brushed against the sensitive skin of her neck only a second before he surged into her, wrapping his arms around her, and driving her past her breaking point.

She broke with him, their harsh breaths of release spiraling as one as they tumbled over the peak, unable to hold on a second longer.

In those moments, when she fell over the edge, all she thought, all she knew, was that she was right where she belonged. Had always belonged.

Addie fought back reality as long as possible. She wasn't ready to drift out of the complete satisfaction surrounding her. A little more time was all she wanted before having to come back down from the high she floated on.

Pushing deeper into the crook of Reed's arm, she flattened her palm against his chest, loving the feel of his heated skin underneath her touch. Her mind wandered, foolishly, to places she'd never allow it to go if she were not basking in the glow of being utterly and thoroughly loved by the one man who stole her heart so many years ago.

Thoughts of finding something more with Reed inched their way forward. They had no place. He wasn't here for good. He'd leave again just as he'd done the last time. And the anger and hurt was still there. She wasn't sure when or if she'd be able to work past that.

It felt good for a brief second to imagine more. To allow one quick fantasy of what it might be like to find a commitment in the strength of Reed's arms. To know their time together wasn't limited to the day when he said goodbye.

Because a nagging truth lingered she couldn't deny—she still loved him. She didn't have a denial strong enough to chase that fact away.

For all that she knew was wrong. For the heartache still lingering. None of it mattered. None of it was strong enough to chase away the love that had never died.

It was that love she never fully chased away that had her turning at his side to look at him.

His answering smile as her eyes met his was slow and sexy. "Are you ready for round two?"

Reaching up, he tucked a stray curl behind her ear, letting his finger linger against her cheek.

"I'm still recovering from round one." She laughed, dropping down and leaving a quick kiss against his mouth.

"I was thinking." She caught his gaze again as she rose. "Maybe you should see your family while you're here."

He tensed beneath her. "I have seen my family. Teddy and I see each other just about every day."

Curling her lips into a scowl, she smacked lightly against his chest. "You know that's not what I was talking about. Your parents obviously want to see you. Maybe you should give them a chance, hear what they have to say."

"It's not going to happen." He rolled out from underneath her, leaving her to fall back to the mattress. She turned to her side, watching as he edged to the side of the bed.

"There's nothing to hear or say." He didn't look at her as he sat out of reach.

Understanding his need for space, she tucked her hands safely at her sides. "How do you know?"

"How do *you* know?" He countered, emotions heating the blue of his eyes. "What makes you so sure it would make a difference?"

"I'm not sure." Taking the risk, she inched closer, resting a gentle hand over his leg. "But I think you need it. I think you deserve a chance to try and find some closure."

Reed turned to face her, dragging a harsh breath through his lungs. Unable to fight the need to touch her, he wrapped his arm around her. "Why does it matter to you?"

He wasn't sure he wanted the answer, but he had to ask. "Because—"

She turned away for a moment, leaving him waiting until she came back. "Because you matter to me."

His answering smile was quick and a bit too confident.

"Don't go there, Reed." She pushed at his chest, breaking free from his hold. "It still doesn't change most of what I feel about you."

He refused to let her get away. Grabbing for her as she tried to slip from the edge of the bed, he yanked her back. "I'll still take it."

She opened her mouth to speak again, and he was sure he didn't want to hear what would come next. Silencing her, he pressed his lips to hers as he encouraged her down until she was under him. Just where he wanted her to be.

"How about I think about it later." He nipped at the edge of her jaw, trailed a slow kiss down the curve of her neck. "After I'm done thinking about what I want to do to you."

CHAPTER TWENTY

S he worried about Rosalie handling the store on her own. But she'd made a promise and she'd keep it.

Reed's partner met them at the door. "We've been waiting. We're ready."

Thoughts of the extended shower they'd shared to start the morning filtered back. Addie could only hope the others weren't able to guess the reason for their tardiness.

Next to her, Reed stepped back into agent mode. Gone was the man who left her limbs feeling like liquid only an hour ago. In his place was the steel-spined, stubborn man who gave his life to the badge.

"You fill the others in?" He pushed past Branson, leading the way down the hallway ahead of them. He paused only long enough to make sure Addie kept up before continuing on.

"I've told them." Branson followed a step behind. "Not that they exactly agree with you."

"Didn't expect any less." He paused at the last door at the end of the hallway and reached out to grab Addie's hand. "You ready for this?"

She had been. Had told herself it was no big deal. All she had to do was describe to some sketch artist the man who'd been inside Magic Moon the day before. It would be easy and done with quickly.

But there was something about being inside the FBI offices. Something about knowing on the other side of the door she would be expected to give details of a man who might be responsible for the horrible deaths of innocent women. Who could now be turning his attention to her.

Catching the flicker of fear in her eyes, Reed tugged her closer, ignoring Branson waiting a step behind.

"You're going to be fine." He brushed a stray strand of hair from her cheek, dropped a quick kiss where it had rested.

She nodded and turned for the door, stepping in ahead of him.

Reed wasn't going to question what changed, he was just going to be thankful something had.

Addie made it through perfectly with the sketch artist and the result was one the Bureau could be thankful for. Even those who doubted his belief, couldn't argue there might be something in finally having a face to put with the one who killed so many. None were willing to dismiss what Addie provided, though they weren't convinced he was the same one they were after.

She'd done good for the hour it had taken, answering questions, closing her eyes and concentrating on what her memory brought back. If he hadn't seen that small hint of fear before she'd entered, he never would have guessed it existed.

Once she was done, he'd offered lunch. Her denial had been quick, needing to get back and help her aunt. So, he tried for a compromise. They'd stop and grab something for themselves and her aunt on the way and he'd hang out and work from there.

She knew why. Didn't need him telling her he wanted to be around to keep an eye on her. He'd expected her argument, nearly stumbled in shock when instead she agreed.

It had been a hesitant agreement but came without the usual pushback. That was enough for him.

He sat in her kitchen, a Po-boy within easy reach and his work spread out over the small table. Not that he had much concentration for any of it. Knowing, within a couple dozen steps, he'd be back at Addie's side was almost too much temptation to resist.

But he would. He had to. Until she was safe, he couldn't afford to let any distractions get in his way.

They battled him as he tried to work. Not just with the need to be close to Addie, but with the reminder of what she'd said to him the night before.

She wanted him to see his family. Claimed he needed closure. He protested, didn't agree, yet the thought continued to nag, growing stronger every time he tried shoving it away.

He'd come back to New Orleans for one reason. This wasn't some journey to settle past hurts or old angers. He wasn't on some quest to find himself. He'd come because the one he sought brought him here. He'd come to finally catch him and make sure not another woman suffered at his cruel hands.

He'd failed already, the minute Amanda's body was found.

He refused to accept another failure, which was why he remained. Regardless of the doubts he faced from others, Addie was wrapped up in this. He wouldn't risk her, or her life. He'd be here until the job was done.

His heart caught for a moment at the thought of what would happen once the job was done. It wasn't something that mattered. Quickly brushing the thought away, he tried again to concentrate on the pile of files spread out along the table.

It only took a few minutes until he was back in his hotel room with Addie's gentle voice encouraging him to see his family.

And well...damn her. Did she really have to bring it up, leaving him wasting time wondering if she could be right.

What good would it do? And why in the hell was he actually considering it?

Giving up, accepting he needed a break, he shoved up from the chair. There was only one thing he wanted. One place he wanted to be.

Not wanting to disturb Addie, he was quiet as he entered through the back of the store.

He found her by the front door, talking with an older couple flipping through hand sketched cards.

What was it about her? Why was she the one he never seemed able to get out of his system?

He ran a thousand miles away, told himself he'd made a new life and was happy with it. And yet, all it had taken was a single look at her again and he was as lost as the first time he'd set eyes on her.

What power was it she held? She pushed him, challenged him, was never afraid to let him know when she was angry with him. She didn't exactly make him feel warm and comfy. If anything, since the moment he'd met her, she'd done the exact opposite.

Which made no sense to explain why he had always been so drawn to her. Why, since he'd returned to New Orleans, he'd only become more needy for her.

For years he'd been convinced he'd move on from his need for her. And then he'd come home.

As if sensing him at the other end of the store, she turned, dark eyes clashing with his. So much hovered in them that neither of them wanted to admit to. While she fought against the emotions in the start, it had come to a place now where she couldn't deny what had never faded between them any more than he could.

He'd bet she was as clueless as he was about what lay ahead.

The smile sneaking across her lips was hesitant before she turned back to her customers.

He was drawn by it. Fighting back the urge to go to her, grab her in his arms, and cart her away to a place where they could just be them again, he found his way back to the kitchen.

The files greeted him as he stared down at the table he'd left only minutes before.

Not yet. Turning instead to the refrigerator, he pulled out a pitcher of sweet tea, pouring himself a full glass.

His mind was rolling with connections he needed to figure out. Connections he'd do no good battling if he sat back down to work.

The courtyard became his only escape. Just a few minutes, he promised, pushing through the door.

Coming back to New Orleans and finding himself tangled up with Addie again wasn't what he'd planned. Telling her the truth of what happened all those years ago wasn't part of his agenda.

He'd opened doors he hadn't planned on. Resurfaced old feelings that weren't so tidily going back to their place.

He supposed it did bring back to the surface his family and the reasons why he left, leaving the possibility of things needing to be settled.

Damn. Slamming his glass on the nearest table with more force than necessary, he paced from the fountain to the gate and back. He didn't like admitting Addie might have been right.

Did he need that? He wasn't willing to weaken himself by calling it closure. But it was something. It was there though he hadn't realized it until Addie spoke up.

And now, he couldn't ignore it, leaving him with little choice. Cursing with the frustration such knowledge left him, he grabbed his glass, finished off the last of his tea, and turned back for the door.

At least he had an excuse for why Addie needed to go out with him tonight. Since she started this whole ridiculous notion that he needed to see his family, she couldn't exactly say no when he asked her to tag along to Teddy's bar.

It was, after all, the most logical way for him to reach out to his family. And since she was the pushing force behind it—

His smile a bit too satisfied, his step a bit lighter, he went back into the kitchen, settling around the files waiting for him, ready, now, to get to work.

He wasn't sure what ate at him more, the curiosity or the frustration.

This wasn't him. This wasn't what he did—following a woman around wherever she went. Always needing to see her. Needing those chances to imagine what it would be like when she finally became his.

He'd followed in the past when he'd found his prey, but never from desire. It had always had a sensible reason. A need to know their ways for his own benefit.

This obsession with Addie was unlike anything he'd ever known. It angered him, pushing the heated emotion deep into his blood.

He hated losing his grasp on control. Hated the threat of being the weak man his mother predicted he would be.

Yet he couldn't stop the need. A need centered only on Addie.

The more he kept her in his sights, the more the anger fed his desperation to take care of what waited for them, especially as McReily continued to be the thorn poking at him.

He wasn't a fool. He didn't have to question what they were planning as he'd followed them back to the hotel the night before. They couldn't keep their hands off each other. Though they were discreet before escaping to the privacy of their room, it was clear that would change once the door closed. That McReily was taking what should be his.

It fueled his impatience, taunting him to act without any more delay. To show Addie where the true pleasure was waiting for her.

He'd thought about it as he'd sipped on a cup of coffee, watching them come out from the hotel lobby this morning.

He chose not to follow them, couldn't bring himself to. It was better that way. Proved he hadn't fallen to the weakness threatening to take over.

But nothing stopped him from making another visit to the store. He figured there was nothing wrong, or weak, in taking advantage of one more chance to be close to her before it became time to carry out what was to come.

The idea teased at him through the morning. He wondered, this time, what he'd claim he was looking for. Perhaps he'd get more romantic, show her he held that side as well. He could draw it out, keeping her with him, helping him as he struggled to make the decision.

The thoughts taunted him, quickening his step as he hurried along the crowded sidewalks. He thought of her sweet scent surrounding him again. Her soft voice drifting in gentle waves as she helped him find what he wanted.

This was right, making another visit to the store, taking another chance to know all that would be his. She called to him, seducing him with her perfection for everything she was.

He glanced through the windows before reaching for the door, wanting a quick peak at her before going in. She was there, just as he'd hoped, long red curls tumbling down her back as she smiled at an older couple.

Anticipation raged through his veins as his gaze roamed deeper into the store, seeking her aunt, knowing he couldn't take the risk of her being the one stepping forward to help him.

And then only a red haze flashed in his vision as his eyes passed over the figure hovering at the back of the store.

McReily.

He watched Addie with the same desire and passion raging through his own blood.

He wasn't supposed to be there. He shouldn't have been there. He'd stolen the chance from him.

Shoving at the couple slowly moving in front of him on the sidewalk, he barreled between them, wanting, needing, to hit something, someone.

This had been his final moment to take and savor before carrying out what waited for him. McReily had ruined it. Stolen it from him.

He would pay. Just as Addie would pay.

No more games. No more putting off what was coming. But first they'd know the wrath of his anger. Understand what it meant to challenge him.

CHAPTER TWENTY-ONE

S he'd wanted a night of sleep. Away from Reed. Away from the reminders of how she'd started the day with the sketch artist.

All Addie had looked forward to while working the shop was the moment when they closed, giving her a chance to head upstairs to her bedroom and hide under her covers.

But, as always, Reed had a way of changing everything.

So, now she sat with the crowds inside Teddy's bar. It was just her and Reed this time. Clay and his band weren't playing and AnnaBeth had a date with some wealthy art dealer she'd met at her latest organized to-do at the hotel.

"You could have called your cousin earlier today." She scowled at Reed as he set a glass of wine in front of her, settling with a beer in the seat next to her.

"I could have." He lifted the bottle and sipped, staring at her over the skinny rim.

How was she drawn to someone who was so aggravating? His smirk was one that should have tempted her to leave and be done for the night. Instead, there was enough spark, enough reminder of the rebellion he'd carried when he was younger, drawing her in even more.

"What are we doing?" She couldn't stop the question. It teased all day, tearing at her, needing to be asked.

"We're waiting for Teddy to get a few free moments so I can talk to him about getting in contact with my family. Like you suggested."

She narrowed her eyes, shook her head. "You know that isn't what I was talking about."

"Maybe." He took another long draw from his beer bottle. "It was the only answer I had."

She wanted to push, get him to give a real answer. But she didn't know what a real answer was. What words she needed to calm the uneasiness and fear brewing inside.

Looking at him over the space of the table, she wondered what ran through his mind. Was he with her, doubting and wondering?

He had a job to do. A set goal that brought him here. She didn't imagine he wondered, as she did, about what would come at the end of it all.

There were those moments when she'd catch a look and think maybe, just maybe, he faced the same struggles she did.

Nothing she played out inside her head came up with anything good. It only served to make her worry and fear more, never getting the answers she wished she had.

He would leave, that was a fact. She told herself a million times she didn't care. That was what she wanted. That was what needed to happen.

Finding herself back in his bed meant nothing other than scratching an itch. She was still mad, he still had a job to go back to, and everything was how it should be.

So, why was she searching for more?

She didn't want to think about it.

"Sorry. It's been one of those nights." Teddy slipped into the chair beside Reed, flashing a smile at Addie.

Reaching over, he grabbed his cousin's beer, taking a long drink for himself. "Sometimes I wonder what possessed me to take on this kind of venture."

"That bad, huh?"

"No. Just that frustrating. Like I said, it's one of those nights." He tossed a final look around the bar, making sure everything was running as he wanted. "That's not what's important right now."

Flattening his palms on the table, he looked hard at his cousin. "What is this, you thinking about meeting with the family?"

Reed's first instinct was to say never mind and change the conversation. He'd second-guessed his decision since he made it. And, being here at the bar, didn't make him any surer.

With Addie at his side, her words echoing inside his head, he knew what he had to do. "It's time I pay a visit to my parents."

Teddy's surprise was quick. "Not something I'd ever thought I'd hear you say. What can I do?"

"Just give me their numbers." Reed washed down the bitter taste rising in his throat with a long swig of beer. "No reason to put you in the middle of this. I can call them once I have a way to reach them."

Teddy's attention strayed to Addie who remained silent then back to Reed. "Everything has come through my mom, sometimes my dad, so I don't have their numbers. But I can get them."

"That's all I ask." Reed finished off the bottle, shoving it out of the way.

Teddy grabbed his empty bottle, raising it and shaking it at his closest bartender. "You sure about this?"

"Hell. I'm not sure about anything." Reed shoved a frustrated hand through his hair. "But I've been convinced it needs to happen."

Teddy didn't need to ask who did the convincing. "I'll get you their numbers."

"Thank you." Reed made room as the bartender approached with his beer as a crash echoed from the back of the bar.

"And that's my cue." With a long, heavy sigh, he pushed back from his seat. "Told you it was one of those nights."

Leaving them alone again at the table, Addie wondered about her chances of escape. She really wanted to go home and crawl into bed for the night.

"I'm glad you're taking the steps to see your parents." She worked on finishing up what was left of her wine. "Even if it turns out to be less than pleasant, I don't think you'll regret it."

"We'll see."

"Now that it's done." She took her last sip, setting the empty glass on the table in front of her. "I think it's time I get home."

"Dance with me first." Reed grabbed her hand before she could leave her seat as the band picked up a slow ballad. The words of love lost and love found surrounded them.

She pulled her hand free. "I don't think that's a good idea. I really need to go."

He stood as she did. "It's just a dance. Didn't you use to be the one who lived in the moment? Enjoyed life as it came to you?"

"Maybe I've changed," she challenged, digging in her heels as he tried moving her to the slice of dance floor in front of the stage.

"No, you haven't." He ran a gentle finger down the curve of her cheek, drawing her in. "Not in the ways that count."

"I think," he lowered to drop a quick kiss on her lips. "You believe you need to change in some sense of protecting yourself. It isn't working. You're still the amazing, wonderful, free-spirited woman I fell in love with all those years ago."

She didn't want to be affected. Didn't want his words to mean anything. Yet, she couldn't stop the slow warmth creeping through, leaving her wondering what it was she really wanted. Who she really was.

"It's one dance, Addie. What harm can it do?"

He pulled her to the dance floor, the gentle fall of the notes and lyrics surrounding them. One dance, she promised silently as he spun her around, collected her close.

One dance with Reed who could send her heart racing by just a look. Who knew where to touch, what to say, to send her blood to boiling and her precautions to the wind.

He proved it again, holding her so gentle curves tangled with hard lines. The press of his hands at the lower curve of her back heated through the cotton shirt she wore, burning against her skin.

He looked at her through those deep blue eyes and everyone else melted away. It was just the two of them, swaying to the ballad.

She was lost. She didn't have the strength left to deny it. Whatever the past was, or the future held, the lies she told herself today no longer worked. She still cared. She still loved him. Losing him again would tear apart the last bit of her heart she'd kept protected.

He sat in the shadows of the bar. Alcohol had never been his weakness, but tonight he couldn't stop his desperate need for it. Anger had him seeing red. Had him needing the beers to cool what burned inside.

Not that it helped. Wrapping his hand around his current beer bottle until his knuckles turned white, he watched the two moving around the crowded dance floor.

It shouldn't bother him. She was nothing to him before he found his way to New Orleans. But she had become his. Planned or not, he was brought to her.

He had an urge to hunt another. To again find a temporary moment of satisfaction before carrying out his intentions with Addie.

The thought of another who wasn't Addie no longer held the same appeal. She was what he wanted.

It was time. If McReily weren't in the way, he'd take her tonight and find what he so desperately desired.

The irritating agent continued to be the thorn in his side. Slamming his empty bottle on the bar, he motioned the bartender for another. He'd become more than an irritation. He was a threat. One who held what was rightfully his to have.

Rage took more force as McReily leaned in close for a kiss. Delusion took hold, shoving at him the conviction she should know better. Should not be lowering herself to the likes of him. Didn't she know she had better waiting for her? That her fate was already accounted for, and it was not in the arms of an irritating federal agent.

As much as he wanted her, he also wanted her to pay. To find punishment for the anger burning inside. She'd caused his obsession. It was time she realized the lessons she had yet to learn about where that obsession would take them.

CHAPTER TWENTY-TWO

Addie didn't fight, didn't argue as she stepped out of the bar, Reed's arm wrapped tight around her shoulders. He turned her toward his hotel, and she didn't hesitate. Didn't try to make excuses.

She didn't have it in her anymore to deny the feelings that returned since the moment she'd seen him again. She'd fought so hard, believed she had done so good. It had all been an illusion. A lie to herself and to her heart.

So many years ago, she became his. And though she'd succeeded in convincing herself she no longer cared during the time he was gone, it never reflected the reality of what simmered inside. It had only hidden it away so she didn't have to live with the truth. So she could continue with life and not be drug under by a love that could never truly be chased away.

Not even her anger from the past protected her anymore. Though she'd fought it, she was beginning to understand he'd genuinely believed by hurting her, he was protecting her.

She struggled with the idea. Stalling as Reed led them through the front doors leading to the lobby, she looked at him, a mix of emotions racing through.

"What?" He encouraged her forward so they wouldn't block the flow of others coming through.

She waited, saying nothing, until he guided them onto the elevator. They were alone as the doors slid closed. "I will never agree with what you did all those years ago. I need to know that you understand you were wrong in hurting me, no matter the reasons why."

He said nothing, letting the silence fall as the elevator jerked to a stop on their floor. The doors opened and he took her hand, staying quiet down the hall and into the room.

Inside, he left her standing by the bed, watching curiously as he picked up the phone. His gaze rested on her before turning to the receiver cradled between his shoulder and ear.

He ordered a bottle of champagne. What was he up to? Had he heard what she said? Did it matter or was he brushing her off while hoping to get her drunk and back into his bed?

He came back to her, cupping his palms softly around both sides of her face. He held her, trapped by the force of his heated gaze. Then he lowered, drawing her into a slow kiss pulling at the need gaining strength.

Once she was breathless and barely able to stand, he pulled away, leaving her wavering on unsteady legs as he sat at the edge of the bed, slipping his shoes off. She couldn't find the ability to speak as one shoe then the other hit the floor.

Sucking in a deep breath, she fought to steady herself again.

With his shoes off, he stayed at his place on the edge of the bed. Slowly he turned, emotions she couldn't figure out darkening his expression.

Unable to take the silence any longer, she took a step toward him. "Reed."

A knock at the door stopped her before she could say anymore. Pushing up from the bed, he came back to her, grabbing her hand and holding it for a moment before letting it slowly slide free.

He opened the door, making way for the man on the other side to wheel his cart into the room.

"Where would you like me to put this?" He waved a hand over the copper ice-filled bucket holding an open bottle of champagne.

"The table will be fine." Reed moved out of his way. Waited while he placed the bucket and two glasses on the table.

The other man offered a smile for Addie as he handed Reed a black, leather holder. "Is there anything else I can get you?"

"No. We're good. Thanks." Reed scribbled over the bill he'd been handed then opened the door for the man and his cart.

Alone again, he walked past her to the table, pulling the bottle of champagne from its bucket. Filling the two skinny glasses, he wrapped long fingers around the delicate stems before coming back to where she stood.

He pressed one of the glasses into her hand before catching her lips in another soft kiss.

"Reed?" She didn't understand any of it. His silence, the champagne, his soft, seductive kisses.

Pressing a finger on the bottom of her glass, he encouraged her to lift it, take a drink. His eyes never left hers as he lifted his own glass, sipping from the bubbly liquid while she did the same.

Lowering her glass, she waited, unsure what to expect next.

Taking a step closer, Reed rubbed his thumb along Addie's bottom lip where a drop of champagne lingered. "I never should have hurt you."

He slid his hand to the side, cupping her cheek. "You deserved more than what I gave you."

"You deserve more than what I can give you now." He teased his lips against hers. The rise of her breasts pressed against his chest as she sucked in a deep breath.

Guilt pressed at him after her words inside the elevator. He'd been speechless. Unable to find a single explanation that seemed right.

Because she was right. Every time he explained it in his own head, made the justifications for what he did and why he did it, the fact remained, he never should have hurt her in the way he did.

To hear her say it, to finally come to grasps with it, was another kick to his gut.

All he could think after that, the only thing coming to mind, was to show her by actions, rather than words, how important she was. How important she had always been.

He'd been afraid to speak. To try and offer some kind of apology for what he'd done. So, he decided to show her instead. To answer the need pushing at him to take her and show her the truth in his heart he couldn't put to words.

But, even with what pushed at him, he understood she still needed to hear that he was wrong. That he had hurt her, and she never deserved it, no matter the reasons he used to explain it away.

He encouraged her to take another sip from her champagne before taking her glass, setting it with his own on the small night table next to the bed.

Coming back to her, he took her hands, holding them at her sides. "I've lived many years believing what I did was right. I wanted to protect you. I thought that was the only way."

Like he had been, she was silent. Only the wave of emotions falling over her dark gaze let him know she was hearing him.

Curling their joined hands behind her back, he forced her closer, soft curves teasing against hard lines. "I was wrong."

He dipped low, finding the sensitive line between her ear and shoulder, trailing his tongue along soft skin. "So wrong."

She arched into him, her head falling back, giving in to the gentle demand of his touch. She struggled to free her hands, but he held tight, wanting her there, unable to do anything but feel.

"You were the best thing that ever happened to me."

He trailed his tongue lower, finding the soft swell of her breasts pushing past her shirt, taking all that was offered above the slim line of cotton keeping the rest of her hidden.

He wanted to love her in a way he never had. To take every luscious inch of her body and show her what she meant to him. Had always meant to him.

She whined when he pulled away. Letting go of her hands, he reached for her champagne glass, pushing it back into her hands.

Surprised, she lifted it to her mouth. He tightened at the sight of her lips gently covering the rim, the tip of her tongue slipping out as she sipped from the bubbly liquid.

He'd never thought of champagne as a turn on, but she was quickly proving how just a simple sip could fuel the desire already tearing through, pushing him to want even more desperately.

She held out the glass for him to take. Shaking his head, he took a step closer, one hand curling around her slender waist while the other encouraged her to enjoy another sip.

Slow this time, she lifted it back to her lips, her brown eyes clouded as they held his. She sipped as his hand slowly made its way over the soft folds of her skirt, down the slope of her thigh and back up.

He cupped his fingers between her legs, heat pushing through the thin material. Her moan caught in the bubbles as her eyes widened.

"Yes," he encouraged when she pushed into him, increasing the pressure. He wanted her here, just like this. Caught by him while the champagne left moisture on her luscious lips, tempting him to take a taste.

He wanted to see the desire flaring in her dark eyes. Feel her press against his touch, seeking more. Her desire for him flared his need even greater. She deserved to know what that was like. To have an idea of the power she held over him.

Finishing off the last sip of champagne, her gaze never straying, Addie cupped the slender glass between her fingers. Of all things she'd expected from Reed, this wasn't close to what she'd imagined.

She was still caught in the hold of confusion, not fully sure of what was happening or why. The heat of his touch, the sensations it raced through her blood, only left her mind less able to grasp on to anything other than her desperation for him.

He took her glass, setting it back with his still full one. Then he was back, pushing his hands under the bottom hem of her shirt, gently gliding them up her sides.

The warmth of his touch trembled through her. He was slow, almost cautious, as his fingers arched around the bottom curve of her breasts. Rubbing the pads of his thumbs against her nipples through the thin lace covering them, he dropped his lips to her. Soft and slow, drawing her up and into him, leaving her breathless.

He fought for his own breaths as he pulled away, resting his forehead against hers before slowly slipping her shirt up and over her shoulders.

"You're beautiful." His voice was a harsh breath as he tossed her shirt aside. Taking a step back, he ran his heated gaze over her from head to toe. It was as if he'd never seen her before though he'd loved every inch of her body many times.

Hit by an uncomfortable moment of self-awareness, she resisted the urge to fold her arms around her front. Though she still wore her skirt and bra, she felt exposed to the slow, lingering force of his deep, blue eyes.

Dropping his hands on her shoulders, he held her for a moment before suddenly turning her. Surprised, and a bit uncertain, it took her a moment to realize what he was doing. His fingers inched up her spine, lingering over the clasp of her bra. He reached around, easing the lace away, tossing it with her shirt on the floor. Curling his hands around her waist, he pulled her back against him.

Warm breath teased against her neck a second before he nibbled against the sensitive line between her ear and shoulder. Cupping his hands around her breasts, he held her closer so not a breath of air separated them.

Addie's head fell back with a moan. She could barely stand, her legs weak, threatening to give up on her. His hands drifted lower, catching at the waist of her skirt, easing it down.

Seconds later, she was completely bared to his touch, backed up and held against the hard-muscled lines of his chest. His fingers barely touched, a tease, as he slid them slowly down her sides, over the swell of her breasts, the curve of her waist.

"You've always been mine." His voice was nothing more than a harsh whisper in her ear. He curled strong arms around her, holding her tighter. She couldn't see him but could feel the hard rise and fall of his chest. The proof of his need pressing against her back.

It only helped to fuel her own need, trapped against him as she was.

"Always mine." He again found the sensitive line in her neck, nibbling his way down, over the curve of her shoulder.

His fingers drifted again, a soft flutter against bared skin as they slid between her legs. She melted into him as he found where she ached. Every touch was slow, gentle, as he slipped inside, then out. Teasing, over and over again.

"Reed...please." Brought to the edge, sure she'd stumble painfully the longer his slow torture continued, she curled her arm behind her, trying to grab at him. Catch him and make him understand what he was doing to her.

Where this night had moved out of her control, she couldn't be sure. Since they'd reached his room, he'd drawn her up, left her confused while building the desire to a point she wasn't sure she'd be able to handle.

It wasn't a sensation she liked. This need to completely surrender to whatever it was Reed was doing to her. He'd always been able to claim her, take her in a way no other man had ever done. But she'd been able to hold on to a small part of herself, never fully sliding under his control.

Tonight, she was dangerously close to crossing that line. The realization frightened her even as it excited her.

Close to powerless, backed against him like she was, she tried moving from his hold. He only tightened his grasp, dropping his mouth, taking a nip from her ear.

"Is it too much, sweetheart?" The warmth of his breath fanned over skin already lit to fire.

Words became harder to form as his fingers continued slowly drawing her higher, leaving her more desperate.

It *was* too much. How could it not be? Trapped against him, unable to do anything but stand there as he built the raging fire through her veins.

Needing to feel him, to let him know what he was doing to her, she rubbed against the proof of his need pushing against her back. She might not be able to find the ability for words, but she could tease. Could give him a small taste of his own torture.

Reed's groan was desperate. It took everything inside him not to throw Addie on the bed and take her with the force of the need driving through him.

But she wasn't there yet. She wasn't where he wanted her. Everything was about getting her to feel what ran through him rather than trying to tell her.

He only wanted her to feel, nothing more.

Raising his hands up her sides, resting them on her slender shoulders, he turned her. In her dark brown eyes was the proof of how far he'd taken her to the edge.

He lowered his mouth, taking hers. He needed it, that intimate taste. Needed to feel her sink into him as his lips roamed over hers.

He'd sworn he wouldn't rush, would take his time, make her feel exactly what he wanted her to feel. The temptation proved harder and harder to fight against as her gentle lines pressed against him, teasing with what waited for them.

Backing her up, refusing to let go, he eased her down over the mattress. She wrapped her arms around him as he eased over her, never letting his mouth stray. Needing the taste of her.

She tugged desperately at the hem of his shirt. Cursing, hating to break the contact between them, he pulled away, quickly stripping away his clothes, throwing them to the floor.

And then he was over her again. Taking in all that she offered, wondering if there would ever come a time when he had enough. When the urges didn't rule, always pushing him to want and discover more.

Digging her heels into the mattress, she lifted her hips from the bed, pushing into him, pleading for the release they both wanted. But he wasn't ready yet, needing more.

Tangling his hands in her long, red hair, he held her for a moment. Just staring. Needing time to see nothing but the passion reflecting back at him through her dark eyes.

He nibbled at her mouth, trailing down over the delicate curve of her chin. The taste of her was a drug he couldn't fight, dragging him under as he lowered to the soft crease between her breasts.

He wanted her. Every inch. Wanted her to feel the burn of his touch rumble through. To know what tore through him with every sight of her.

Her groan was desperate as he trailed his tongue slowly around a hardened nipple, loving the feel of her rising into him, needing more.

His hands leading a gentle path lower, he followed with his mouth, never giving her a chance to drift back down. Keeping her tense and needy underneath him, her hands grasping for the mattress, hips pushing up, seeking more.

"Reed...no. I can't." Her words surrounded him on a breathless gasp as his mouth and hands teased at her most sensitive spot. Like vices, her fingers grabbed his shoulders.

He drew her up. Her body shook beneath his. Every soft gasp, every moan, only fueled the fire in his veins. Yes, this is what he wanted. Her complete surrender to him. Letting him take with all the greed burning inside, making her his in ways he never had before.

She'd never forget. Never want another like she wanted him.

Her nails bit into his skin as her hips vibrated under the tease of his mouth and hands. He took then took some more. Drawing her up, letting her slowly slide down only to pull her back again.

"Please." Her voice caught close to a sob. "No more."

And she was his, completely.

Her hands fell from his shoulders as he came away, slowly working his way up until his face hovered over hers. Refusing to give her a chance to come back down, he curled his palms around her red-stained cheeks, holding her, claiming her mouth as he slid inside.

She shuddered as he filled her, nearly pushing him over the edge. He couldn't move, didn't dare risk it, taking her with only his mouth as he sucked in a harsh breath.

Slowly, achingly slow, he moved inside her. She closed around him, and he lost himself in her. In all that she was. All that she tore through him with a look, a touch.

He'd surrendered to her just as much as he'd hoped to get her to surrender to him.

He didn't know where she began and he ended. Didn't know whose heart he felt beating frantically against his chest. Which one gasped desperately for a breath as he slowly pulled out only to bury himself deeper.

He needed. He took. He wanted.

It would never be enough.

Folding his arms behind her, he lifted her from the mattress, holding her close so that not an inch of space came between them. One with him, she looked into his eyes, so much in her brown gaze he felt it into the core of his bones.

Never had he known a connection so strong it passed all else but the feel of her melted against him. Surrounded him so that every bit of air he sucked in, every sensation rocketing through him, was taken over by her. By what she was, had always been, to him.

He didn't do weak. Didn't do desperate. Yet she did that to him. Made him struggle. Left him realizing even the greatest strength couldn't fight against what she brought into his life.

Losing the last bit of control, he moved inside her, folding her body tight with his. He needed her to feel, to know, everything tearing through him.

She tensed in his hold as he drove them higher, desperation taking over, seeking the release building so hot inside.

"This, Addie." His voice was harsh as he pushed in deeper. "This is what matters. This is what we've always been."

She didn't speak, only tightened around him, drawing him in with every thrust. With a tortured groan, he took her, over and over, until she shuddered under the force of his hold.

"Reed." His name was a frantic plea as she tumbled, closing around him. Drawing him in so that he was one with her as he fell into his own frantic release.

Just a few blocks from Bourbon, there was no sign of the lively chaos he'd left behind.

He'd stayed, nursed another couple beers, after watching McReily and Addie leave the bar together. With each sip, his anger built, becoming almost blinding as his mind replayed the two of them so close on the dance floor. Like lovers who only had eyes for one another.

Feeling deceived, he had no room for reasoning or sane thoughts. His mind worked only around making her pay. Punishing her for her betrayal.

He'd left the bar knowing what he had to do.

Standing across the street from Magic Moon, he was alone on the sidewalk. There was no sign of life inside. No sign of anything but a store shut down for the night, waiting until the next day and the next surge of customers to come through the door.

This was Addie's livelihood. He wasn't sure why such a place would hold importance to anyone, but for her, it did. He'd watched her work. Seen the dedication in her eyes when she'd helped him. For whatever reason, here was where her heart was.

So here was where he would strike.

Crossing over, pausing long enough to make sure he was still alone, he pulled out the lock picks he carried in his pocket. The ones that had come in handy when his prey wasn't always so easily accessible.

He'd never thought he'd use them for tonight's purposes but figured he was a regular old boy scout, always prepared.

The lock was fairly new and well-constructed, giving him a challenge. It didn't help that, even on an empty street, he was exposed if someone were to come by.

Fighting back the dangerous combination of anger and liquor, he fumbled with the pick, cursing as he dropped it. He bent to pick it up, catching a flicker of movement through the corner of his eyes. Quickly shoving the pick into his pocket, he hurried down the sidewalk, stopping a few stores down, looking around as if a tourist lost as a couple, wrapped tight in each other's arms, came at him.

They barely noticed him as they stumbled past, turning around the next corner.

It was too much of a risk. He should go. He didn't make these kinds of mistakes. That was why McReily ran around like a dog chasing his tail, trying to catch him. He knew better than to put himself in situations that would give him away.

The knowledge of it didn't stop him from turning back, pulling out the pick as he again reached the door to Magic Moon.

Something different burned through his blood this time. Addie did that to him, leaving him careless and reckless. The thought only made him angrier as he fought the lock.

He should have never seen her. This wasn't supposed to be about her. If she had stayed away, hadn't tempted him in the way she had, he wouldn't be here. Wouldn't be taking such dangerous risks.

Like his mother, she pushed at him, teased him, taunted him. Just like her, she was out to destroy him. Make him pay for mistakes he never made.

As a boy, he'd had his time of feeling out of control, as if the world was spiraling away from him. It had taken time and dedication to become what he was. To carry a level head that knew how to act and when to act.

She'd pushed him back to this point.

The satisfying click echoed quietly around him. Again, he checked the empty street before shoving on the door. It gave easily, allowing him inside.

Silence greeted him. He stood in the dark, making sense of the shadows surrounding him. He thought of Addie inside the store. The sight of her. The sound of her gentle voice filling the space.

Those things were meant to be his. Only his.

She needed to know that. Understand it.

He ran a heavy hand over the display on his left, tossing whatever hung there to the ground.

Yes. She needed to understand.

He turned to his right, swiping an angry hand through what was there. The dark kept him from seeing what clattered against the floor, but the sound fueled what burned inside.

Shoving his way through, he kicked at the thick shadows at his feet, the crash and shatter echoing through the quiet. He turned, throwing an arm in the air, hitting whatever he could reach, finding satisfaction in it.

The destruction gave him purpose, pushed him for more. If this was what she loved, he'd take it from her. Show her what it meant to deceive him.

His anger grew deeper, darker. His eyes adjusted to the lack of light as he moved toward the heart of the store. Shoving, throwing, breaking anything that came into his path. A wooden shelf, full of books, landed with a heavy thud. Crystals shattered at his feet. Tapestries tore under the force of his hands.

He wanted nothing untouched. Every broken, ruined item was another addition to the suffering he wanted her to know.

Through his fury, a strange sound echoed. It took a moment to realize it was the squeak of door hinges. He was no longer alone inside the store.

She stood behind the counter. He remembered the older lady from his visit to the store. Fear shimmered in her eyes, but she stood strong, defiant, a baseball bat clutched in her hands.

"I've called the police." She waved it at him though he was far enough away there was no chance of making contact.

The sight of her only made the rage greater. She was a part of this. A part of what Addie cherished. What he wanted to strip from her.

The bat doing nothing to frighten him away, he took a step closer, kicking the disaster at his feet. She stood her ground, swinging the bat again, still missing him.

He wanted her. Wanted her broken like everything around him. The force of that need, the anger boiling in his blood, rushed through as he stepped into the range of her attack.

She got in one shot to his arm, but he barely felt it under what raged over him. Her next swing never made contact. Reaching up, he wrapped his fingers around the thickest part of the bat.

They stood frozen. Fear thickened in her gaze, washing over her as he yanked hard on the bat, taking control.

"The cops will be here any minute." Her voice shook but she remained firm where she was.

He didn't bother answering. Didn't bother with a single word. Raising the bat above his head, she didn't have a chance to get away before he brought it down, lodging it hard against the side of her head.

She cried out, stumbling back, fighting to stay on her feet. Her hands flailed for something to grab. Something to keep her up. She hit nothing but air for her desperate efforts.

He came at her again. The bat hit her in the side, sending her down. Terror flashed as she looked up at him. It fed him, giving him a satisfaction close to what he felt with the other women.

She was his. He'd do with her what he wanted. She'd be his punishment to Addie. Beyond the chaos he'd already created inside the store, she'd be his final stand.

With a vicious roar, torn from deep inside, he came down again and again, each strike harder than the one before it. She curled into herself, trying to protect flesh and bone as best as she could.

It didn't stop him. He hit with fury. With the need to make Addie pay. Over and over again. Seeing only red in his vision. Feeling only anger surging through his veins.

Through the ringing inside his head, he heard another sound. Holding the bat above his head, staring down at the beaten woman at his feet, he prepared to come down again, but the sound grew stronger.

Sirens. Getting closer.

Dropping the bat, he kicked her aside, running toward the back of the store and the door she'd left open. He stumbled through shadows lingering in a dark kitchen, finding another door.

The echo of sirens surrounded him as he stepped into a courtyard. With the close set of the buildings around him, his only way out was the gate leading to an alley. He'd be exposed, vulnerable.

But there was no other way. No other choice.

Thankful for the darkness of the alley, he slid through the gate, staying in the deepest of shadows, working away from the flashing lights.

The urge to run was great but he fought it. Shoving back the anger ruling only minutes before, he grasped for rational thought, understanding a desperate flight would be sure to get him caught.

Staying in the darkest corners of the alley, he pushed back thoughts of how dangerously close the sirens were, concentrating only on being unseen.

He would not give himself up now. Not when there was still business to finish. Still prey he had yet to conquer.

Finding another courtyard, he slid slowly past an untended tumble of shrubs, barely avoided tripping over old patio furniture scattered along the torn-up path.

Every step took him further away from the risk he'd left behind. Through the alleys and the courtyards, he worked his way toward the sounds calling from Bourbon.

Life still thrived. He only had to join the crowds and he'd be safe. More sirens screamed and he wondered how long he had before they started searching for him.

It wouldn't be much longer. There was no question they'd reached the store. Once they'd assessed the situation they'd be on the hunt.

But he'd never be found. Releasing a relieved sigh, he stepped into a crowd working their way down Bourbon Street, becoming one of them.

Drunk as they were, they welcomed him with a cheerful toast sloshing over the tops of their plastic cups, never once wondering about the stranger who joined them.

CHAPTER TWENTY-THREE

The jarring ringing of his phone pulled Reed reluctantly from sleep. Pressed tight to his side, Addie mumbled, turning away from him and the intruding sound, burying deeper into her pillow.

At least one of them could still sleep.

A glance out the small slit in the curtains told him it was still dark out. Nothing good ever came out of calls that came before daylight.

Glancing at the clock, noticing it was barely four in the morning, he reached for his phone, pulling it free from its charger as it rang again.

Addie didn't move. It took everything he had not to stand at the edge of the bed and stare down at her. At the beauty she was while in sleep.

He didn't want to disturb her more than she'd already been. His bare feet silent along the thick carpet, he hurried into the bathroom, closing the door behind him.

"McReily." He flipped the switch by the door, light burning his eyes.

"It's Perry. We have a problem. I just got a call from the locals. There was a break-in and altercation at the Magic Moon."

The last trace of sleep quickly disappeared as Perry's words hit. "What kind of altercation?"

He moved away from the door, not wanting his voice to reach the bed where Addie slept. Not yet. Not until he knew exactly what happened.

"Sounds like, from the information I've been given, whoever broke in was confronted by the owner. She was beaten pretty bad. Those on scene said she was clinging to life."

"Damn." Reed shoved a heavy hand through his hair, thought of Addie sleeping in the other room. Of what this would do to her. "Where is she now?"

"They took her to University. The LEO I talked to said it was a miracle she made it there." Perry's long draw of breath pushed through the phone. "It doesn't sound very good."

Everything inside Reed turned cold. "Did they catch the perp?"

He already knew the answer. Asking was a waste of time.

"He was gone by the time they arrived. They have a force looking for him. But with no clue who he is, it's about useless at this point."

Reed didn't have to wonder who they were looking for. He didn't need the evidence of who he was, his mind was already set.

"Thanks for letting me know." He didn't wait for a response before ending the call, his mind already on how he was going to tell Addie.

His first instinct was to protect her from this. To do whatever he could to spare her the pain that would come once she learned what happened.

He could let her sleep, go out himself, and learn what he could before telling her the truth. But doing so would only cause more problems. She needed to know. He couldn't put it off, no matter how desperately he wanted to.

She looked so peaceful asleep, red hair contrasting against the white pillowcase. The luscious curve of her breasts peeked out of the top of the sheet. It made what he had to do that much harder.

Settling on the edge of the bed, he rested a hand on her slender hip. Gentle, he leaned over, dropping a kiss on her cheek as he gave her a shake, waking her up.

Her lids fluttered, giving him a peak at brown eyes misted with sleep. She looked so innocent, so at peace, he considered again not telling her the truth.

But she had to know.

"I need you to wake up." He gave another gentle shake when her eyes slid closed again. "I have to talk to you."

The strange tone in his voice caught Addie before she could slip back into sleep. Forcing her eyes open, she fought through the murkiness lingering, finding Reed's hard-lined face hovering above hers. The somber look in his eyes reflected back at her.

Staring up at him, the last bits of sleep falling away, she knew whatever he had to say wasn't going to be good. "What's wrong?"

He only looked at her, saying nothing for a moment. Tugging on her arms, he urged her up to sit beside him. "I just got a call from one of our local agents."

He took her hand in his, held it tight. "Somebody broke into the Magic Moon last night."

"What?" She tried pulling away, but he tightened his hold. In his gaze, she saw there was more.

"Rosalie?"

He put his arms around her shoulders, pulled her close. Her heart stopped. She struggled for a breath, fighting back the fear of what he wasn't telling her.

"They believe she confronted whoever broke in. She was beaten pretty bad."

"No." This time he couldn't stop her as she bolted off the bed. Memories came tumbling back, clashing with the present. Her mom. A break-in. A shooting. She was back in a place she never wanted to be again.

Knowing she was close to losing control, she sucked in a deep breath. "Where is she? How is she? I have to get to her."

She searched frantically for her clothes. It was hard to concentrate, to focus on anything but the harsh swirl of emotions tumbling through. She found her skirt, threw it on the bed then turned with a desperate need to find the rest.

Reed caught her from behind, pulling her back against him. "We're going to get to her."

His warm breath fanned against her neck. His strong arms curled around her, drawing her close. "I'm going to call my partner, send him over to Magic Moon to check on things. And then I'll get your clothes together while you go into the bathroom and get ready."

"I can't. I have to go now."

He turned her, closing his palms around her cheeks, holding her still under his heavy gaze. "Take ten minutes, Addie. Give yourself that. Toss some cold water on your face. Suck in a few deep breaths. Whatever you need to do and then we'll go."

He was right, though she hated admitting it. Every second away from her aunt was a second too long. But she needed to gather herself. Calm the nerves scrambling through. Now was not the time to fall apart.

Her aunt needed her. That was all that mattered.

"I wish I had better news for you." Standing under the harsh glare of the lights, the stress lines cutting over the surgeon's face were deep. "The beating was severe. We had to rush her into surgery. She had blood collecting between her chest wall and lung that immediately needed to be drained."

Addie nearly fell into Reed. Fighting back a wave of nausea, she forced her legs to hold her up. "Is she—"

The words wouldn't come, fear of the answer holding her hostage.

"She's hanging on. We have her in a medically induced coma right now. In addition to the dangerous bleeding, she also has three fractured ribs, a ruptured spleen, a broken leg, and multiple lacerations. There's also some swelling in the brain we will be watching closely."

Addie wanted to turn and run from it all. She wanted to throw her hands over her ears and scream so she didn't have to hear the truth.

She couldn't avoid it. Couldn't deny it. Not surrounded by the overwhelming scent of disinfectant mixed with the underlying smells of illness and death, dragging her back to another time, another break-in, and another hospital.

No. As much as the memories of her mother's death pushed at her, she couldn't let them take over. Rosalie needed her. That was what mattered. She would not mix the present with the past.

"I need to see my aunt."

"We'll have her moved into the ICU within an hour or so. Once she's there, I'll send a nurse for you. If something happens or changes before that, I'll be sure to let you know."

He gave a quick smile before turning, leaving her and Reed alone in the long, bleached-white hallway.

"There's coffee in the waiting room." Dropping an arm around her shoulders, he urged her away from watching the surgeon disappear. "I think we could both use a cup."

She didn't argue. Found it hard to do anything more than let him guide her back down the hall to the small room crammed with chairs. A television hanging from the wall droned on with the early morning news. An older couple sat huddled together in the far corner.

He led her to a nearby chair, waiting until she was settled before disappearing long enough to grab them each a cup of coffee.

There were no windows. Nothing to let her know if morning had come or if they were still in the darkness that had brought such a horror. The thought of what her aunt suffered sent a shiver straight down to her toes.

Why had she confronted the intruder? She knew better. A hint of anger surged as Reed encouraged a cardboard cup into her hands.

She should have stayed safe upstairs. She had no reason to go down. No reason to put herself in the same position that killed her sister so many years ago.

Why hadn't she stayed where she was? Why?

Tears came. Addie quickly brushed them away. Sucking in long deep breaths, she took a sip from the bitter coffee Reed put in her hand.

"Why would somebody do this?"

It was a question she wouldn't get answers to. Just like with her mother. There were never answers, only more questions.

"I wish I knew." He curled his arm over her shoulders, pulling her close. She almost fell apart under the gentle weight of his hold. Fighting back tears, she took another sip from her coffee as the heavy glass doors slid open.

AnnaBeth came rushing through, a whirlwind of fear and worry. Seeing Addie, she hurried over, grabbing her from her chair. "Are you okay? What happened? How's Rosalie?"

She held her at arm's length for a moment then yanked her close. "I'm so sorry, Addie."

The tears she'd been fighting broke free under the force of Anna-Beth's hold. Fear surged, leaving her a weak mess in her best friend's arms. She was helpless to stop it.

AnnaBeth held her, knowing no words would help. Slowly finding the ability to come back to only sniffles, Addie stepped back.

"How did you know?"

Annabeth looked over her shoulder.

Addie turned, discovering Reed standing right behind them. "You did this?"

"I called Teddy while you were in the bathroom, asked him to let the others know."

For reasons she couldn't explain, it touched her deep, knowing what he'd done. He'd been the solid rock at her side since she'd learned what happened. He'd kept her steady when she'd needed it. Held her when she came close to sliding down. Never leaving her side. Always there. And yet still knowing and finding the time to do more for her.

She couldn't go to the feelings such thoughts brought up. Not now. It was too much. She reached for him, drawing him close. Pushing to her toes, she took his mouth, hoping he felt in her kiss what she couldn't share in her words.

His arms wrapped around her, holding her before she pulled away. He kept her there, his chin resting on top of her head, arms tight on her sides. She didn't fight it. Didn't want to. She held on with him, needing the connection.

It wasn't until the sweep of the glass doors broke through that she finally eased away. Turning, the tears returned as Clay and Teddy walked through.

Like AnnaBeth, they hurried over, grabbing and holding her with the understanding only old friends could.

She didn't have to ask this time. Because of Reed she was surrounded by the best support and comfort she could have. The fear was still there. More tears wanted to come. But she wasn't alone.

She knew, no matter what happened, she wouldn't be.

CHAPTER TWENTY-FOUR

S he looked so pale, so fragile.

Addie was barely aware of the hours passing as she sat with her aunt, holding her hand through the barrier of the rails on her hospital bed.

The doctors said the first twenty-four hours would tell them the most. In a medically induced coma, Rosalie was lifeless, only the blips and beeps on the machines hooked to her giving any signs of life.

Addie willed her own life to her. She couldn't go. She was too vibrant, too full of all the joys of life, to give in now. It wasn't her time. It just wasn't.

"Here. You have to eat." AnnaBeth shoved a Po-boy into her hands. It was the first time she'd left her side, grabbing food she insisted Addie needed.

She barely acknowledged the sandwich. The thought of even a bite made her stomach turn.

Resting a gentle hand on her shoulder, AnnaBeth bent over, unwrapping the Po-Boy. "It's your favorite."

Addie shook her head. Taking it away without another word, Annabeth set it on the small table beside her. Putting her own beside it, she pulled the chair shoved in the corner, settling at her side.

"Rosalie is one of the strongest women I know." She took Addie's free hand, holding tight. "She's a fighter. She always has been. If anybody can make it through this, she can."

Addie wanted to believe her. Wanted her words to be true. But the fear was great. The memories continuing to haunt her only made the doubts grow and the tears threaten.

"I want to know why." She glanced at Annabeth. "Why would somebody do this?"

"Reed will get the answers. You know he won't give up until he does." AnnaBeth's voice was soothing but did nothing to calm what raged inside.

She was right. If there were answers, Reed would find them. "I wish he'd call with some news."

"He will. Give him time. He's only been gone an hour."

Addie was surprised by that. It felt like it had been so much longer since he'd left her in AnnaBeth's care to find out what was happening at the Magic Moon.

She looked back to her aunt, praying she'd come out of this. Without her, there would be no Magic Moon left to worry about.

Rage fueled the destruction inside the Magic Moon.

Standing in the middle of it, Reed saw the proof. This was not about any kind of theft. It was a need to destroy. A need to take away what meant so much to others.

It was personal. Of that, he was sure. Whoever did this wanted to make either Addie or her aunt pay. He'd wanted them to suffer.

"We may have something." Branson made his way through the shattered glass and porcelain at his feet. "Art gallery across the street has a security camera. Jackson's over there now, working with the owner to get last night's footage."

Reed hoped for the best but knew better than to expect it. In his mind, he already knew who had done this. There was no proof. Nothing more than his gut telling him it was true. Shaking off the crap he didn't need distracting him, he walked over shredded tapestries and torn clothing, following the path the intruder made the night before.

It was behind the counter they'd found Rosalie's lifeless body. Standing over the spot, he fought back the thought of what would have happened if Addie had come home last night rather than going back with him to the hotel.

It could have been her beaten close to death. Her fragile body fighting for life in that hospital bed.

The horror of it was too much for him to grasp. He couldn't afford to go there. Not now. Not when she was still suffering with her aunt fighting for life.

"They checked the apartment?" He turned to his partner.

"Nothing's disturbed or out of place. The belief is, he escaped through the kitchen and into the courtyard but was never upstairs."

Reed bit back a curse as his phone rang. "McReily."

"I hear you've had some interesting developments out there." His SAC's deep voice broke through the line.

Not surprised by Marshall's call, Reed moved to the door behind the counter, leading to the kitchen. "You could call it interesting. We have a victim fighting for her life and a store destroyed."

"This is our concern, why?"

Reed didn't believe for a minute that he didn't already know the reason. There wasn't much Marshall didn't have his thumb on when it came to his agents.

"The owner of the store is Rosalie Monrose. Her niece is the one I believe our unsub has targeted."

"I'm guessing you've decided they're connected."

"My gut's telling me it's too much coincidence for there not to be a connection." He eased open the door leading to the courtyard, looked back at the door he'd come through from the store.

It would have taken only seconds to get where he now stood. Even in panic mode, the route was straight and easy.

"Or it could be a simple break and enter with a tragic ending."

Stepping into the courtyard, he tried getting a sense of what it had been like, standing in the dark. Adrenaline running. Fear of being caught raging through. His only way out would have been through the gate and down the alley. The fact he'd made it told Reed he'd had enough time between the attack and when the first on the scene arrived.

"What happened was personal. It wasn't some random attack." He worked his way toward the gate, pushed it open. He looked down the alley, wondering which way he'd escaped.

"You and Branson work it but let the locals take the lead. This isn't for us, at the moment. If we get more evidence leading us another way, then we'll make some changes."

As much as he hated to, Reed agreed. He had no argument good enough to push for different. Stepping back and closing the gate, he turned back for the door leading inside.

"In the meantime," Marshall continued as he found his way back inside. "I have some information directly related to why you're there in the first place."

Interested, Reed stopped in the middle of the kitchen. "What is it?"

"We got a match on the familial DNA we ran. A hit from a former convict in Tennessee. The relations weak, but it's there."

It was the kind of news he waited for. The hint of a break after all this time was better than what they'd been working on for so long. "Who is it? Have we made contact?"

"Name's Jeremiah Barrow. He served eight of a fifteen-year sentence for robbery and assault. Got out a few years ago. Our agents tried contacting him at his last known address. He hasn't lived there for over a year."

It was no longer a surprise. For every step forward, they ended up with a push three steps back. "I'll do some records search, see what I can find."

"I've got Tennessee agents working on that. It might do you good to put some time into it, too. Work this case, find what you can before looking for answers you want that might not exist."

Reed wasn't going to lie. Wasn't going to make promises he'd never keep. "I'll do my best to take care of what needs to be done."

Marshall's grunt on the other end made it clear he knew exactly where Reed's mind was at. "I'll be in touch with you if I learn anymore from my end."

With that, he ended the call.

Pocketing his phone, Reed found his way back through the door into the store. Branson was coming at him with his first step behind the counter, determination hard in his expression.

"Jackson has the tape from the security camera last night. She says it's worth the time to take a look."

He enjoyed watching the chaos. Liked knowing he was the cause of it.

He'd known better than to come back too soon, though the urge had been strong. Instead, he'd slept, knowing he needed it, letting the morning hours come around before daring to venture out.

By the time he made his way back, he was just another one of many onlookers crowding the sidewalk. He was there to see McReily walk in. To find some satisfaction in knowing he'd been keeping the agent busy while still beating him at the game.

He wondered how long it would be before McReily gave up. Before he finally realized, once and for all, he would only come out on the losing end no matter how long he kept at it.

Once he had control of Addie, McReily's loss would be even greater. It was something he looked forward to with great anticipation.

Standing across the street with a group of strangers, his attention was drawn to the door of the Magic Moon as McReily came out with his partner.

Their heads were dropped low in conversation. They turned away from him and he wondered what had them so involved. Perhaps it was another false lead that would get them nowhere. A clue that still wouldn't lead to him.

He wasn't worried. Stepping away from the group on the sidewalk, he made his way toward the music floating from Jackson's Square. Whatever interested McReily and his partner, it wasn't a threat to him.

He'd beat them long enough to know they'd never find him. When he was done, McReily would regret ever trying.

CHAPTER TWENTY-FIVE

"Her vitals are showing improvement. She's doing better than expected."

For every word her aunt's doctor shared, Addie felt a small glimmer of hope.

He reminded her of a concerned grandfather as he used his forefinger to push up the nose of his glasses while reading through her chart. Gray hair was an orderly tumble around his wrinkle-filled face. Blue eyes sparkled with understanding.

"Let's see how she does waking up." He smiled, his gaze resting a moment on AnnaBeth before returning to Addie. "It's a bit earlier than planned, but I think it would be best to take her off the medication keeping her in a coma. Let's give her body a chance to do what it needs to do."

Though optimism hinted in his words, Addie knew better than to let it go too far.

"And as for you," he rested a gentle hand over her shoulder, squeezed. "I would suggest getting some sleep. It will still be some time before your aunt comes around. She's going to need you well-rested when she does."

Addie nodded, but the only sleep she'd be getting would be whatever she could steal in the chair at Rosalie's side. "Thank you for everything."

"I'll check in later, see how she's doing." He moved around her and AnnaBeth, leaving them alone once again as he slipped out the door.

"You should go home and get some sleep." Addie looked at her friend. She'd put aside her day, cancelled all she had needing to be done to stay by Addie's side, leaving only long enough for food or much needed coffee.

"Giving advice you won't take?" AnnaBeth slung an arm around her shoulders, pulling her close. Addie rested against her friend, thankful for her.

"Reed will be here soon. Once I know you won't be alone, I'll sneak away for a bit. But I'll only be a phone call away."

And she'd come running again if she were needed. Knowing words would never match what she felt inside, Addie turned, sweeping a soft kiss against her friend's smooth cheek. At the side of Rosalie's bed, they stood, two friends who spent nearly a lifetime counting on each other.

Reed paused in the door, sticking out an arm, stopping Branson from going through.

Sometimes he'd forget how close Addie and AnnaBeth's friendship was. Until times like this, watching them together, holding on for the comfort and support they needed.

His gut twisted, remembering he'd been allowed to be part of such a friendship and had made the choice to turn away from it.

Giving them a few seconds more, he cleared his throat before coming into the hospital room, Branson a step behind.

Addie turned, dark eyes catching his, causing a quick catch in his heart. Yeah, it was getting bad. At some point, serious decisions would need to be made.

But not now. For the time being, it was business as usual.

"How is she doing?" He stepped up closer to Rosalie's bedside, seeing no changes since he'd left.

"Her doctor says she's showing some improvement. They're going to let her come out of the coma." Beside him, Addie wrapped her arms tight around her middle.

He reached for her, gathering her against his chest. He wanted to chase away the sadness, the fear, reflecting in her gaze. Wanted to make all of this go away so she could go back to the life she'd known only a few short weeks ago.

What he was about to ask from her would only prove to cause the opposite of everything he hoped for. "I know this is the worst time."

He stepped back, holding her at arm's length. The grief looking back at him nearly made him change his mind. But it had to be done. "I have something important I need you to look at."

"What is it?"

He waved Branson over from where he hovered by the door. "I need you to look at some video. The quality isn't particularly good, but I want to know if you recognize someone."

Holding out his hand for the small player Branson brought along, he moved to Addie's side.

"This was taken last night from a security camera across the street from the Magic Moon." He pushed play and the grainy black and white images began flashing over the tiny screen.

A few seconds in and he paused it as a dark figure came into view. "This is the man who broke in last night and attacked your aunt."

He let it play until the moment when the man checked the street, giving the camera its best shot. Swiping his fingers over the screen, he zoomed in on his face, caught in shadows and half-turned.

Addie leaned in close, focusing on the grainy image. Without color, it was hard to recognize anything. But something was there. Something in the shape of the face. In the eyes, even from so far away. It was familiar, stirring a memory.

Gasping, she pushed back from the player in Reed's hands. "I know him."

She didn't need to look again. Didn't want to look again.

"That's the man who was in the shop the other day. The one you had me describe to your sketch artist."

"Are you sure?" Reed moved the player closer.

Though she didn't want to, she stared back at the face caught on the screen.

"I'm sure." Turning away, she folded her arms tight around her middle, fighting off a sudden chill. "He's the one. But I don't understand why."

Reed handed the player back to his partner, reaching for her, folding her against the warmth and strength of his chest. She wished she could stay caught in his hold and forget everything.

"Why would he do this? Who is he?"

The heavy shift in Reed's expression left little doubt about his answer.

"You think it's that killer you came after? The one who left that woman in the cemetery?"

He didn't need to respond, it was in his eyes.

"It doesn't make sense." Shaking her head, she pulled away, looking down at her aunt. The sounds of the machines echoed eerily around her. The room suddenly felt cold and airless.

This nightmare had to end. It was too much. She struggled for a breath. Gasping as it became close to impossible to draw in air. "I can't do this anymore. I can't."

Waving Reed away, AnnaBeth came to her side. She grabbed her hand, folding it between both of hers. "Do you remember when we had the bright idea to go boating down the bayou in the dark, just you and me? Two foolish teenage girls without a clue."

Confused at why she'd bring up the memory, Addie looked at her friend. "I remember."

"Do you remember going too deep and losing our way? We were so afraid. So sure we were done for."

It had been so dark. A thick black sheet settling, stripping away their sense of direction.

The sounds of the bayou buzzed, gathering an eerie feel the longer they were out there. The water moved around them, creatures rippling past, making the fear even greater.

"I was terrified." Addie shivered with the reminder of how strong the feeling of doom was. "I didn't see any way we would get out of that. We were going to die in that boat. I was sure of it."

"So was I." AnnaBeth tugged on her hand, smiling softly. "We both believed we were about to face the worst but still we never gave up, even in the darkest and most frightening moments."

"No, we didn't give up."

She thought again of that long, terrifying night. They'd worked themselves around in circles for hours. The heavy darkness kept them from finding anything familiar. Anything giving hope they would find their way.

They'd made it, refusing to give up, just as AnnaBeth said. Fear might have held them, but it didn't take them under. For so long, the beam of their flashlight caught nothing in its weak light. Until the strange reflection when their exhaustion was so great they wondered if they'd been reduced to seeing things.

It had been real, the light reflecting off the headlights of an old truck.

It was their beacon. Their first hint of hope that they wouldn't become yet another disappearance in the bayou.

The truck had been empty, but the feel of solid ground under their feet was enough reason to sigh in relief. They had no idea where they were. How far they had drifted away from where AnnaBeth left her car.

They followed the skinny dirt road behind the truck, finding the run-down shack. It looked like it was straight out of a horror film. The heavy set, thick-bearded man who answered their frantic knocks could have easily been the villain.

"You didn't give up then. You didn't let fear take control."

"And I won't do it now," Addie finished for her, resting her head on her shoulder.

Easing away from AnnaBeth, she grabbed her aunt's hand, holding it tight. She was afraid. She was terrified. But she couldn't run and hide. Couldn't avoid what was happening.

AnnaBeth was right. She had to be brave, refuse to give up. Whatever the reason, whoever it was, she'd fight until the end.

"AnnaBeth told me Addie hasn't left her aunt's side." Teddy sat across from Reed at the skinny table inside the hospital cafeteria.

Cupping his hands around his cup of coffee, Reed nodded. "She refuses to leave until Rosalie wakes up. It's been over twenty-four hours since her doctor decided to cut off the drugs keeping her in a coma. Her vitals are good, but she's showing no signs of coming around."

"Rosalie's tough. Always has been." Teddy sipped his own coffee. "I can't imagine what it would do to Addie to lose her. Especially after she lost her mom in such a similar way."

It was a thought Reed didn't want to give any weight to. Thinking of the pain such a situation would cause for Addie was more than he could handle. What he wanted was to be a miracle worker. One who could make all of this go away.

He'd brought this to her. Though some in the Bureau were still hesitant to follow his belief, Reed didn't doubt the killer he hunted was the same man terrorizing Addie.

He couldn't blame it on coincidence. He had to face the fact Addie was targeted because of her connection to him.

Everything they knew about him no longer mattered. He'd broken out of his usual ways with his attention now on her. Nothing made sense anymore. It was a new game with the same killer.

Guilt weighed heavy on his shoulders. He needed to do more to make this right, outside of his duties as an agent.

For the first time in the years he'd been away, he thought of his trust fund, sitting untouched. He had the means to provide the best of doctors for Rosalie's care. Could give Addie a secure place better than anything the Bureau had to offer to keep her safe.

Old angers shoved him back from the idea. Addie was right, it was time to settle things from the past. "I don't suppose you got those numbers."

"I have them." Teddy looked at him over the rim of his coffee cup. "Wasn't sure you'd be ready for them with all that is going on."

"It needs to be." Reed couldn't deny the truth.

"Your parents still have a landline. The home number hasn't changed. You could have called without me getting the other numbers. I have a feeling you already knew that, though."

"I figured it. But I was hoping to stall for as long as possible."

"And now?"

Reed didn't say anything for a moment, sipping slowly from his coffee. "Now, I think it's time to take care of things."

CHAPTER TWENTY-SIX

T he first flutter of movement left Addie wondering if she was imagining things. After three days of waiting, hoping for some sign of life, it didn't seem real.

But another twitch of her aunt's fingers against her palm and she knew she wasn't imagining it. It was small but it was something.

"I think we should get the nurse." She looked at Reed in the chair beside her.

"Is something wrong?"

"No. She moved. I felt it."

The same doubt she'd felt reflected back at her through Reed's gaze. He didn't argue, pushing up from his chair and disappearing out the door.

"Don't you make me look like a fool." Pushing up from her own chair, she dropped a soft kiss against her aunt's forehead. "I know you're in there, trying to come back. Make sure you let them know that, too."

A soft ripple fluttered beneath her eyelids. So quick, she would have missed it if she hadn't been looking down at her aunt. "Yes. Just like that. You let them know you're there."

The shuffling at the door pulled her attention. Addie was happy to see Grace coming through. With the many nurses who had come and gone out of the room, Grace was one of her favorites. Curly blond hair and bright blue eyes matched her bubbly personality. Her smiles and laughter were easily given and needed in the days Addie stayed at her aunt's side.

Reed followed a step behind, his gaze coming right to her, concern clear in the weight of it.

"So, I understand we might have a patient who decided it's time to wake up." Grace's smile was gentle as she came to Addie's side. "Why don't you tell me what happened."

"I was sitting there," she nudged her head to the chair, "holding her hand. And her fingers moved. At first, I didn't believe it. But I felt them move again and, right before you walked in, I saw something beneath her eyelids when I was asking her not to make a fool out of me."

"Let me check some vitals." She squeezed her fingers around Addie's arm before encouraging her to move aside with a slight shift of her shoulder.

"Don't worry. If there is no change, that doesn't mean she isn't coming back. It just means her body isn't responding at the same speed as her need to wake up."

The minutes passing felt like hours as Grace carefully checked the machines crowding the side of the bed. She knew better than to get her hopes up. But it was hard with the tiny glimmer she'd been given.

Grace tapped her notes into the pad in her hands. "I don't see any change but, like I said, that doesn't mean she isn't starting to come back. You keep talking to her and encouraging her. That's the best help she'll have."

Addie hoped to hear different. It didn't change what she felt and saw. Whether there was proof in the machines, she knew the truth. Her aunt was coming around.

"I brought sweet, glorious caffeine." Both hands wrapped around a cardboard tray, Clay burst into the room, looked at those hovered around the bed, and stepped back. "I'm sorry. Am I interrupting something?"

"Of course not." Addie reacted before the others could.

Smiling, she joined him at the door. "I'm hoping one of those are for me."

Looking a bit uncertain, he held out one of the cups. "I thought we'd do a coffee day while we hung out with Rosalie."

He was the next one to come in to spend time with her. Reed made sure she was never alone. If he couldn't be with her, somebody else always was.

He'd also made sure Magic Moon was secure after the police finished their investigation. Had brought her clean clothes and the necessary toiletries she needed to at least give off the semblance of clean.

He'd held her when the worry and fear brought tears. Reassured her when she wanted to give up. Sat with her in silence when it was what she needed.

It was a strange thing. Something she'd have to sort through when her fear and worry for her aunt wasn't the ruling part of her life.

She'd spent years swearing she'd never fall victim to believing she could ever count on or trust Reed again. Yet, the temptation to do just that was growing stronger by the day. She wasn't sure if it was a good thing or another mistake.

"We'll do coffee and gossip." She slung an arm around Clay's shoulders, encouraging him in. "We know how Rosalie loves that."

He smiled, relaxing under her hold. "She always did love to chat."

"And we'll have some really good things to talk about."

"I guess I'll take that as my cue to go." Easing her away from Clay, Reed grabbed her hands in his, holding them tight as he turned her to face him. "I only need a few hours and I'll be back."

Needing to do it, regardless of the doubt, she pushed to her toes, dropping a soft kiss on his lips. "Thank you."

"For what?"

"Just—"

She shook her head. "Just, thank you."

Slowly, he bent his head, taking her mouth with his. Not caring that they weren't alone, he melded her body with his, hands pressed tight against her back as he took her with his heated kiss.

She wanted to protest when he pulled away. Wanted to forget they were in the middle of her aunt's hospital room, leaving them no other choice.

"I promise I won't be too long." He dropped one more quick peck to her lips before turning away. Waving goodbye to Clay on his way out the door, he disappeared down the hall.

"Do you need a cold shower after that?" A teasing smile spreading over his face, Clay nudged her with his elbow. "Cause if you don't, I might."

It felt good to laugh, even with all the worry and fear surrounding her.

"So," Clay took the chair Reed vacated as Addie reclaimed her own at her aunt's side. "Things are looking pretty serious between you two. Something we should know?"

"We?"

"The way I see it, AnnaBeth and I, and Teddy too, have a vested interest in you two. So, I ask again, is there something we should know?"

There wasn't. Not really. And how could she explain any of it when she didn't understand what was happening between her and Reed?

"It's complicated." She tossed out the excuse, knowing it was worthless even before Clay's brows bunched over doubtful eyes.

He didn't ask again. Just stared and waited, knowing exactly how to get to her.

"I don't know." Finally giving in, she let out a long, heavy sigh. "I'm still wondering if there is something *I* should know when it comes to Reed and I."

Reaching across the space between them, he took her hand. "Almost sounds like old times."

"I don't remember it being so confusing back then. I remember meeting him, falling madly in love, and then having my heart broken."

"And now?"

"And now, we're all grown up and it's different. It's not so easy anymore."

"If love was easy, everybody would do it." A tease sparked in his bright blue eyes. "Or at least I would."

"I never said anything about love."

"You didn't have to. That part's easy to know by anyone who looks at you and Reed together."

Uncomfortable with his words, knowing they were a truth she couldn't deny, Addie pulled her hand free, turning her attention back to her aunt. "None of it will matter in the end. Reed will go back to Washington, I'll be here, and our time together will become another memory between us."

"Is that what you want?"

She didn't have the answer for him. It was one she couldn't give even to herself.

"What I want is to have some of that coffee and gossip you promised. I think it will be just what Rosalie needs."

He took the hint with an easy-going smile. Settling back in his chair, he changed the subject. "I've heard some juicy stuff about one of Teddy's waitresses. We're talking two boy toys with another in consideration."

Addie relaxed, thankful for him and the break from discussing, or thinking about, her and Reed.

"We have prints from the baseball bat." Sipping from the black sludge they called coffee around the New Orleans's office, Jackson sat forward in her chair, resting her hands on the table.

Across from her, Reed already knew the rest of it. "You didn't find any matches?"

Shoving a hand through her hair, she shook her head. "Not one. We ran the prints through every available database and came up empty."

It was as it always had been. Glancing at his partner, the same acceptance was in Branson's gaze. They'd already traveled the same road many times, coming up with the same results.

"He was careless, leaving behind evidence," Perry joined in, pulling Jackson's coffee from her hands for a drink of his own. "Tells me he already knew there was no trail to follow that would lead to him."

"We've come to the same realization."

Perry shoved the file across the table. "If this is your guy, you tell us what we're missing."

Slow and thoughtful, Reed flipped open the file, sorting through the papers inside. They had the basics but not much more. It was, sadly, about the same he and Branson had been able to collect over the time they'd worked the case.

"He needs to be isolated." Closing the file, Reed rested a hand over it. "What he does to the women requires privacy. He can't risk being somewhere he might be overheard or walked in on."

"He's cocky," Jackson added. "If this is one in the same person we're looking for, he doesn't let fear of being caught rule him. He does what he does and shows no signs of being afraid of discovery."

"True. He's also smart enough not to take unnecessary risks if they can be avoided. We've been looking at some more of the remote places around here. Places where he'd have complete privacy. I think it would do good to extend that search."

"We're a bit short handed in agents at the moment but I think we can make it work." Perry reached across the table, pulling the file back.

"What else needs to be done?" Jackson picked up where her partner left off.

Knowing they were starting to listen to him and agree with him left Reed hopeful they'd nail the one who was creating such a hell for Addie.

"We've got a familial DNA match. Agents are already following up on that. The most we can do here is process every bit of evidence we collect and pray for a miracle."

"A miracle?" Jackson's was doubtful. "How has that worked so far?"

"It hasn't. But there is always room for hope."

"Did you see that?" Unable to remain sitting, Addie nudged Clay at her side before jumping to her feet. "Her eyes opened."

Slower than she'd been, he pushed to his feet, stood with her at the side of the bed. "Are you sure?"

"Of course, I am." She shot a dirty look his way. "It's not something I'd make a mistake about. I saw it. She opened her eyes."

Grabbing her aunt's hand, she held tight, desperate for another sign of life. "Come on, Rosalie. I know you're fighting to come back."

Though they didn't open again, she caught the flutter behind her eyelids.

"I saw that." No longer doubtful, Clay beamed a smile at her.

Curling his hands over the railing of the bed, he leaned closer, nearly pushing Addie out of the way. "I'm guessing, wherever you are right now, you can still hear me."

The emotion in his voice gripped at her heart.

"We still need you here, just so you know. I know we're all grown up now, but not a one of us is ready to go on without your guidance."

He wrapped his hand around Addie's and Rosalie's. "Imagine the trouble we could still get into without you keeping us in line."

Looking over his shoulder, he shared a smile with Addie.

"Clay is a troublemaker." She nudged him with her elbow. "Without you here, who knows what he'll get me into."

Her fingers flexed under Addie's hold.

She looked at Clay, nodding her head, letting him know they were reaching her, wherever she might be. Unlike before, when her aunt first started to show some life, she had more hope. It felt different this time.

"Should I get the nurse?"

Addie shook her head. She didn't want the intrusion of the nurse this time. "I think it's better just the three of us, right now."

"Rosalie wouldn't want us embarrassing her by telling some of her old stories in front of strangers."

The flutter came again a second before her eyes opened, giving Addie another look at her aunt's deep, brown gaze before they slipped closed again.

It took everything inside Addie not to lean over the bed rails and start shaking her aunt until she came around. She was so close. Addie could feel it.

"Is everything okay?"

Intent on waiting for another sign of life from Rosalie, neither one of them heard the movement by the door.

Turning, Addie's heart did a quick flutter at the sight of Reed coming up behind her. Cursing her reaction to him, she forced a smile. "Everything is better than okay."

She waved him over to where she and Clay stood at the edge of the bed.

Letting go of his hold around her hand, Clay stepped to the side, giving Reed room. "Seems our Rosalie's trying to come back to us."

"Is that right?" Reed looked from Addie to Clay before resting his gaze on Rosalie.

Addie vibrated with excitement beside him and he prayed she wasn't getting her hopes up. "What did the nurse say?"

"We haven't called the nurse. I didn't want anyone here. Not this time."

"Are you sure that's wise? If there's some kind of change, they'd have the best ability to let you know what's going on."

"No. They won't tell me anything more than they did the last time. She's coming back. I know she is. I don't need a nurse here to tell me to wait and see."

Arguing wasn't worth it. The truth of it was in the strength of her words. In the determination in her brown eyes.

"Okay." He pressed closer to her side, hoping for the best.

For Addie, if he could do it, he'd find a way to force her aunt back. Anticipation sparkled in her gaze. Hope teased in her voice. The thought of her being crushed if the results weren't what she was hoping for, left him desperate to do something to save her from that.

Time seemed to slow as he stood with her, staring down at her aunt. It wasn't in him to suggest maybe they sit down and wait. Addie was so intent on watching her, any such suggestions would only be met with resistance.

A light flutter moved behind her lids. So brief and quick, if he hadn't been staring as hard as he was, he would have missed it.

Addie turned to him, hope brightening her eyes. He nodded, letting her know he'd seen the same as she had.

There was another flutter before Rosalie's eyes opened. It was as if she was looking right at him. He didn't know what to say. If there was anything he should say.

Addie knew.

"Stay with us." Her voice was a desperate plea. "Don't go away again."

Her shoulders sank in disappointment as her aunt's eyes slid closed again. Draping his arms around her slender shoulders, he pulled her close, hoping to comfort.

Rosalie's eyes slowly opened again. Moving from his hold, Addie leaned over the side of the bed. "Yes. Keep your eyes open."

She fought it. Her lids started to close again before she forced them open. Looking from Addie to him, a hint of life slowly sparked in her gaze.

Though she had protested before, he turned for the door. It was time to get the nurse.

He'd only risked two visits to the hospital. It frustrated him, knowing he hadn't killed the woman. And more knowing the beating robbed him of his chance to see Addie.

She hadn't left the hospital once. After the police finished their investigation at the Magic Moon, it had been locked up tight without any sign of life inside. He'd caught McReily coming and going but never her.

It only helped fuel his desperation, threatening the control he clung to. The control he needed to keep him from making mistakes.

His need for her was becoming more of a hindrance than anything else. It burned at him. Left him aching for a chance at her.

Making himself unnoticed in the long hallway, he lingered near the door McReily entered not long ago. His first visit to the hospital had been a failure. He hadn't discovered any information about Addie or her aunt. He'd only roamed the halls, hoping for a sign for where they were.

Today he'd planned better, waiting outside the entrance until he'd caught sight of McReily entering. Falling in a few steps behind him, he'd entered as one who looked like he had a purpose for being there while carefully following the irritating agent.

It had proven to be much more helpful than his last visit. He'd heard Addie's voice outside the room where McReily disappeared, the soft sultry fall of it pulling at him, tempting him.

He pretended interest in a room listing hanging from the wall near the nurse's station as McReily came back out through the door, turning in his direction.

He turned, pulling the baseball cap he wore lower over his face. In jeans and a simple T-shirt, he blended in with most of the others moving through the hall. McReily spared him no more of a glance than anyone else he passed as he came up to the counter surrounding the nurse's station.

"Can I help you?"

With his back turned, he guessed the voice belonged to the older woman he'd seen sitting there. She was the grandmotherly sort who offered a quick smile when he'd walked past but didn't ask any questions.

"We need a nurse in Rosalie Monrose's room. She's starting to wake up."

It took everything in him not to react to the news. He wasn't sure if he welcomed it or resented it. Knowing he killed the woman would have been an extra bonus to his ego.

But with her aunt coming around, maybe Addie would finally leave the hospital. He'd gone too long without so much as a glance at her. She was like a drug now. One he needed to keep his high.

A flutter of activity erupted at the nurse's station. McReily turned back for the room, his gaze again landing on him as he passed.

He had the ridiculous sense that he lingered longer. A pause unlike the first time he passed. But McReily continued, the nurse behind the counter following.

They disappeared into the room, and he turned for the elevators. He shoved down the flicker of worry, knowing it was foolish. McReily didn't know him from the next man on the street. He'd made sure of it.

He would not waste time worrying about something that held no meaning. Only one thing demanded his concentration. After hearing her voice today, being given the hope she might finally find her way out of the hospital, he was certain he and Addie would find their shared time together very soon.

CHAPTER TWENTY-SEVEN

I t sat uncomfortable with Reed for hours.

The man he'd seen, the one standing by the nurse's station, bothered him but once the nurse reached Rosalie's room, a wave of controlled chaos took over. She hadn't slipped back again, following the nurse with her eyes as she came around to the side of the bed.

He stood with Clay, out of the way, until Addie's tears pulled at him. All she'd held in escaped once the nurse had news that wasn't wait and see.

The first few tears broke into a downpour when her aunt moved her head. A long, heavy stream of release from the fear and uncertainty she'd held inside.

Reed held her, tighter with each tear that fell. He thought of nothing else. Only her.

Clay called the others. Before long AnnaBeth rushed into the room, grabbing Addie from him. Her own tears flowed as she wrapped her arms around her friend.

Teddy wasn't far behind.

The room was crowded and full of hope, even with the warnings of not expecting too much from the nurses and doctors flowing in and out through the door.

He'd fought back the itch at the back of his mind, knowing Addie needed him. Refused to let anything take away from her relief.

The day stretched into late afternoon before the excitement began to calm. As it slowed down, his mind began to work again.

Teddy came to his side, slapping a firm hand to his back. "Now all we have to do is catch the bastard that did this to Rosalie."

It hit then, with a clarity pushing urgency through his veins. Reed went back to that moment in the hallway. Saw again the face that nagged at him.

And he knew.

He hated doing it, but he didn't have a choice. Wrapping a firm hand around Addie's arm, he urged her away from her aunt's bedside. "I have to go."

Disappointment flickered in her dark eyes. He hated it. "Okay."

He grabbed her, holding her tight. "I swear to you, if it wasn't important, I'd stay."

She pulled away enough to look up at him. "Can you tell me what's going on?'

"Not yet." He dropped a kiss on her lips. "All I can do is ask that you trust me."

He caught the quick flicker of doubt in her gaze. She pushed onto her toes, catching his mouth in a quick kiss. "Okay."

He wished he could stay longer. Wished he could tell her what was going on. It wasn't the right time. She needed to concentrate on her aunt and her recovery.

Much as he hated to, he stepped back, turned her, and encouraged her back to her aunt's bedside.

He didn't like the feeling settling in his gut. Feared what he suspected was correct. But he wouldn't react. Wouldn't do a thing until he knew for sure.

"I'm going to say it again, I think you should go home and get some real sleep." At her side, AnnaBeth tightened her hold around Addie's shoulders.

Her aunt had slipped into sleep. This time, the nurses and doctors assured her, was different than the coma. This was a sleep needed to regroup and refuel after the stress and energy it took for her to come back.

It was a normal sleep, they promised. One she didn't have to worry about.

"Not yet." She looked at her aunt, so still in the bed, hoping those in charge of her care were right.

"Are you afraid of going home?" AnnaBeth came to her side at the bed, looking down at Rosalie with affection in her eyes.

The question hit at something Addie had done her best to deny. "Why would I be afraid to go home?"

AnnaBeth wasn't fooled. "Nobody could blame you, you know, after what happened?"

"I can't leave Rosalie right now."

"I understand that. It's exactly what I'd expect from you. But—"

Her look said more than words ever could. It tugged at Addie. Shoving a hand through her hair, she resisted the urge to turn away. "I am afraid. But not for the reasons you might think."

She looked back to her aunt, smoothing stray strands of hair from her face. "I almost lost Rosalie just like I lost my mom. Magic Moon is the tie to both.

"That store has been my entire life. It's all I've ever known. I love it with the same passion my mom and aunt have always loved it.

"But what happens when I walk back in there after what happened? How do I know, just the sight of it won't make me hate a place I have always loved? What do I do if I've lost my heart for it?"

"Oh, honey." AnnaBeth threw an arm around her shoulders, pulling her close. Addie collapsed against her, fear and uncertainty she'd fought back for days finding strength.

"I'm not ready to face it." Her shoulders sagged under the weight of it all. "Not yet. Especially not with it still holding proof of what happened to Rosalie. I can't bring myself to see how much damage was done."

"You don't have to. You'll do it when you're ready. Until then, you are always welcome at my place, though I have a feeling I won't be able to compete against crawling under the covers with Reed."

She tossed Addie a knowing smile, easing the mood. They didn't need more words. In the comfort of their friendship, they stood and watched over Rosalie while she slept.

Reed didn't bother with greetings as he barreled down the hall of the Bureau's office.

"I need the sketch of the man Addie saw in her shop," he threw at Jackson as she stepped out of her office. "And a still of the man from the security footage."

He continued to the conference room. Perry caught him right before he reached the door.

"What's going on?"

"I have a bad feeling." A step ahead of him, Reed entered the room. He headed for the coffee, desperately needing the caffeine.

"Care to share." Following him to the pot, Perry poured his own cup. Together they found a seat at the table.

"As soon as Jackson is here."

As if on cue, she came through the door, dropping what he'd asked for onto the table, pushing it toward him. Aware of both Perry and Jackson's curious gaze, he looked at the sketch first then the image caught from the security tape the night Rosalie had been attacked.

It was the same man he'd seen in the hospital. "We need protection on Addie. I want at least one, if not two, agents with her at all times."

"Burke's going to need a good reason for it." Jackson leaned a hip against the edge of the table.

"Where is he?" Reed could call Marshall, get his own SAC to agree, but it would be much easier to have Burke agree to do it himself.

"Last I saw him, he was in his office, doing some half-hearted arguing on the phone," Perry answered before Jackson could.

"I'll see if he's still there." Jackson pushed away from the table.

Perry watched her go then turned back to Reed. "What's got you so worked up? Burke's a good guy but I can tell you, he's going to need more than one of your feelings to make such an order."

"He was at the hospital today." Reed stuck a finger on the corner of the still from the security video, pushed it Perry's way. "Right outside Rosalie Monrose's room."

Perry picked up the still for a better look. "You're sure it was him?"

Before Reed could answer, Burke stepped into the room, Jackson right behind him. "Good to see you, McReily. Jackson said you needed to see me."

Reed nodded at him, waiting for him to take a seat across from him. Moving the still away from Perry, he turned both it and the sketch in Burke's direction.

"This is the rendering from the sketch artist done from Addie Monrose's description of the man who entered Magic Moon." He pushed it closer.

"And this." He dropped a finger against the still. "Was taken from a security camera across the street from the Magic Moon the night Rosalie Monrose was attacked."

Burke glanced at both pictures then lifted his gaze back to Reed.

"This same man was at the hospital today while I was there, hanging around outside Rosalie Monrose's room."

That got Burke's attention. He took another look at the sketch and still in front of him. "The sketch and the still are similar but they're far from being exact matches."

Reed didn't figure he needed to respond since Burke was only stating the obvious. A witness's memory replayed to a sketch artist was never exact to the person.

"But this." Burke flipped the still around. "This is the man you saw at the hospital?"

"It's him. I'm sure of it."

Burke said nothing for a moment, looking at his own agents, silently assessing what Reed was telling him.

"If my belief that this is the same guy I have been after is wrong, which it's not. This man," he stabbed an angry finger against the still, "has proven he's a threat to Addie and her safety. She needs protection."

Silence fell around the table. Reed and the other agents waited until Burke slowly nodded. "I'll get it in place."

The relief running through Reed was swift. "I'll let Addie know."

Which would be another thing, all together. Getting Burke to agree was going to be easier than getting Addie to.

CHAPTER TWENTY-EIGHT

"You worry too much." Still weak, it took effort for Rosalie to lift her hand, dropping it over Addie's resting on her arm. "Before you know it, I'll be out of this bed and irritating you again."

For the first time in the weeks her aunt had been in the hospital, Addie was beginning to believe it. Though still tired and held back by her injuries, strength was coming through. And stubbornness as she fought each day to do more. To reach the point where she'd be allowed out of the hospital and back to the life she knew.

"If I don't worry about you, who will?" Addie threw back the line her aunt used on her many times.

She earned a soft smile. "Still no reason for you to spend all your time stuck here with me. I'm doing better every day. You heard the doctor say so. No need to hover anymore."

Even with the reassurances, the thought of leaving the hospital didn't feel right. It was a mix of loyalty to her aunt and the fear she'd admitted to AnnaBeth. Both had a hold on her that wasn't easy to shake.

Plus, there were the babysitters Reed put on her, claiming the man who'd done this to her aunt was lingering around the hospital. Only because the thought of it unnerved her did she pull back from the worst of her arguments when he introduced her to the agents assigned to guard her.

Which wasn't too hard for them since she never left the hospital. And she didn't have any plans to.

"You just want me gone so you can have my Po'boy when Anna-Beth gets back with it."

It felt good to hear Rosalie's laugh. For so long she'd feared she never would again. Her aunt was going to be okay. Relief was like a ton of bricks lifted from her shoulders.

Still, she worried. Worried about what was to come. About the future of Magic Moon. About the one who stalked her without reason and his intent if he ever truly reached her.

For now, she wouldn't let those worries weigh her down. Not when the worst of them was eased with the strength her aunt was reclaiming. The rest could wait for another day.

Though he'd dreaded it, he finally made the call.

His steps slow and measured, Reed made his way to the large, sweeping doors of the hospital. It had been his father who'd answered. Even after all the years, the rough briskness in his voice remained, threatening to pull Reed back to the teenage boy he'd been.

He hadn't expected any different. Not with Christopher McReily. He was true to his blood and heritage. The McReily's hadn't become what they were by emotions. It was cold determination, a hard belief to dismiss anything that didn't fit into their world, creating what they were.

It was also what he'd run from.

Until now.

A wave of cool air hit as he pushed his way inside. Cutting through the bright lobby for the elevators, he wondered what it would take to convince Addie to finally leave the hospital. Though he'd seen her every day, he missed her.

Missed time alone with her. Missed having her in his bed.

Tomorrow morning, he was set to meet with his parents. He wanted Addie there. Didn't have any qualms using it against her that she'd created this in the first place. But could he play it into dinner and a night together?

He could only hope.

An older couple joined him in the elevator. The man carried a flower bouquet of roses and lilies. The woman a soft teddy bear, the chocolate brown fur making Reed think of Addie's eyes.

"Our first grandchild was born this morning." The woman's smile beamed.

Realizing he'd been staring at the bear, Reed drew a smile of his own. "Congratulations."

"She's been telling everyone." The man shook his head, though his eyes sparkled with their own delight.

"Just as it should be." Reed softened his look for the woman as the elevator stopped at their floor. Excited for what waited for them, they pushed through before the doors fully opened.

They hurried down the hall, side by side, giddy with the thought of seeing their first grandchild. The doors slid closed and his thoughts went to Addie. To what it would be like to share such an experience with her.

He jerked back from the idea. He didn't know if they had a future together. Much less one that involved hurrying through a maternity ward to see their first grandchild.

Hell, the only future he was hoping for was convincing Addie to dinner and back to his bed. And even that was uncertain.

The elevator reached the next floor. Reed stepped out into the hall, noticing the absence of the agents who were to be stationed outside Rosalie's hospital room.

A hint of fear battled with irritation. He could only think of two reasons why the agents weren't where they belonged. He didn't like either one.

His steps much quicker, strides long, he made it past the nurse's station before the laughter came. It floated out the door of Rosalie's room, drawing him in.

The missing agents stood at the foot of the bed, Addie and Anna-Beth at the sides. It was good to see Rosalie sitting up, propped against pillows at her back. It was even better to hear her laughter mingle with the others.

All heads turned as he stepped further into the room. It was Addie he made a line for, needing to be near her. "Did I miss an invitation to the party?"

Her brown eyes shimmering from laughter, she shook her head. "AnnaBeth bought all of us Po'boys. Didn't feel right expecting the agents to be stuck in the hall while eating theirs."

"They've been telling us some interesting stories." Buchner's gray eyes lit with the knowledge he'd gained.

"Very interesting." Brown nodded, her own smile leaving little doubt Reed was better off not knowing what was shared.

"Don't suppose you saved my dignity while you told your stories." Unable to help himself, he pulled Addie to him, caught her lips under his.

The surprise of the kiss left Addie stumbling for a moment, trying to understand the words he'd said. He stepped back, giving her a chance to draw a breath.

"No deep secrets shared," she finally found the ability to speak. "I promise."

She shifted a step away, in need of space. It wasn't good, her reaction to him. The lies she'd told herself weren't working anymore. It was more than she'd wanted. More feelings. More need. More emotions she didn't dare try to accept.

Seeing him every day now became something she thrived on. Watching him come through the door, catching her in his deep, blue gaze, was quickly becoming the drug she wasn't sure she'd ever break free from.

"You're looking much better." Effectively doing away with the space she craved, Reed moved in, brushing against her as he leaned over the side of the bed, taking Rosalie's hand in his.

"I'm feeling better. If they'd let me, I'd go home today."

"You haven't even tried standing on your own yet. Don't rush it."

"And she hovers." Tenderness mixed with impatience in the look Rosalie tossed at Addie. "Worries, too. A bit too much if you ask me."

"Getting out of the hospital might help her ease some of that worry." Annabeth flashed a smile at the scowl Addie shot across the length of the bed.

"I can help with that." Reed slung an arm around her shoulders, pulling her close.

She would have moved away if she weren't aware of every set of eyes resting steadily on them. "I don't want Rosalie to be alone."

"Actually," her aunt was cautious as she looked at her. "I think some alone time is what I need. Some time, maybe, to process everything that happened."

The need was clear in Rosalie's eyes. She didn't want to leave her. Didn't feel right leaving the hospital without her. But she wouldn't stay if it was what her aunt wanted.

"How about dinner? With me?" The understanding in Reed's voice slid over her. "I was already planning on finding a way to convince you."

She looked at him, wondering at her options. She didn't want to go back to the Magic Moon. Wasn't ready for it yet. But a night with him, with all the emotions finding more strength every day that passed?

She could go with AnnaBeth. Her friend wouldn't have a problem with it. But she'd only be avoiding what she didn't want to face, whether it was the Magic Moon or Reed. And she'd know it. AnnaBeth would know it, and in the trueness of their friendship, would challenge her with the truth of it.

It felt as if all eyes rested on her, waiting for her response. She already knew her answer though she fought it. A night with Reed was what she craved, even in all the confusion running through.

Dangerous as it might be, it was what she needed when she was honest with herself.

"Okay. Dinner it is."

His answering smile held more than she cared to see. It reached inside her, warming her with the strength of it.

"You have your things here?" He asked a question he already knew the answer too since he'd been the one bringing her what she'd needed the past week.

She nodded.

"I need a couple more hours to work. I'll pick you up later this afternoon. You can bring what you need from here and get ready at the hotel."

Whether he intended it or not, she was relieved she wouldn't have to return to her own home to get ready. And his hotel room was much better than the small confines of the hospital.

"I'll be ready."

She saw the heat in his eyes, was prepared this time as he lowered for another kiss. Once he waved himself out the door with quick goodbyes all eyes come back to her.

"That's looking a whole lot more serious than I thought it was." Rosalie's gaze was a mix of curiosity and concern.

Addie wasn't going to discuss it, not with the agents there.

"Just a kiss or two." She shrugged, making it clear she had no desire to discuss it further.

They understood and turned the topic again to old stories. Ones of laughter and fun. Of the days when she and AnnaBeth were young, and Rosalie spent a good share of her time keeping them in line.

The easiness of it helped keep her calm as she waited for her night with Reed.

CHAPTER TWENTY-NINE

He'd planned ahead. While Addie stood inside the door, Reed cut over to the small tray waiting for them, filling two flutes from the bottle of champagne resting in a bucket of ice.

"Well," accepting the flute of bubbly liquid he held out for her, she took a slow, savoring sip. "This wasn't what I expected."

"I figured, after all the time you spent inside the hospital, this might help take the edge off while you get ready."

She enjoyed another sip. "It does. Thank you."

She moved further into the room. With all that had happened and changed in such a short amount of time, it still looked exactly as it had when she'd rushed from it, fearing for her aunt's life.

Why wouldn't it? The rest of the world hadn't changed, hadn't experienced some great shift while she'd been praying desperately for Rosalie to recover. The fear, desperation, might have made her feel different. But it didn't affect life continuing as usual while she'd sat at the edge of the hospital bed, day after day, night after night.

Dropping her bag on the edge of the bed, she went to the window, sipping from her champagne as she watched the excitement slowly building along Bourbon.

She'd missed the life, always full of so much heart and energy, within the Quarter. In her worry and fear, everything else faded away, ceased to exist. It felt right now to be back to it, even if she had hesitated and second guessed her decision.

The warmth of Reed pressed against her. Needing it, she moved back into him. His arm curled around her waist, holding her against him as they stared out the window, sipping from their flutes.

It was all she needed. The worry, the fear, the stress of so many long, painful days found its release. It shook through her, draining what she'd held for so long.

Reed didn't need to see them to know the first tears began to fall. He didn't move. Didn't try to offer words of comfort. He held her against him, letting the emotions pour from her as they needed to do.

She made no sound with her tears. Against the glass of the window, their reflection came back at him, one crying, one holding, forgotten flutes of champagne in their hands.

It was odd, realizing this was a memory he'd carry with him. It touched him somewhere deep. In a part of his heart he wasn't ready to open yet.

Holding her close, he felt the change in her. The shift from the emotions gripping her to the realization of their bodies pressed tight.

She stiffened, and for a moment, he wondered if she'd try to move away and break the hold he had on her. Instead, she turned, bringing them face to face, pushing into him.

"I should get ready." She rested the hand holding the champagne flute over his shoulder, pushed the other between them, flattening it against his chest. "But you're making it hard to do."

He arched a brow at her, careful not to spill his own champagne. "I can't bring myself to say I'm sorry. Not when I'm enjoying this."

Pushing to her toes, she brushed a soft kiss against his mouth. "I've missed you. I've missed this."

She was so beautiful. So close he could feel every delicate curve. Every soft line drawing her into the beauty she was.

Stepping back, he closed his fingers around the slender base of the flute caught between her fingers, encouraging another drink. She did so, her eyes never leaving his, making him thirsty for much more than the champagne they both finished off with one final sip.

He took their flutes, setting them on the small table pushed into the corner. Before she could move, he was back. He wanted her there, at the windows. Wanted to take her, make her his as he'd done before.

Hunger for her burned through. She didn't speak, only watched, her brown eyes wide as he wrapped his fingers with hers. With a tug, she was pressed against him. Arching her neck, she took him in with her luring gaze, rushed the hunger into desperation.

He wanted slow. Wanted to savor—here at the window, looking out over the place that first drew them together. Brought them back again.

He brushed his lips slow against hers. Her soft sigh pressed into him. It was here he belonged, she belonged. They fit like they were made for each other. Just as they always had.

She opened to him, more than ever before. He felt the shift of it. The trust. The belief in him, in them.

It poured through him. Drove him with a power, a thirst, he'd never known before. She was his. His in every way he had ever dreamed. Wanted.

Pushing her back until she was flush against the window, he took her mouth, claiming it as his own. She gave back, meeting the same need burning through his veins.

Untangling her fingers from his, she brushed her hands over his sides, curling them around his shoulders, holding on tight.

Pushing his hands through the long fall of her red hair, he pulled her away, holding her face captive. His breathing heavy, heart pounding, he said nothing as he stared into her dark eyes, a harsh truth taking over.

He'd run so far only to find where he belonged right back where he started.

He yanked her back. Desperation found a new strength, a new force, as he claimed her mouth again. Then there was nothing but the heat surrounding them so the kiss was not enough. Not nearly enough.

His mouth trailed, needing to taste her, down the curve of her chin, the gentle slope of her neck. His hands roamed, needing to feel her. The round of her shoulders. The gentle slide and dip along her sides.

Sighing, Addie fell into the sensations he created. She'd missed this. Missed him. He'd been there every day at the hospital. But this was different. This was what fueled her. Brought her to life.

He tugged at the hem of her shirt. Helping him, she slid her arms free of the sleeves, tossing it aside once he had it over her head. Then his hands were back, roaming over bare skin. Licking to life fires with every place he touched.

His thumbs brushed over her nipples through the lace of her bra. She sucked in a breath, dropping her hands over his shoulders, needing to hang on.

He smiled, quick and seductive before taking her mouth again, his hands curling to her back, flicking at the hooks for her bra.

He broke the kiss. Her bra dangled for a moment from his finger before he flicked it on top of her shirt.

"So beautiful." His deep whisper washed over her. She pressed into him, wanting more. Controlled by it.

He took. His rough palms closing over her breasts. Lips trailing over the sensitive line between her ear and shoulder, teasing, drawing more heat, more desire, until she was sure she'd burst from it.

She fumbled against the button of his jeans. He laughed at her frantic attempts. Covering her hands with his, he helped her then continued until he had them both stripped of all the clothing barriers between them.

And she realized, through the heat and desire coiling around them, she was standing naked in front of the window. Making a move for the bed, Reed wrapped a hand around her wrist.

"No. Here." He tugged on her arm. "I want to take you here."

She shook her head, but he only turned her so that she looked out the very window she was trying to avoid.

"Here," he repeated in a whisper as his strong arms wrapped around her sides, hands coming up to close around her breasts.

"Nobody can see us." He nipped at her ear, sending shivers down her spine. She saw them in the reflection against the glass. His hands on her. His mouth tasting her.

The thrill of it ran through her. For all she wanted to back away, something more kept her there, watching through the reflection as his hands slid lower. Down her sides, the firm slope of her stomach. Lower still, brushing softly against the inside of her thighs.

And they watched, eyes held against the window.

She leaned back into Reed. If it were not for his hold on her she'd be a puddle at his feet. He teased, fingers sliding slowly, so close only to drift away again. Nibbling at her neck, down her shoulders, he drove the tension until she was sure she'd burst.

"Oh...Reed. Please." She hated to be reduced to begging but she desperately needed all he promised in just his touch.

Cupping his hand around her cheek, he turned her face to him, claiming her mouth as his fingers slid inside. She moaned under the kiss, every part of her trembling.

He took, driving her higher, drawing her slowly back down. Over and over again. She couldn't get enough. Violently craved the release he so carefully kept from her.

Pressed to him, she forced her hand between their bodies. He belonged with her, as out of control as he was making her.

His own groan vibrated through the kiss as she wrapped her fingers around him, stroking the length of him. Breaking the kiss, he touched a finger to her cheek, turning her back to the window to see the torturous flames of their passion in their reflection.

The image tumbled her to a new level. Took the desire claiming her, sparking it to a new life, out of her control. She couldn't do it anymore. Couldn't last through another second of the torture. Turning away from the window, she pressed tight against Reed's chest.

"No more." She pushed on to her toes, nipped at his bottom lip. "I need—"

She didn't get to finish. Growling, Reed curled his hands behind her, lifting her from her feet, moving her until her back pressed flush against the window.

Without a chance to catch her breath, he was inside her. She sucked in hard, fighting back the quick hit of desire, tempting her to tumble before they ever got started.

Locking her legs behind his back, trusting him to hold her up, she closed around him.

He nibbled at her bottom lip. "You rule me."

Pleasure mixed with frustration in his words. It struck her hard, shoving the ache for him deeper. To places she could no longer keep protected.

He moved. A slow shift, drawing out only to smoothly slide back in. She stayed with him, clenching around him, rising higher and higher with each push deeper.

Somewhere in the back of her mind was the reminder they were bared at the window. It no longer mattered. Not now. Not when Reed took her higher and higher until tension pumped hard, driving her to the edge she craved on a primal level.

"Look at me." His words were a snap through the heated air surrounding them.

She did as he asked, her gaze tangling with his deep, blue eyes. She saw so much. Felt so much. The fire coming back at her pushed her closer, desperately craving all he offered.

He held her with his body and his gaze, loving her with both. Higher and higher he took them. Every thrust burning a new fire. Every flash of desire sinking deep inside.

And then there was no room for thought. No room for anything but how he made her feel. How her blood sizzled with him tight inside her. Taking her, over and over, until she was sure she'd go crazy from it.

She didn't want it to end. Didn't want to release what built inside. But she didn't have a choice. It came at her, raging and fierce, seeking escape, driving her over the edge with a tortured gasp of pleasure.

Reed went with her, calling out her name, tightening his hold around her. The room spun as they tumbled, air sucking in around them, leaving them the only two in the center of the fierce heat they'd created.

It was a slow ride back to normal breathing. Her heart pounded against her chest, matching the beat of Reed's as she clung to him, her head buried in his shoulder.

Something tangled inside her. Lifting her head, she caught his eyes, still burning hot.

"I love you." The words poured out. She couldn't stop them or the emotion bursting inside.

Time froze. Reed only stared, his gaze hard and fierce. Then his mouth was on hers, taking her in, claiming her.

He said nothing. No return of the love she'd declared.

She fought back the hurt. It had been a risk. Perhaps, a foolish one. The words came because the feeling left her no other choice. She would not let it be ruined because he didn't share the same.

It wasn't like she was fooled into believing anything was different between them. She reminded herself of that as he slowly eased her back to her feet, his hold on her still strong.

"I should probably get ready."

She couldn't look him directly in the eye. It was foolish. After some time alone, she'd be back to her normal self. It's not like she was the only woman who had declared her love for a man only to be met with silence. And with her and Reed, it wasn't like she should be surprised by it.

He held her, tightening his arms around her sides when she made a move to get past. His eyes shadowed with emotions she couldn't read, she waited, foolishly hoping.

The silence soon weighed too heavy. Needing space, she gently slipped from his hold and escaped into the bathroom.

Reed made sure she'd have her favorites for dinner.

Grabbing an oyster from the platter between them, he watched her across the table. She'd been quieter since they'd left the hotel. He didn't need to be a genius to know why.

Hearing those three words come from her mouth had nearly knocked him over. He'd never thought he'd deserve them again.

He'd not only heard them but felt the power and truth behind them.

She loved him. It did ridiculous things to him to know that. To be able to live in that reality again.

And yet, he hadn't been able to give her back what she had given him.

"It feels wrong to be here, enjoying this," Addie swept her hand toward the balcony where they sat, looking down on the slowly quieting sidewalks along Royal, "with Rosalie stuck in the hospital."

Reaching across the table, Reed took her hand. "She needed time alone. You heard it yourself."

"Still feels wrong." Picking up an oyster, she dropped it on the small plate in front of her.

He wished he could chase away the struggles running through her, especially knowing he held his own blame for them. If he could, he'd reach across the table, take her hand and promise all she wanted to hear.

But it wasn't fair. Wasn't right. He couldn't promise what was in his heart until he had answers. She still had a crazed killer after her. He had the meeting with his parents looming over him. And who knew what the future had in store. He couldn't imagine leaving her again. But there was nothing certain. Nothing sure. To give her love only to rip it away a second time wasn't something he was willing to do.

"She's a tough woman. I know where you get it from." Grabbing the wine bottle at the edge of the table, he topped off their glasses. "Maybe you'd loan some of that toughness to me tomorrow."

She sucked on her oyster, curious eyes meeting his over the shell. "What do you mean?"

He hesitated, second-guessing his decision to bring her along. The past week had been enough for her. Did he want to add to it?

But he couldn't fight the feeling he needed her for this. "I'm meeting with my parents tomorrow. At their house. My childhood home."

Picking up his wine glass, he watched her carefully over the rim. "I was hoping you'd go with me."

"Do you really think that's a good idea?"

"I do." He didn't question what he felt was right. His family judged her, shunned her. If they showed signs of repeating that past, there would be no reason for any further discussion. He'd leave, happily take Addie with him, and never look back.

Running her finger along the top rim of her wine glass, she stared at him for several silent minutes. "I suppose, since I encouraged this, I can't really argue."

"There's that. But that's not why I'm asking you to go."

Addie wasn't sure she wanted to know the reasons. Wasn't sure she should even go. She'd pushed for him to see his parents again but had never thought she'd be part of it. Was pretty sure she didn't want to be.

Reed reached across the table, grabbing her hand. "I want them to see you. Who you are. Who they so wrongly attacked all those years ago."

She felt the old anger in him as he sucked in a harsh breath, easing it away.

"I need to see how they react to you now." He let go of her hand, turned away so she couldn't see what lingered in his gaze. Distracting them both, he grabbed another oyster from the middle of the table and dropped it on his plate.

She wanted to reach for him again, wishing the contact between them was back. She folded her hands in her lap, understanding it was for the best.

"Years ago, I screwed up. I won't do it again."

He sucked the oyster from its shell then wrapped his long fingers around the stem of his wine glass. His eyes never left hers as he took a sip.

"I need to see their reaction to you. I need to know before I let anything go any further."

And in that, how could she argue. All she'd once hoped he had done, he was offering it now. "I'll go."

"Thank you."

She nodded, doing her best to accept what she'd agreed to. She wasn't sure it was the best decision. But it was done. There was no going back.

Maybe meeting his parents, seeing where he came from, would give her a better idea of the man she'd never stopped loving. Feared she'd lose all over again.

He'd thought he could protect her from what was meant to come.

Sitting on the balcony, watching the couple a few tables down, he sipped slowly from his beer. They didn't know he was there. Didn't know he watched.

He saw all of it. Not even those pesky guards McReily set into place could deter him from what was his.

And Addie was his. He couldn't deny the truth burning stronger and stronger inside him with every passing day. That same smile she gave to McReily, sitting across from her, would soon be his. The softness in her voice, traveling to him with the gentle breeze, would be only for his ears when he was done.

For as wise as McReily believed himself to be, he would always be a step behind. Always find himself on the losing end when it came to what needed to be done.

They'd have tonight. They'd have the coming days given to them. But the time was drawing closer. Fate was calling. Soon Addie would be his. Soon all that was meant to be would finally come to reality.

CHAPTER THIRTY

Addie sipped from her coffee, staring past Reed into nothing. The streets filled with tourists faded away, leaving only the blank canvas of her own thoughts.

She should be floating, hanging on to the wonder the night had brought. After dinner, Reed took her back to the hotel, loved every inch of her body as if they hadn't thoroughly enjoyed each other only hours before.

Every time she told herself she didn't care, that she hadn't expected anything different, it tore at her knowing her vow of love wasn't met with an equal sharing.

She wasn't going to dwell on it. What had been done was done. She didn't regret telling him. But she'd be more careful from now on. Her mind was already heavy with so many other things. She didn't need to take on more.

Worry for Rosalie continued though she'd seen for herself, earlier in the morning, her aunt was getting better and stronger by the day.

She'd been insistent on stopping at the hospital before they did anything else. Reed hadn't argued, understanding her need to be there after her first night away.

The doctor had been there when they'd arrived, finishing his check-up. A few more days, he promised, before Rosalie would be free to go. For Addie, it brought worry. For her aunt, a hopeful glee to her dark eyes.

And then she'd been shooed away again for the day she had planned with Reed. A day she continued to second guess the decisions she'd made.

"Trust me, meeting my family on an empty stomach is not a good idea." Reed pushed the omelet she'd barely touched closer.

She wasn't sure meeting his family with a full stomach was a good idea either. She picked up her fork and turned away from the sidewalk, taking a bite while Reed nodded with satisfaction.

So much of her wanted to back out. To tell him she'd changed her mind. For reasons she couldn't explain, she didn't. Instead, she picked at her omelet, sipped from her coffee, and dreaded the time that passed, bringing them closer to heading off for a part of Reed's life she'd never known. Wasn't sure she wanted to.

Uptown may have been his home while he was growing up, but the Quarter would always have his heart.

Suffocation from his younger years returned as he drove down streets lined with thick heavy trees standing guard over old, majestic homes.

Turning onto Audubon, he brought them into the heart of where the wealth and prestige of a family name weighed heavy. Along this quiet exclusive stretch of road entitlement reigned, drawing in those with old money. With a history to New Orleans and the businesses and industries that helped build it.

Old resentment, anger, threatened to return, drawing him back into the young man who'd turned and walked away all those years ago.

He glanced at Addie in the seat next to him, taking it all in. Twisting her fingers in her lap, she tried to smile, but it didn't do much good. "I always knew your family was rich. But I don't think I ever realized just how rich."

He reached over the middle console, resting his hand on her leg to calm her. "Having money isn't always what it's made out to be."

She looked at him, dark eyes probing deep. "How did you end up so different? You and Teddy?"

Reed shrugged. "Teddy's family was far enough removed, he wasn't born into the same dynamics and expectations. There's still money. He has a share of the McReily fortune. But it's nowhere close to what the immediate family claims."

"And you?"

He wasn't sure of the answer. "I don't know how different I really was. Not to start. It was the only life I'd ever known, so it felt normal."

"For you, it *was* normal." Addie looked at him as he slowed for the upcoming drive. "Just like my life growing up in the Quarter was normal for me."

"It was. Still, I was suffocated by it. That's when I found my escape with Teddy."

"I remember, but...oh my."

Distracted by the old, majestic Oaks arching over the drive, she turned away, staring out the window as they slowly passed.

The house had changed little over the years he'd been gone. Long, sturdy columns rose to the black slate roof. White brick shimmered under the rays of sun breaking through the tree branches.

He stopped in front of the gray-stone path. More flowers had been added in the years he'd been gone. Bright vibrant colors everywhere. Hanging from the long, wide terrace. Curled around it in patches of bright yellows and vibrant reds.

They had a gardener, but the flowers were her his mother's work. Tending them was one of the rare occasions where she didn't take advantage of the help they had.

Beside him, Addie let out a nervous breath. "It's—"

She looked at the large house, the surrounding grounds, where he'd grown up, taking it all in. "It's beautiful. But a bit intimidating."

She shook her head, trying to grasp this part of Reed's life. It was one thing to hear his tales of the house he grew up in. It was another to see it for herself.

It was more than the size of it and the proof of the many generations that had aged it far beyond a century. You didn't grow up where she had and not come across the old, stately homes. She used to look at the windows, and the lights glistening beyond them, and wonder about those who lived inside. About what their lives might be like in something so different than anything she'd ever known.

This was different. Reed was one of those she'd wondered about. He came from a life so different than hers. One she'd only been able to guess about until now.

"You ready for this?" Resignation and reluctance tumbled in his voice as he turned off the car, staring hard at the house.

"Wait." She laid a hand over his arm, keeping him in his place.

He dropped his hand from the door handle, looking at her, curiosity in his gaze.

"I asked you what made you different and you never gave me an answer." Sliding her hand down his arm, she curled her fingers around his.

"It wasn't about your childhood, not really. It's about who you are inside. The man you became when you walked away from all of this."

She used her free hand to wave at the house. "Like you said, this was your normal. Most people, myself included, stay with our normal. With what we know. You didn't."

He tensed. He wasn't so easily accepting what she had to say. She wanted him to hear it before they walked back into the house he'd avoided for so many years.

"That's what makes you different. When most would have come running back to this, you didn't. Instead, you made a new life for yourself. You faced obstacles you didn't have to face to be someone else."

"That matters." Leaning over, she pressed a gentle kiss to his rough cheek. "I hope you'll remember that."

He grabbed her before she pulled away. Cupping a hand around both cheeks, he held her, staring into her eyes, his gaze full of so many different emotions. His lips found hers, sharing with her what he couldn't with words.

He hadn't expected to see his mother on the other side of the door.

He'd have first guessed Jack, their butler of so many years, was no longer working for the family if he hadn't caught sight of him hovering behind his mother's shoulder. His surprise matched Reed's.

Someone other than Jack welcoming those who came to the door rarely happened.

It had been that way since his childhood. His parents in the front parlor whenever guests came to call. Jack always at the door, greeting them, leading them to where his parents waited.

This was different, setting him off from everything he was prepared for.

She was beautiful standing in the open door, the lights behind haloing her in an almost glorifying light. He was swept back to the small boy he'd been, so in awe of his mother. Of the grace and beauty she carried.

It was an awkward moment. Neither seemed to know how to react. How to step out of the past and greet one another in the present.

"Mrs. McReily, it's so nice to finally have the chance to meet you." Addie pressed in front of him, holding out her hand.

It surprised his mom as much as it did him. It was what was needed. He didn't doubt they'd both agree on that. Finding her normal self, she flashed a proper smile, held out her own hand.

"It's nice to meet you as well. Please, come in."

She moved aside, giving them room. Addie waited until he stepped up beside her before entering with him at her side.

Stepping into the foyer, crystal chandelier hanging, wide, curving staircase leading to the open floor above, he was swept back to childhood.

There was no running into the house as a small boy, dropping whatever he might have carried along the way. Clutter wasn't allowed. Dirt of any kind, taboo.

Not that he'd been given too many chances to get dirty. Life growing up had been a constant schedule of all that was right and proper for a young boy who carried the McReily name.

He shook the memories off. Now was not the time to go back.

"Rosie set us up some drinks and snacks in the back parlor. Your father is waiting for us there."

Grabbing Addie's hand, he followed his mother down the long hallway. She had a slower step than she'd once had. And though he was sure she fought it with all the money at her disposal, he didn't miss the lines of age slowly finding their way to her face.

It struck him odd, having a touch of sadness at the realization his mother was growing older. It shouldn't matter to him. He didn't think he'd care. But he couldn't deny the small part inside where it mattered. Where it became a reality, facing the fact his parents weren't immune to the natural flow of life and the aging that came with it.

Where he noticed the change in his mother, there wasn't much change to be seen through the house. It was a strange sensation, passing rooms so familiar yet so foreign. So much was still the same as his memories.

The crisp white walls his mother insisted on, claiming it didn't take away from the colors of the artwork she hung. The gray marble floors softened by elaborate Persian and Oriental rugs.

Some of the furniture and décor had changed. But it still carried the same high cost and discomfort. The pieces he'd been scolded for being too rough with as a boy. You sat properly or you didn't sit at all. And there was no rough-housing or running allowed out of fear of breaking one of the dynasty vases or sending the Tiffany silver tea set to the hard floor below.

Like the rest, he shook it off, reminding himself again it wasn't the time for it.

He caught Addie's curious glance as he made a visible turn away from the dark wood filled dining room. Tugging on her arm, he kept her moving with him, knowing she had questions he simply couldn't answer.

His mother paused at the arched entryway to the back parlor, a silent invitation for them to enter ahead of her. He barely made it a step in before being grabbed and pulled away from Addie.

"Look at you. Just look at you." Rosie held him at arm's length for a moment, her eyes misting with unshed tears, before yanking him in for a hug.

All kinds of emotions rushed over him as he closed his arms around her, holding her tight. Of all his memories growing up inside this house, it was the ones with Rosie bringing the smiles, the laughter.

He was only two when she'd come to them as their housekeeper. He wasn't part of her responsibility. His parents always faithfully employed nannies for that. For Rosie, it didn't matter. She'd loved him and spoiled him from her first day.

The chocolate chip cookies made just for him and snuck into his hands when his newest nanny believed sweets were the destruction of all children. The secret nights of watching movies together in her room when another nanny stuck strong to only educational programming.

She'd been his savior, his partner in crime, and most importantly, his friend.

"You're all grown up." Backing away, she brushed at the tears sliding down her cheeks. "And you brought a beautiful lady with you."

She slowly let go of him, turning for Addie. He caught her wide-eyed look a second before Rosie grabbed her in a hug.

And then he saw neither of them as his father pushed up from his chair.

His show of age was much more than his mother's. He looked more like Reed's memory of his grandfather. A man with money to help ease the lines but still edged with the hardness of life. He didn't smile. Didn't show any emotion as he approached.

He knew Rosie released Addie when her hand slid into his, offering support. He didn't turn to look at her. Didn't move his gaze away from the man slowly coming his way.

What he expected he didn't know. What he wanted was even more unsure. The most he could do was stand and stare at the man who looked so much like the person he saw every morning when he looked in the mirror.

He stopped with only a few feet between them. Reed forced out the breath caught in his lungs, feeling like a small child all over again facing the fierce power of his dad, wondering what would come next.

For all he had prepared for the moment, he wasn't ready when his dad reached out, curling his hands over his arms, pulling him close.

Time stopped. Nobody else was there. Just the two of them as his dad pulled him into an awkward hug, a show of affection once so unlike him.

Rosie sniffled beside him as his dad pulled away. Feeling like he was in some sort of time-warp where nothing was as it was supposed to be, it took him a moment to regain his footing and think straight.

"I...it's good to see you, dad."

"And this must be Addie." He stepped over to where she continued to stand close at Reed's side, holding out his hand.

He took advantage of the moment, getting his balance again. No matter the greeting, he couldn't afford to let his guard down. Not yet. It was one thing to miss each other and have the emotions. It was another to figure out how the past was going to sort itself out for the present and future.

She was treading through new waters.

Addie took a long look around the room where they'd gathered, sunlight washing over her.

It wasn't a room exactly. More a large open space at the back of the house. Long windows brought in warmth from the sun, rays dancing over the polished oak table where they sat.

Freshly cut flowers spilled from crystal vases in the middle of the table and the long bureau centering the opposite wall. They were the only splash of color in the soft greys and blacks of the furniture, the rug stretched over the marble floor.

Nothing was out of place. Everything was perfectly set to create the right balance. The proper appearance.

Blanche, Reed's mother, held out the silver platter carefully lined with tiny cakes and cookies. "Rosie's been baking since she learned you were coming."

Though nerves caused her stomach to roll uneasily, Addie took a chocolate frosted cake from the platter, setting it on the small plate in front of her.

Coming up behind her, Rosie poured coffee in her cup before moving on to the others. There were small glasses for juice as well, if she preferred, but the cake and coffee were already enough for a stomach that didn't feel exactly right. She wasn't going to risk more sugar to aggravate.

Under the table, Reed squeezed a hand around her leg. He looked better than when he'd first entered his childhood home. More put together than the hint of confusion and heart-deep emotion she'd seen when his father grabbed him in a hug.

"How is your aunt doing?" With the finest polish of a well-raised, wealthy woman, Blanche softly pinched two fingers around the handle of her coffee cup, lifting it to her lips. "I heard the news about what happened. I am so sorry."

"Thank you." Knowing she'd never be able to match the dignity and grace of Reed's mother, she decided it wasn't worth trying as she cupped a hand around her own cup. "She's doing much better. Her doctors say she'll be home soon."

"It was a sad thing. I saw the story of it on the news." Christopher McReily, a mirror image of his son, shook his head.

He turned to Reed, carefully watching him. "This is what you do now? Take care of cases such as this as a police officer."

Stiffness pushed through Reed. She reached over and dropped a comforting hand on his leg.

"I'm not a police officer." Without looking at his dad, he grabbed a cookie from the tray. "I'm an agent with the FBI."

"And I'd bet you're the best they've got." Standing behind him, Rosie dropped a quick kiss on the top of his head, making Addie smile. He was still the little boy she'd always known. It was in the tenderness and love in her eyes whenever she looked at him.

Reaching behind him, Reed grabbed Rosie's hand, giving a gentle tug before letting go. "I like what I do. It's good for me."

His dad looked at him, a long, probing stare. For a moment there was only silence. Lifting his coffee cup, he pushed it at Reed in a half toast. "Then, I'll have to agree with Rosie. I'm sure you're the best they've got."

Across from Addie, his mother said nothing. A mixture of disappointment and uncertainty lingered in her eyes. Still, she drew a smile for her son before turning away.

Addie looked at Reed. He noticed too. A bit of doubt hit. She'd wanted this for him. Had encouraged him to have this moment with his parents. But she wondered now if his mother would ever see the amazing man her son had become. If she'd ever be able to accept that what she expected for him and what he needed for himself were two things that would never meet.

"So, how long will you be in town?" Reed's dad took his own cookie from the platter.

It was a question with no answer. Reed shook his head.

"Don't have a set time. I need to take care of some things here before I think of going back to D.C."

"Do you like it there?" His mom sipped from her coffee, watching him carefully over the rim.

Reed didn't answer. Grabbing a cake to join his cookie from the tray, he used the excuse to stall for time. A month ago, if the same question had been asked, his answer would have been quick and true.

He loved working and living in D.C. He'd set up and created a new life there he didn't regret. But now—

"It's a good place. I like the years I've been there."

It was an answer, even if not the one his mom might have been seeking.

He didn't have more of an answer for himself, much less his parents. The thought of leaving Addie, going back to D.C. and the life he left behind, clawed at him. Left him wondering where he would ever find what he'd twice found with her.

There was nothing he could promise or commit to yet. If he could, he'd have already returned Addie's words of love, giving back to her the precious gift she'd given to him.

As if reading the contradictions warring inside his head, Rosie dropped a gentle arm around his shoulders. "New Orleans is a good place, too."

She held him close while resting her gaze on Addie. "What's here might be even greater than what you had."

He couldn't answer. Didn't dare to answer.

He couldn't give any of them what they wanted. Not yet. Not while so much uncertainty still lingered over him. Over Addie, her safety, and the place she found again in his heart.

CHAPTER THIRTY-ONE

After leaving Reed's parents, Addie insisted on going back to the hospital, only to be chased away again. Her aunt's friends had come, smuggling in two bottles of their favorite red wine. Boiled crawfish, and a pan overflowing with bourbon bread pudding covered the small bed tray. Enticing smells filled the room, teasing every stomach, whether empty or full.

The nurses turned a blind eye after a promise of getting their own share of the goodies. It would be a party of old friends. And Addie was again convinced by her aunt to go out, enjoy herself, and stop worrying so much.

She sat in Teddy's bar, sandwiched between AnnaBeth and Reed while Clay created his magic on stage.

"Enough." AnnaBeth stuck a bony elbow in her side, lifting her wine glass and pushing it into her hands.

"You're worrying," She picked up her own glass, held it out to tap against Addie's. "Just enjoy. You deserve it."

She caught Reed's answering smile beside her. She was outnumbered. It would never go completely away, not all the worry she carried with her aunt still in the hospital. But she reminded herself Rosalie would be out in a day or two. That she had her own friends surrounding her just as Addie did.

It was enough to know. To relax. To enjoy the night she had with those closest to her heart.

And Clay providing the entertainment made it that much better.

By the end of his set, it was time for another round.

"I'll take care of it." Reed pushed away from the table. "Need to talk to Teddy, anyhow."

Addie felt the tension that had been with him since leaving his parents. "I think he's in need of some family input."

"How did it go today?" Catching Clay's attention, AnnaBeth waved him over.

"It was," she struggled for the right words. "It was needed."

"So, no out crying of love or begging for a decade worth of forgiveness?" AnnaBeth pushed out the chair next to her, making room for her brother.

Addie thought of Rosie. She definitely loved him. "I think it was hard for both Reed and his parents. I guess I can't say it would have been any other way, considering the circumstances."

She smiled at Clay as he sat down. "It was his dad, more than his mom who seemed willing to heal old wounds. I'm not sure she's ready to let go of the Reed she wanted him to be instead of the one he's become."

"So, it's more wait and see." AnnaBeth set her empty glass back on the table, her fingers lingering around the stem. "At least it's a start."

"Yes. It was a start. A good one, I think."

AnnaBeth's curious gaze pierced deep. "Reed and his parents aren't all. I can see it."

No. Addie wasn't going to go there. She refused.

AnnaBeth turned a charming smile on her brother. "You should join Reed at the bar. Let him know you expect him to include a drink for you in the next round."

Clay looked from his sister to Addie, getting the hint. "I think I'll do that. Would hate to waste what break I have thirsty."

And he was gone, leaving Addie alone with AnnaBeth and her probing eyes, looking deep into places she wasn't ready for anyone to see.

"So, you can tell me easily. Or I can push and irritate you until you explode and end up telling me anyways."

That would be exactly the way it would go. Addie wasn't foolish enough to believe otherwise.

Desperately wishing for another glass of wine, she sucked in a harsh breath, letting it out slowly. "I told Reed I loved him."

"And?"

"And nothing." She fought back the hurt threatening to rise. "Absolutely nothing. He kissed me and that was it."

"He loves you. I don't doubt that."

Addie tried brushing it off, but AnnaBeth shook her head. "You need the words. I get that. I understand it, especially when you say it first."

"Maybe we're both reading him wrong. Maybe whatever this is between us really is nothing more than a fling for him. A way to pass the time while he's here."

"Oh, bullshit." AnnaBeth's voice rose, catching the attention of those seated next to them.

"You've got some pity going. I can't blame you for it. I figure, if there ever came some crazy time when I actually told a man I loved him, I'd want it back, too."

Addie stared into her empty glass. "I feel weak, like I did when he first left. I don't like feeling that way. I've already fought it in the past. I don't like fighting it again."

"Oh, hun." AnnaBeth leaned over the side of her chair, wrapping a tight arm around Addie's shoulders.

He felt off tonight.

Reed couldn't pin it down to one thing.

His mind buzzed, with Addie, his parents, the killer who'd brought him back here.

Waiting for Teddy to bring the beers and wine he'd ordered, he turned, catching AnnaBeth as she swung an arm around Addie's shoulders, pulling her close.

He wondered what they talked about. What brought the show of affection. He wanted to be there. To hear them. Know what they discussed.

It wasn't for him. It was the reason, he was sure, why Clay was with him now instead of at the table. He'd been sent away to give them privacy.

"You've got some serious brooding going on." Clay pushed a beer his way as Teddy set them down on the bar.

"I know I'm not blood," he tossed a look at Teddy as he turned to get the wine. "But I'm here if you need an ear."

"Thanks." He lifted his glass, tapped it against Clay's. "I appreciate it. I think, right now, we need to get the wine to the girls before they start getting cranky."

He took the glasses as soon as Teddy slid them across the bar. "I will definitely remember the offer. It means a lot to me."

He pushed up from his stool, carefully balancing his beer and the two glasses of wine between his hands.

AnnaBeth and Addie separated as he and Clay returned.

"Oh, thank goodness." AnnaBeth took her wine before he had a chance to set it down.

Setting Addie's down in front of her, he took his seat at her side. A hint of sadness shimmered in her eyes. She quickly shook it away, smiling. "We needed this."

He didn't want to think of the sadness. Didn't want to admit to the guilt, knowing he was most likely the reason for it.

"You guys sticking around for a bit?" Clay worked quick on his beer, minutes ticking away until he was due back on stage.

"Don't plan on going anywhere for a while." Proving her point, AnnaBeth settled back in her seat.

Reed glanced at Addie, got the nod. "Seems we'll be hanging around, too."

"Good." He finished off the rest of his beer in one large gulp. "I've got a surprise coming."

He looked at his sister, his smile a bit too cocky. Too full of something it was clear only he and AnnaBeth shared.

"Want to tell me what that's about?" Reed tossed his head in Clay's direction as he headed back for the stage.

"Let's just say, I'm glad I didn't have to make up some reason to keep you two around. That was plan B if you'd decided to leave."

"What in the world are you talking about?" Addie looked from Reed to AnnaBeth. "What am I missing."

AnnaBeth smiled. Reaching over, she pressed two fingers to the bottom of Addie's glass. "Drink up and enjoy yourself. That's all you need to worry about."

Only because she suddenly had a need for it, Addie did as she was told, taking a sip from her wine. She knew her best friend well enough to know there would be no getting anything out of her.

Reed glanced at her over the rim of his own glass, letting her know he had no more idea than she did.

Clay broke into his next set of songs, drawing the dancers back to the floor as the beat pierced through the bar. One song led directly into another. Addie drank from her wine, wishing she knew what to expect.

Teddy joined them, his own beer in his hand. He shared a look with Annabeth, pulling the chair out next to her and settling in.

So, it was only her and Reed being kept in the dark. Addie's curiosity peaked more. On stage, Clay continued to sing, easily flowing from a heavy rock song to a love ballad.

When he finished the last note, he looked back at his band members with a nod. Applause broke out and he waited, his eyes falling on Addie for a moment before turning back to the heart of the crowd.

"Thank you." He wrapped his hand around the pole for the microphone, placing it back into place. "We'll be back with more in just a few. But first, I have some news to share."

He waited until the roar settled to a reasonable volume. "Here in the Quarter, we have many things that make us great. Make us unique. One of those things is an amazing little shop called Magic Moon."

His gaze came back to Addie. Others stared, following his lead.

"The store is owned and run by my amazing childhood friend, Addie. And her wonderful aunt, Rosalie."

She tried not to fidget. Reed rested a hand over her leg under the table, squeezing lightly. Through the corner of her vision, she caught AnnaBeth moving closer, smiling wide. Across from her, Teddy looked from his cousin to her, his gaze as excited as the others.

"Not too long ago," Clay drew the attention back to his place on stage. "Somebody tried to destroy all that was good about the Magic Moon. In the process, they terribly injured Rosalie."

Tears threatened. Addie fought them back. Picking up her glass of wine, she used it to soothe back the emotions threatening to escape.

"I'm so very happy to say Rosalie is going to be okay."

Applause erupted and Clay stepped back, allowing it for a moment before coming back to the microphone. "Unfortunately, Magic Moon hasn't yet had the same recovery. So much was destroyed and ruined. And, because Addie has dedicated her time to her aunt's recovery, it remains that way."

He looked back at her, his eyes softening with the memory of old friendships and the love that comes with them. "So, myself, my sister," he pressed a hand to his lips, blew AnnaBeth a kiss.

"And Teddy, the owner of this wonderful bar." He pointed a finger to where Teddy sat across from Addie. "Came together and decided we needed to do something for one of our oldest and dearest friends."

She wasn't going to cry. Even as she demanded it, the first tear slipped free, slowly sliding down her cheek. AnnaBeth took her hand and pulled it into her lap, holding tight.

"Tonight, and tomorrow night I'll be here." Turning back to his band, he waited while his drummer pulled out a bright red plastic bucket. "And we'll be raising money for our wonderful friends and the Magic Moon."

He set the bucket on the edge of the stage and pulled out his wallet from his back pocket. Pulling out a twenty-dollar bill, he waved it at the crowd before dropping it into the bucket. "Every little bit will help."

Some stepped up to drop in money before he ever finished. Addie's throat tightened.

"We're not done there." Clay's gaze came back to hers as AnnaBeth's hold tightened more.

"On Saturday, once we've gathered some much-needed money to help them out, we're going to put in some of our own time to get them back on their feet.

"My sister and I, my band here," he swept his arm behind him, "will be joining Teddy and the workers from the bar to help rebuild Magic Moon. Together, we will show whoever did this horrible deed that they can't and won't win."

The answering applause shook the bar. Addie couldn't speak. Couldn't do anything but sit with tears running down her face as the weight of many eyes turned to her.

"I just—"

Choking on a sob, she looked at AnnaBeth.

"And this, ladies and gentlemen," Clay went back to the crowd in front of him. "Is truly a historic event. We've made our dear Addie speechless."

Laughter and applause mixed, swirled around her. AnnaBeth let go of her hand, grabbing her in a hug instead.

Addie cried. Because, at that moment, she could do nothing else.

In the far shadows of the bar, he clapped, not wanting to draw attention for being the only one who didn't.

So, they were doing a fundraiser for her. Helping her and her aunt rebuild Magic Moon. It was a nice sentiment, he supposed. Not one he'd ever lower himself to.

It was an opportunity, he realized, nursing his beer.

He looked for Addie through the dim light, found her with tears running down her cheeks. Yes, there could be something here. A chance opening its way for him.

The applause died down. The band picked back up the music, filling the bar with a pounding rhythm. From his place in the shadows, he watched those around the table. McReily and that cousin of his. Addie and her friend.

While he watched, his mind worked. He had a plan. Things needed to be taken care of. Ideas needed to be meshed out. This rebuild of the Magic Moon was exactly what he needed to finally bring about what he had in store for Addie.

CHAPTER THIRTY-TWO

A ddie was restless. She hated it.

Forcing a smile, she shifted from foot to foot where she stood inside her aunt's hospital room. It was a full room, overflowing with anticipation.

Rosalie was being released. The wonderful nurses who had tended to her worked hard to get her back to the Magic Moon before those coming to help rebuild would arrive.

"She's going to be fine." Draping a comforting arm around her shoulders, Reed lowered his mouth to her ear so only she could hear. "Her doctors are right, home is where she needs to be. She'll do better at her recovery in her own surroundings."

Addie nodded. He was right. The doctors were right. Still, she worried.

How could she not?

She looked at Rosalie, sharing a private joke with AnnaBeth. Her smile so real, so true. They both lifted their gazes together, looking directly at her.

"I told you." AnnaBeth gently pushed an elbow into Rosalie's side. "She's a mess from worrying about you."

The look in Rosalie's eyes was soft and tender. "She'll worry for some time, I'm sure."

Using the cane they'd given her, she worked her way around the foot of the bed, reaching out for Addie with her free hand. "Just as I'll continue to worry."

It took effort. Addie's heart ached as her aunt leaned forward, sweeping a soft kiss over her cheek.

"Hey, what's this?" Clay burst into the room, Teddy a step behind. "I thought you'd be celebrating getting out of this place."

"I am." Rosalie reached up as Clay came closer. Curving a palm around the side of his face, she gave his cheek a pat. "I don't know how to thank all of you for what you're doing."

"Consider it a thank you for not kicking our butts all those times we deserved it."

Addie hugged him, thankful for her friends and what they were doing. Clay's efforts raised over five thousand dollars. And with AnnaBeth's experience and knowledge, today was organized down to the very last detail.

And her aunt would be okay. A glimmer was coming back to her eyes. A spark of life shimmered around her.

"We've got a throne set up for you, Miss Rosalie." Teddy came around her and Clay, wrapping an arm around her aunt's waist and dropping a kiss on top of her head. "You'll get to sit inside the Magic Moon and keep us all in line."

"Ha." Rosalie swatted at him. "Like that has ever worked."

Things were going to be okay. With those she had around her, how could they not be?

Agents were posted at every entrance to the Magic Moon and the apartment upstairs. Reed refused to take any chances.

The Bureau had more than it ever had before, and still there was nothing leading them in a direction to find the man terrorizing Addie. No matter what lead they had, it always proved to go nowhere, leaving him more and more frustrated as every day passed.

"You're going to scare away those coming to help." Branson jabbed a bony elbow into his ribs. Standing together on the sidewalk in front of the store, they watched the crowds.

"Not so sure that would be a bad thing."

"You're letting your worry get the best of you. Not a good idea. We know who we're watching for. He won't get past us."

Reed wanted to believe him. Wanted to take his words as truth. But the nagging fear continued, leaving him wishing he could steal Addie away, hide her somewhere safe until this was done.

"Well, doesn't that figure." Teddy pushed out the door, coming to a stop at Reed's side. "You Bureau types too good to participate in some actual hard labor?"

"It might scuff our wingtips." Branson held up a foot.

Teddy shook his head. Smiled. "You two do what you have to do and make the excuses you need. Meanwhile, we're ready to get started."

He turned, leaving them alone once again as he disappeared through the door.

"Almost sounded like a challenge to me." Branson flicked at a non-existent speck on his shirt. "Sure would hate to disappoint him."

The moment easing some of Reed's worry, he shook his head at his partner. "We can't have that. Imagine the embarrassment we'd cause the Bureau."

Laughing, Branson swung an easy arm over his shoulders, turning him back to the door. "No, we can't. Guess we better get busy."

Addie had a hard time taking it all in.

All these people, some she barely knew, gathered to help.

They filled the Magic Moon, creating a buzz of excitement inside the walls that poured out onto the sidewalk, catching the attention of those who passed by.

AnnaBeth slid an arm around her waist. "You doing okay?"

Addie looked around the store she'd dreaded coming back to. The many people working hard to repair all that had been ruined. Her aunt seated in a thick comfortable chair, set out of the way, watching the progress.

"I am." She rested her head on her friend's shoulder. "Thank you for this."

"It was a group effort."

AnnaBeth moved her gaze to Teddy and Clay, cleaning up the glass shattered along the floor. To Clay's band members picking up a destroyed display of handmade cards. She nudged her shoulder where Addie's head rested. "What are friends for?"

Reed came through the door, Branson a step behind. His eyes caught hers, holding on over the small stretch of space between them.

She wondered, for a moment, if it was love reflecting back at her. Or was her hope for it simply creating an illusion that didn't exist?

She wasn't going to worry about it. And though it was the same repeat of what she'd told herself many times, she had to believe one of these times it would stick and mean something.

"You look more like you were the one just released from the hospital." Rosalie patted a gentle hand against Addie's arm. "Maybe it's time for a break."

Shoving the disheveled hair back that had worked its way free from her ponytail, Addie looked over the organized chaos exploding through the store.

As the hours stretched, more continued to arrive. Complete strangers worked side by side with the others. AnnaBeth's co-workers. Friends tagging along with the band members, bar employees.

Then there were the ones who were there that night at the bar when Clay shared the horror that struck Magic Moon. Some of them tourists, giving up their own vacations to help. To be a part of rebuilding all that had been destroyed.

It was unlike anything she'd ever experienced in her life. So many giving up so much. Strangers and friends giving of themselves in a way she never would have imagined.

It brought wonder, and a few tears. It gave her hope. A belief that even with the ugly evil she faced, the good would always win in the end.

"I might sneak away for a few minutes." The exhaustion was a good one but a bit of quiet to regroup didn't sound like a bad idea.

"You go. I can take care of things here. I don't want you wandering off alone. Make sure you get someone to go with you."

"I'm only planning on going out to the courtyard and grabbing some fresh air. Nothing to worry about."

Rosalie smiled wide when she caught sight of Clay coming towards them. "I think Clay could use some fresh air, too."

She grabbed his hand once he was close enough, pulling him toward her.

"I...ummm." He looked at Addie, his eyes wide, brows cocked. "I suppose some fresh air would do me good."

"You've always been a good boy." Leaning forward, she patted his arm. "You two go take a break. I'll watch over things."

Shaking her head, Addie slipped her arm through Clay's, leading him through the door into the kitchen. She waited until she was sure they were out of hearing range before stopping and turning to him.

"You don't have to tag along, no matter what my aunt might have railroaded you into." She freed her arm from his. "I really don't need a babysitter to slip outside for a moment."

Turning for the door leading to the courtyard, there was a moment of silence before the sound of Clay's footsteps echoed behind.

"Who's to say some fresh air really isn't what I need."

Catching up with her, he slipped his hand through hers, leading the way.

Reed resisted the urge to follow Addie as she slipped through the back door. She wasn't alone. Clay was with her. And, as the crowd had grown, he'd called in more agents. They mixed with the others, always watching.

So many strangers made him uncomfortable. His first instinct had been to grab Addie and get her out of there. But he'd known better. She would have fought him. Would have never left easily.

So, he'd called in more help while spending his time always knowing where she was. And he'd worried, as he was now, during those brief moments when she was away from him.

Glancing over his shoulder, he caught Rosalie's knowing look. With a quick jerk of her shoulder, she gave him an excuse to step away from the ruined tapestries he was put in charge of.

"She only stepped out to the courtyard for a moment." Rosalie looked up at him when he reached her chair. "The poor girl's exhausted. She needed a break."

Reed glanced toward the door where she'd disappeared.

"No. She needs a break from you too and all the emotions you're bringing her way."

He wanted to protest. Wanted to tell her she was wrong. Her hard, leveled stare made it clear she wasn't foolish enough to believe him.

"My niece, she loves you."

She only shrugged as Reed quirked a brow. "She hasn't told me the truth of it, but I can see it. Anyone close to her can see it."

"I can see you love her, too." She narrowed her eyes, daring him to argue.

When he didn't, she reached out, taking his hand in hers. "She needs to know. It will help her."

"She needs to be safe. That's what's most important, right now."

"She deserves better than more dishonesty from you."

The accusation hit him hard. He wasn't being dishonest with her. He was protecting her.

When he'd lied to her before, he'd used the same excuse.

The realization wasn't one he wanted. He didn't have the time to think of such things, not while her life was threatened.

Easing his hand from Rosalie's, he bent down, brushing a soft kiss over her cheek. "I just want to keep her from getting hurt."

Disappointment lingered, but he chose to ignore it. He couldn't go there. It wouldn't help. He did love Addie. His heart swelled with it every time he rested his eyes on her.

But now was not the time for that. He wouldn't put her at any more risk. He had no answers for her. No idea if he could offer her a future.

What mattered most was making sure she lived for whatever future was to come. The rest, he'd deal with later.

He glanced toward the door where Addie and Clay disappeared. Though he hated having her out of his sight, now wasn't a good time to go after her. Not with the raw emotions and uncertainty Rosalie drew out of him.

She was with Clay. And Perry was keeping an eye on things in the alley, right outside the courtyard gate.

It was better for him to stay inside and work off the unsettled nerves taking hold. He'd give her ten minutes. If she wasn't back inside by then, he'd go to her.

CHAPTER THIRTY-THREE

"I may have been forced into it," Clay nudged Addie's shoulder. "But I have to admit, I needed a moment."

"What you did here," she waved her hand, "is more than I can ever thank you for. I don't have the words to tell you how much this means to me."

With the soft flow of the fountain behind them, he dropped an arm around her shoulders, pulling her tight to his side. "This is what you do for family."

"And to me," he tapped a finger against her nose, "you've always been family."

"I'm so thankful for you." She rested her head against his chest, the steady thud of his heart beating against her ear.

It really was going to be okay. In that moment, standing in the courtyard with Clay, she didn't see how it could be any different.

At some point the one they called the Kissing Killer would be caught. She had to believe that. And though it would tear her apart, Reed would go back to D.C., and she would go on with her life as usual.

She'd still have her friends. She'd still have Rosalie and the Magic Moon. She would be okay. Of that, she was sure.

It would take time, and plenty of tears, to get past losing Reed again. She didn't imagine she'd ever move on to find another to share her heart with. It was something she'd live with because what was truly important was right here with her, surrounding her. Reminding her there was so much more than matters of the heart to keep a life going.

The ringing of Clay's phone broke into the soft silence settling around them. With his free hand, he pulled it from his back pocket. "It's AnnaBeth. I'm guessing she wants to beat me into going back to work."

"You should go." She lifted her head from his chest, arching her head back. "I'd hate for you to risk your safety."

He was hesitant.

"You're fine." She pulled away, giving him a shove. "Go. I'm in my own courtyard with agents literally bleeding out of every corner. I think it's safe to say I'm okay without another babysitter."

"You won't stay out here much longer?"

"Just a few minutes more, I promise. Now, go." Pushing to her toes she brushed a quick kiss against his cheek.

Hesitating for only a second more, he eased around her, heading for the door leading back to the chaos.

He disappeared inside and she was thankful to truly be alone—or at least as alone as she could get considering the circumstances.

It was good not to have someone hovering. The relief tugged a weight off her shoulders. It felt like years, rather than weeks, since she'd been able to turn, to move, without bumping into another person carefully glued to her side.

She liked people. She was a sociable creature by nature, just like her mother and aunt, which played a part in Magic Moon's success. She also liked her privacy. The stretches of time with only herself and her thoughts keeping her company.

If ever she realized how important those times were, it was now.

And she'd make sure she didn't lie to Clay. A few minutes more and she'd go back in. She'd enjoy what time she did have. Be thankful for it.

She groaned when the door Clay disappeared through opened again. So much for hoping for a few minutes.

It was Reed she'd expected to see coming through. Surprise came when he wasn't the one stepping into the courtyard.

She shoved a smile to her face. They were all here to help her and Rosalie. Showing any sign of frustration for her private time being interrupted would only be rude.

"I'm sorry. Am I interrupting you?" He paused at the door. The sun glinted off his glasses, making it impossible to see his eyes.

She wanted to say yes. Wanted to ask for more time alone but it wouldn't be right.

"Of course not." She forced an invitation to her voice she didn't feel.

He took a step her way and something in her tightened with uncertainty.

Nerves. That's all it was. After weeks of all that had happened, she was reduced to seeing everything and everyone as a threat.

"It sure is busy in there." He smiled as he came closer and her heart lurched. She'd seen that smile before, she was sure of it.

Taking a step back, her legs brushed against the edge of the fountain. Maybe she was wrong. His hair was a dirty brown not the pale blond she remembered. He had glasses and a pouch at his waistline that didn't match her memory.

"Yes, it is."

Slowly, as casual as she could, she scooted to the side, her eyes flashing quickly to the door he had come from. "I should probably get back in and do my share to help out."

He nodded as he moved between her and the door. He stopped with only a few feet between them, close enough for the sun glare to no longer be a problem. His glasses were clear now. Through them she had a clear view of his eyes.

And she knew.

Fighting hard not to let on that she recognized him, she tried inching around him. "Feel free to stay out here and enjoy the courtyard."

She needed to get away from him. Once she was inside, she'd let Reed and his agents take care of him.

Flashing a smile she hoped didn't show the fear building inside, she moved around him. Her steps were long, heading for the safety the door promised.

She was almost there, only another couple feet to go, when he was suddenly at her side, twisting a tight arm around her waist. "I have other things I'd rather enjoy."

Her first instinct was to scream but the sharp poke in her side stopped her. Glancing down, she caught the glimmer of the sun bouncing off the gun pushed below her rib cage. "You start calling out for help and I'll put a bullet through anyone who comes through that door."

The look he settled on her left little doubt to his threat. Too many she loved were inside. She couldn't put them at risk. Somehow, she'd figure out another way.

"Good girl." He nodded when she didn't utter a sound. "Now, you and I are going to take a casual stroll out the gate."

He moved the gun from her side long enough to wave it toward the alley. "You're going to tell the agent you and I are old friends going off for a quick bite to eat."

The gun was back to digging into her side. He loosened his hold on her waist so it appeared to be nothing more than a casual gesture. Still, he held tight enough to steer her toward the gate.

He stopped her before she pushed it, angling his body so the gun couldn't be seen. "Whether or not he lives depends on how good you are at convincing him."

Fear and desperation twisted through her. Her heart thundered against her chest, the frantic beat making it hard to breath.

"Open the gate."

She didn't want to. Everything in her resisted.

He thrust the gun harder into tender flesh and she had no choice. She'd either die or someone around her would die.

She couldn't explain her sudden need to remember the name of the agent on the other side of the gate. But it meant something to her. Something close to desperation as she wrapped her hand around the handle of the gate, pulling it toward her.

He was on the other side, just as she'd knew he'd be. Part of her carried the irrational hope he'd been called away. "I wasn't expecting to see you out here."

His gaze passed from her to the man at her side. She wanted to move so he could see the gun. Wanted to tell him the truth. Both options would get one of them killed, or both of them.

"I'm a bit hungry." She wondered if he heard the shakiness in her voice. Felt the fear rolling off her. "We're going to grab a quick bite to eat."

His blue eyes came back to her. She caught the hint of doubt. "I figured McReily would be insisting on tagging along."

Swallowing hard over the knot in her throat, she prayed he saw the truth in her eyes she couldn't put into her words. "He's busy inside."

A quick flicker tightened the lines in his face, understanding filled his gaze. "Perhaps, I'll join you. Haven't had a thing since I grabbed a stale doughnut on my way out of the office this morning."

The gun dug deeper into her side as she caught the slow shift of the agent's hand, working toward his own gun.

"We prefer this to be a more private affair." The slow drawl from the man beside her rushed a chill up her spine. The gun was yanked from her side at the same moment the agent's hand grabbed for his.

Though it happened quick, it felt as if everything ran in slow motion, her head a mess as the man beside her lifted the gun. He pressed his finger to the trigger before the agent was able to do anything more than get his own released from its holster.

The sound of the shot echoed in her ears. The smell of it burned her nose. The agent was thrown back, falling hard and lifeless to the ground.

She screamed with a terror she'd never known before while her mind fought to resist what happened.

"Shut up or you'll be next." It was an ugly hiss in her ear as the gun again dug into her side. Half dragging her down the alley, he tossed his head frantically side to side, looking for an escape.

He yanked on a gate leading to another courtyard and, finding it unlocked, shoved her through.

She hadn't realized she was still screaming until he stopped long enough to wave the gun in front of her face. "I've killed a damn agent, I have nothing left to lose. You either shut up or your dead body will be the next one lying on the hard ground."

He was going to kill her, anyhow. She forced a breath through her lungs, fighting back the screams.

Tightening his hold, he moved them through the courtyard, using the cover of the Magnolias growing untended between the gate and the house.

What was he planning? She couldn't imagine a way he could get out of this. They were already looking for him. She was sure of it. The gun shot would have been heard by those inside the store.

There wasn't a way out, not that she could see. The only question she imagined was whether she'd be alive or dead when it was over.

Reed caught sight of Clay coming back into the store. He'd expected to see Addie right behind him.

But he was alone.

He fought back the uneasiness coming with the thought she was alone in the courtyard. He was overreacting. Perry was out there, at the gate. She was safe.

He set down the broom AnnaBeth shoved into his hands only minutes earlier. He didn't see any harm in checking on her.

He caught Rosalie's knowing look as he passed. Her words came back. He quickly shoved them away. Now was not the time to put thought into what she'd said. Maybe it was avoiding a truth he couldn't deny. With all that was going on, it was better to deny than waste time that couldn't be afforded on such matters.

Stepping into the kitchen, he found his partner at the table, a fully loaded sandwich halfway to his mouth. His smile was close to pathetic as he took a bite.

"Good to see you working hard. Who gave you permission for a food break?"

"Came straight from Rosalie." He swiped at the mayonnaise caught on his bottom lip. "She even had someone make it for me."

"Aren't you lucky." Reed reached out, grabbing the sandwich. He took his own big bite before handing it back to his partner.

"It's what happens," Branson shrugged, "when you make an effort for people to like you rather than getting them pissed off at you."

Reed only scowled. His partner took another bite and he considered reaching for the sandwich again but thought better of it, afraid Branson might take off his hand if he tried.

But damn, now he was hungry.

"Have you seen Addie come through here?"

Branson shook his head. "Only one I've seen come through here was that Clay friend of hers a few minutes ago."

He made a move for the door, his mind playing around the idea of how to convince Addie they should sneak away for something to eat. Promising her one of her many favorites seemed to work best. It just depended on what favorite to pick.

A loud crack pierced through the kitchen seconds before Reed had his hand around the doorknob.

"What the hell?"

His partner's voice was behind him but he didn't stop to look back. There wasn't a law officer who didn't recognize the sound of a gunshot.

His heart stopped as he threw open the door, praying he'd see Addie.

The courtyard was empty. Fear took hold, pounding hard through his veins as he ran for the open gate leading into the alley.

She'd be there. Whatever the explanation was, it didn't involve her. Maybe she'd heard the shot as he had and run out to check. Or Perry had taken the shot, protecting her and she was safely with him on the other side of the gate.

Branson was only a few steps behind him but he didn't stop to wait. He needed to know. Needed to see she was okay and unharmed.

He burst through the gate and his entire world shifted. Perry laid lifeless on the ground. Addie was nowhere to be seen.

Reed stopped long enough to rip open Perry's shirt, a sigh of relief ripping through when he saw the bullet flattened against his vest.

"Go." Branson skid to a stop at his side. "I've got him."

"Addie." Reed tossed his head from one side to the other of the alley, hoping for a sight of her. "Tell the other agents, he has her."

Where the hell had he gone? He was somewhere close. But where? Images of the other women he'd taken roared to life. Their lifeless, abused bodies. The kiss left against their breasts.

No. He wasn't going to let those thoughts get to him. He'd get to her. He'd find her. And when he did, he'd make sure the son of a bitch suffered like he had never done before.

CHAPTER THIRTY-FOUR

He'd drugged her.

Addie fought to come out of the fog. She sensed movement beneath her. Fighting back the throbbing in her head, she turned, caught thick trees sweeping past.

Sucking in a deep breath, she pushed back the lingering darkness, forcing the memories back.

The courtyards and fences he'd shoved her over, always holding the gun on her, making it clear he'd kill her like he did the agent if she so much as uttered a sound.

So often, she was sure she'd heard Reed's voice. But she could never be sure. Could never know if it was worth risking calling out to him, knowing the one who held the gun on her had no problem using it.

And then there'd been a car. Down by the river, she remembered, parked right off Canal. He'd shoved her in, and she'd felt the prick in her arm.

Then nothing.

"So, you're back." His voice, though smooth and easy, crawled over her skin. "That's good. I was hoping I hadn't given you too much. I want you aware for what's coming."

The fog lingering, speaking was too much of a challenge. She turned her head away from the window at her side, catching him in her gaze.

He'd removed the glasses, giving her a clear shot of pale blue eyes she'd never forget. Especially not now.

"Bet McReily's feeling like a fool right about now." Self-satisfaction brought an ugly sneer to his face. "After all this time he's been after me, and I slip right past him."

Sparing her one last gloating look, he slowed, turning onto a small, hidden road. They were heading into the swamps. Cypress trees curled around them, long, gnarled branches snaking up, blocking the sun. The Spanish moss was thick, threatening to take over.

Desperate, she tried moving her hand for the door handle. She'd rather risk the dangers of the swamp than what he had in mind. The drug still claimed her, leaving her motionless, helpless.

As if sensing what she was trying to do, he looked back at her. "It's an unpleasant feeling, I know, not being able to will your body to move at your command. My own mother used to leave me with the same feeling, though it wasn't drugs she used. Just a good old beating."

He laughed, an odd ripple holding more anger than anything else. "She believed it was the only way to gain control. Thankfully, I'm much wiser. Drugs are a much quicker answer to make sure someone does exactly as you want."

Fear raged. She was sure she was going to be sick, right on the floor of the car. He drove them deeper, engulfing them in the gloomy loneliness of the swamps where it was much too easy to hide and never be found.

Wherever he was taking her he meant for it to be where she'd spend the last moments of her life. She didn't doubt Reed. Didn't doubt he was good at what he did. But as had been pointed out, the man who had her had been successful in hiding himself for a long time.

Finding him, here in the swamps, seemed impossible.

A tight knot formed against her chest. This was not going to be the last moments of her life. It couldn't be. Too much still waited for her. Her aunt and Magic Moon. Her friends. Reed.

She nearly choked over the swell of emotions. For all he'd once taken from her life, he'd brought back so much more. She'd foolishly believed she'd be fine when he left again but the thought, now, of not having him every day in her life clutched a painful fist around her heart.

She'd expected him to stay with her in New Orleans. Had hoped he might give up the life he'd created to be with her. She could give the same. To be with him, she'd make the sacrifice. It would be hard. It would tear at her to be away from so much she loved. But she'd do it.

Or she would have done it.

Reality hit harder. For all that she could or would do, none of it mattered now. Those chances were quickly proving to be gone.

Caught by helplessness, she couldn't stop the tears pushing at the corners of her eyes. Moving her head was the only motion she had so she turned back for the window. The last thing she wanted was for the monster beside her to be witness to any weakness.

Reed paced the same halls he'd come to know so well while Rosalie had been in the hospital.

Burke and Jackson sat together in thin plastic chairs at the far end of the hall. Other agents circled them, worry clear in their eyes as they waited for more information.

For Reed, it was answers he wanted. He wasn't here for support. He was here to find out whatever he could that might help him find Addie.

The fact that Perry had been smart enough to wear his vest was the one thing that saved his life. The doctors said it more than once. Had he not, the bullet would have gone through his heart, taking with it the last beat.

The force of the bullet at such close range threw him back violently against the hard ground. It had not only knocked him unconscious but had also shattered bones and left him with a concussion worrying the medical team taking care of him.

Yet Reed couldn't afford to let worry for a fellow agent take away a second of his desperate need to find Addie.

He'd run through every alley, every courtyard. Through the bars and restaurants. The art galleries and gift shops. He'd run until his lungs ached and still kept going. Caring about nothing except finding her.

They were still searching, even now, though the hope of finding her was close to gone. Not an inch of the Quarter had been missed. Then they'd turned back and repeated searches they'd already done.

All with the same outcome. No sign of Addie or hint to where she might have been taken.

He only hoped Perry had something for them.

The double doors at the end of the hall swung open. One of the nurses who had been keeping them updated came through, stopping first where Burke and Jackson sat.

Reed moved closer, needing to hear. Needing to know when Perry could give him answers.

"We have him stabilized. He's awake and aware." The nurse laid a comforting hand on Jackson's arm as she fought back tears. "He's already demanding to speak to an Agent McReily."

Burke and Jackson's gazes turned to him and the nurse's followed. "I take it you're Agent McReily."

Reed nodded, biting back impatience.

"He's pretty insistent he needs to talk to you. Usually we discourage such a thing, but I'm afraid the stress of needing to see you and being denied will actually prove worse for his recovery."

"I'll go with you." Burke pushed up from his chair. He took a moment to reach down and grab Jackson's hand in his, giving a quick squeeze before moving to stand beside Reed.

The nurse looked between them. Reed feared she'd change her mind. Her brows furrowed together. The lines of her mouth pulled down. "I'm going to allow ten minutes, no longer."

She turned back for the doors, Reed and Burke following.

Every step down the long hall was a hollow echo. He wanted to move faster. Wanted to get to Perry and find answers. Each second passing was another second Addie was in danger. The truth of it ate at him, leaving a cold chill running up his spine.

The nurse stopped at the door at the end of the hall, pushing it open. "Ten minutes."

Reed entered first, Burke a step behind. The lights were dim, casting shadows over the bed centered in the room. Machines beside the bed glowed, their rhythmic beats echoing between the walls.

Perry was as pale as the white sheets he laid on. He pushed up on the bed when he saw them. "I was afraid—"

He fought for a breath, the mere effort of sitting up draining him. "I was afraid they were going to keep fighting me about seeing you."

Though his gaze brushed across and acknowledged his SAC, it was Reed he concentrated on. If it wasn't Addie's life hanging in the unknown, Reed would have turned and walked out, giving Perry the time he needed to recover. But, where they were, he couldn't risk it. The sharpness in Perry's eyes told Reed he felt the same.

"He changed his appearance." Every word pushed out on a labored breath. "That's how he got to Addie without us noticing."

Reed figured that was the case. He wanted to push Perry for more but battled back his impatience. The man had taken a shot to the chest. Vest or not, it was a hit he'd face some struggle getting past.

"His hair was darker." He turned away, staring at the ceiling as if seeing him there. "He had glasses and was heavier than what we originally believed."

It was information they needed. He'd send out an updated profile as soon as he left the hospital. If they were lucky, somebody might have seen him with his new look.

"Did he say anything?" Reed curled his fingers over the bed rails, knuckles turning white from the force of his hold. "Anything at all that might give us an idea where he took her?"

"I wish he did. I keep going back over it in my mind. Addie was coming through the gate with him and telling me they were going to get a bite to eat."

"It wasn't right." He shook his head on the pillow. "I knew it when I saw the look on Addie's face.

"I should have drawn my gun quicker. I never should have given him a chance to get away with her."

Reed knew better. Of all the things he'd felt, doubt about Perry's actions was not part of it. He was a good agent. He hadn't failed.

Shoving back the violent emotions he'd battled since hearing the gunshot, he took a quick moment, leaning over the side of Perry's bed, wrapping a firm hand around his arm.

"You saw the threat and you reacted. Had you not, it would have been much longer before we realized he had Addie. Don't forget that."

Perry's doubtful look followed him as he turned to leave. The guy had slipped by and fooled all of them. This was not a guilt to rest on anyone's shoulders.

All he cared about now was finding Addie before it was too late.

He'd had to drug her again though he'd hated to do it.

He couldn't take the risk. Not when fate had finally delivered what he wanted. The smallest mistake could ruin what he'd waited for.

He didn't need her fighting him when he tried getting her into the cabin. He guessed she was still weak. Her first dose had been so light he didn't want to take the chance she was trying to play him for a fool.

Not that she had much of anywhere to escape. Even if he hadn't decided to drug her again and she'd, by some miracle, been able to get away, they were secluded away in the swamps where the only signs of life were whatever slithered around in the grimy water.

Even at a dead weight from the drugs, it was an easy feat getting her out of the car. Her body limp in his arms, he was tempted to take from her right there. On the dirty ground between the car and the cabin.

He wouldn't do it. Patience was a must. He had to wait until everything he'd carefully planned was ready.

Only then would he allow himself to take what he'd waited so long for.

CHAPTER THIRTY-FIVE

R eed's fist hit the wall, shoving a hole through it.

The other agents in the room fell silent, constant chatter suddenly cut off in mid-sentence.

Good. He wanted them to shut up. Every one of them. They had nothing. Not a single clue to figure out where Addie was. All they had was speculation and a whole bunch of crap that didn't help.

And meanwhile, Addie was in the hands of a man who enjoyed torturing the women he captured. A man who first destroyed them then killed them.

Where the hell was she?

From the corner of his eye, he caught Branson pushing back from the table. The only one daring enough to approach him.

He swung an easy arm around Reed's shoulder, urging him back from the wall before he lodged another fist through it. "Let's take a walk."

"A damn walk isn't going to save Addie." He shook out of his partner's hold.

Refusing to be deterred, Branson grabbed his elbow, his hold tight. "It's going to do better than what you're doing now."

He lowered his voice so only Reed heard him. "I get it. I have a new wife who I haven't seen since our honeymoon. If something happened to her, I'd be crazy. But you need to move. You need to process your mind past the anger, or you aren't going to do Addie any good."

"So," he eased his hold. "Either you realize I'm right and take a walk with me or I shove your ass through the door and give you no choice."

Though Reed glared at him, Branson was right. His anger wasn't helping. If he was the agent he prided himself on, now was the time to prove it. Addie needed him. Needed the very best of him.

Sucking in a deep breath, he looked at the man who wasn't just a partner but a friend. "Let's walk."

Branson's answering nod was quick. Letting go of Reed, he turned for the door.

The stares from the other agents fell heavy as he moved through the room. He ignored them. Getting out of there suddenly became the only thing he cared about.

In the hall, he sucked in another breath, knowing it was the bone-chilling fear pushing the anger. Every time his mind went to what Addie might be suffering through, he came close to losing control.

Branson was right, it wasn't doing any good. It wasn't getting him any closer to finding where he might have taken her. He needed to walk it off. Needed to center and refocus so that Addie didn't become another dead woman left for him to find.

In the way only partners understood, Branson didn't bother with words as they made their way down the hall toward the doors leading out of the Bureau office. It was the silence Reed needed to work through what ran so frantic through his head.

They were only a few steps from the doors when they burst open. Sure his mind was playing tricks on him, Reed had to take a second look to be sure.

Of all the people he'd expected to step into this part of his life, his parents were at the very bottom of the list.

His dad reached him first, dropping two firm hands over his shoulders, squeezing tight. "We saw the news. They said Addie was taken by the same man you suspect tortured and killed other women."

Caught in shock by the sight of them, Reed nodded as he reached desperately for the ability to speak. They shouldn't be here. Why had they come?

He sensed Branson easing out of the way as his mother rushed to him. Though she didn't grab for him like his father did, the emotion darkening her eyes held the same power. "Is there any news on where he might have taken her?"

Reed struggled, his mind unable to accept his parents were there, asking about Addie. They looked at him, waiting for a response he was having a hard time giving.

"We don't know where she is." He finally managed, his voice sounding hollow even to his own ears. "Our agents are working on it."

It was the same response he'd repeated to the press and their many questions. To the point and without a hint of emotion.

For his parents, it didn't bring the same reaction.

"I'm so sorry, son." His dad's hold tightened a second before he pulled Reed forward, wrapping his arms around him and holding him close.

Reed was lost. He was a grown man who escaped to live his own life and yet, caught in the hall by his dad's arms, he found a comfort he'd never believed he'd feel again.

The anger he battled slipped away into desperation. The fear became more real. Caught in the arms of the man he'd spent so much of his life pushing back against, his need to deny the truth of his emotions failed.

He sensed his mother coming closer, the warmth of her hand resting against his arm. "What can we do to help?"

The tenderness in her voice was nearly his undoing. He shook his head, having no answers.

"There has to be something that can be done." His father pulled away far enough to look at him. "All the McReily resources, it has to mean something. It has to be able to *do* something."

Of all times he'd wished his family's wealth and power could help—

The thought struck even as he was shaking his head. McReily Industries employed some of the very best in security, in private investigators. With the high-priced dealings they worked in, they could never afford to be too trusting or too lax. Every situation, every business contact, was considered suspect until their experts proved otherwise.

As private investigators, their hands were never tied in the same way as those in law enforcement. His father was right, their family had resources the Bureau couldn't imagine.

"There's a person we desperately need to find." Pulling himself back together, he stepped back from his parents' hold. "One the Bureau hasn't yet been able to locate."

He caught Branson's look, letting him know he might be hearing but would forever deny any knowledge of Reed sharing information from an ongoing investigation without the Bureau's permission.

He didn't care. Didn't give a damn what rules he might be breaking. The only thing that mattered was Addie. He'd give up not only his position with the Bureau, but his own life, if it meant finding her before it was too late.

"Give me whatever information you have. I'll make sure our investigators do nothing else until they have what you need."

It was what Reed wanted to hear. Later, once Addie was safe, he'd put thought to what it meant to have his parents show up, offer to help. For now, he couldn't afford such distractions.

"His name's Jeremiah Barrow. Last known residence was Tennessee. I'll need to get back to my notes," he jerked his head in the direction he had just come, "to get you the full address."

"Let's go." His father slapped a hand against his back, turning him in the right direction.

Her mind was foggy.

Addie forced her eyes open, trying her hardest to understand why her lids were so heavy. A dim light hung above her, disorienting her. This wasn't right. She couldn't process the why, but she felt it. Knew it.

She tried turning but couldn't get her body to do as her mind commanded.

What was happening?

Closing her eyes again, she struggled for some sort of focus. She wasn't at home, in her bed. That much she knew. She shoved hard at the fog holding her mind captive.

Images came. She was in the courtyard, talking to Clay. And then—

It flooded back. The gun at her side. Shooting the agent. Running through the Quarter. It was all there, redone in vivid memories.

She remembered turning for the swamp, going deeper and deeper in, shoving more fear through her veins. And then nothing.

He'd drugged her again. The knowledge angered her even as it frightened her. What had he done to her while she'd been out?

Opening her eyes, relief swelled as she realized she was still dressed, down to the leather sandals she'd put on earlier that day.

It was still the same day. She had to believe that.

"You're awake." The voice, drifting from a place she couldn't see, raked over her, causing chills.

She tried desperately to get her bearings, but it was impossible when she couldn't move. Couldn't take a single look where she was other than staring at the dim light bulb above her, feel the press of a thin stretch of material beneath her.

"I had hoped this would be our place. It was planned so perfectly. Then I got you here and nothing was right."

What was he talking about?

Again, she tried. But her body refused to obey. To do what she wanted.

"This isn't what it should be. Not what I'd anticipated for us."

Was he talking to her? She couldn't be sure.

All she was sure of was that she was caught in a living nightmare. One she currently had no ability to escape.

He was there then, staring down at her. "Why couldn't this be enough for you?"

His anger burned over her, leaving her more desperate to find some way out of whatever held her captive. The crazy in his eyes surged a greater fear, making it hard to pull a breath through her lungs.

His hands grasped her wrists, squeezing tight. Unable to move away from the pain spearing up her arms, she could do nothing but stare back into the fury of his heavy gaze.

He'd taken her, brought her here to who in the hell knew where. Now he was angry about it. She didn't understand any of this.

She wanted to be home. Wanted to be back with Reed. With her aunt and friends. Back to the Magic Moon.

"I had it all planned." He jerked away. Before she grasped what was happening, the shatter of things hitting the floor filled the room.

He came back again, his anger more potent than before. "What is it about you that makes it all so much different?"

She sensed he didn't expect an answer. Not that she could have given him one if she'd wanted to.

More crashes echoed around her. She wondered what it was he destroyed. Feared what his anger meant even as she didn't understand it.

And then there was silence.

She wasn't foolish enough to believe it meant anything good for her. Something was very wrong in his soul. It was clear in his eyes.

Whatever angered him, she would never know. She feared, whatever it was, it would only prove to be worse for her.

Which seemed ridiculous to consider when she was already facing the fact her life would soon end.

They still had nothing.

Reed sat in the same office he'd been in for hours. He pounded keys until he was sure his fingers would bleed. Flipped through and searched every shred of evidence the Bureau had, hoping desperately to find a clue to where Addie was.

None of it did a damn bit of good.

She'd had a night with him. The thought terrified him. He knew what happened to the women he took under his control. Couldn't bear the thought of Addie experiencing the same.

He felt helpless. His position with the Bureau, his badge, the oath he stood under, none of it meant a damn thing. How could it when he'd failed at protecting her?

Cursing, he shoved away from the desk. Self-pity wasn't doing a damn thing to help.

He needed something other than the stale air circulating through the building. Something besides pounding desperately away at a computer refusing to give him any clues.

He needed answers, and he wasn't finding them here.

Between the agents and the local police, there wasn't a part of New Orleans and the surrounding areas that wasn't being searched. Branson was out with a team now, searching some of the more remote bayous.

Shaking his head, frustration growing, he stepped into the quiet hall. Most were gone, doing their searching. His gut told him it wouldn't do any good. They weren't going to find the bastard by combing through swampy waters and remote cabins.

They needed to find Jeremiah Barrow. Nothing else had worked. Not in all the time he'd been chasing this sadistic, twisted killer.

They needed more.

Images of Addie, frightened and tortured, struck without warning, sucking the breath from his lungs. He couldn't go there. Couldn't allow his worst fears to control him.

He would find her. And it would not be too late as it had been for the other women.

He shoved out the door, almost tripping over Teddy trying to come through.

"Hey. I was just coming to see you." He stepped back, making room for Reed to move away from the door.

Reed didn't have time for a visit. Didn't have time for anything but finding Addie.

"I have to go." He didn't bother hiding the frustration in his voice. Every second spent talking with Teddy was another second lost in getting Addie back safe.

"She was ours first." The quick spark of anger in his cousin's voice stopped him. He turned back. Teddy stood there, emotion carving hard lines over his face.

"I know you love Addie. I know you're terrified for her." His voice lowered though a hint of anger remained. "That doesn't give you the right to shut the rest of us out."

The disappointment in his eyes was like a punch in the gut. "We loved Addie before you ever came into her life. We loved her when you left. We love her still. Do you not think we are just as desperate and frantic to find her? To have some clue what is happening? She's one of us, too."

And he'd shoved them all off, ignored them. Teddy didn't have to say it.

"Rosalie and AnnaBeth are a mess. They've closed themselves away inside the Magic Moon. All they do is cry and pace the store."

"And Clay and I." He shook his head, his eyes showing the first true signs of his own struggle. "We try to help but we have nothing to tell them because we don't know a damn thing. You won't talk to any of us. You've shut us out and forgotten there are others who are as terrified as you are."

He deserved the painful hits. Though they were only words, Reed felt each one.

"I just want to find her." His heart and his head hurt. "I can't stand the thought of losing her."

Fear threatened to take over again. He couldn't allow it but struggled so hard to keep it at bay.

Teddy's hard expression eased. Stepping closer, he wrapped a firm hand around Reed's arm. "We won't lose her."

It was easier to say, harder to believe. Reed stared at his cousin, the one family member he'd always been closest to. He was right. They had loved Addie first. Had allowed him a part in that life they shared with her.

"Let's go." Pulling away from his cousin's hold, he turned for the sidewalk only a few steps away.

It took only a second for Teddy to catch up with him. "Where are we going?"

"To the Magic Moon." Reed stopped for a moment, looking at him.

Teddy nodded, falling into step beside him. "I'll call Clay."

Reed hated even a minute of putting off his search for Addie.

But Teddy had been right, he hadn't given a thought to how the others were struggling, especially Rosalie. He'd ignored their calls. Hadn't put any time into considering how they might be doing.

Clay met them in the alley behind the courtyard. Reed's attention strayed to where he'd found Perry after he'd been shot. He looked around again as if he might somehow find Addie there.

Fear shoved hard against his chest, tightening it. He fought it back, knowing he'd already face enough of it as soon as he walked through the gate.

"I called on my way. They're waiting for us." Clay's expression was somber, worry etching lines over his face. A need in his eyes that couldn't be fulfilled.

Teddy pushed on the gate, letting Reed and Clay enter ahead of him. They walked in silence through the courtyard. Each with their own thoughts and worries.

Reed glanced at the fountain, his mind going back to the night he'd had Addie there in his arms, so ready to carry her upstairs to her bed.

He wanted her now, right back there. Wanted her in his arms, enjoying the taste of her. The feel of her.

The door opened before they reached it. AnnaBeth came out first, her eyes red and swollen. She moved past Teddy and Clay, her eyes set firmly on Reed.

"Where is she?" Desperation brought a shrill tone to her voice. "Where is Addie?"

Her pain tore through Reed, threatening to toss him over the cliff he was trying to avoid. "I don't know."

He hated saying it. Wished he had something more. Something better to offer.

"That's not good enough."

She came at him, her hands in fists, hitting his chest. Rosalie came up behind her. Reed shook his head, stopping her.

He understood she needed this. Just as he had when he'd put the hole through the wall back at the Bureau office.

Slowly, her punches weakened as tears began to flow down her cheeks. With one last, half-hearted hit, she collapsed against him, sobbing.

He wrapped an arm around her and held her, knowing there was nothing he could say or do to make it better.

Eyes red and puffy, she looked up at him. "I'm sorry. I shouldn't have exploded on you like that."

"It's okay." He held her close for a second more before letting go.

She stepped back with Rosalie who looked at him with the same red, puffy eyes. The sight of them together, their fear and worry so clear and urgent, reached deep, yanking at his heart. A part of him, so strong it was almost overpowering, wanted to lie to them. Give them false assurances he couldn't ever back up.

Dealing with the family of victims was part of his job as an agent. He'd always been kind but truthful. This time, it was different. This time it meant so much more with those who were looking to him for answers.

Addie's voice was inside his head, reminding him what happened the last time he'd lied to try and save another from knowing the painful truth. He could see her as if she were standing in front of him. That thoughtful look in her brown eyes, the quirk at the corners of her mouth, expecting him to do the right thing, no matter how difficult it might be.

And...damn. He wanted to start throwing his own punches again as the emotions threatened.

"Why don't we go inside." Teddy stepped up, swinging an arm around Rosalie's shoulders.

With his lead, they made their way through the door, into the kitchen.

"Sit." Rosalie waved them to the table, turning for the refrigerator. "I'll get us something to drink and eat."

"You don't need to do that," Reed protested.

She waved him off. "I need to."

While she reached into the fridge, pulling out a pitcher of sweet tea, he took a seat between Teddy and Clay at the kitchen table.

They waited for her. She set the pitcher and glasses on the table, centering it between them before turning back.

"I've had to keep busy, or I'll go crazy." Her back to them, she pulled a platter from the cupboard by the sink.

"I made some of Addie's favorite Snickerdoodles." From the bread box where, to his memory, there had never been bread stored, she pulled out a covered tub.

She pulled out cookies, arranging them on the platter. So much of him wanted to leave all of this. But he couldn't. They deserved whatever he could give them.

And he'd do it over a glass of sweet tea and cookies reminding him of Addie with every bite he took.

Setting the platter in the center of the table, she pulled out the chair next to AnnaBeth, looking at Reed over the width of the table. "You don't have any idea where she is, do you?"

The question, so direct and unexpected, set him on edge. Again, the urge to lie became a force.

He couldn't. Wouldn't.

"You're right, we don't know." The words were bitter as they left his mouth. He should be out there searching until they did know instead of sitting here at the kitchen table with tea and cookies in front of him.

"But you're trying." Desperation darkened AnnaBeth's eyes.

It was a question they all knew the answer to. "With everything I have. With every resource the Bureau has. I've even brought in outside help."

"What kind of outside help?" Teddy's curious gaze pushed at him.

Turning to his cousin, he didn't figure he had a reason to hide what he'd asked of his dad. Not from any of them. "McReily Industries' private investigators are following a lead for me."

Surprise flashed in Teddy's eyes. Though Reed clearly saw the questions lingering, he didn't say a word.

Thankful for it, Reed turned his attention back to Rosalie. His heart ached at the vibrant fear lingering in her eyes. Of all of them at the table, he guessed her heart weighed the heaviest. She'd already lost her sister. Had faced her own terrible attack only to find herself now facing the reality of her niece missing with no answers as to where she was or what might be happening to her.

"I promise you," he reached across the table, taking her hand. "The only thing I care about is finding Addie. You said some things to me the other day and you were right. She needs to know and I'm going to make sure that I have the chance to tell her."

Understanding lit in Rosalie's eyes, pulled the corners of her mouth up in a slight smile. "You should never waste the chance to let someone know you love them."

And he'd done just that. The truth of it hit hard.

"Do you think she's still alive?" Tears gathered in the corners of AnnaBeth's eyes. She reached across the table for him, grabbing the same hand holding Rosalie's.

The pain reflecting at him was almost his undoing. He didn't have to lie though he didn't need to reveal why he knew the answer. "I'm sure of it."

Her shoulders fell with relief, and he knew then it was good she didn't know the rest of it.

He knew Addie was alive because the one who had her never killed right away. He had become unpredictable, changing everything they knew about him, but Reed was certain that was a fact he wouldn't change.

He'd keep Addie alive only to enjoy the fear and horror she was suffering before it came time to end her life.

CHAPTER THIRTY-SIX

I t was all wrong.

He couldn't go back into the cabin. Instead, he paced. Around the cabin. Over and over again. High-growing reeds grabbed at him. Prickly branches scratched against bare skin.

He felt none of it, his mind centered on his own complete failure. *Because of her.*

Sometimes that *her* was Addie. Sometimes it was his mother. They both held his frustration, his disgust, as his steps sunk into wet ground and his bare skin welcomed every stinging insect.

For two days she'd been his. Two days of finally finding the freedom to do with her whatever he chose. To find the pleasure he'd spent so long promising himself was coming if he'd just be patient.

His hands clenched to fists at his sides.

Every time he was inside the cabin with her, the horrible weight of failure nearly choked him. He hadn't been able to find the urge to undress her. To discover the luscious beauty waiting underneath her clothes.

He'd never failed before. Never suffered the clutching reality he was unable to do what fate called from him.

The sun began to dip, casting shadows. His mother's condemning voice roared, reminding him he was no good. A failure. An embarrassment.

The terrible whisper of it was an itch digging deep inside, refusing to let go.

No. He chased the irritating, grating voice from his thoughts. She would not take him down with her. She was in her grave now, where she belonged. She wouldn't win.

He pushed back at what grabbed him, clearing his mind.

It hit him, standing in the gathering dark, the buzz of insects a constant drone around him.

It was the cabin in Tennessee calling to him, not this one lost in the Louisiana swamps. He'd taken Addie somewhere she didn't belong.

It was back to the place of his childhood, to those memories that haunted him, where he'd find all that he'd waited for.

She'd been different from the start. Wanting her demanded more since the moment he'd put his eyes on her.

He needed to go back there with her. Back to the memories that created him, made him what he was. That was where she belonged. Where he'd no longer be frozen by whatever it was grabbing at him, keeping him from doing what he'd planned.

Realizing the answer, it felt like a ton of bricks had been lifted from his shoulders. He had the answer. Now he needed to carry it through.

Addie lost track of time. She didn't know if it had been hours or days since he'd taken her.

He kept her drugged. Whenever it felt like she might be coming out of whatever he fed into her veins, might actually have a chance of moving and getting away, he was there, sticking another needle in her.

She stared at the warped and dirtied ceiling, having no other choice, her mind full of wandering thoughts.

Though the drugs made it hard to concentrate, they didn't make it hard to remember. In those moments when she couldn't fight it back, fear grabbed her, threatening to drag her under.

That's when the horrible thoughts came, telling her she was facing the last days of her life. Reminding her of all the horrors the women before her faced.

In the rare moments she found the strength to shove them back with her fear, other thoughts kept her going. Kept her from giving up, holding on to the small hope she'd get out of this alive.

The sound of AnnaBeth's laughter. The love in Rosalie's eyes. The encouragement Teddy always brought. And Clay with all that was so uniquely him. She could see him snapping his suspenders and smiling at her. That big, beaming smile that always brought a smile to her lips.

Then there was Reed. Always Reed.

It was his voice she heard, telling her to hold on and not give up. It was his deep blue eyes she saw. The way they darkened with desire when he hovered over her. The spark that lit in their depths when he smiled.

He was out there doing everything he could to find her. She knew it. He wouldn't give up. Would never walk away.

In that, the crazy who took her messed up. She'd come to accept her fate wasn't a good one. There wasn't much hope of being found. Not out here, in the middle of nowhere with more life crawling around in the swamps than the cabins scattered through.

If having to realize death was what waited for her, she also knew, no matter what happened, Reed would push and fight to know what happened. The killer was already more than just another case to him, and now, he would become more.

Reed would find him. She was sure of it. He'd signed that reality the minute he'd shown up in her courtyard.

Staying alive to see it was all she could hope for. Knowing it would happen, no matter what her fate would be, offered some satisfaction in the hell she faced.

"Good, you're with me again."

The deep timber of his voice washed an icy chill over her as his footsteps echoed in the tiny space.

She turned her head, watching him move deeper into the room until he hovered over her. The look in his eyes washed cold over her. A dark emotion lingered. One she felt down to her bones.

He looked at her hard, as if reading her thoughts, before shaking his head. "We're leaving. Today. As soon as possible."

Leaving? It was the last thing she expected. What was going on? Something was wrong.

She wanted to ask, wanted to know where he was taking her. But the ability to form a single word was still out of her ability. She could only stare at him and wonder what he was planning.

"I don't want to have to drug you again." He leaned lower, the warmth of his breath washing over her. "I think I should be enjoying more of your company."

She didn't dare show any emotion. The risks were too great. The less he drugged her, the more chance she had of finding some way out of this horror.

He trailed a finger down her cheek. Inside, she cringed but held a blank stare, thankful the drugs helped keep her from showing anything more.

"I made a mistake bringing you here." His finger trailed back up and nausea rolled in her gut. "But I know how to make it right. I know what needs to be done."

He lingered for a second more before turning away, disappearing out the door he'd come through.

Addie didn't know what to think, what to expect. She could only hope. Moving her out of the swamps might prove to be the chance she needed to stay alive.

CHAPTER THIRTY-SEVEN

"We have a lead."

Reed knew better than to get his hopes up as his father's voice drifted over the phone.

"I sent my investigators to Tennessee, figuring they'd have more luck on the ground than working from a desk here in Louisiana."

It was more than Reed expected. Within the Bureau, the leads were being followed by agents behind the desk. They wouldn't put them into action until there was a justifiable reason to do so.

"What have they found?"

"Jeremiah's got a job where he's being paid under the table. Probably why your agents couldn't secure a lead on him."

"Makes sense." Reed sipped from his now cold coffee, forgetting when the last time was he'd filled it. "No taxes paid, no trail to follow. How did your investigators figure it out?"

"Don't know. Didn't ask."

It was no less than what he figured he'd get for an answer. There was a reason why the most successful companies had some of the best investigators on their payroll. Getting information without certain restrictions was a driving force behind the success of many.

Hopefully it would give some of the same results in finding Addie before it was too late.

His heart caught at the thought. It would never be too late. It couldn't be. The thought of losing her now was too much to bear.

"I'm guessing your investigators will be paying a visit to this under-the-table employer."

"The plan is this afternoon. Just wanted to keep you informed."

"Thanks for that."

"I'll let you know what they learn. And son," his father's voice gentled, "take care of yourself."

Reed shoved back the strange reactions trying to find a hold. Ending the call and shoving back from the desk, he grabbed his coffee cup, figuring a walk to refill it would do him some good.

Considering he'd barely slept since Addie was taken, another hit of caffeine was essential, especially when it came from the Bureau's black sludge.

He didn't bother returning to his desk before taking the first sip. It hit hard in his gut, falling on top of the gallons of coffee he'd already consumed.

Stepping back into the hall, Branson nearly knocked him over.

"Let's go." Taking Reed's cup from his hand, he took his own sip before stepping back into the conference room, setting it on the table.

"I was drinking that."

"Not anymore, you're not." Not waiting for him, Branson started back down the hall in the same way he had come.

"The locals got a call," he supplied when Reed caught up with him. He barely spared him a glance, his attention set on the door leading outside. "Seems some old guy from a place called Houma is suspicious about a cabin out there in their swamps."

Reed knew Houma. It was a small place about an hour away from New Orleans. Far enough away to be private but close enough to travel back and forth without problem.

His heart kicked up a notch as he followed his partner out the door. "What kind of suspicion?"

"He lives in one of the cabins out there and swears he saw a dark sedan heading for one of the more desolate cabins around him. Claims he's had problems in the past with the owner renting it to shady characters. So, he's been watching who comes and goes, wanting an excuse to put an end to it."

Branson only shrugged at Reed's raised brows. "Just telling you a repeat of what I was told."

He picked back up his pace along the sidewalk, heading for the rental car he'd left parked against the curb in the closest spot he found. "He put a call into NOPD after watching the news coverage of Addie's disappearance. According to him, he saw a female looking like her in the passenger seat of the dark sedan."

Reaching the car, he punched the fob in his hands, unlocking the doors. He waited a moment before crawling in, looking at Reed over the space of the roof. "Not sure there's much credibility to this old guy's rantings, but I figured you'd want to be there when they checked it out, just in case."

He did. At this point, he couldn't get there fast enough.

Giving his answer by climbing into the passenger seat, Branson followed behind him, slipping behind the steering wheel. "You have to know, this sounds like a long shot. Like nothing more than an old, grumbling guy finding a reason to complain."

Reed only stared at him.

"Just don't want you getting your hopes up." Branson punched the button, starting the car. "Figured it was important we be there, but I can't promise anything."

Reed didn't care about promises. Didn't care about long shots or credibility. All he cared about was finding Addie before it was too late.

"It's empty. Somebody's been staying here but we haven't yet received confirmation on who it was."

The fresh-faced officer stood in the open door of the cabin. Flashing lights reflected eerily along the dark waters surrounding them, catching him in their strange swirl of color.

Reed pushed past him. He needed to be inside. Needed to see for himself.

It was nothing but a musty space of old, weathered wood. The kitchen, if one could call it that, consisted of nothing more than an antique stove and refrigerator, a rusting sink sunk into the yellowing countertop between them.

A sagging door on the other side led to a bathroom. With the state of the rest of the cabin, he could only imagine what it looked like. Was thankful the locals had already done their search, saving him from having to find out.

The rest of the small dingy room held an old, broken recliner and a long metal table crammed into separate corners. A long, skinny cot centered the worn and beaten floor.

There was nothing else. Not a blanket for the cot or a single dish in the sink. It was empty. Too empty. As if someone had made a point of clearing out any hint of who might have been there, leaving it nothing more than a cold shell.

And yet standing in the dust swirling around him in the dirty light, Reed knew. Addie had been there, and they hadn't come in time to save her.

He didn't know how he knew and didn't give a damn to try and figure it out. But he'd bet his own life, she'd been on that cot, a prisoner inside this dilapidated cabin.

"I want to know who owns this place." He turned back to the others hovering at the door, urgency rushing hot through his veins.

The officer who'd greeted him took a step away from the rest. "We're working on that."

"Work faster," he snapped, pushing his way outside. "You'll have every resource the Bureau can offer at your disposal to find out who was here."

He stopped only a few feet from the cabin, turning to look back at it. This was not like the man he'd chased for so long. Nothing he'd done since he set his sights on Addie made any sense to what they knew about him.

Fear tore at Reed's gut. He'd been an agent long enough to know, when things started to change this drastically, it was never a good sign. Serial killers needed, thrived on, the same routine. For every situation, every victim.

Breaking that routine usually only meant one thing—something inside had snapped, making a crazy mind more frightening.

CHAPTER THIRTY-EIGHT

He hadn't drugged her. At least not until they'd hit the interstate, leaving the cabin and swamps behind.

Sluggish from the drugs lingering in her system, Addie hadn't realized what he was doing until she felt the tiny prick in her neck. Though it had been many hours since he'd last dosed her up, the most she could do in response was a pathetic, protesting whimper.

"We have a long drive ahead of us, you might as well relax." The humor in his voice sickened her. She didn't want to play his games anymore. Exhaustion took over, mentally and physically. Whatever he had planned for her, she had a desperate desire to get it over with.

"We have a name, but it still doesn't mean a damn thing." Jackson threw the paper clutched in her hand to the table, shaking her head.

In the hour it took to get back to the Quarter, information began to churn. Burke met Reed and Branson at the door as they returned to the Bureau office, ushering them back to the conference room.

Jackson's frustration was clear as she looked at the others in the room.

Pushing past her, Reed picked up the paper from the table. He read over the type, realizing it was a rental agreement for the cabin they'd left behind.

It was short and to the point. A week-to-week deal providing nothing more than an old, dusty space for whoever chose to pay for it. The date at the bottom fell right into line with the time Reed arrived in New Orleans. The signature belonged to a John Smith.

"The owner of the cabin is Presley Waters," Jackson explained while Reed handed the paper to Branson. "He's been in a retirement home in Baton Rouge for almost a decade, has rented out the cabin even longer."

She shook her head. "The guy doesn't care about anything but the money in his hand. He doesn't check, or ask for, identification. You give him money and sign his joke of a contract and the place is yours."

Which meant they had nothing.

He had the urge to punch another hole in the wall.

"We're digging further for whatever information we can find." Burke moved to the head of the table, looking down at the other agents.

His gaze landed on Reed. "The locals took a picture of Addie to the man who made the original call. He confirmed it was her he saw. He also gave us a description of the car they were in. The Bureau issued a BOLO for it."

It wasn't enough. Not while every second of Addie's life slowly ticked away. No matter what his plans were, his final goal was to kill Addie just as he'd killed the others. Of that Reed was sure.

He needed to go back through his notes, through every bit of information he'd collected. There had to be an answer in there. Something that would lead him to Addie before it was too late.

She must have slept.

When Addie came back, she was surrounded by darkness. For a moment she was disoriented, unsure of where she was.

"You're just in time." The voice slid coldly over her skin, yanking back the reality she'd briefly escaped. "We're almost there."

She didn't want to look at him, not yet. In the heavy dark, she hoped he couldn't see as she tried moving, praying all the drugs he'd pumped into her had worn off.

Frustration surged when the most she achieved was a slight twitch in her fingers. How much damage had the constant flow of drugs done? The thought frightened her. Not that it would matter in the end since his plan was to kill her.

The car slowed. Long, thick shadows of trees slid past along an exit ramp. Through the inky black, a small spread of lights broke through.

"Welcome to Bear Forks." The heavy weight of his eyes settled over her.

It was easy to guess they weren't anywhere close to New Orleans anymore. Or still in the state of Louisiana. But, falling asleep took away her chance to have some idea where they were.

He turned onto a quiet, empty street, dim lights shimmering in the brick buildings. They were old, stretching along both sides of the street. A bank. A diner and a feed store. One by one they passed by, ending with a post office tucked back from the street.

"It's not much of anything." Disgust was clear in his voice. Through the edge of her vision, she caught the sad, slow shake of his head. "Just a nothing small town in the middle of more nothing."

He turned at the end of the street, taking them past houses on small patches of land. Some well cared for, white fences and old trees edging the street.

Others were beat up, forgotten in what their beauty once was. Peeling paint and sagging porches dimly illuminated under the weak light from the streetlamps.

He kept on until the houses fell away. She could see the shadows ahead. Didn't understand it was the edge of mountains looming until they drew closer.

The engine churned as they started the climb. Leaving the lights behind, the darkness thickened as the road twisted.

She wished she had the ability to speak so she could demand he tell her where he was taking her. Wish she had control of her limbs so she could find a way to escape.

The helplessness returned with more force as the road climbed higher. Not only was she drugged with a madman, but now she was in unfamiliar territory, having no clue where she might be or what to expect.

Even if it was her death that brought it, she wanted it to end.

His breathing beside her changed as he slowed for a turn, each breath so harsh she heard it from her place next to him. Felt the struggle as he fought for the next one.

The road beneath them changed. She tumbled in her seat as deep ruts caught the tires, shifting them from one side of the road to the other.

He muttered under his breath, words she couldn't understand. She dared a look, catching his heavy stare ahead, the tight hold of his fingers around the steering wheel.

As if sensing her gaze, he turned, the whites of his eyes flashing.

She felt the fear—not her own, but his—and tried desperately to make sense of what it meant through her drug-hazed mind. What would frighten him about a place he'd been set to bring her?

He took a curve in the road too fast, tossing her against the door. Her arm hit the handle, shoulder ramming against the door. Pain hit then slowly slid away.

He grumbled something under his breath she couldn't make out. Sucking in air, he let it out slowly, easing off the accelerator until the car slowed to a safer speed.

Something about where they were headed was setting him off balance. That much she figured out even with the sluggish pace of her thoughts. Was it enough to use to her advantage?

Not that she really had any kind of advantage, trapped like she was under the hold of the drugs.

He slowed for another turn, crossing between old Dogwood and Birch trees edging both sides of the skinny drive. The car slowly worked its way up a steep climb, the crunch of tires grabbing against pebbles echoing beneath them.

When the car leveled out again, she caught the shadowed shape of what looked like another cabin. This one bigger, more livable. A long, red-brick chimney crawled up one side. A sagging porch stretched the front of it.

He stopped the car, sitting in silence for so long she began to wonder if he was changing his mind. She didn't know where they were or what his next plans were. She sensed, straight down to her bones, he was on the edge and the littlest shift might send him over.

Which, she guessed, would be a worse situation for her.

He looked at her, an inner battle clear in the depths of his pale, blue eyes. "Here you go."

His half laugh held an eerie darkness. "My childhood home."

She didn't know what to think. Was thankful she didn't have the ability to react. Looking from him to the cabin and back to him, the cold reality settled over her.

Whatever drove him to bring her here wasn't good. Something burned inside him she was afraid would take over. And in the depths of her she knew, coming here, made him more dangerous.

CHAPTER THIRTY-NINE

He'd given in and gone back to his hotel room, but he hadn't slept.

Standing at the window, Reed looked down on one of the rare moments of quiet along Bourbon. The time when the partiers had finally found their beds and the daily tourists had not yet ventured out. Even the crews who came out every morning to soap down the streets from the night before had not yet made their appearance.

In that moment, he felt like the only one awake within the Quarter, staring out over where lively chaos would again come racing through.

He thought of Addie. It was all he did anymore. He saw her on the very street he looked down on. He wanted her back there. Would give anything to make it happen.

The fear of what she was facing, of the fate he felt helpless to protect her against, was threatening to become too much. Too much time had passed. Too many strange turns had come into play. He didn't know anymore what to expect. The truth brought anger. A frustration of teetering on an unknown ledge with Addie's life hanging in the balance.

He needed her back. Having her back in his life had shown him so much he hadn't realized. He couldn't lose her now.

His phone rang, vibrating against the end table beside the bed. He glanced at the clock beside it. It wasn't yet five. His heart caught, refused to take a beat as his mind battled what such an early call meant.

"You're up." His father's familiar voice drifted from the other end.

"Haven't slept."

"I just got the word, thought you should know. My investigators found Jeremiah Barrow. He's agreed to meet with them."

"When are they meeting him? Where?"

"In Tennessee. In a few hours."

"Tell them I'll be there." His mind began playing through his options. Driving wouldn't get him there in time. He'd have to fly. Burke wouldn't be happy, but he would be the next call. The Bureau would get him there or he'd find his own way.

"I figured as much. If you want the company jet, it's ready for you."

It wasn't what Reed expected and his first reaction was to deny the offer. But just like when his father offered to bring in his own investigators, it was thoughts of Addie ruling him. The jet would get him to Tennessee quicker and without the hassle of working through the Bureau's necessary channels.

"I appreciate it. I can be at the airport within the hour." Already he was turning away from the window, heading for a quick shower.

"The jet will be ready. I'll let my investigators know you're on your way."

Thanking him, Reed ended the call, reached the bathroom, and typed another number in as he flipped the controls for the shower. On the other end, Branson's phone rang until finally slipping into voice mail.

"I don't have time for your two calls to wake you up requirement." Holding his phone to his ear with one hand, he used the other to test the temperature of the water. "Wake up and meet me at the airport in an hour. We're headed to Tennessee."

Addie wiggled her fingers, swallowing back a cry of relief.

He hadn't drugged her again.

He'd hauled her through the dark cabin, her feet dragging against the worn wood floor, body lifeless in his harsh hold. His steps quick, frantic, he seemed almost desperate to be away from her. Kicking open the door tucked deep into the back wall, he dumped her on a bare, stained mattress sagging on a metal frame pushed into the corner.

And then he was gone, disappearing through the door.

She'd been confused, unsure of what was happening. From the main room, the thud of his steps passing back and forth echoed as if he paced right outside the door.

And then silence. It stretched so long, Addie began to wonder if he'd left, leaving her alone inside the cabin.

Then he was back, footsteps echoing a second before he stepped into the room, rope hanging from his right hand. He didn't say a word, never looked her in the eye.

He was quick but jumpy, wrapping the pieces of rope around her wrists and ankles, securing them to the frame of the bed.

He left again and the silence returned.

She had no way to track time, but sensed hours had passed since then. No sight, no sound of him. Just an eerie quiet shifting through the cabin, thick enough she could hear the beat of her heart, the shift of air through her lungs.

She could move. Only her fingers so far, but it gave her hope for more.

The sluggishness from the drugs kept their hold. She fought it. The smallest of movements gave her a determination to try for more. It had to be now, while she had the chance.

Listening carefully, waiting for the drop of footsteps, of any kind of movement in the other room, she closed her eyes, concentrating on getting her limbs to obey the commands of her brain.

Still and drugged for so long, pain shot up her right arm when she finally found the ability to lift it an inch from the stained mattress before the rope tied at her wrists restricted her.

She tried again, biting back a cry of joy when the second try was easier than the first.

It was harder with her left arm, the pain worse. She was able to move it. And it only pushed her for more. After days of being trapped in her own body, what rushed through her was a different kind of drug. One carrying a glimmer of hope.

She could move her legs. The more she moved the more she realized the ropes holding her down were giving way, loosening with each yank.

If she could free one arm.

Feeling more give in the ropes tying down her right arm, she bit down on her bottom lip, refusing to care about the pain rumbling through, knowing this might be her only chance.

He was everything his mother told him he was.

Outside the cabin, he paced through the Maples banking the edge. His mother's shrill voice echoed inside his head. The words, the insults, the hatred, never ending, repeating until he was ready to scream.

He'd made a mistake. He had to admit it. From the moment he'd set his eyes on Addie, she'd set all he'd accomplished on end, tempting him in ways he never had before.

Back in New Orleans, he'd been sure the only problem was their location. Was sure this old, creaky cabin with so many dark and angry memories was calling to him, presenting a chance to finally silence all that tortured him here.

He'd been wrong. So very wrong.

Because what he'd hoped to make better only became worse.

The sun began its peek over the eastern skyline, fueling the anger burning in his gut. Another day, more time wasted, and Addie was still untouched. His own needs, always so hot and potent, refused to come to life as they had in the past.

A failure. Just as his mother said.

He screamed into the silence. A guttural sound full of the frustration. He would not have this. Could not have it.

A mistake might have been made but he could make it right and prove again he was the man he was born to be, not the one his mother tried to make him into.

Having Addie was proving to be different than he expected. But he would find a way to change it.

"Tell me again why you gave this up?" Branson sipped from the espresso in his cup as he looked out the tiny window while the airplane began its descent.

Reed shot him a dirty look. His partner knew enough of the story. Was only poking now because he was awe-struck by being flown around on something other than what the Bureau afforded its agents.

"Finish it up." He jerked his head to the weaved, porcelain cup caught almost awkwardly between Branson's thick fingers. "We're about to land."

His partner's answering scowl didn't hold much threat. Sprawled in his reclining seat, he sipped slowly from his espresso, watching out the window as the plane glided lower.

Reed watched too, his nerves on edge. Since the call from his father, his mind had not stopped running through everything he knew. Everything he'd learned from the moment the body of the first woman was found.

His gut told him there was something here. Something in the meeting with Jeremiah Barrow. He couldn't say what. Couldn't say why other than the fact this was a lead they'd never had. One he hoped would lead to Addie.

The landing was smooth, only a slight jolt when the tires hit the runway. Branson still looked like he was caught in a moment of awe as he set down his cup, pushing up from his seat beside Reed while the flight crew swung the door open.

"I'm assuming that's for us." His partner jerked his head toward a black SUV parked only a few feet away from the airplane.

Reed nodded, leading the way. His father promised to have a company vehicle pick them up. Just another perk, he thought grimly, for being a McReily.

Everything he'd run from so long ago seemed to now slap him right in the face.

An early morning chill wrapped around them. The day had barely begun and yet, to Reed, it felt like an unending circle of hours with no end as long as Addie was in the hands of a killer.

The driver of the SUV, his suit a crisp, professionally tailored black, smiled from his place against the front fender.

A step ahead of Reed and Branson, he opened the doors along the passenger side of the SUV, stepping back to give them room to climb in. Closing the doors, he circled around the hood, crawling in behind the steering wheel.

"I've been instructed to let you know, Crayers and Mallow are waiting for you." He dropped the names of the investigators who found Jeremiah.

Punching a finger to the button kicking the engine to life, he glanced over his shoulder. "We've got about a forty-five-minute drive into Gatlinburg. Plenty of time before your meeting."

And yet too much time in the desperation grasping at him. Every minute counted and nothing was happening fast enough.

Reed thanked him, his attention drawn to the window at his side. Tennessee was the first killing. Where they suspected he had his ties, though they never had enough to prove it.

He watched what rushed by as they left the airport, wondering what was here to give him some answers. They passed streetlights flickering off as the morning sun took over. Traffic filling the streets as the workday began. Coffee shops that were busy. Café's filling with breakfast crowds.

It was all so normal. So expected for the start of another day in another city.

Yet, something was different here. It had to be. Tennessee had to hold a secret he had not yet found. It wasn't in the day to day of those who called it home. But it was there. He was sure of it.

CHAPTER FORTY

H e was back.

The echo of footsteps jarred through Addie's heart. She looked frantically at the knotted rope around her right wrist, the progress she'd made in loosening it.

She was so close. Every muscle ached. Her skin screamed from the rub of rope against skin. Just a bit more and she'd be free.

Unless he came into the room and figured out what she was doing.

She stilled, barely breathing, listening to every move he made.

He was coming her way. She heard it in every thud against the floor. She wanted to be wrong. Wanted to believe he was back for something other than her.

The hinges creaked. Her breath caught painfully in her chest. Morning light snuck through the blinds of the only window in the room, casting him in an eerie light as he hovered in the door.

Every slow step toward the bed pounded new fear into her heart. There was something different about him. It was in his eyes. Those pale, blue eyes already so cold. They held a hard, grim shadow, chilling her to the bone, making her wish for the dark of night again rather than the sun streaming through the window.

"You're turning out to be a dilemma." Anger hinted in his voice. He took the final step, stopping at the side of the bed. "Whatever I expected from you, this wasn't it."

Careful not to move, afraid if she did he'd realize how loose the rope around her right wrist was, she tried making sense of whatever it was he was saying.

He raised his hand, light catching against the blade of the knife he clutched between his fingers. "I will finish what I started. I am not a failure."

Her head spun. She wanted to yank and pray the rope would come free. Wanted to kick and hit, fighting off whatever it was he had in mind.

A small rational voice remained in her head under the weight of fear, insisting she stay still and not give away what might be her only hope until she had no other choice.

He lowered over her, his warm breath fanning over her face, forcing her to fight back the sickness in the pit of her stomach.

"We're going to have some fun."

Pressing the dull side of the knife below her chin, he trailed a line down the slope of her neck. Cool steel slid against her skin, dipping at her breasts until meeting the collar of her thin, cotton tank.

She couldn't breathe. Terror pushed hard against her chest, trapping the air in her lungs.

Lifting the knife away, he locked his gaze with hers. She couldn't turn away, trapped by the dark emotion staring down at her.

He didn't move, his eyes probing as they glared into hers. The lines on his forehead creased hard. His mouth pulled into a harsh scowl.

"Damn." He yanked away, shaking on his feet as he looked from her to the door and back.

He lifted his knife, rage heating his pale gaze. "I will have you. I will not prove her right."

She could barely place her thoughts on who he was talking about. It all seemed to be happening so fast and yet in such slow motion.

One second he was standing over her. The next he curled the bottom hem of her tank into his fist, pulling it tight. "I only need to know the pleasures you hold."

The sharp tip of the knife cut into cotton above the dip in her breasts. She couldn't fight back the scream. It echoed through the room as the blade cut through the thin material.

The need to get away became too hard to fight. She yanked on the ropes holding her down, feeling more give.

He didn't notice. Didn't glance at her right hand getting so close to slipping from the knot around it.

"This should be enough." He shoved aside what was left of her tank, running a slow finger around the edge of her pink lace bra. "How could any man not be tempted?"

She tried jerking away from his cold, disgusting touch but the ropes holding her were too tight. She felt more give in her right wrist, but not enough to do any good as he came back over her. His mouth pressed against hers, hard and demanding.

"You will be mine," he growled through his lips taking hers.

No. She yanked her head to the side, breaking his hold. Nausea threatened. Terror grabbed her.

She couldn't lose it now. Doing all she could not to be obvious, she continued to work on the rope holding her captive.

It was her only hope to escape.

He grabbed her face between his rough palms, holding her gaze to his. The pressure of his fingers pushed into her cheeks hard enough to bruise. He hovered above her, as if frozen in place.

What ran through his mind, she didn't know. But the proof of it was in the tense lines creasing his face. The thin push of his lips.

For a moment, it felt as if time stopped.

His hot breath swept over her. The frantic beat of his heart pounded against the thin barrier of her lace bra as his weight seemed to grow, pinning her to the mattress.

She was helpless, lost to do anything while the press of his body kept her trapped. Her mind scrambled for something to get her through as he shifted against her, pulling back enough to stare down at her breasts, thinly covered.

When his pale blue eyes met hers again, so much anger burned there she recoiled from it, pushing deeper into the mattress.

He raised his hand, and she didn't have a chance to brace as his palm slapped hard and painful against her cheek.

She hated that she cried out against the fierce sting.

"What the hell are you doing?" Rage tore through his voice. He shoved away, pushing back to his feet at the side of the mattress.

"You want to prove her right, don't you?" He curved his fingers around her shoulders, biting into her skin as he shook her. "You're trying to prove I'm the failure she said I was."

"Bitch." He slapped her again. This time with the backside of his hand. Hard enough her head jerked to the side.

Biting back the cry of pain, refusing to give him another sign of weakness, she bit hard on her bottom lip, fighting the pain pulsing through her cheek.

She turned her head back, meeting his gaze with her own, refusing to turn away. He'd kill her, she was sure of it. But she wouldn't cower.

If he wanted her dead, he'd do it with the memory of her eyes boring into his.

Though only minutes passed, it felt like hours as his gaze locked steady with hers. His hands came around her neck, only a hint of pressure where his thumbs pressed into her skin, fingers wrapped around the curves below her ears.

Instinct kicked in and she shifted frantically beneath him, desperate to break his hold. He only increased the pressure the more she struggled, a sick smile spreading over his face as she gasped for breath.

This was it. She couldn't fight him off. Couldn't do anything but yank frantically at the ropes until even that became too much effort as she gasped for the smallest hint of air.

Black spots crept into her vision. Her lungs ached. Fear slid away under the acceptance she couldn't stop her death.

"No. Not yet." His voice was a low growl as he yanked his hands away.

She gasped. The first intake of air burned through her lungs. Desperate, her breaths were quick and frantic. Her heart beat frantically against her chest, the rush of blood a hard echo in her ears.

He stared down at her, as if needing to make sure he hadn't gone too far. Once her breathing slowed, he spun around, his steps hard and determined, leading him out of the room.

They continued through the cabin, the loud slam of a door leaving no doubt she was alone again.

Her throat raw, lungs aching, she fought back the need to close her eyes and slip away from reality.

He'd be back. She was sure of it. And when he did come back, he'd finish what he'd started.

The diner wasn't more than a tiny hole in the wall set on a crowded corner of downtown Gatlinburg.

As promised, Crayers and Mallow took up two seats around a small, scarred table inside, waiting for Reed and Branson. Half-finished plates of pancakes and an omelet sat in front of them. Coffee cups, getting close to needing a refill, were in easy reach.

They stood when Reed reached the table, offering outstretched hands.

"You made good time." The one Reed recognized as Crayers, his black hair cut and shaved as if he was still in the Army where he'd served for two decades, gave a quick, brisk shake of his hand.

"Your father said you took the company jet in."

Reed nodded and turned his attention to Mallow. His tall, looming form made Reed feel small.

"We've got about fifteen minutes before our man is supposed to show," Mallow informed him, reclaiming his seat at the table.

Picking up his coffee cup, he held it for the waitress to see. "He didn't seem all too eager to talk to us but, when we explained the situation, he claimed he'd be here."

"Might be best if you don't flash your badges around," Crayers added. "I have a feeling he might not take too kindly to it."

Understanding, Reed unclipped his badge from his waist, shoving it in a pocket as Branson did the same. "You're the lead on this."

The waitress reached their table, coffee pot and extra cups in her hands. At their nod, she set a cup in front of Reed and Branson, filling their cups along with Crayers and Mallow.

"Can I get you some breakfast?" She set the pot on the edge of the table, pulling out a pad from her apron.

Reed shook his head, the thought of food the last thing on his mind.

"How about one of your cinnamon rolls." Branson jerked his head to the display case on the counter.

Tucking her pad back into her apron, she flashed a quick smile. "You make it easy."

She grabbed the coffee pot, tucking it back in place before sliding a plate from the stack teetering by the order counter. Seconds later, she slid a fresh cinnamon roll in front of Branson with the reminder to let her know if they needed anything else.

They waited.

Fifteen minutes turned to twenty then thirty. The waitress returned, filling their cups again. Branson finished his cinnamon roll, Crayers and Mallow picked at what was left of their own breakfast.

Reed watched the time, desperation and frustration growing with every passing minute.

"He's here." Mallow's attention turned to the door as the bell above chimed through the tiny space. He stood while the others remained seated, crossing between the cramped booths and tables toward the worn and beaten man looking cautiously around at those inside.

The lines creasing his face deepened when he spotted Mallow coming for him. Reluctance was clear in the sweep of his gaze. Hesitation slowed his steps to almost a crawl.

He kept at it, following Mallow to the table.

"Didn't figure there'd be a party waiting for me." He trolled his gaze over the others, displeasure clear in the turned down corners of his mouth.

"As I explained over the phone," Mallow pulled out the empty chair at the end of the table for him before returning to his own. "This matter is of the most importance to McReily Industries. Reed McReily is here personally, for that reason."

The other man's eyes followed the wave of a hand Mallow sent across the table, landing heavy on Reed. "You the one writing me that check?"

Caught unprepared, Reed pulled his expression into a tight line, hoping he didn't reveal he had no clue about any check. The slightest bit of suspicion would send Jeremiah Barrow running back out the door he'd just come through.

"I have your money." Crayers tugged a briefcase to the table, snapping it open. Pulling out a plain white envelope, he set it on the table.

He looked at Jeremiah as he finally took a seat, resting a hand over the envelope. "As you requested, we have five thousand for you, providing you have useful information for us."

Jeremiah eyed the envelope. So did Reed, from across the table. In the reality of things, such an amount wasn't even a drop in the bucket for McReily Industries. Still, knowing his father had to approve such funds going out in this kind of situation, he found himself more off balance by all the changes since Addie pushed him to take that first step with his parents.

"Don't suppose a meal is part of the deal, too." Jeremiah looked around at the plates cluttering the table. "Haven't had myself any breakfast yet and I've got to go from here to work."

Mallow waved down their waitress. "Order whatever you'd like."

Reed's impatience grew while they waited for the waitress to bring him a menu and for him to decide what it was he wanted. Finally, with his own cup of coffee joining the others and his breakfast choice ordered, he turned his attention back to those waiting for him.

"Don't understand exactly how it is you found me." He sipped from his coffee, staring at them over the rim. "Not that I suppose it much matters, now. You found me and I'm here. So, what is it exactly you want to know?"

Crayers reached into the briefcase where he'd left it on the table. "You have a DNA connection with this man."

He pulled out the sketch created from Addie's memory of the man who had been in the Magic Moon and the still caught from the video the night Rosalie had been attacked. He pushed them across the table toward Jeremiah. "We need you to tell us who he is."

Looking at the envelope rather than the pictures in front of him, Jeremiah seemed to need the reminder of what his true motivation was. Avoiding the four different sets of eyes resting on him, he finally looked down at the pictures, grabbing one in each hand.

"Don't think I recognize him." He tossed the pictures back to the table.

Crayers placed his hand back over the envelope, sliding it away. "Maybe you should take another look until you know."

Watching the risk of his money slipping away, he yanked at the pictures again. "I probably got more blood folks around here than I'll ever know. We don't exactly stay close. Haven't seen my own ma in over a decade."

He continued to look at the pictures. "Meant it when I said I don't recognize him."

He set them down as the waitress reached the table with the steak and eggs he'd ordered. "But I'll admit to some resemblance to a cousin of mine. One of the few I actually knew."

Grabbing the hot sauce from the edge of the table, he drowned his eggs. Reed wanted to grab him. Shake him until he told him what he knew about this cousin of his.

He knew better, though. If he had any hope of finding Addie before it was too late, he had to play the game.

It was one Jeremiah seemed to be taking a new interest in, and enjoying, as he cut into his steak, slowly chewing his bite, washing it down with a long sip from his coffee.

"Mikey was what we all called him." He waved his fork at them before spearing it into his sauce covered eggs. "He preferred Mike once he got into his twenties."

None of his information meant a damn thing. He knew it. It was clear in the self-satisfaction gleaming in his blue eyes, staring at them over the huge bite he shoved into his mouth.

"So, this cousin, Mike," Mallow pushed him on. "Do you know where we can find him?"

"Sure." His smile was cocky. "He's six feet under at Our Lady of Grace cemetery where he's been for over twenty years."

"Well, then—"

Crayers grabbed the envelope, tossed it into the briefcase. "It seems this has been a waste of time. We'll leave you to finish your breakfast."

The sight of his check being taken away seemed to be the push Jeremiah needed. Setting his fork on the table, pushing his food out of the way, he eyed the briefcase. "He had a son."

That caught their attention.

Crayers flattened a hand over his briefcase, waiting for him to go on.

"He married some girl right out of high school." He shrugged under the weight of four sets of eyes settled on him. "Only met her a couple times but always knew something wasn't right about her."

Satisfied his chances of getting his check were again on the right track, he pulled back his food. "They had a boy a couple years after they married. He'd have been about five when Mikey died."

"Where's this wife live?"

Jeremiah shook his head. "That I don't know. Like I said, Mikey's been gone for over twenty years. I never saw a reason to get to know her while he was married to her, much less after he died."

"How about names?" Crayers opened his briefcase but left the envelope sitting inside it. "For the wife or the son."

"The son's name is easy." Jeremiah poked at his eggs. "Samuel. It's a family name."

He took a bite, washed it down with coffee. "The wife, though, that's a harder one. Mikey was from my ma's side, so he was a Holkman. I'm sure she'd have taken his last name. Her first name I can't be sure of. I'm thinking it was either Victoria or Vivian."

Reed pushed up from his chair, pulling his phone from his pocket on the way to the door. Whatever was left to be said or done, he didn't have time for. Crayers and Mallow would handle it.

Marshall's voice boomed through the phone before Reed made it outside.

"I have names." He didn't bother with small talk, pushing his way out the door.

He felt it deep in his bones, the knowledge that this latest information was his only chance of finding Addie. If it was real, he had a chance. If it was a wild goose chase—

The reality was one he couldn't bring himself to think about.

CHAPTER FORTY-ONE

S he was free.

Even with urgency raging through her veins, Addie had to take a minute. Her entire body shook. Her heart pounded. Every breath was painful to grab.

She lifted her right arm, waving it in front of her, needing to see the proof she wasn't still trapped to the bed. The cry of relief was almost too strong to hold back. But she had no other choice. Couldn't take the chance of being heard.

Not that she believed he'd been back since he'd come close to strangling the last breath from her lungs.

The cabin had been eerily silent. She strained again to hear something, anything that might give a clue where he was. Only the hollow echo of emptiness came back.

Realizing she was losing precious time, she curled over on the mattress, quickly going to work on the rope holding her left hand down.

She worked her fingers frantically over the careless knot. The first hint of give fueled her desperation. Pushing past the strain in her muscles, she battled the rough cords around her wrist.

Tears came when both her hands were free. After coming so close to losing her life, she suddenly had hope.

Being able to sit up on the mattress rushed a new strength through her. She finally had some control over her own fate.

With the use of both hands, freeing her ankles was quick and easy. Swinging over the edge of the bed, she pushed to her feet. Her legs buckled underneath her, sending her tumbling back.

Sucking in a deep breath, she tried again. Her legs threatened to give out. She bit hard on her bottom lip, fighting it.

Every muscle cried out for her to give up. To simply collapse on the bed and stay there.

She refused to give in to the pain. She dared a step. Her entire body shook, and for a moment, she was afraid she'd end up a useless pile on the floor.

Dragging up every ounce of strength from inside, she stayed standing. She listened, heard nothing from the rest of the cabin, and dared another step.

Where was she going? Sucking in a deep breath, fighting back the pain, she looked at her options.

She could go back through the door. It had been quiet since he'd stormed out. The door slammed and she'd assumed he'd left. But what if she was wrong? What if he was still somewhere inside? Or if he came back in while she was trying to get out?

The only other choice was the small, dirty window cut into the wall across from the door. She didn't know if she could get it open, much less fit through it.

She had to try. It was better than taking the risk of walking through the cabin and being discovered.

Every step was a new shot of pain racing up her legs. Once she started, she refused to stop, forcing all the strength she could grab to get her to the window.

Age and neglect were clear around the old wooden frame. She feared it hadn't been opened in decades. Flipping the old lock, fighting the catch in it, she prayed it would work.

It didn't. But there was some movement, giving her hope. Every muscle screamed as she tried again. Her heart hammered against her chest from the worry of being found before she could get away.

There was more give, the window beginning to slide in its frame. Another inch and she got her fingers under it for more leverage.

Her legs continued to threaten to drop her to the floor. Biting hard on her lower lip, she thought of Reed. Saw his face, heard his voice, letting it be what she needed to bring a new strength to her efforts.

Another push and it was as if whatever had been fighting her suddenly broke. The resistance was gone. Curling her fingers under the bottom ledge, she shoved it up, thankful when she let go and it stayed in place.

The screen was nothing. Torn and ripped, it took only a slight shove to have it falling out to the ground below.

Listening again and finding only silence, she stuck her head through the small, open space. It would be tight, but she'd fit through. The drop though, left her thinking again about going through the door instead.

It wasn't too far, in the reality of things. A bit higher than she expected but still only a first-floor fall.

Her legs were already protesting at the thought. It was a struggle to get them to simply hold her upright. The tumble out the window would be so much more.

She didn't have a choice. Knowing the risk of the fall from the window was still better than trying to get through the cabin, she sucked in a long, determined breath.

She'd go headfirst, working her body through the skinny space. If she could hold the edge of the window long enough, she might be able to break the worst of the fall.

It wasn't as easy as her mind created. Putting her head through while holding on was impossible. She worked it until she was half sitting, half hanging out the window. She'd have to go legs first. The idea of hanging on for as long as possible would still work, just from a different direction.

The old and splintered wood frame caught at the cut edges of her shirt. Damning any sense of modesty when her life was at risk, she yanked it off, tossing it to the ground.

In her bra and skirt, she worked awkwardly through the limited space, trying to turn without launching herself to the ground before she was ready. Weathered splinters caught at bare skin. Her arms ached from the fight of holding on. Her hip hit hard against the outside wall of the cabin as she lowered herself, sending a new wave of pain raging through.

She dangled, still a good drop to the ground. Sucking in a long, deep breath, holding it, she let go.

Her feet hit first, the thrust of it tossing her back, knocking the wind from her lungs. She couldn't move. Could only lie there while her body trembled. Something slithered against her bare back, and she bit back a scream.

Between the drugs lingering in her blood stream and having the air choked from her lungs, she worried about having the strength to keep on. But she didn't have a choice. It was that or death. And she really didn't want to die. Not like this.

Drawing on everything she had left inside, she rolled over, pushing to her hands and knees. She could see the thick wall of trees surrounding the cabin. If she could get to them, stay under their cover, she might have a chance.

A crack echoed from somewhere close. An animal hanging out or a human foot along the ground? She didn't know. Didn't want to find out.

Rocking forward then back, she made it to her feet. She centered her attention on the trees, willing her legs to work under her. She might not know where she was or where she'd go, but the thick trunks and branches waiting for her offered hope. And for that she'd keep moving.

"Vivian Holkman is dead."

Marshall's familiar voice boomed from the other end of the phone. Still at the same table in the same diner, Reed pushed back his chair, stepping away from the others.

They'd waited it out while Jeremiah took his sweet time finishing up his breakfast. And even then he hadn't been done, ordering one of their cinnamon rolls to go and sipping slowly from his coffee.

Crayers sliding his check across the table hadn't encouraged him. He merely laid a hand over it, as if needing a minute to savor the feel of it, before folding it in half and stuffing it in the back pocket of his jeans.

Once he'd left, they'd stayed, going over what he'd told them, debating the chances of whether or not he'd been truthful and where his information might lead.

"She died three months ago," Marshall continued while Reed stepped out of the diner. "Heart failure was the cause. Coroner states in his report, it was inevitable."

"So, a natural death." Reed stared at the traffic slowly easing by on the street, giving proof to the time that had passed as the frantic beat of rush hour was no longer evident. It was another reminder of how quickly time was ticking away, putting Addie's life more at risk.

"Seems that way. Her son is the only living heir. A Samuel Holkman. Dad was Michael Holkman."

Which was exactly what Jeremiah told them.

"Didn't inherit anything more than a load of debt and an old cabin in the Smoky Mountains. My best guess, it's where he grew up."

"Do you have an address?"

He was quick to get back to the table, waving his hands at the others, in search of a pen and paper.

Crayers pulled both out of his briefcase, shoving it in front of Reed as Marshall read off the details.

"I've already alerted the locals. They're on their way."

Beside him, Branson grabbed the paper, started punching it into the GPS on his phone.

"Forty-five minutes." He looked from Reed to Crayers and Mallow across from them. "Thirty, if you're not afraid to drive fast."

Marshall continued but Reed barely heard him, leading the way as they hurried out of the diner.

"The son didn't bother to claim the body," Marshall filled him in as he climbed into the SUV. "I'm guessing there's more we need to know there."

Reed agreed. But not now.

His gut told him they needed to get to that cabin and worry about the rest later.

He'd been so close.

So close to ending it all. To taking her life and walking away.

How could she have been so wrong when she was so perfect?

He'd been so ready to take her life and end it, hovering above her, watching as she struggled for those final gasps of life. It would have been all that was left. The final act in ending the mistake he'd made.

Then he'd heard his mother laughing at him, mocking him. He was done with it. She was dead. Gone. He refused to let her continue to control him.

He knew what needed to be done. Addie was nothing more than a problem to be dealt with. A mistake he'd take care of without having to hear his mother's disapproval.

She wasn't meant for him, though every part of him ached for it to be different. It was time to finally be done with her. No more excuses. No more weakness. He'd block the whining voice of his mother echoing so loud in his head and prove the man he truly was.

Addie wouldn't get a second chance. He set the truth of it in his head, refused to let it go as he threw open the door of the cabin.

It was now. She needed to go. He would not let anything sway him this time. He'd carry out what was meant to be.

Determined, his heavy steps were quick, taking him back to the room. He wanted to see her face when he came in. Wanted to see the realization settle that she was facing the final seconds of her life.

Throwing open the door with more force than needed, he stepped into the room with a satisfied smile stretching his lips.

It quickly disappeared when only an empty bed greeted him.

"What the hell."

Empty ropes dangled from the bedposts. He walked to them, grabbing one in his fist, clutching until the rough cord burned against his palm.

His own dumb mistake. Stupid. He should have drugged her again. Should have had the sense to check the ropes holding her down.

Where the hell was she?

His eyes were drawn to the open window, and he had his answer. Sticking his head through the opening, he stared down at the screen below, out to the twist of trees behind the cabin.

Cursing, he turned from the window, hurrying back through the cabin. She couldn't be far. He hadn't been gone long.

Storming out the door, he ran around to the back, stopping where the screen rested against dirt and old pine needles. Going still, listening, he was sure he heard a rustling from the trees directly ahead of him. He started that way, refusing to second guess himself.

He'd find her. And when he did, he'd make her pay.

CHAPTER FORTY-TWO

Behind the wheel, Mallow paid no attention to the speed limit along the interstate, cutting between cars, keeping their speed fast and desperate.

It wasn't enough for Reed.

His mind played horrible games. Images of a frightened Addie—the empty cabin they'd found in Louisiana, of what they might find in Tennessee—raced like a fire through his head.

Marshall had his agents digging further on Samuel Holkman. The information trickled in as they raced down the interstate. School records portrayed an isolated student, barely slipping by with his grades. A file opened by Child Protective Services reported suspicion of abuse within his home that could never be fully proven.

And then he'd simply disappeared. It was as if he reached twenty-one and no longer existed. No more hits to his social security. No more employment records to be found. Nothing to show he lived anywhere, owned anything, worked a job or existed, in any way, in the normal ways of life.

He was just gone.

Reed didn't believe it was a coincidence that a few years after that, the murders began.

He still had no proof. No way to provide any evidence that Samuel Holkman was the man they'd been hunting for so long. But he knew it. Felt it deep inside.

And he had Addie.

"The locals are going in quiet." Branson ended the call he'd taken only minutes before. "If they find anything they'll let us know."

Reed could only nod, his mind running in so many different directions. He needed to suck it in. Needed to be the agent he prided himself on if he had any hope of finding Addie in time.

His love for her threatened everything that usually kept him going and level-headed. The thought of never having her again in his life was more than he could deal with.

She'd always been his everything. Coming back to New Orleans, seeing her again, had only proven it to be true. He needed her like the next breath through his lungs. Couldn't think of anything but her and the horror she was facing.

He'd get her back. He couldn't believe otherwise. And when he did, he'd never let her out of his arms again. He didn't have to have the answers he'd thought he needed. He only had to have her.

Addie could hear him. He was close.

He hadn't tried to be quiet, coming after her through the thick trees. He'd taunted her. Calling out her name. Promising what he'd do to her once he caught her.

Her heart pounded. Her lungs ached. Her legs were like rubber ready to give out on her at any minute. Still, she ran, trying to work her way around the long, thick roots sticking through the ground, threatening to trip her.

The trees were thick. They crawled like a wall around her, leaving her with no idea where she was or where she might be heading.

Heavy branches hid the sunlight, casting her in shadows. Unknown things slithered and crept around her. Dead leaves crushed under her feet. Twigs snapped.

"You have nowhere to go." His voice echoed from behind. "Run. Run. Run. You won't get away."

Her pulse thundered through her ears. The rumble of his voice was closer than it had been. She forced her legs to move faster. But where was she going? She was lost in an endless sea of nothing but trees, branches hanging low, grabbing at her. Roots pushing through the ground, threatening to take her down.

There was no end. No sign of anything but the craziness. She couldn't stop. Couldn't take the time to try and figure out where she was or where she should go.

She could only run. Run and pray she'd make it out of there alive.

"The cabin's empty. But you need to see this."

The fresh-faced deputy who met Reed and Branson at the door, waved his hand behind him, into the dim interior. He stepped aside, letting them through the door, leading them toward the back.

"At least one person wasn't here by choice." He pushed through a door, Reed and Branson only a step behind.

The small room was empty except for a bare mattress on a frame pushed into the corner. Stepping up to the edge of the mattress, the deputy lifted a short rope tied to the edge. It matched the others on each corner.

Fear clutched at Reed's heart. Looking past the ropes, he trailed his gaze around the room to the open window on the far wall. Stepping past the deputy, he stuck his head out the opening, saw the screen on the ground below.

The thought Addie might have had a chance to escape jolted through him. "Where are the rest of your officers?" He spun around on the deputy.

"Already out there searching."

"Call the Bureau," Reed barked at Branson as he rushed past. "Have them bring in more resources. I want everything and everyone we have."

He didn't wait for a response, his steps at a run as he left through the same door he'd come in only a few minutes before. Unclipping the Glock from his waist, he rounded the side of the cabin, coming to the back where the screen rested on the ground.

The ground was too dry to keep the imprints of footsteps. He could only guess which way she'd headed. Placing Addie in his mind, he tried imaging what it must have been like for her, pulling free from the ropes that bound her, escaping through the window.

She'd have taken the most direct route, he was sure. Desperate to get away without thought to the direction she was headed.

He started off in what he hoped was her path, cutting into the trees. Thick branches closed around him. Silence surrounded him. He put his mind to Addie again, trying to imagine her standing where he was, terrified, running for her life.

Keeping the image with him, he tried following every step he thought she would take, praying he was right. Knowing, if he wasn't—

It wasn't a thought he wanted to hold.

CHAPTER FORTY-THREE

There was nowhere to go. She kept running only to find nothing but more trees surrounding her.

She couldn't stop and try to get her bearings. For every step she took, Addie heard his steps getting closer. His voice a threat continuing to gain space, creeping in until she wasn't sure if she was escaping him or only providing more enjoyment in his sick, twisted mind.

Ahead, a flicker of light hinted at a break in the trees, allowing the sun to sneak through. It was a whisper of hope. One she hadn't had since climbing through the window.

She could hear him behind her. But other sounds were breaking through. The rustle of dead foliage. The crunch of tree branches breaking. The sounds came at her from both sides, making her wonder if it was reality or her mind starting to slip away.

It didn't matter. Losing her mind was better than what waited for if he caught up with her. The hint of sun ahead was her beacon, leading her through the branches grabbing at her. The roots threatening to trip her up.

The echo of his chase seemed to get louder with every footfall. Willing her legs to move faster, fearing it still wouldn't be enough, she kept her attention on the hope of sun shimmering ahead. She cut through the trees, always keeping the glimmer of rays breaking through in her sight.

She hoped for another cabin or a road where a car might pass by. Sucking in a hard breath, she surged forward, breaking through the thick branches.

"No."

It wasn't a cabin, a road, or anything to give her hope. Instead, she was surrounded by boulders, taking over where the trees had been, only a few feet away from a rocky ridge. She edged close enough to look down. A river tumbled hard below, white caps crashing against rocks along the bed.

A flicker of noise came from behind. She tried to turn back for the trees, to run, but she was too late. In the few seconds she had stopped, she'd sealed her fate.

His hand grabbed hard around her arm. Yanking her back against him, he lowered his mouth to her ear, his warm breath sliding like oil over her skin. "I told you, there was nowhere for you to go."

She tried yanking away, looking at the ridge only a few steps from where she stood. Falling to her death in the river below seemed a much better choice than letting him do to her what he had in mind.

His hold tightened more, rough demanding fingers biting into flesh. The temptation to give up, accept the fate waiting for her, rushed in strong and fierce.

She couldn't do it. Refused to simply let it happen without some kind of fight.

Kicking back with her foot, she felt the hard hit of his shin as she made contact.

"Bitch," he growled in her ear, but his hold didn't weaken.

He moved at her back. One of his hands slipped from her arm while the other tightened more. Seconds later, sunlight bounced off the smooth blade he waved in front of her.

"I'll tell you how this is going to work." His voice an eerie shift in her ear, he waved the knife again, bringing it closer. "You and I are going to go back to the cabin. You aren't going to try and run again, or I'll leave you for dead right here in the middle of nowhere."

He'd leave her for dead no matter where they ended up. She nodded weakly, knowing better than to dare a word. If she made him believe he had her weak and willing, maybe she would still have a chance.

"Drop the knife." The deep voice broke through only a second before two uniforms burst from the trees around them.

Addie had only a second of relief before the sharp edge of the knife pressed against her neck, cutting into skin.

"I'll have her neck slit before you get a shot off." He backed away, bringing them closer to the ridge, the roar of the water below a constant drone. "Or maybe we'll take a jump together."

He stepped closer to the ridge, looking down before piercing his gaze on the officers in front of them.

She was going to die. The realization hit with a jolt of icy fear settling deep in her bones. She couldn't fight anymore. No longer had any more hope of escape. Her moment had come.

The reality tore a horrified scream from deep inside.

Reed couldn't run fast enough. The frantic beat of his feet running through the trees matched the desperate rhythm of his heart pounding against his chest.

Others searched through the trees, trying desperately to find Addie. He couldn't see them, couldn't hear them, but they were out there.

It did nothing to ease what clawed inside. He kept seeing the mattress, the ropes. Images of Addie trapped—thoughts of what might have happened while she was vulnerable to the monster who had her—ran rapid through his brain. Pushed desperation heavy through his blood.

Still trying to put himself in Addie's head, he kept his path straight. She wouldn't know, wouldn't have any experience to guide her to zigzag through the trees. She'd have only instinct carrying her along.

He was beginning to wonder if he was wrong when Addie's scream broke through the silence. The fear in it grasped a tight fist around his heart.

Branches grabbed at him. Rocks and roots tried to take him down. He didn't care. All he knew, all that ran wild through his mind, was Addie and whatever horror she faced.

The sun broke through the trees ahead. That was where he'd find her.

Hard-earned agent instincts kicked in, taking over his frantic fear before he broke through the trees. He couldn't let his feelings for Addie draw away from the one chance he had at saving her.

He shifted through the last wall of trees, cursing the crunch of his shoes against old leaves and fallen twigs littering the ground. Low limbs, pine needles scratching at bare skin, gave him cover as he took in the clearing only a few steps from where he stood.

From his place, he had a view of two officers standing with their guns drawn. The thick stretch of trees prevented him from seeing more. Moving around a trunk twice as big as him, he was careful with every step, not wanting to give himself away.

He saw her then and his heart stopped.

He couldn't see Addie's face, only the small slice of her back where Samuel had her trapped against him, his arm raised and wrapped around her neck.

Inching around for a better look, his worst fear was confirmed as sunlight reflected off the knife he held at her neck.

A sound from behind pulled him from the terrifying sight. He spun around, gun raised and ready.

Branson held up a hand. "No reason to shoot. It's just me. Been running my butt off trying to catch up with you."

Though his voice was no more than a whisper, Reed still motioned for him to be quiet. Without saying anything in response, he waved his partner to where he stood in the barrier of the trees. The officers a few steps closer, coming into his view.

"Don't be foolish." The larger of the two kept a steady point on Samuel with his gun. "You don't have a way out of this."

To Reed's horror, Samuel inched closer to what he realized was a ridge just past the line of trees. Understanding the roar he'd heard pass through the branches had to be a river below, he didn't have long to decide his next move.

He motioned to Branson, pointing through the trees to a place directly behind where Samuel held his knife to Addie's throat.

It was a risk. A *terrifying* risk. One wrong move from him, the smallest of hints of what he was trying to do, and Addie's life would be done. Whether by the knife or by the fall over the ridge.

He wished he could let the other officers know he was there. He had to take the chance they wouldn't have a knee-jerk reaction and try to take him down while he tried to save Addie.

With Branson only a step behind, he stopped short of coming out of the trees. He didn't dare utter a word, too close now to risk being heard.

But Branson knew what ran through his mind. They'd been partners too long for him to need to question what it was Reed intended.

"Come any closer and I'll kill us both." Cold resignation echoed in Samuel's voice. He took another step closer to the ridge and Reed didn't have another second to waste.

Palming his badge in his hand, holding it up with the hope the other officers would see it, he raised his Glock and stepped out from the cover of the trees.

He had only seconds. Even the best trained officer was going to react to the sight of him suddenly stepping into the clearing. Once that happened, he'd no longer have surprise on his side.

If he moved fast enough, knowing Branson was right behind him, backing him up, he'd have a chance at saving Addie.

The taller one who'd spoken only seconds before noticed him. He was good. Reed would give him that. If one wasn't watching closely, they would have never caught the sudden shift in his eyes. The acknowledgment flickering for a brief second when his gaze passed over the badge.

Thankful for it, Reed inched closer to where Samuel held Addie, terrifyingly aware of the knife he held to her throat. One wrong move and he'd be helpless to stop the blade from cutting through.

The other officer noticed him then. And though he tried, his reaction was not as smooth as his partner's. The moment of surprise sweeping over his face was clear. He tried chasing it away, but it was too late.

Samuel spun around, the sudden jerk pressing the blade into Addie's neck, drawing blood.

Reed's heart stopped. Desperate to control the emotions surging inside, he kept a firm grip on his Glock, his finger pressed to the trigger.

Just one shot. That was all he needed. But it was too risky with Addie held against him.

Relief and fear mixed in Addie's dark eyes when she saw him. It killed him that he couldn't reach for her. Simply grab her into his arms and let her know she was safe.

"Well, isn't this fitting." A sick, twisted smile grew over Samuel's face. "After all the time I've kept you running and guessing and here we are, finally, face to face."

"If it wasn't for you, Agent McReily," his pale eyes shimmered with the craziness of one who had killed many. "I never would have been led to Addie. How does that feel, knowing you handed her right to me?"

Though he'd already known it, the truth settled heavy in his gut. Everything inside pushed for him to take the shot and end the life of the miserable man he'd sought for so long.

He couldn't do it. Not with Addie's dark brown gaze resting on him, trusting him.

"It feels like you made a fatal mistake."

Something flickered in his eyes, so quick Reed didn't have a chance to figure out what it might mean. He didn't have the time to wonder more as Samuel took another step closer to the ridge.

"You'd be smart to let her go." His words would do nothing, but he needed to stall, aware Branson was somewhere behind him in the trees.

He had to count on his partner, now. Draw from all those years they'd worked together and know he was back there somewhere, doing what needed to be done to save Addie.

It was so damn hard. Hard not to risk a shot. To take him out. So close to her now, he could see the bruises around her neck. His mind played horrible images of what she must have endured. Her shirt was gone. Fear burned in her dark eyes and her delicate skin showed proof of the pain she'd been put through.

He wanted Samuel to pay. Wanted him to know the hell he deserved.

The other officers kept their ready stance across from him. Whether they were aware of Branson's presence, he couldn't be sure. Had no way of finding out.

Pure evil darkened the look Samuel threw back at him. "I think I'd be smart to kill her here." His knife dug into tender skin, drawing more blood. "While you're forced to watch."

Addie's tortured cry tore deep into him. Before he could stop himself, he took a threatening step forward, his mind only on getting Addie away from him.

"Careful." Samuel took another step toward the ridge, bringing him so close even an inch of movement from him would send them over.

He looked down at the river roaring below, back at Reed with a sickening smile stretched across his face. "Figure I could throw her over now before you'd have a chance to react."

He turned so that it was Addie who hovered close to the edge. Terror catching her, she tried, uselessly, to struggle free from his hold.

Dirt and rock fell beneath the toe of her shoes. It would take nothing to throw her over as he threatened. Her side ached from where he kept his arm so tight around her. Blood dripped down her neck, warmth cooling as it slid down.

Only the look in Reed's eyes kept her from giving up completely. In their deep blue depths, he pleaded for her to trust him. To know he'd give his own life to save hers.

It was hard to hold on to hope when there didn't seem to be anything Reed or the officers could do. The way he held her to him, she was a human shield, making sure she'd take the bullet before he did.

And that was added to the fact she was close to dangling over the ridge, the river a violent rush beneath her. The smallest step from him and she'd go down.

"He can't save you now." His breath was a warm crawl over the sensitive stretch of skin between her shoulder and ear. She cringed, trying again to wrestle her way free.

He only tightened his hold. "You're only wasting your time. I either kill you or we die together."

She looked at Reed again, needing to see him. Needing the reassurance of the strength and love she found inside him. Her eyes caught something as she turned her gaze. A hint of movement. Quick and barely there, a brief rustle in the trees behind him.

Fearing he saw what she had, she braced for his reaction. When nothing happened, she grasped on to a last glimmer of hope of getting out of this alive.

"I tell you what." Holding his gun in one hand, Reed held the other out toward them. "You let Addie come to me and I promise you, I'll make sure you walk out of here alive."

His answering laugh was a harsh echo in her ears. "See, that's your problem Agent McReily. You've believed, all along, I was a fool."

His attention firmly on Reed, he didn't catch the other officers carefully getting closer. Or more movement in the trees.

Addie couldn't react. It would be the end if she did. She had to trust Reed and the others would give her a chance to stay alive.

"Only a fool would scoff at my offer." Reed's voice remained steady, calm. "It's your only chance of staying alive."

Addie felt the tension. Something was about to happen. The other officers dared another step closer. Reed looked at her, his hard gaze spearing through the fear to a strength she thought she'd lost.

"Already told you." He was close to dangling her over the ridge. "I might just kill us both."

Addie bit back a scream. She had to believe in Reed. Had to trust him.

"Not much use for me to stick around now." His hold on her tightened painfully. The blade again bit into her neck. "You've made sure of that."

Anger vibrated from him, and she feared how far it would lead him.

Reed came closer. His gaze stayed locked with hers, giving his own strength to her the only way he could. Another rustle again, this time closer. A flicker through the branches only a few feet away.

She felt the strength flowing from Reed. And the hope in whoever or whatever still lingered in the trees. A chance was coming.

She had to be ready. Had to do her part. There would only be one chance. If she missed it, it would be the worst failure of her life. A failure that would cost her the very life she wanted to continue to live.

Though it brought her closer to him, she inched back from the edge. Slowly, hoping he wouldn't notice the subtle shift of her body, moving her away from the threat of tumbling over.

Reed knew, though. In his eyes she saw the knowledge and the slight nod of his head, encouraging her.

"How about we make a trade, Samuel. You let her go and I'll take her place."

The roll of his disgusting laugh brushed over her. He shifted, giving her hope he was more about what Reed was saying than what she was doing.

Going on that, she curled around further, relief a quick breath through her lungs when her toes no longer dangled dangerously over the roaring river below.

"I think you're better suffering with what I take from you." A slur echoed in his words she hadn't heard before.

He leaned forward and for a moment she feared he was moving her back to the edge. Instead, he took a step forward, closer to Reed, taking her further away from the threat. "You trade places, and I don't get the satisfaction of knowing you get to watch her die."

He remembered her then. His hold around her tightened. The blade of the knife dug deep again, drawing more blood.

She saw him then, Reed's partner breaking through the trees. He hovered where Samuel couldn't see him.

The time was now. No second guessing.

"Sounds like a weak excuse to me." Reed kept him distracted, giving Branson time to move behind without notice.

Samuel snapped around, facing Reed directly, moving Addie further from the edge. She arched away from him, feeling a slight pressure, but nothing more.

Only the knife at her throat gave her pause. She didn't have a choice. She had to take the chance.

Reed took his own step closer as Samuel seemed to sway behind her. "I'm not—"

The growl of his voice drifted off behind her. His hand holding the knife to her neck slipped lower. "I'm not...I don't do excuses."

There was definitely a slur to his words, she was sure of it this time. Jerking her hand free from where he'd had it trapped by her side, surprised for only a moment by how much easier it had been than she expected, she twisted her fingers around his wrist, doing everything she could to pull the knife away.

She was aware of Branson moving fast from the side. Of the sudden echo of movement from the officers behind them. But it was only Reed she saw. Only Reed she cared about as she twisted in his hold and yanked on his wrist.

He stumbled for a moment, and she was hopeful.

Then it all happened so fast, it was a blur. Behind her, Samuel regained his footing. He fought the pull on his wrist, yanking back, the blade slicing painfully above her collar bone.

The burning pain of cut flesh too much to handle, she cried out, losing her grip and her fight to free herself. A warm flow of blood pooled between her breasts. She fought the blackness creeping into her vision.

"No." The echo of Reed's voice tumbled inside her head. Through blurred vision she saw him rush forward, a strange roar coming from behind.

And then a pop, vibrating around her, leaving an acrid scent burning her nose. The blackness grew as Samuel's arms slipped away, freeing her.

Fear burned in Reed's eyes as the darkness took over, tumbling her to the ground.

CHAPTER FORTY-FOUR

He couldn't stop the blood.

On the ground beside Addie, Reed pressed the shirt he'd ripped off against the long gash slicing her delicate skin.

He'd wanted her to move and give Branson a better chance at taking a shot. He hadn't expected her to take it further. Hadn't been prepared when she'd tried to free herself.

"Here." Kneeling beside him, Branson tore off his own shirt, held it out for Reed. Tossing aside his own blood-drenched shirt, he grabbed for his partner's, pressing it hard against the gaping wound.

Sirens registered in a distant part of his brain.

"They're close." Branson dropped a firm hand over his shoulder. "Medics were already on standby."

The knowledge didn't ease the worry. Didn't weaken the fear. Addie's blood stained his hands. Seeped through his partner's shirt as fast as it had his own.

Losing her this way would be the end of him.

"You have to fight, Addie." He swallowed hard over the painful knot lodged in his throat as he applied more pressure. "Don't you give up."

He willed his own life to save hers as a swirl of frantic movement kicked up behind him. He barely registered it until Branson gave him a gentle shake.

"Sir." On the other side of Addie, another man was kneeling, reaching for where Reed's hands pressed hard against her neck. "I need you to let go so I can help her."

A swarm of bodies surrounded them, dropping equipment, barking out orders.

Letting go of Addie, backing away so the others could get to her, was the hardest thing he'd ever done. A part of his heart yanked free, left beside her as he watched the paramedics in a daze.

"We have a DRT."

Even in his lost state, Reed picked up on the words echoing inside his head. The paramedics gathering around Samuel's body determined what he'd hoped. He was dead, his cruelty finally ended.

The news registered only a moment before he put all thought back to Addie and the frantic rush to keep her alive.

"Clay and I have Rosalie. We're stopping to pick up Teddy and we're on our way to the airport." AnnaBeth's voice held a painful strain as it drifted through the phone.

Reed made his first call to AnnaBeth while Branson drove, flying down the interstate behind the ambulance rushing Addie to the hospital. He'd pulled himself back for a moment, remembering the pain he'd already caused those closest to Addie when he'd allowed his fear and desperation to silence him with those who cared about her with the same force he did.

He'd known AnnaBeth was the one he needed to reach out to. The news would paralyze her as it had him. But she'd hold it together, for Addie, for everyone who loved Addie, to take care of what needed to be done.

He hadn't been wrong.

She'd had a moment. Such a strong, pain-filled moment when the emotion was so raw in her voice, he felt it through the distance separating them. He'd heard the sobs, knew the tears were there too. But she'd sucked in a deep, harsh breath, so clear through the phone, and promised she'd take care of things.

He'd promised the company jet, even without speaking to his dad first, knowing it only added to more help he'd have to ask for that he'd so strongly sworn off.

Such a promise meant he'd had to stay grounded longer so he could call his dad, make the preparations.

His mind, his heart, never ventured far from Addie in the ambulance ahead of him, fighting for her life. He could see clearly by the looks passed between the paramedics, keeping her alive was a battle.

Samuel hit a vital artery when the blade of his knife cut into Addie's flesh. The paramedics fighting to save her life didn't sugarcoat it for him, understanding, as an agent, he'd know better.

They'd shared the awful truths. The doubts and odds of her making it through. The risks that came with such a violent loss of blood.

Truths he chose not to share with AnnaBeth when he'd made the first call. Truths he couldn't keep back from his dad when he'd made the call asking for use of the company jet.

Truths continuing to haunt him as he paced the waiting room, his phone held tight to his ear while he struggled to concentrate on what AnnaBeth was telling him.

"I've arranged for a driver to meet you when you land," he forced out by sheer will with his second call to AnnaBeth. "He'll bring you straight to the hospital."

"Reed—"

Her sobs echoed through the phone, piercing through his heart. "Tell me she's going to be okay."

He wanted to. With every bit of his soul, he wanted to tell Anna-Beth her best friend would make it. That there was nothing to worry about it.

But he couldn't do it. Couldn't give false promises, no matter how much he was tempted to.

"The doctors are doing all they can." It was the best he could offer. "Having all of you here will help."

He heard the sniffs. The quick breaths trying to regain control. "You tell her we're on our way. And—"

Another sob escaped. "And that we love her."

She ended the call, leaving Reed standing numbly at the edge of the waiting room, staring blindly out the bank of windows bordering it.

"Drink." Branson shoved a steaming cup in his hand. "Don't argue."

Too lost in fears and worry, he lifted the coffee swirling in the cup to his lips. "The whole crew is on their way. They'll want answers when they get here. Especially her aunt and AnnaBeth."

"Might not have them by then. They'll understand."

Maybe they would, but he wouldn't. He wanted those answers now. Wanted the doctors to come through the double swinging doors only a few feet away and tell him something...anything.

The waiting, the not knowing, was enough to take him down.

She ran down a dark tunnel, seeing nothing, feeling only the claws reaching for her, brushing against her flesh. A wind howled but didn't reach her, an echo of something fierce and frightening.

She was cold. So cold. The chill went straight through to Addie's bones.

She wanted to stop. Wanted to find warmth and rest. But something she didn't understand, couldn't grasp on to, pushed at her. Kept her running. Kept the fear raging inside so strong it controlled her.

There was a whisper of something. Her name, she thought, but couldn't be sure.

Nothing made sense. Nothing was as it should be.

So, she kept running. Into the darkness. Into the cold.

CHAPTER FORTY-FIVE

T he sun was gone for the day, leaving only the dark night reflecting back at Reed as he stared out the windows from the waiting room.

A ding from the double doors at the end of the corridor pulled him away from the windows. He turned that way, as he'd done for hours, always hoping it was news about Addie. Always being disappointed.

But this time the older man in scrubs didn't turn away from him as the others had done. Pulling his mask from his face, leaving it to dangle around his neck, he turned for Reed.

"Agent McReily."

Even with all his years with the Bureau, Reed couldn't read the tone of his voice. Had no idea if what he brought was good news or news that would drop him to his knees.

"Yes." Branson came up behind him. He was thankful for the strength of his partner when he suddenly felt so weak.

"I wanted to let you know we have Miss Monrose stabilized though her condition is still critical."

Closer now, Reed saw the stress lines around the doctor's deep blue eyes. The stain of red on his cheeks. "Can I see her?"

The older man shook his head, tossing gray hair over a wrinkled forehead. "Not yet. We struggled to stop the blood. It will be some time before we feel comfortable moving her."

Reed wanted to protest but it would do no good. "Will she—"

He swallowed back the fear of the question he had to ask. "Will she be okay?"

"We're hopeful. The next twenty-four hours will tell us more."

In the way of answers, it wasn't much. Reed craved more, knew he wouldn't be getting it.

"I promise to have one of the nurses come get you as soon as you can see her." The doctor dropped a comforting hand over his shoulder. "Until then, I promise we'll take good care of her."

Understanding it was the doctors, not his badge, ruling here, he nodded slowly. "Thank you."

The doctor disappeared back through the double doors. Branson slung an arm around his shoulders. "Let's go get a refill on coffee."

Reed shook his head, but Branson turned him toward the waiting room door. "It's a quick walk to the cafeteria. I promise, right there and right back. The walk might do you some good."

He didn't want to go. The last thing he wanted was to be further away from Addie. But Branson was already moving them toward the door, letting Reed know he wasn't going to take no for an answer.

A mix of voices poured out of the waiting room.

"You okay?" Branson slapped a hand to his back.

Realizing he was standing in the middle of the long hallway like a fool, Reed nodded, finished the final steps taking him into the waiting room.

All eyes turned to him the minute he took his first step in. Anna-Beth was the first to come rushing forward. She grabbed him, held on for a moment before stepping back. "Tell me she's going to be okay."

"We don't know yet." He looked from AnnaBeth to the heart-broken look darkening Rosalie's eyes as she came up from behind. "The doctor said we'll know more in the next twenty-four hours."

Clay came up beside him, dropping an arm around his shoulders.

He saw them then, near the long row of chairs lining the back wall. "Dad. Mom. I didn't expect you to come."

The concern in his mom's eyes grabbed at him as she took a cautious step toward him. "I—"

Her voice shook. "I'm so sorry, Reed."

She reached for him, wrapping him close. He couldn't remember the last time she'd held him in such a way. Surprise held him still and silent for a moment. It was the care in Teddy's eyes, catching him over the slender curve of his mother's shoulder, bringing him back. Lifting his arms, Reed wrapped them around his mother, accepting what she offered even with the strangeness of it.

It lasted only a few seconds, though in some ways it felt much longer. She pulled away as his dad approached, holding his hand for a moment before slowly letting it slip free.

"I didn't expect you to come." He leaned easier into his dad's quick hug.

Stepping back to stand with his mother, his dad gave him a long, probing look. "Felt like we needed to be here. Hope that's okay."

Reed was caught, not knowing what to say. It was hard enough grasping on to what was happening to Addie. Trying to figure out this new, weird relationship between him and his parents was almost too much.

He never would have thought—

"I'm glad you're here."

He looked at all of them together, his two worlds he'd tried so hard to keep separated, colliding inside a tiny hospital waiting room. Coming together for the one person who'd always been at the center of every decision he'd made...Addie.

Reed took Addie's hand the minute he was allowed to see her.

When they moved her from recovery to a room of her own in the ICU, he stayed at her side, his fingers tightly grasping hers.

And that's where he'd stayed, as day turned to night and back into day again.

"I need more coffee." Clay pushed up from his chair in the corner of the room.

"What do you two want me to bring back for you?" He ran a comforting hand down his sister's hair while his gaze strayed to Reed. "And don't be telling me nothing cause I'm not listening to that."

"I don't suppose they'll have wine in the hospital cafeteria." AnnaBeth tried a smile and failed. "Just a juice for me. I can pretend."

Clay kissed the top of her head, looked at Reed.

"Coffee."

With a nod he was out the door, leaving only Reed and AnnaBeth holding tight to Addie between them. The long stretch of waiting and not knowing wore on Rosalie and Reed's parents. It was best for them to get some rest outside of the solemn, sanitized air hovering inside the hospital.

He'd sent Teddy and Branson off with the task of getting them settled, thankful to both of them for understanding as they found excuses to usher them out the door of Addie's room and down the hall toward the elevators.

"She's always been so stubborn." AnnaBeth's voice caught on the sob she choked back. "She won't give up now."

Reed tightened his grip on Addie's hand, wishing he could grab her and shake her until she came back. She'd made it past the first twenty-four hours. Her vitals were showing improvement. The doctors were optimistic.

None if it meant anything until she came out of whatever held her under.

And she would. He had to believe it just as AnnaBeth was doing her best to believe it, because the alternative was something neither one of them was willing to accept.

Addie felt the first stirring of something needing to be done though she couldn't understand what it might be.

A familiar comfort drew her from where she was lost. A touch she knew but couldn't place. A sound as familiar as her own heartbeat.

What surrounded her was heavy, weighing on her as she fought through it. She was so weak, so tired, still she pushed on what tried holding her back, knowing she had to break past.

"Addie."

Her name echoed around her. She strained for it.

What held her weakened, lost its force.

"Come on, Addie." Reed tightened his hold on her hand. He'd seen the soft flutter behind her lids. Felt the slight curl in her fingers caught with his.

He bent lower, his mouth close to her ear. "Come back to me. Please come back."

Her fingers twitched under the force of his hold. Though her eyes stayed closed, he felt her coming back. Knew she was with him.

AnnaBeth looked at him from the other side of the bed, her eyes misting with tears. "Adelaide Scarlet Monrose, you come back now, or I'll be sharing every secret I know about you, starting with why you had no clothes the night you came home from Billy Jorgen's Mardi Gras party."

Something behind her eyelids fluttered. Her hand jerked in his.

Through her tears, AnnaBeth smiled. "I knew that would get her."

Another flicker behind her lids, a twitch in her fingers, and then she was there. Her deep brown eyes looked out for a moment before she drifted back.

For Reed it was enough. She was still in there. She was coming back. It was a hope he'd been afraid he'd never find again.

"You need some rest." Christopher McReily laid a gentle hand over his son's shoulder.

Reed glanced up at his father, lack of decent sleep weighing heavy on him. He'd lost track of whether it had been four or five days he'd sat at Addie's bedside. It didn't matter. He'd stay as long as it took.

She was doing better. At times she'd open her eyes and he was sure she was fighting to stay with them before they closed again.

And so, he stayed, waiting for more. And AnnaBeth stayed, waiting for the same.

"I'll be all right." He flashed what he hoped was a convincing smile but from the look in his dad's eyes he hadn't succeeded.

"How about a few minutes then, for a talk." He shifted his head toward the hallway.

Reed was hesitant. Leaving Addie's side for any length of time brought the risk of her coming back without him there.

"I'll be right here." His mom moved in close to his side. "I promise to come get you if anything happens."

"And I'll be here." AnnaBeth looked at him from the other side of the bed.

No more than five minutes, he silently promised, pushing up from his chair. He followed his dad to the door, stopping before stepping into the hallway to glance one more time at Addie.

"Go." AnnaBeth waved a hand at him. "She'll be fine."

He hated leaving her, but he wouldn't be far. His dad waited for him a few feet from the door, leaning a shoulder against the wall.

"I'll be quick," he promised when Reed joined him. "Just have some things I want to discuss that I didn't figure others needed to hear."

Curious, Reed drew his attention away from the open door taunting him back to Addie's side.

"I was talking to your partner earlier. Branson, right?"

Reed nodded.

His dad looked toward Addie's room then back to him. "He mentioned the Bureau allowed you to take a leave."

Reed's first thought was to curse Branson for opening his mouth. But what did it matter who knew that he'd asked for, and received, time away from the Bureau so he could make Addie his only responsibility?

Marshall didn't ask questions. He'd filed the paperwork himself, knowing such a request didn't come easy.

"Addie needed me more than the Bureau." He shrugged it off.

"And when she's better and back in New Orleans?" His dad's questioning look was hard and long. "What will you do then?"

Reed already knew the answer. Had known it, deep inside, since before Addie had been taken. Going back to a life without her in it wasn't something he could do again.

He didn't know what it meant from there. Didn't know what the future held outside of the hospital. He only knew, if she'd have him, he was sticking around. And if she didn't want the same—

It was a worry for another day. "My only concern now is Addie. The rest will come later."

His dad looked at him, so much in his eyes Reed had to look away. Silence lingered before his dad cleared his throat. Reed caught the hesitation when he looked back at him.

"I know I made mistakes in the past. I never stopped long enough to ask you what you wanted for your life. I pushed for what I expected without thought to the fact it might not be what you wanted."

Reed wasn't sure he liked where his dad was going. He thought about walking away. Back to Addie. Away from whatever was about to be said.

He heard Addie's voice so strong in his head. If she'd been beside him she'd have told him he needed to stay. Needed to hear what his dad had to say.

He wouldn't be standing there with his dad if she hadn't pushed him to be a better person. To take steps he'd never have taken on his own.

He owed it, not just to her, but to himself, to hear his dad out. "Suppose we've both made our mistakes in the past."

"We have. I'm hoping not to repeat some of mine." His dad pushed away from the wall, taking a step closer.

"I have an offer to make. But I want you to know it's nothing more than a possibility for you. I don't expect anything, and I don't want you feeling as if you'd be obligated."

He drew in a deep breath, released it. "I didn't arrange or plan it, I want you to know that from the start, but we're in need of a Head of Security. Bart's retiring in a month. We're going to need somebody to fill his position."

Reed said nothing, absorbing what his dad said. Bart had always been there. The rock his dad counted on. He had memories of his office when he was a young boy, the strong scents of leather and cigar smoke mingling in the air. His deep voice and twinkling gray eyes welcoming him.

Pictures of his children and grandchildren lined his desk, Reed remembered. Plaques lined the wall behind him, awards he'd received while in the Marines and serving on the police force before coming to work for McReily Enterprises.

Reed couldn't imagine him gone. And more, he couldn't imagine being the one to step into the legacy he'd leave behind.

"It's not about any expected obligations to the family," his dad quickly added when he remained silent.

His gaze strayed for a moment to the open door leading back to Addie. "I didn't understand it all those years ago. Figured you were being a stubborn teenage boy who wasn't seeing the big picture.

"It took losing my son for me to realize how ridiculous it is to worry your life around a commitment to the McReily name. To expect your own child to walk away and defy their own heart to please such demands."

Shock held Reed frozen. He didn't know what to say. How to react. Of all things he'd expected to come from his dad, that was something he never would have imagined.

"Your mom is getting there, too," his dad continued before he could come up with a single word. "So much was expected from her when she married into the family. It's hard for her to imagine any different, now. She loves you and she knows you love Addie. That's what matters most to her, even if she doesn't always know how to show it."

Reed was left at more of a loss for words.

His dad waited, saying nothing more. It was up to Reed, now. What he wanted. What felt right for the life he lived. The future he had ahead of him.

It was honesty that needed to be said. Any less would only take them back to the past they were both trying to work past.

"I appreciate the offer. But I don't have an answer I can give right now."

"I understand." His dad laid a hand over his shoulder. "None of it was meant for immediate answers. Just as things to know and consider."

It was a hell of a lot to know and consider. His mind ran with all of it, but he pushed it back. Addie was his first concern. The rest, no matter how shocking, could wait.

"I should get back." Hesitant, not wanting his dad to think he was brushing off what had been said, Reed reached out, gave his dad's arm a firm squeeze.

It was his first true show of affection since he'd returned. The softening in his dad's eyes let him know the gesture wasn't unnoticed.

CHAPTER FORTY-SIX

A ddie knew the voices surrounding her. Recognized them as she fought against what kept her trapped.

Her aunt's soft, gentle voice, reminding her she was a Monrose, and they never gave up. Clay and Teddy, bantering over one another.

And AnnaBeth. Always AnnaBeth. Fear in every word she spoke. The tug of so many memories shared pulling her back.

And another voice, one she was drawn to with such strength. The one she clung to, needing it every time the urge to give up and slip away threatened to become too strong to fight.

She clung to it. Every time Reed's voice made its way through, she felt stronger. Felt the desperate need to fight back the darkness and open her eyes to the light that waited for her.

It was drawing her forward again. She didn't want to lose it. Didn't want to slip away again, grasping desperately for it even as she was taken back under.

"I know you're there, Addie." Reed's slow drawl surrounded her. "I feel it every time you try to come back. Stay with me this time. You can do it. I know you can."

She wanted to. Oh, how she wanted to. Pulling up whatever strength she could find, she fought against the dark clawing at her, put her mind to the warmth of his voice.

The light was blinding when she forced her lids open. Her first instinct was to close them against the glare, but she fought it. She wouldn't slip away again.

It burned through, searing against her eyes as she struggled to keep them open. Pain roared through her body, the fight to stay aware taking its toll.

She could do it, for all those voices drawing her forward. For AnnaBeth and for Reed.

"Stay with me, Addie." His familiar face was above her. His smile creasing the lines around his eyes, drawing her in.

She wanted to reach out and touch him, feel the warmth of him beneath her fingers. But she was too weak.

Too weak to do anything but stare back at him.

He bent lower, dropping a soft kiss on her lips. A kiss she felt all the way through, battling against the pain.

It gave her a burst. A hope she could do more. The strength seemed so fleeting. She fought, needing to give him something

Shoving back the dark wanting to pull her back, she concentrated on her hand held by Reed's. It was a battle, getting her mind to do what she wanted, fighting against the pain spearing through.

If she'd had the strength to cry out, she would have as she curled her fingers in his palm, turned them so they twined with his.

He looked at their joined hands, lifting them from the edge of the bed. "There you are."

She couldn't do more. But she'd done something, letting Reed know she was with him and didn't plan on going away again.

"Heard they're in need of agents at the New Orleans office." Branson leaned a hip against the edge of the wall to the side of where Reed sat at Addie's bedside. "You thinking about it?"

Reed had been thinking about it and so much more over the last few days, ever since his dad made his offer. The news about the New Orleans' office needing agents came only a day later.

And in it all was Addie, resting now beside him but every day doing so much better. She'd said his name the last time she'd come back—a sweet whisper reaching deep inside, easing the fear he'd lived with since the moment Samuel had held his knife to her neck.

"Not sure what I'm thinking about now, other than Addie."

"I understand that. I have to admit, I've been thinking about it. Before we got married, Marjorie was talking about wanting out of D.C. Seems to me this might be good timing."

Surprised, Reed looked at his partner. Branson leaving D.C. was never a thought. The man had never lived more than an hour from the Bureau office his entire life. "It'd definitely be a change for you two."

Looking at Addie, he thought of the change he'd made so many years ago. Thought about the new changes waiting for him if he chose to take them.

"My dad offered me a position." He looked back to his partner. "Head of security for McReily Enterprises."

That got Branson's attention. Pushing away from the wall, he moved closer to the edge of Addie's bed. "You'd leave the Bureau?"

"Haven't decided yet."

"Can't say," he scratched at the stubble darkening his chin, "that leaving the Bureau would be a bad thing. You can love being an agent and still find it time to move on to something else."

"You talking about me, or you?"

"Not sure."

It was interesting to think his partner might consider leaving the Bureau, something that wasn't a thought for either one of them a few months ago.

"You know, as head of security, I'd need a partner I can trust."

Branson's eyes widened as he shook his head. "Shouldn't be getting me thinking about such things, especially since I haven't mentioned any of this to Marjorie."

"I don't have any answers either. Just playing around with different ideas and decisions to be made."

He looked at Addie. His biggest decision was already made. Leaving her again wasn't something he had any intention of doing. What that meant for him, and his future, their future, he didn't know.

He didn't even know if Addie's wants would match his. If she wanted him gone, he wasn't sure what his next steps would be. He wouldn't be going back to D.C. That much he'd decided.

New Orleans was where he'd stay. If that meant being there and fighting for Addie, he'd do it. He hadn't fought for her before. He'd do it this time if that's what it took to make her part of his life.

CHAPTER FORTY-SEVEN

T he dark that held her finally eased.

Addie was no longer a prisoner to it, fighting for a few seconds of awareness before slipping under again. She understood she was in the hospital. Small teasers of memory were coming back, giving her answers to why she was there.

Reed was there every time she opened her eyes. His gentle smile greeted her while worry clouded his deep blue gaze.

AnnaBeth was never far, poking at her, challenging her not to give up while tears shimmered on her cheeks.

The comforting scent of Rosalie's perfume lingered in the room. The familiar rise and fall of Teddy's and Clay's voices tumbled over one another.

She grabbed on to it all, wrapped it around her like a security blanket, giving her comfort and strength. And the will to fight past what held her.

It brought her back again as the familiar sound of her name coming from Reed drifted to her.

"Hello beautiful." His smile greeted her as she forced her eyes open.

"Reed." The feel of his name on her lips gave her a surge of strength.

"You're looking better." He tightened his hold on her hand.

She wanted to respond but her mouth was so dry it hurt to try. Noticing her struggle, he reached for a cup at the side of her bed.

"No water, only ice chips." He pulled out the spoon stuck in the center, tiny chunks of ice centering it. "Nurses orders."

She wasn't going to argue. Ice was wet. That was all that mattered.

He curved a gentle hand around her cheek, guided the ice-filled spoon to her mouth. It took effort to open her mouth but the minute the cold wet rested against her tongue she was thankful.

It was easier the second time, as he refilled the spoon, bringing it back. She swallowed and felt little pain.

"Better?" He kept his hand resting against her cheek.

She nodded, thankful she found the strength to do so without much effort. "I—"

Her words caught, harder to get out than the smile or nod. "I'm much better."

The three simple words exhausted her even as they energized her. It was the most she'd been able to manage, and it felt good to find her voice again.

"Yes, you are." Leaning closer, Reed dropped a soft kiss on her lips. He reached for the cup and spoon again, giving her another glorious taste of ice cubes, cooling her mouth and throat.

"Oh, Addie." AnnaBeth's familiar voice exploded inside the small room. Fighting back the pain, Addie turned her head, watched her best friend shove a insulated cup into Reed's free hand.

"And you insisted it was my turn to get coffee." Holding a matching cup in her hand, AnnaBeth shoved against his shoulder before hurrying around to the opposite side of the bed.

Grabbing Addie's hand in hers, holding on as if her life depended on it, she dropped a firm, hard kiss on her lips. "You couldn't wait five minutes till I got back."

Her smile was full and bright when she pulled back. "And damn, you need a beauty day."

Addie laughed, a bit rough and painful, but welcome all the same as it escaped.

"You," she sucked in a harsh breath, fought past the pain, "too."

"Been sitting on my butt by your side for days, haven't even had a decent shower. Just tells you how much I love you."

It did, more than she would ever know.

Sleep pulled at her again. She didn't bother to fight it. Love surrounded her. A love that would bring her back again.

She could go. She could rest. It was okay because she'd be back, and she'd be stronger.

Standing in the hall outside Addie's room, Reed kept half a foot at the crook of the door, listening for her.

"She's doing better, I hear." His father, standing on the other side of the door, nudged a head toward her room. "I'm sorry I've missed her while she was awake."

"You'll get the chance. She's getting stronger every day."

And more and more back to the Addie he knew and loved. The doctors were hopeful she'd be released soon. Rosalie had already started plans to get her home to New Orleans. And AnnaBeth was carrying on about scheduling a beauty day with all the fixings as soon as they were back.

It was all moving forward. Soon she'd be home, and the future would be ahead of her.

A future he wanted to be a part of. One it had come time for him to make some decisions about.

"Got a call from Burke the other day." He looked at his dad, slow and thoughtful. "He heads up the New Orleans Bureau. They're short on agents and he thinks I'd be a good fit."

Of all things, even with the changes between him and his dad, Reed didn't expect the flash of pride in his eyes. "That's great news. I'd guess just about any place within the Bureau would be pushing to have you as part of their team."

Reed couldn't respond to that. Didn't know how.

"I turned him down." He let his words sit and settle, watching his dad closely.

"You did? Does that mean you'll be headed back for D.C.?"

Was that a hint of loss in his father's gaze? Reed couldn't be sure, decided it was better not to know.

"No." Shaking his head, he glanced inside the room, taking in Addie sleeping peacefully in her bed. "New Orleans is where I belong. I'm coming home."

His dad reached for him, grabbing him into a hug he wasn't expecting. "I know it's selfish to say, but I'm happy to know my son will be close again. Especially if it's your choice and not one you feel forced into."

"It's my choice. I loved my time in D.C. Loved being an agent. It defined me for many years, and I don't regret it. I could go back to D.C. and back to the Bureau and be happy."

Sensing he needed the space, his dad stepped back, dropping his hands.

Reed sucked in a deep breath. More needed to be said and he wanted it done before Addie woke up.

"But other things are more important now than the badge. I'm not going to lay blame on my being an agent, but the fact is, Addie is where she is because of that. He targeted her because of me. Because my job led him to her."

His dad opened his mouth to speak. Reed held up his hand, stopping him. "Like I said, not putting the blame on my being an agent, or on myself. Just stating facts that can't be denied."

"And those facts need to be considered in where I want to go from this point forward. What life I want. Who I want in it." He smiled at his dad. A genuine smile rather than the forced ones he'd become good at when around his parents.

"I'm thinking it's time to finally step into the family business. If that job offer is still available, I'd like to take it. But I've got one request."

"What's the request?"

"I'd like to bring my partner, Branson, on as my right-hand man. There's nobody I trust more to have my back."

"It's done."

Reed released the breath he hadn't been aware he was holding. "I'll need some time. Addie needs to be home and recovered first."

"I wouldn't expect any different. You get her better and we'll go from there."

Reaching out, his dad wrapped a hand around his arm. "I would have understood and been happy, no matter your decision. But I'd be lying if I said I wasn't hoping you'd take the position. We'll make it a new, better start for all of us."

Reed had hope for it, though it would be day by day and take some time before old hurts faded completely. They'd already come so far since he'd come back to New Orleans, and he didn't doubt they'd make it the rest of the way.

The room was dark.

Addie was disoriented. A voice, similar to Reed's, but not his. He was talking but it took effort to concentrate on the words he was saying.

"...wasn't easy convincing those two to leave your side."

Yes, like Reed's, but a little deeper. Hardened more by age.

His dad—Christopher.

"Those two needed a break, even if it is just dinner in the hospital cafeteria. And I'm thankful for a chance to be with you alone."

He didn't know she was awake. The dark covered the fact. She laid still in her bed, sensing it was what he needed.

"You've got something special about you." He shifted in the chair Reed usually occupied. Though she was tempted, she didn't dare turn to look at him.

"You've always been the best for my son and I'm so sorry I didn't realize that for so long. It's hard knowing we did everything we could to shove you out of Reed's life and yet, you're the reason he's back in ours."

He sucked in a harsh breath. She wished she could see his face. But letting him believe she was asleep was best for both of them. She didn't know what she could give back.

"I need to thank you. You gave me my boy back when I was sure I'd never see him again. He'll be home now and my worrying for him will take on a much lighter load."

He'll be home.

The words caught in Addie's head. Reed was moving back to New Orleans?

She worked her mind around how she felt about it. Wondered what his plans were. Did they include her? Did she want them to?

Her heart said yes. Swelled with the answer.

But she worried. And the worry pulled back the exhaustion. Reed's dad still talked but his words slipped away, barely heard as she drifted back to the comfort of sleep, healing her as it gave her an escape.

For the first time it was just him and Addie alone.

Clay had finally put his foot down, forcing AnnaBeth back to their hotel room to get a real night's sleep now that Addie was doing better.

She'd gone kicking and screaming, but she'd gone, leaving Reed alone, sitting beside Addie's bed, wishing he could crawl in beside her and hold her close.

He missed that, the feel of her in his bed, those luscious curves of hers fitting so right, so perfect, against him.

If she'd have him, he'd know that pleasure again. The doctors wanted a few more days before they were willing to let her go. A few more days and they'd be back in New Orleans. Back home where they belonged.

And where he hoped he'd belong with her.

She shifted in her sleep, and he watched her, loving the sight of her, feeling the relief of knowing she was going to be okay.

Her eyes slowly opened, and he was lost in their deep brown depths, his heart swelling with love.

He was truly a lost man. It was something he'd come to realize he didn't mind at all.

"Hi." Her soft voice was a whisper, heavy with sleep.

"Hi, yourself." Bending over, he dropped a kiss on her lips, enjoying the taste of her.

She smiled and he loved seeing it no longer drained her as it once did. Her eyes trailed slowly around the quiet room. "We're alone?"

"We are. Everybody's off to get some sleep for the night. Even AnnaBeth, though she didn't go happily."

"No. I don't suppose she did."

He knew she'd be thirsty, as she always was when she woke. Grabbing the small green pitcher at the side of her bed, he filled a plastic cup and dropped a straw into it.

"We've got the whole room and the whole night to ourselves." He handed it to her. "What do you suggest we do with it?"

She wrapped her lips around the straw, watching him over the bend in the plastic, drawing forth all kinds of ideas he had no right to while she laid in the hospital bed.

"I have thoughts. But I'm thinking this bed might be too small for most of them. And the rails might be a problem."

He wanted to grab her, right there and then. Damn the bed, the rails. He wanted her. All of her.

He clung to enough self-restrain to know better. "I'm going to hold you to whatever those thoughts are as soon as you're sprung and feeling better."

"I'm feeling better now." Though she smiled, a hint of something more below the surface chased back the images running wild inside his head.

Standing from his chair, he nudged her over with his elbow. With one leg planted on the floor, he half sat on the bed, stretching his arm behind her, pulling her close.

He didn't say anything, sensing it in her when she remained silent that something brewed inside. Something she needed to work through before a word was spoken.

He held on, knowing he'd do it for a lifetime if that's what it took.

"I remember," she finally spoke, resting her head on his shoulder, diverting her gaze to the wall in front of them. "I remember all of it."

He tightened his hold, wishing he could spare her from what was running through her head. The all too familiar guilt threatened to surge back but he pushed it away, knowing it would do no good for what Addie needed from him.

"He's dead." It was a statement, not a question. "I know he is. Maybe it makes me terrible, but I'm glad to know it."

"You don't have it in you to be terrible." He pulled her closer, held tighter.

He knew this would come. It was a part of healing, accepting. If he could, he'd have done whatever it took to spare her from reliving the dark memories.

"He's dead, like you said. He'll never be able to hurt you again."

Her head resting against the strength of Reed's shoulder, Addie let the memories come, knowing she couldn't fight them. "Who was he?"

It was the question she needed an answer to. The one haunting her since the images started coming back.

"His name was Samuel. He was a sick man with a sick mind."

It was a start, but Addie waited, needing more.

Reed didn't disappoint.

"From what the Bureau has learned," he pulled her closer, dropping a kiss on top of her head, "he grew up in an abusive childhood. Reports from schoolteachers, old family members, show an unstable mother who was nothing close to the loving sort."

Her mind replayed what he'd said while he'd held her captive. "He wasn't right, I knew that. How could he be with what he did?"

"After he grabbed me," she shivered, and he tightened his hold around her. "He kept telling me it wasn't right. I don't know what he meant, will probably never understand it. But I believe it was what kept me alive. Whatever he had in his mind, whatever sickness pushed at him, he was thrown off from what he planned."

The fear came back, as fierce as if she were still held captive by him, wondering if she'd live through another day. Reed so close, holding her tight, helped chase some of it away, reminding her she was safe now.

"He didn't hurt me. Not in the way he hurt those other women."

The relief was a hard one to hold, being thankful she hadn't experienced such a horror while knowing others had. It was something she couldn't dwell on, for her own sanity.

"He hurt you enough." Reed rested a hand against her cheek, turning her toward him. He waited until her eyes met his. "As an agent, I learned there is no meter on which victim might have suffered the most. It's not about what he did to the others and not to you. It's not about whether you might have been spared something they weren't."

His words settled, soothed. Maybe they didn't fully convince her, but they gave her comfort. For that she was grateful.

"I miss New Orleans." She turned away, staring out the window where the inky darkness of the night looked back at her. "I want to go home."

"By this time next week, you'll be home." She looked at him and he smiled. "We'll both be home."

"Are you coming back, Reed? Are you coming home to New Orleans?"

He didn't answer right away. It wasn't hesitation she sensed but more of a need for thought before answering.

He pressed a finger beneath her chin, lifting her face to his, drawing her into a kiss holding a depth of emotion she'd never felt before.

Breathless, she watched as he pulled away, staring at her with those deep blue eyes of his. "I'm coming home to you, Addie, wherever that might be."

Her heart caught. A moment of uncertainty hit as old hurts from the past came back.

"Why?"

He didn't answer right away, just stared at her while she waited.

"Because leaving you was the worst thing I ever did."

His words, so slow, so true, hit deep. Turning away again, she let the night ground her. Keep her from reacting to the roll of emotions tumbling through.

"I didn't come back to New Orleans for you. You know that and it would be an insult to us both if I tried to suggest different."

He tugged on her hair, drawing her attention back to him. "But coming back brought you back and made me realize how much I need you. Made me finally admit I woke up every morning missing you and went to bed every night wanting you."

It was all the words she'd wanted.

She'd had doubts. She'd had fears. And she'd sworn to herself, when she wondered if she'd ever see Reed again, she wouldn't let them rule her. Wouldn't let them take away what she wanted. Had always wanted.

She smiled at Reed. He needed to hear what was in her own heart. "I never thought you'd come back. Spent many years telling myself I didn't want you to."

She reached up, rested a hand against the stubble lining his cheek. "I was wrong. I did want you back, I just couldn't admit it or accept it."

He took her then, a slow, passionate kiss full of love. She trembled when he pulled away, not sure if she was still on her bed or floating above it.

"I'm going to marry you, Adelaide Scarlet Monrose. You might not agree now, but I'll wait. And I'll do all I can, while I'm waiting, to prove to you we're meant for a future together."

Her heart swelled. Warmth settled over her. He wanted to marry her. Wanted to spend the rest of his life with her. The knowledge of it drifted soft and gentle inside her, pushing at her own love for him, making it grow.

She knew her answer but still had questions. His dad's words from earlier returned, making her wonder. "Would I be the wife of an agent?"

Caught in the crook of his shoulder, she couldn't see his face. But she felt the long breath he pulled through his lungs. "Ex-agent."

It was matter of fact. Needing to see him, she shifted carefully. "Is that a good thing or a bad thing?"

"Not good or bad. Just a choice that was made."

"And what's the next choice? I know you well enough to know you wouldn't make one without having another already there."

He looked at her, hesitant to answer.

She worried. Wondered what held him back.

"My dad offered me a position as head of security." He watched so closely the heat of his gaze burned. "I accepted."

It fell into place, his dad's words finally making sense.

It took only a moment for the realization to sink in. She didn't have a chance to respond before Reed was pulling her closer. "If it's not good for you, I want you to tell me. I haven't burned my bridges with the Bureau. It's still a choice I can make and be happy with."

She let that sink in, the fact he'd walk away from his family business again, for her.

It took some doing, shifting in the small bed without crying out in pain. Pressing a hand to his chest, she took a moment to stare into the eyes of the man she loved. The man she was going to marry.

"I'm happy with you. I don't care how you come to me." She pushed up, kissing him. "I'll marry you. I'll be the happy, proud wife of whatever you do in your life."

Wrapping his arms around her, he folded her in close. "I love you, Addie. My life is complete knowing I'll spend the rest of it with you."

She ignored the twinge of pain as she pushed closer. "My life was complete the first day you walked into it."

She rested her head against his chest, the steady, comforting beat of his heart letting her know she was right where she belonged.

9 798218 504526